Other Women

Other Women

KIRSTY CRAWFORD

ORION

First published in Great Britain in 2005
by Orion, an imprint of the Orion Publishing Group Ltd.

1 3 5 7 9 10 8 6 4 2

A CIP catalogue record for this book is
available from the British Library.

ISBNs 0 75286 657 5 (hardback)   0 75286 893 4 (export trade paperback)

Typeset at The Spartan Press Ltd, Lymington, Hants
Set in 12/14.5pt Apollo MT
Printed in Great Britain by Clays Ltd, St Ives plc

All the characters in this book are fictitious, and any resemblance
to actual persons, living or dead, is purely coincidental.

The Orion Publishing Group Ltd
Orion House
5 Upper St Martin's Lane
London WC2H 9EA

www.orionbooks.co.uk

To my parents
Dennis Fowkes and Katharine Adams

Acknowledgements

My thanks go to the brilliant editorial team behind this book, in particular Jane Wood, Sara O'Keeffe, Hazel Orme and Susan Lamb; and to everyone at Orion in sales, marketing, editorial, art, publicity, production and rights who welcomed the book so warmly. They are a splendid bunch – the best.

My thanks also go to my agent, Lizzy Kremer; to my friends, who have been so encouraging; to my famly, who have been so excited for me; to little Barney, who was cooking at about the same time as this book. But most of all to my wonderful husband, James Crawford.

Chapter One

Her last day.

Bella woke feeling leaden. That was all wrong, for a start. She was supposed to be feeling like a prisoner on the brink of liberation, wasn't she? Instead it felt as though a heavy weight had been placed in her chest overnight. Beside her, the bed was empty; Iain was up already. Good God, what on earth was the time? She struggled over to look at the alarm clock: it was almost six a.m. She flopped back on to her pillow and growled with annoyance as the morning sounds of the house filtered through to her: the children running about and calling to each other, the plumbing system doling out the hot water for showers, the faint tinny voice of the radio in the kitchen. Above it all was a high, piercing, tuneless sound.

For Christ's sake! she thought. He's whistling. Who actually whistles when they're cheerful, apart from the Seven Dwarfs?

It was typical of Iain to be at the opposite end of the emotional spectrum to her. As she grew more depressed at what lay ahead, he became more elated, his good mood making him unbearably energetic and upbeat. Every little thing he did at the moment set her on edge and grated on her nerves.

The tower of boxes near the bed looked precarious, a manilla-coloured Cubist mountain, filled with clothes and books and hangers and shoes and all the thousands of things she didn't even know she'd managed to cram into one small bedroom. Around them, the room looked stripped and bare. She could tell just by looking at them that the drawers and the wardrobe were empty — they seemed lighter somehow. In three hours, the movers would be here to hoist it all up, the boxes and the furniture, and take it down the stairs and out through the front door. And that would be that. They would scoop up their possessions and the Balfours would be gone from here for ever.

She ought to be used to it by now, this moving on and abandonment of places, but this time it was different. Before, she had always looked ahead to what awaited them. This time she was looking back at what she was leaving behind. She felt like a dog pulled reluctantly along on its leash by an over-enthusiastic owner – Iain had chivvied and bullied, persuaded and commanded until finally she'd agreed that they would leave, and now the time to go was here.

She closed her eyes and tried to drift off again, but it was no good. Sleep was not going to come back now. The next time she slept would be in the new house, in a strange room in a tiny Cotswold hamlet miles from anywhere – certainly miles from London, from her friends, and from everything that was comforting and familiar. Well – it was too late to change her mind now. Everything had been set in motion, and all she could do was try to stay in control as far as she could.

'Morning, love!' said Iain briskly, coming through the bedroom door. He was vibrant with energy. 'Chop-chop! We're all up and dressed. I'm just making some breakfast for the kids.'

'The movers aren't arriving till nine,' Bella said wearily. 'Why do we have to get up so early?'

'Well, we'll need to clear up and pack the last of the boxes, won't we? We ought to strip the bed. And I want us all ready to go the minute they arrive. You know what the traffic's like getting out of London on a Saturday, and with a great removal van, it'll be twice as bad. I'm aiming to be in Rawlston by lunchtime, if possible.'

Bella scowled but Iain refused to notice. 'Come on,' he said brightly. 'There're cheese toasties and tea all ready in the kitchen.' He turned and bustled off.

Why would he think that either of those things might tempt her down? she wondered. She was a coffee and muesli person and always had been. She'd started to notice that, lately, Iain appeared to be finding it harder and harder to distinguish her from the children. She admitted defeat and climbed reluctantly out of bed.

This move was just the kind of thing her husband thrived on: a monumental project, entailing lots of organization and getting everybody sorted out. Yet, despite all his enthusiasm, Bella couldn't help noticing that the actual work – packing the boxes, making the children sort out their things, cleaning the house for the next occupants   had been done by her. Still, perhaps that was for the best: they'd moved so often that Bella had her system down to a fine art. When Iain tried to be helpful he mucked everything up, muddling the boxes by putting bathroom stuff in the bedroom crate, glasses in with the toolbox and stopping to read the books as he packed them. Once she'd found him carefully wrapping the tins of food in newspaper – 'to stop them knocking each other,' he'd explained. If only he'd taken so much care of their wedding china, which had almost become extinct over the years and many encounters with removal men.

She found Katie and Christopher bouncy and excited in the kitchen, eating their breakfast, and Iain humming and cheerful. Her husband's good humour was sending her plummeting downwards in inverse proportion but, at least, she thought, he had stopped whistling – minor mercies and all that. By the time they'd all finished, tidied up and done the final packing it was still only seven-thirty and they had to sit about with nothing to do, the children haring about and jumping on boxes. Bella was cross and sleepy. Iain was triumphant that they were so ahead of schedule.

Life had been a series of endings lately, thought Bella, as she locked the front door of their house for the final time after the removal men had taken out the last box. There had been leaving her job – admittedly, not exactly a wrench although she would miss some of the people she'd worked with over the past five years. They'd held one of those awful leaving parties for her, where everyone stood about and drank warm white wine and only talked to the people they usually talked to anyway. She'd got a card signed by everybody – *Keep in touch! It won't be the same without you! We'll miss you!* – and a little sheaf of Argos vouchers.

3

The thought was kind, but she knew they wouldn't miss her. Why would they? In a month or two, someone might say, 'Has anyone heard from old Bella? What's she up to? Does anyone know how she's getting on in the country?' and after that she would be forgotten, just as she'd forgotten the people who'd worked with her for a while and then moved on.

'Excellent. We can buy a lawnmower with those,' Iain had said, when she'd shown him the Argos vouchers. 'We'll be needing one now.'

'Mmm, I suppose so. I just . . . I can't help thinking it would have been nice to get vouchers for Liberty, or Heal's, or Harrods. Somewhere like that. So I could get something a bit frivolous.'

'I expect you'd like to spend it all on kumquat bath oil or something equally ridiculous. This is much more practical. Useful.'

The removal truck, loaded with all their possessions, made its slow way down the street, heading for the road out of London. Iain and the children waited for her in the car, while Bella walked round to the estate agent to deliver the house keys. It was a fine late May morning and Chiswick looked fresh and pretty. The streets seemed alive with young families out for a stroll, taking the children to the green to play or doing some Saturday shopping. She passed the knick-knack shops with the colourful toys and ornaments that drew the eye like candy, and the smart delicatessen with its array of cheeses and continental chocolate. Then there were the exclusive boutiques, four different types of supermarket, the branch of Snappy Snaps she used so often, the dry-cleaner's, the off licence. Here was everything she needed for a civilized life, and she was leaving it all for a hamlet miles from the nearest village. No dashing out for a bottle of new world Shiraz there. If she popped out, it could well be days before she returned.

She felt a stab of panic. Had she made the right decision? When the company had offered voluntary redundancies, she'd wondered idly if this was the get-out clause she'd been waiting for, after five years of working in computer training. Then, when she'd mentioned it to Iain, he'd pounced on it with excitement and begun to rhapsodize on it like a composer with a theme. What had been a way to change her job became an opportunity for them to pursue Iain's cherished dream to move to the country, her redundancy money providing the injection of cash they'd always needed to make it a reality, but never had.

At times, she'd had to admit, Iain's dream had seemed attractive: times when she was stuck in fumy traffic, or her train came to a frozen, unexplained halt in the fusty darkness of a tunnel somewhere below Gloucester Road; when she saw a gaggle of dangerous-looking youths loitering and menacing passers-by; when her car window was smashed again, leaving glittering chunks of glass everywhere. And that was before she thought about the children. Really, this move was for them: to give them fresh air and freedom and a sense of what lay beyond concrete and Tarmac and straggly commons covered in dog mess; to move them away from London schools to somewhere they might be able to cling on to childhood a little longer. They were beginning to pester her and Iain for more and more expensive toys and gadgets because their friends had them. They were on a bit of a hiding to nothing with that one, especially where Iain was concerned. His favourite reason for saying no to something was because everyone else did it or had it or was going to get it. Katie, who was just ten, was hankering for a mobile phone for Christmas. She might as well forget that right now.

Bella handed in the keys at the agent's, trying to ignore the people scanning the photographs of properties for sale, and fighting her sense of gloom. She'd come to love their house, even if they'd never quite got it finished. Like most of their houses, it had been a wreck when they'd bought it and at first they'd gone at it with enthusiasm, but that had gradually waned and she'd got used to living with bare plaster and untreated floorboards. At least the new place didn't need much beyond some decorating.

The family were sitting obediently in the car waiting for her return. She climbed into the driver's seat.

'Right, then,' she said, trying to sound upbeat. 'Say goodbye to the house everyone!'

'Goodbye, house!' chorused the children.

'See you soon,' added Christopher, waving out of the window at their front door.

'No, you won't,' said Iain. 'We're not coming back, don't you remember?'

'Aren't we?' Christopher blinked his huge blue eyes in surprise, as though no one had mentioned such a thing to him.

Bella twisted round to look at him, smiling encouragingly. 'You know, Chrissie, you can't have forgotten – it was only the other day. We went to see the new house in the country where we're going to live. And we went round your new school – don't you remember the lovely classroom and all the paintings and the special nature reserve they've got?'

'Course he does,' said Katie. 'You remember, stupid. Remember the stream?'

Christopher's face lit up. 'Y-y-y-yes!' he stuttered with excitement. 'And I can have a hamster, you said! A hamster called Stephen.'

'That's right, darling.' Bella started the engine. 'Now, the sooner we get going, the sooner Stephen will become a reality.'

They put some story-tapes on the radio to keep Katie and Christopher amused, and headed west. Before long, they were on the motorway.

That's that, then, thought Bella. The end of my life in London. It felt as though she was leaving behind everything that defined her, and sailing out into the unknown towards a whole new version of herself that she could discern only blurrily at the moment.

The thing she feared most was the loneliness. Her girlfriends had organized a large, chatty farewell lunch at the Clapham house of one of them; they had all enthused about the move, cooed over the photos of the new house and said how lucky she was, how much they envied her and how they would all be visiting. They'd given her a present of a pair of wildly flower-patterned gumboots and a rainbow umbrella – 'no danger of you disappearing into the rain and mud with those,' they'd told her. She'd been very touched and had hugged them all tightly when the time came to say goodbye. That had been bad enough but worse had been saying goodbye to Nicky, her closest friend. When they had met for a quiet farewell drink in Soho, Bella had embarrassed herself by crying.

'Hey, hey, hey! What's all this, honey? It's not so bad,' Nicky had said, clasping her hand. 'You're only going to Gloucestershire, you know, not the Orkney Isles.'

'I know,' said Bella, damply, sniffing into a tissue. 'But we find it hard enough to meet up when I'm here in London. How are we going to manage it when I'm miles away?'

'We just will. And now you're a lady of leisure, you can come up and visit me. We can have lovely weekends together, doing all the things you promise yourself you'll do when you actually live here and never get round to. And you'll have that wonderful place to live in. Holly Lodge. The picture makes it look beautiful.'

'It is,' Bella admitted. She'd forgotten how pretty it was until she'd driven there the previous week to measure up and inspect the rooms. A red-brick Victorian house, it stood sturdily at the end of a long lane, just at the turn that led up to the big house shielded behind its high hedges of rhododendrons. The lane was pot-holed and dirty and she'd been cursing it when she'd pulled the car to a halt. Then she'd been startled, first by the extreme quiet – no traffic noise, no wailing sirens, just the distant buzz of some farm machinery – and then by the picturesque house, with its white sash windows and carved wooden porch, a spray of jasmine curling up over it. 'But it's not just a holiday home – I have to *live* there. And what am I going to do?'

'Isn't there a town nearby?'

'Well, Oxford's about thirty miles away.'

'There you are, then. You can find something there, can't you? It won't be as bad as you're expecting.'

Bella stared into her glass of wine. 'It's just . . . we'll need money. I have to find a job. And I can't help feeling weary at the thought of starting again. We keep moving, we never seem to settle. It's as though we believe that life is going to be better somewhere else, if only we can get there. We've been in London four years, and that's the longest we've spent anywhere.'

'Iain wants to better himself, doesn't he? I thought that was why you're always buying these old ruins and doing them up and selling them. I assumed there must be money in it.'

Bella smiled crookedly. 'You'd *think* so – it seems perfectly reasonable. But it never works quite like that. We always spend far too much on the houses because Iain insists on doing the work himself, rather than paying someone. It all goes wrong and we have to bring someone in to fix it. Iain gets the cheapest builder he can find, who naturally makes a mess of it, so we have to bring in someone else or just hope that whoever buys it won't notice, but they always do. Then we find out that we're just outside a catchment area, or on the wrong side of the street, or our area has just gone down in value . . . so you're looking at one of the few people not to make any money out of buying and selling property. We're just about breaking even. We could never have afforded the lodge if I hadn't had the redundancy money.'

'Oh, Iain . . .' Nicky laughed and shook her head. 'He's such a funny old thing.'

'Funny, unless you're married to him.'

'You picked him – you must have seen something in him.' Nicky refused to take Iain seriously, pretending that Bella had married him as some kind of joke in order to amuse her friends. 'Come on – you two seem happy together. I mean, he's a bit eccentric but you have a laugh together, don't you?' She frowned. 'Is everything all right with the two of you?'

'Oh yes, yes. We're fine, really. But sometimes I feel as though I just don't know him, even after all these years. In fact, it seems to be getting worse as he gets older, as though he's retiring inside himself and cutting off from the outside world. That's why I've got this theory that the move is about getting away from everything that he doesn't like, so he can construct his own way of life in the solitude of the country.'

'Most moves are about getting to something better, aren't they? There's nothing unusual in that.'

Bella frowned. 'I suppose so – but it's different with Iain. It makes me think of someone retiring into a monastery.'

'Oh. Yes. I can see that's not too good.'

'But it's his dream. It's what he wants. I can't stand in his way because I owe it to him to give it a try.'

'You'll be fine,' Nicky said firmly. 'Just don't forget about what you want, okay? I don't like to think of you suffering in the middle of nowhere so that Iain can indulge his fantasy of country life. You can call me, or email any time. Okay?'

'Okay. Just promise you won't forget me.'

They arrived in Rawlston soon after lunch, having made good time down the motorway. The removal men had got there before them, making Bella suspect that the lumbering van had gone far too fast down the M40, and the lawn in front of the house was already crammed with furniture and boxes where they had unloaded the truck. Iain got out quickly to let them in. Katie and Christopher scrambled out in excitement to start exploring their new territory, while Bella sat for a few minutes longer in the car, watching. She ought to get out herself and make sure that Iain knew where things should go but she couldn't quite face it.

The children ran past the front door, a flash of bare legs and a slap of flip-flops up the path, and skirted round the side of the house towards the back garden. Bella took a deep breath and got out of the car. The air was warm and sweet with the smell of grass.

'Bella, I need you!' shouted Iain. 'I can't find my keys. Have you got your set?'

The men carried on stacking furniture on the lawn, oblivious to Iain's buzzing.

'Yes,' she said, 'and yours is in your jacket pocket.' She handed him hers anyway.

'Thanks. Right. Let's get sorted out.' He hurried to the front door and started fiddling with the keys. Bella watched him with a sort of irritable fondness. Iain was in his summer weekend uniform: tatty old shorts, ancient sandals and a sagging blue Aertex shirt. His hair, thinning on top, was still more brown than grey but it was growing wispy and fluffy, which Bella suspected had something to do with the long years of using the very cheapest shampoos. Iain would never buy anything but the supermarket own-brand and he insisted on getting that in bulk, great tubs of over-scented pink gloop. Well, if it made him happy. Bella preferred her nice herbal stuff.

Iain opened the door. 'Let's do a quick tour of inspection.'

She followed him inside and up the stairs. They'd both come to see the house originally, before they'd put in their offer, but Iain had little recollection of it. He could vaguely recall the kitchen and the garden but hardly anything else. It was one of his peculiarities, his inability to remember things. He forgot people, places, names, even words.

He went into the first bedroom, the largest, with the fireplace, the bathroom next door and a view that showed green fields and dark copses for miles.

'Now, this is it!' he cried. 'Look at that! Fantastic.'

'I thought this might do for us,' Bella said casually, from the doorway. 'Imagine waking up to that every day. What do you think?'

'Oh, yes. We'll have this one.' Part of the trick with Iain was making him think everything was his own idea. He strode to the window and opened it. 'Kids! Come in and see the house. You need to choose your bedrooms.'

Bella tensed. 'I've chosen their rooms. Christopher is on this floor, Katie's upstairs in the attic. She'll like being a bit separate but Chrissie's too sensitive to be far away.'

'No harm in letting them decide,' Iain said. 'I don't think it makes much of a difference.'

'All right,' Bella said, realizing that she would have to steer the children into making the right choice. She was too tired and the day too fraught to start taking Iain on.

The movers left as the afternoon turned rich and golden. The beds were in the appropriate rooms, after furtive persuasion by Bella, and the furniture deposited haphazardly around the house. Bella wondered what the movers had made of the Balfours' mish-mash of things, most of it second-hand, picked up in junk shops and at sales; the old travel trunk that served as their coffee-table, the battered wardrobes, the cartons and cartons of books. How did all this define them, she wondered. It looked both familiar and strange in its new setting and for a moment, she had a sense of distance about who they were as a family. Delightfully shabby, perhaps? Messy? Unconcerned with expensive trinkets and family heirlooms? Or just too poor to afford anything decent?

She went into the kitchen at the back of the house. This was an extension to the original so it lacked the high ceilings and tall windows of the rest. It was long and low, with a dirty old Rayburn set into the far wall. God only knew how she was going to cook on that thing. The plain units were serviceable, the Formica bland and only a little chipped. Grey-tinged net curtains swung from a piece of elastic over the windows that gave on to the back garden. Those will have to go, thought Bella. Why are they there? It's not as if anyone can look in. There are no houses for miles.

She was absorbed in unpacking when she heard a strong rat-tat-tat on the knocker. She turned her head to listen and it came again, so she went to the front door and opened it.

A tall man, smartly dressed, stood on the doorstep smiling. He was imposing with his height and air of confidence, a well-lived-in face, deep blue eyes and silver-and-black hair. Behind him in the lane Bella could see a sleek, expensive-looking sports car.

He said, 'Hello. You've just moved in, haven't you? I've come to say welcome.'

'Thank you, that's very kind of you,' said Bella, conscious of her chaotic moving-day hair and her torn old jeans. He was very good-looking – you'd have to be blind not to see that.

'My name's Ben Clarke. I'm from the house at the top.' He gestured up the lane to where the big house was just visible, its roof and chimneys emerging above the trees.

Bella was puzzled. 'Where Mrs Fielding lives?' She and Iain had met Jane Fielding when they'd come to view the lodge and knew she lived in Rawlston House.

'Yes. But we don't live with her. The house is divided and we're in one half. I live there with my wife Sam and my daughter.'

'Oh. I see. Well, it's very nice to meet you. I wasn't sure how many other people live around here.'

'There are the folks in the cottages –' Ben Clarke nodded over his shoulder towards the small houses on the other side of the lane '– but most of them are well past retirement age, so I don't know how much of a social whirl you'll be enjoying with them. Do you have any kids?'

'Two. Katie and Christopher.'

'Good,' he said emphatically. 'We need some more children round here. How old are they?'

'Ten and seven.'

'A bit on the young side for Emma, she's nearly eighteen. Never mind, you must all come up and have a drink soon. What do you think of the place so far?'

'Lovely. Quiet. Compared to London, anyway.'

'Which part of London are you from?'

'Chiswick.'

'Don't know Chiswick.' They stood and smiled politely for a moment longer. Ben said, 'Well, I won't keep you – I'm sure you're busy. Just wanted to say welcome to Rawlston. Do come by any time and let us know if we can help.' He turned to go, then swung back. 'What's your name?'

'Balfour. Bella and Iain.'

'Great – well, here's my card. Call or email and make a time to visit. I mean it. 'Bye. Happy settling.' He handed her the card, then walked off down the path. A moment later the car disappeared smoothly up the lane.

By nine o'clock the children were mute and drooping and went up to their bedrooms without protest. Bella felt the floating tiredness of a hard day's work when she followed upstairs. Outside, darkness was falling, a thicker, deeper kind than city darkness, and the night was full of sound: the chirrups of night insects and the rustling of branches. In the city, she understood the perils of the night, the knifers, muggers, the speeding traffic. Here, inside their bedroom with the lamp lit and the curtains drawn, she felt as though something massive and unknown was moving outside as it willed. She reminded herself that those farm cottages were only over the road, their small windows glowing yellow, proof of other people about.

In bed, she said to Iain, 'Did you know that the big house has got two families living it?'

He looked up from his book. 'I might have. Did Jane Fielding say something about it? I don't remember.'

Why *does* he forget everything? she thought. It's as though his mind is a sieve and he can't hold anything in it. 'A man called round while you were in the garden. Ben Clarke. He lives in the other half. He wants us to go up and visit.'

Iain brightened. This was part of his fantasy of what living in the country would be like, as they were clasped to the bosom of the new community. 'That's great. When?'

'I've got to call him.' She poked her foot out from under the duvet. The night was really too warm for such a thick cover but it was all they had.

'You must. The sooner we get to know our neighbours, the better. What was he like?'

'Nice enough. Distinguished. But not grand. I liked him.'

'Good.' Iain turned back to his book. 'Then give him a call in the morning.'

Chapter Two

'What a racket!' said Jerry crossly. 'What do they want to go and spoil a nice quiet afternoon like this for?'

They were sitting having tea on the terrace and Jerry had gone to a lot of effort. He'd baked his special healthy Victoria sponge with brown flour, diabetic jam and half-fat *crème fraiche* instead of cream. It had a consistency and taste that reminded Jane of old paste but, as Jerry said, 'Anything that keeps the calorie count *down* and the life expectancy *up* has to be worth it.'

Jerry threw a filthy look over his shoulder in the direction of the roaring engine, as though it could somehow pierce the thick rhododendron bush and reprimand the driver of the lorry now reversing with loud beeps down the next-door driveway. 'Blasted neighbours,' he said bitterly.

'It has rather tried my patience recently,' Jane admitted. 'The builders get here at the crack of dawn and start banging and hammering away, great trucks come up the lane, and it doesn't stop all day. They must be leaving now, though. It's almost four.'

'What on earth are they doing?'

'I don't know. I haven't asked – I haven't laid eyes on either of them for weeks. One day I'm expecting to look round the corner and see that they've replaced the whole thing with a glass penthouse or something.'

Jerry looked horrified. 'No!'

'No, they couldn't do that,' Jane said quickly, 'I don't think planning permission would be allowed. The council hasn't yet got to the stage where they're allowing Grade II listed mansions to be demolished.'

'Not yet,' Jerry said darkly. In a huff, he took another bite of his sponge cake. Jane knew that he felt a proprietorial sense towards Rawlston. His own tiny cottage in a village several miles away could not be more different from the large, gracious, golden-stoned house that had been in the Fielding family since the 1920s when Theo's great-grandfather had bought it with the money he had made from manufacturing rubber tyres. It sat, beautiful and peaceful among its rhododendrons, at the top of the lane in the hamlet of Rawlston, a reminder of an age now past, when people like him had lived lives of elegant luxury. 'It's all changing,' he said gloomily. 'First you lose half the house, now you've had to sell the lodge. What will be next?'

'I don't know,' said Jane. 'I can really only think about one thing at a time, these days. The main aim is to stay here if we possibly can. You know it's what Theo would have wanted.'

'Of course. Of course he would. I'm not criticizing you, it's just . . .'

'I know. It's horrible to watch things change. But it isn't always bad.' Jane looked fondly at Jerry. As usual, he looked dainty and neatly turned-out in a blue blazer, pressed trousers and well-knotted tie. For a large and quite fat man, he always created an impression of trim perfection. He had been her husband Theo's friend at university, and after Theo died, she and Jerry had become closer until she supposed that he was the nearest thing she had to a best friend, always there, always ready for a chat, usually bubbling with ideas and enthusiasm. He had helped her more than he could ever know when Theo had died so suddenly and left her floundering in a world of which she was completely ignorant, where there were taxes and debts and pension rights and lawyers' fees. Sometimes she wondered whether Theo had done the right thing in keeping all that from her for so long, making her so helpless and so frightened in the face of the thin, official letters from the bank that made her stomach swoop and her palms damp when she saw them on the hall mat. Even driving past the branch in town, she kept her eyes averted and her shoulders hunched, as though if anyone inside spotted her, they'd come out shouting and pursuing her down the high street. It was hard to remember now the Jane Fielding who'd existed before Theo died: that creature seemed so far away, so carefree and frivolous, worrying only about the children, the village fête and the church flowers, never stopping to think when she wrote a cheque or used the cash point. Now she pondered over every penny before she spent it.

But, she reminded herself, she was off the hook now, for a while at least. She'd rung the bank's automated phone line that morning and, after keying in endless codes and options, had heard the mechanical voice telling her the account balance. She'd laughed, hung up and called again just to hear it repeated. It seemed so fabulous to be in credit. Holly Lodge was sold and the funds were now in her account ready to be transferred into savings and investments, a new roof and gutters to stop the leaks in the upstairs bedrooms, the university fund for Alec and Lucy, perhaps something for grandchildren, if they ever came along. Most importantly, it meant they could stay at Rawlston for a while longer.

They sat in enforced silence for a while as the lorry roared away, fading into the distance as it went down the lane. The terrace caught the afternoon sun and it was restful to sit there looking out at the lawn that sloped gently to the woods.

'What are they like, then, these neighbours?' Jerry asked. 'Have you met them properly?'

'The Clarkes. I called round when they arrived, of course. They were very friendly – at least, he was. Ben. The husband. Great big bear of a man, very confident. His wife is extraordinary-looking. I've never seen anyone so tiny.'

'Like a dwarf?'

'No, no, just amazingly thin, like someone in a magazine. She had a pair of jeans on with the waist virtually skimming her pubic bone, skinny legs and matchstick arms, and bright yellow hair. She also had very brown skin, as though she was just back from the South of France.'

'Mmm, fake tan, no doubt. Ghastly stuff. Makes one look vaguely grubby – at least, that's what I found. How old is she?'

'I couldn't tell. You know how women all dress alike now, forty-year-olds wearing the same as teenagers. But if she's mother to that girl I see moping around, she has to be at least in her mid-thirties and even then she must have started very young.'

'Oh dear. How very common.'

'Don't be a snob – you know I hate it. Anyway, they're obviously doing a lot of work to the other side of the house.' She looked over towards it wistfully. 'I wonder what it's like now.'

'You must go and see, of course. Why not have a dinner party and have them over? I'd love to meet them, and then they'd ask you back and perhaps me as well, and we'd get a good look-see round the new doings. Go on, Janey!'

Jane laughed. She couldn't be cross with Jerry for long – or with his terrible snobbery: he was so harmless with it and so frank and open about what he liked in life. '*Beauty*,' he would say, 'is the only thing in life worth anything. That is what I care about.' It seemed to cover an enormous range of things, from the clothes he adored and cared for so meticulously to the exquisite decoration of his cottage. His job running the picture gallery and rare-books department of an Oxford college meant that he was surrounded by beautiful things in a beautiful place all day long, and as he lived alone, he had enough money to indulge himself in the arts he loved.

'Perhaps,' said Jerry, with badly disguised cunning, 'they might even invite a nice man for you.'

'Well, they might,' said Jane, 'but let's not get ahead of ourselves. We haven't even put phase one of the plan into action yet. You're right – I must invite them over. I've been meaning to for ages. I'll do it right away.'

'Good. I like to see things progressing. It's my mission to find you a man this year. You've been on your own far too long.'

'So have you,' Jane pointed out. 'And you seem perfectly happy.'

Jerry sighed. 'I've put all that behind me. Too much trouble, if you ask me. It's never gone right since that rat Max did the dirty on me. He was my last great passion. No. I just comfort myself with the fact that I get to feast my eyes on an endless procession of delightful young undergraduates, many of whom invite me to charming little parties, even if it's a case of water, water everywhere.'

17

'It sounds so sad.'

'Well, it's not. It makes me happy. I think I'm better off on my own. And when I really hit my dotage, you can put me up in the attic. I'll be quite happy up there.' He smiled at Jane. 'I'm not like you, darling. You need someone, I can tell. I'm an independent sort, happiest by myself – but you're different. You've got the air of someone with a pent-up store of love they want to pour out. Not just want – *need* to pour out on someone.'

'Have I?' said Jane, surprised. She thought of herself as rather self-contained and independent. After all, fifteen years of widowhood were behind her.

Jerry nodded. 'And it's just not right that you haven't got someone. That's my opinion, anyway.'

Jane drove to the small town ten miles from Rawlston to do her usual Saturday shop. The farmers' market was on in the mornings and she liked to go along and see what they had. The superstore was closer but she disliked those giant, chilled places where there was an eerie lack of smell and an excess of frozen food and plastic packaging. At the market she could poke about and pick up what suited her, and most of the stallholders recognized her and flattered her by holding back special little somethings for her, although she knew it was just salesmanship. She bought a game pie for her and Lucy's lunch, fresh bread and some ripe, smelly cheese, then wandered across the marketplace to the grocer's to pick up some washing powder and tea-bags. On her way into the little shop, she almost collided with a woman coming out in a hurry, smoking a cigarette and muttering under her breath something that sounded like 'fucking provincials'.

'Oh, Mrs Clarke!' Jane said. She grasped for a first name but couldn't quite remember what it was. A man's name – Bob? Nat? Georgie? None of those.

The woman stopped and seemed to stare hard, although it was difficult to tell with the giant pair of sunglasses she was wearing. She looked quite unusually glamorous for this place, with her white jeans, pale vest top and blonde hair in two girlish plaits. 'Yeah?' she said.

'I'm Jane Fielding – from next door? We met a while back, when you'd just moved in. Do you remember?'

'Oh.' Mrs Clarke frowned. 'Oh, yeah, hi.'

'Are you all right?'

The other woman took off her sunglasses, revealing china-blue, rather bloodshot, eyes and a sulky expression. 'I've driven all the way over here for some shampoo because I forgot to get some last time I was at the salon, and everything here is absolutely revolting. I wouldn't wash my dog with it, if I had one.'

'Oh dear. Have you tried the hairdressers round the corner? They seem very upmarket.'

Mrs Clarke pouted. 'Worth a try, I s'pose.'

'Let me walk you there.' They set off together, skirting the market-place and the town hall. 'I'm afraid we must be a bit different from . . . Where was it you lived before?'

'Cheltenham.'

'You must find us very countrified after that. But it's not all bad, I promise. Actually, I'm glad we met. I wanted to ask if you and your husband would come round some time.'

'Oh. Yeah. Okay, then.'

'Good. We really ought to get to know each other a little more now that we're neighbours. You could bring your daughter.'

'Who?'

'Your . . . your daughter?' Jane was confused. What was the girl if not a daughter? A niece? A sister?

'You mean Emma. Don't worry, I won't inflict that on you. Ben and I will come though. Just let me know a date and I'll check the diary. We're going to France in July.'

'All right. Well, I'll think of something and let you know.' They stopped in front of the town hairdresser, a pink and white confection called Lottie's. Mrs Clarke stared at the display of bottles in the window and made a small snorting sound. Jane felt a little uncomfortable as they stood in silence, looking at the rows of treatments and lotions. Then she said brightly, 'Oh, I meant to tell you. Don't be surprised if you see a removal van in the lane today. There are some new people arriving.'

'Yeah?' Mrs Clarke's interest appeared to be awakened ever so slightly.

'Yes. The Balfours. You know the lodge at the corner of the lane, opposite the cottages?'

'That red place?'

'That's right. Well, it belongs to the house – at least, it did, before I sold it. They seem like a very nice family from London, and they've got two young children. Perhaps they can come over when you do.'

The other woman sucked a last drag from her cigarette, threw down the butt and ground it into the pavement with the heel of her stiletto. 'Yeah,' she said at last, sounding unimpressed. The air of boredom descended on her again. 'Great.'

'I'd better get along. My parking ticket is about to run out.'

Mrs Clarke didn't reply.

'All right, then, goodbye.' Jane clutched her carrier-bags a little more tightly and smiled.

''Bye,' Mrs Clarke said, and returned to staring at Lottie's window.

Jane turned back to the bright bustle of the marketplace, letting out a long breath as she did so. 'Golly,' she said to herself. 'Miss Charm she isn't.'

Jane knew that the market was hardly a seething metropolis but it was still a relief to get back to the peace of Rawlston House. As the car bumped up the driveway, she felt the usual calm return at the approach of home. How long had she lived there now? It must be twenty years, only five with Theo and the rest on her own – with the children, of course, but still essentially alone. The odd thing was that it was getting harder and harder to leave the place. She was beginning to feel glued to it.

In the kitchen, she covered the table with a red gingham cloth and set out her purchases. It looked just right – the wonky golden pie in the middle of a white plate, the tomatoes and cucumbers bright beside it and the fresh bread on a wood board. She went to the back stairs and called up to Lucy to come down for lunch. There was no reply so, after a few minutes, she went up to the first-floor landing and along the corridor to the attic stairs door, which was firmly shut with the faint sound of music coming through it. She opened it. No wonder Lucy couldn't hear her: she had a stereo on full blast. She went up to the next flight and hammered at the door at the top. 'Lunch, Lucy!' she bellowed.

'Coming!' was the muffled reply, so Jane went back to the kitchen, stopping to pick out a pile of washing from the basket on the landing where Lucy dumped all her dirty clothes. How anything got washed when her daughter was at university with no one to do it for her, Jane couldn't think.

It was twenty minutes before Lucy descended, by which time Jane had made inroads into the pie and salad while she read the Saturday newspaper supplement. Lucy sat down, looking fresh and young in her jeans and off-the-shoulder top, her brown hair pulled up into a messy bunch on the top of her head and speared with a chopstick.

'Have some pie,' said Jane. 'It's very good.'

'Is it veggie?'

'No. It's a game pie.'

'Oh God – what's in it?'

'Game, I imagine – pheasant, rabbit, venison, pigeon, that sort of thing.'

'Christ,' said Lucy, looking ill.

'When did you go vegetarian?' Lucy was always springing this kind of surprise on her.

Lucy rolled her eyes. '*Mum*. I've been veggie for ages. I eat fish and chicken and sometimes bacon but not rabbit and all that stuff, and especially not in a pie.'

'Is the pie format somehow crueller?' enquired Jane.

'It's the pastry – chock full of fat.'

'Oh, I see. Well, I'll get some fish in for you, then. And chicken and bacon. No wonder I didn't notice. You eat an awful lot of meat for a vegetarian.'

'It's all in the context. But this looks good.' Lucy reached over for the bread and cheese. 'I'm going out later. Work.'

'So they gave you your old job back at the hotel?'

'With knobs on. I'm deputy restaurant manager now. But don't get excited. It doesn't mean a medal or anything – about fifty pence an hour more and the honour of cashing up at the end of a session if no one else is about. So I'll be in and out at all hours – don't expect to see too much of me.'

'Oh. Maggie will be disappointed.'

Lucy looked up quickly. 'Maggie's coming? Wow – she's never here. That's great. When's she arriving?'

'At the weekend, I think. I know it's hard to persuade her down but I managed this time. I just didn't think I could face a trip to London with the tourist season beginning and all the terrible traffic. I told her you'd be here and that helped.'

Lucy grinned. 'Good old Aunt Mags. I bet she wants to hear all the gossip.'

Jane felt mildly hurt. 'Is there gossip? Has lots been happening at university? What haven't you told me?'

Lucy's gaze slid away. 'Well, you know, bits and bobs. You wouldn't be interested, Mum. Anyway,' she changed the subject deftly, 'I bet that means we won't be seeing Jerry around for a while. It's hilarious the way they can't stand each other – I can't say I blame Maggie either. I don't know how you put up with all that affectation and puffing about, pretending to be something out of PG Wodehouse—'

'Lucy – that's unkind. He's a good friend of mine, and what's more, he's very fond of you.'

'Sorry. It's just he's so funny. Do you remember the last time he and Maggie met?' Lucy giggled. It had gone into family lore. Maggie liked to infuriate Jerry, whom she considered a foolish anachronism, and knew just the buttons to press. At lunch, she had launched into a long speech about how the aristocracy should be forced to give up their estates and the land shared out among the poor and the homeless. Jerry had risen beautifully to the bait, gone quite violently red in the face and spluttered, 'They wouldn't have the *first idea* how to manage a stately home!'

Jane smiled. 'I have a feeling Jerry will keep well away.'

'Let me know exactly when Maggie's coming and I'll arrange some time off. Shame Alec's not going to be here – he loves seeing her.'

'Yes, I know.' It hadn't escaped Jane's notice how much more animated and sociable her children were when her sister visited but she tried hard not to mind. 'He's not back from school for weeks yet.'

'Enjoy it while it lasts,' counselled Lucy. 'The longer we can avoid the Beast in the Bedroom the better.' She got up, taking a hunk of bread and cheese. 'I'd better get ready. I'm due at the hotel at three. See you later.'

'See you later, darling.'

Silence fell on the house after Lucy had cycled off to the Station Hotel. The day was bright and sunny. Jane washed up the dishes, then decided to take the radio out to the garden and see what needed doing. It was a rule that she did no housework at the weekend. There was so much to do during the week, keeping this great old place even vaguely in order; she seemed to spend her life dusting and vacuuming and tidying, even though most of the time she lived there alone. She'd grown used to it now – the long periods when the children were away. It had been worse when the place had been one big house: then she'd had to shut up great swathes of the place and try to forget about dust, cobwebs and the damp creeping into the unused, unheated rooms. At least Rawlston was more manageable now that she had half the bedrooms to worry about, half the heating bill, yet still had plenty of space and most of her beloved garden. And if she hadn't divided the house, they would have had to sell up and lose the place completely.

She changed into her gardening trousers and an old shirt, then took her ancient Roberts radio and a gardening mat outside. The grass seemed to glow in the sunlight and the lawn, which stretched away down to the woods at the bottom, appeared almost juicy in its greenness. The grass would need cutting soon – she must ask Mr Foster from the cottages if he'd look after it regularly over the summer, as she usually did. Alec would protest violently if she asked him, so it wasn't worth trying.

Jane wandered over to the kitchen garden, a large square plot surrounded by crumbling, mossy brick walls, one of which pressed up to the cool dark woods beyond. She arranged everything carefully so she could begin weeding, then remembered with annoyance that she'd left her hat in the kitchen. With the sun beginning to beat down, she ought to wear it if she didn't want a headache. She hauled herself to her feet, went back inside, collected the floppy straw hat and was heading out again when the phone rang. She debated with herself whether to answer it, then went to the kitchen extension and picked it up.

'Jane Fielding,' she said smoothly.

'Mum – it's me.'

'Alec.' She was surprised. He almost never rang home, except to request more money or tell her where he'd be spending the next exeat, which was rarely with her. 'Hello, darling. How are you?'

He ignored this and said tersely, 'Mum, I need you to pick me up at the station this afternoon.'

'This afternoon? Why? Aren't you getting ready for your exams? Did you get my good-luck card?' It felt as though Alec had been preparing for his end-of-year exams for months, not that he ever mentioned them or appeared to do any work.

'I just need you to pick me up with the truck. I'm gonna have all my stuff with me. I'll be on the six-thirty train.'

'Alec, why on earth are you coming home? I'm not expecting you for weeks. What about your exams?' she said, exasperated. 'Just talk to me for once, can't you?'

There was a pause before Alec said roughly, 'Look, I've been expelled, OK? Just pick me up later.' He cut the connection before she could say anything else.

It was a long, tiring conversation with Alec's housemaster but, in the end, she had to accept that her son had been expelled, and would be leaving school that afternoon.

'The headmaster and I would like you to come in and discuss everything at some point,' the housemaster had said, 'but at the moment there's nothing to be done except remove Alec immediately.'

'I don't understand,' Jane had protested. 'It doesn't sound so bad to me. Don't lots of boys get up to this kind of thing? I can't believe that it warrants expulsion.'

'Rules are rules, Mrs Fielding, and Alec has had a fair number of warnings. We are strict about how our pupils behave when they are in our care and, occasionally, it goes beyond a point where such behaviour is excusable. In those circumstances, we must insist that the pupil's tenure here comes to an end.'

Oh, talk like a human being, can't you? she thought furiously. Then said, 'All right, all right. But I'm not at all happy.'

The housemaster was evidently relieved to get Jane off thc line. She put the phone down and swore hard, slamming the dresser with a palm. She said again, 'Shit, shit, *shit*!' It made her feel bettcr.

That was the worst of living alone, she thought. There was no onc to share this with, talk it over with. Shc considered calling Jerry but, really, she couldn't inflict her troubles on him in good conscience.

It was already four o'clock. She changed out of her gardening clothes, took the keys to the old Land Rover that she usually only used when the weather made the lane almost impassable and set off in it towards the village.

The station bore the name of the village but it was a couple of miles outside, the kind of place that would have been shut down years ago except that it was on a main commuter route linking the Cotswolds to London. Intercity trains flew through without stopping while the turbo trains that served the villages chugged in and out every hour or so, heading up and down the Thames valley. Beside it was the hotel, lonely in its isolated position, with only the railway line for company. For years it had resembled the setting for a Gothic novel or fright movie: huge, ragged at the edges, grey and dismal. Then last summer some eager new owners had moved in and tried to make it over, hopeful that somehow they'd attract people from the surrounding villages. Now it had the appearance of an elderly lady smeared with makeup, dressed in clothes far too young for her venerable age, with a trail of fairy lights festooned across the front below the gaunt-looking windows and gaudy flower baskets hanging at the sides.

Jane went inside. The old floral carpets and dingy paint had gone – well, that was an improvement anyway – and everywhere was now blond wood and halogen spotlighting and helpful little signs full of quotation marks.

She went to 'Reception', where a smiley woman in a blue jacket was shuffling leaflets and arranging pens in a row.

'Hello,' said Jane. 'I'm here to see my daughter, Lucy Fielding. She's working in the restaurant.'

'Through to your left,' answered the woman brightly, pointing to a sign that read 'Café' and 'Carvery'.

Jane went to the café, which was almost empty, apart from a man reading a paper at a far table. She looked about for Lucy and then spied her bustling out of the swing doors at the back, unfamiliar in her black-and-white uniform. Lucy saw her and came over, looking anxious. 'Everything all right, Mum?'

'Have you got a moment? I'm sorry to disturb you at work.'

'Sure. It's empty here. What is it?' Lucy beckoned her to a table and they sat down.

Jane got straight to the point. 'It's Alec. He's been expelled and he's coming home this afternoon.'

Lucy looked dismayed. 'What? Why? This afternoon? Bloody great! What's he done now?'

'Well, that's just the thing. It doesn't seem much at all. He sneaked out of school and went to a pub in the town. A master caught him there, drunk and ordering brandy. Alec tried to brazen it out, then ran off and was found by the housemaster climbing up the side of the boarding house, apparently trying to creep in at a window. So they sacked him.'

Lucy stared at the pink tablecloth and ran a finger along the damask pattern. She looked up, her expression cross. 'That's it?'

'It's not the first time, apparently. He's been warned before – not that they've ever mentioned it to me. They're adamant that they want him out.' She sighed with agitation. 'What am I going to do, Lu? He'll never get into another school for just a year to finish his A-levels. God knows what his grandparents will say when they find out. I'll have to tell them or they'll just ask me why the bills have stopped coming. They'll probably refuse to pay any more fees at all. They only stumped up for that place because it was Dad's old school.'

'Don't bother with them,' Lucy said brusquely. 'Who cares what those old bastards think.'

'Lucy—'

'I mean it. They don't give a shit about us, and never have. Who knows why they decided to pay our school fees in the first place? They've never done anything else for us. I've not even laid eyes on them since Dad's funeral. Mum . . .' Lucy looked down at the pattern she was tracing with her finger. 'I didn't want to say this before but Alec's not happy. I don't know why, I'm the last person he'd confide in, but I can tell. That school's probably glad to have an excuse to get rid of him. He's been in trouble for the whole year, he's going to fail his exams and bring down their grade average and league-table place and all that stuff. So if you're thinking you can persuade them to have him back, forget it.'

'He's going to fail?' Jane was astonished. She'd always thought of Alec as bright and capable, maybe not Oxbridge material but certainly above average.

'Yep. Badly. And I think that's just the start of it.'

Jane leant back in her chair and studied her daughter's serious face. Her heart was racing and her stomach churning. 'This is a bit of a shock, Lu. I thought everything was fine.'

'Sorry, Mum. I suppose you had to know some time.'

At six-thirty, she was sitting in the Land Rover in the station car park across the way from the hotel. She'd sat for over an hour in the hotel café trying to read a paper and eking out a filter coffee until it turned cold and scummy. Then she'd given up and come to watch the trains pull in and out. Eventually the train drew in, and a few minutes later, after the stream of commuters had gone by, she saw Alec pulling his luggage out of the gate by the ticket office. He looked taller and skinnier than she remembered, his hair was absurdly long and dishevelled, and he was smoking a small, tight roll-up.

He frowned as she pulled up beside him and only grunted when she greeted him. He allowed her to kiss his cheek and then, his little cigarette clamped between his teeth, threw his bags into the back of the Land Rover. They set off in silence, Alec blowing sour smoke and staring out of the window as they followed the narrow, hedge-lined lanes back to Rawlston.

'Did you have a nice trip?' said Jane at last, unable to bear the moody silence. Now she came to think of it, Alec hadn't had a conversation with her in years. She'd put it down to normal teen-age reticence but what Lucy had said was turning over in her mind. Had she missed signs that Alec was suffering? That he was miserable? Should she have done more?

'It was okay.'

'Lucy's home from uni. She's looking forward to seeing you.'

He didn't reply.

'Do you want to talk about what's happened? You must be feeling rotten about being expelled like this. Missing out on the end of term.'

'Mum,' he said sharply, 'I don't want to talk about it. Okay?'

'All right, darling. Whenever you're ready. Just say the word,' said Jane unhappily, and they drove on without talking any more.

Chapter Three

Sam Clarke sat at her dressing-table, brushing her hair. It was something she did very slowly these days since she'd noticed that her hair was starting, very slightly, to thin. It seemed crackly and coarse and she was sure she could see more pale pink scalp than she used to. Her hairbrush was always thick with long coils of bright yellow strings. Was it the dye, she wondered, gazing at the carefully graded highlights applied by her hairdresser every six weeks. Her hair contained eight shades, ranging from honey beige to silvery ash blonde, and she'd been dyeing it since she was fourteen so she supposed that it might have an effect after a while. All those chemicals right next to the skin. Leaking in. I'm sure I read about it, she thought. Was it in *Marie Claire*? Or *Cosmo*? I must ask Mitch about it next time I get my hair done. Perhaps there's something organic they can use.

Organic seemed to be the answer to everything. Organic meant healthy – it was an insurance policy against grisly cancers and chemically induced agony. Anything that said 'organic' automatically seemed bathed in a rosy glow of wholesome goodness – even those organic chocolate gateaux they'd started selling. Silly, really.

Sam looked at her face, scrutinizing it from every angle. I'm looking good, she thought. Her face, in a certain light – daylight, probably – was a touch haggard and hollow in the cheeks, but with her full makeup on and in artificial light, she looked about twenty-one. I should think so too, she thought, with the amount I spend on all those lotions and potions. The previous week she and Becky had gone for one of their periodic trips to London for a girls' day out: the hairdresser, massage, beauty treatments, a lovely lunch with champagne at Harvey Nic's, a romantic comedy at the cinema. Becky was a bad influence: she had her husband's corporate platinum credit card – what were they going to invent when platinum seemed a bit ordinary? Was there a diamond credit card? And what about after that? Perhaps a moondust card or something – and she was almost encouraged to spend on it in order to rack up air miles, then it was wiped clean at the end of the month, just like that. Sam's credit card had plenty of bounce in it, but she was supposed to manage her allowance. Ben never liked it when she came pleading for more money even though he was the first to enjoy the way she looked, the beautiful clothes she wore, and the careful condition she kept herself in. All that cost money in a way men just didn't understand. She and Becky had been in the cosmetics department and Sam, after much smooth persuasion by the sales girl and urging from Becky, had ended up spending over a hundred pounds on one pot of luxurious face cream made from seaweed, packed with minerals and said to be the favourite of famous actresses.

Sam stood up and turned slowly in front of the mirror. The other day she'd been depressed when the scales had touched just over eight stone. When that happened she went on the hot water and grapefruit diet for a couple of days. Apparently Hollywood stars in the old days used to do that before they started filming. Of course it was very nasty and made her feel sick and dizzy, but it did the trick. Otherwise she simply used a combination of all the celebrity diets she read about, which meant she was on a low-everything regime: low fat, low carbohydrate, low protein, no wheat, almost no dairy. Basically, she was on the low-food diet. Breakfast was fruit – though she worried about the sugar in that – or sometimes muesli; lunch was cottage cheese on a Ryvita and some bare salad. Dinner was a tiny bit of whatever Ben cooked for him and Emma, but strictly without the carbs.

God, no wonder she smoked. She had to put something in her mouth, just to remember it was there.

But she had to keep in shape – it wasn't a matter of choice. It was her duty, to herself and to Ben, to look as good as she possibly could. When the time came, she'd be first in line to have her eyes lifted, her face sculpted and her thighs sucked out, and she wouldn't feel vain about it. You only got one life, so what was the point of spending it looking fat and ugly? Sam couldn't understand women who let themselves go. Look at the woman next door, Jane Fielding. When she'd introduced herself the first time, Sam had thought she was collecting on behalf of some charity, she was so dowdy. When Sam had realized she was the woman who'd originally owned the whole house, she couldn't believe it. She'd seen enough pictures of the upper classes in those glossy magazines to know that a lot of them looked as good as any film star. But this woman – what was she thinking of? She'd been wearing a baggy old tweed skirt, a jumper covered in what looked like cat hairs, and a dreadful sleeveless Puffa thing over the top. It was a bit like Sam's sheepskin gilet, only made of green stuff. Her hair was a neat, slightly wavy bob but it had streaks of grey in it, was almost white at the front, and she wasn't wearing a scrap of makeup. Ben said that her husband had died and now she was a widow. Well, she'd be one for the rest of her life if she didn't make an effort.

Sam went downstairs, admiring her fresh interior decoration as she went and wondering idly if she could give Mrs Fielding a makeover and, if she did, what she'd do with her. A dye job first. Nice rich chestnut brown. A full makeup session at the Shiseido counter, then a trip down Bond Street for some new clothes . . .

'Mrs Clarke?'

Sam jumped. It was her head builder, Pete, who'd been overseeing the final bits and pieces they were having done. He'd poked his head round the living-room door, giving her a fright.

'Hi, Pete. Everything okay?' She liked getting on well with workmen, although she didn't let them forget who was paying for all this. Too often they acted like they were doing some great act of charity, instead of fleecing her for all they could get.

'Just to let you know that the boys expect to finish putting in the kitchen today, so you'll be able to use it tonight.'

Sam clapped her hands, delighted. 'That's great! Is the range cooker going to be in?'

'All eight burners, separate frying plate and wok stand, and three ovens plus grill,' Pete replied, with a grin. 'You must enjoy cooking.'

'Oh, I don't cook. Can't hardly boil an egg. It's my husband who's the chef.'

'Right,' said Pete. 'Get him to give you a lesson then, you look like you could do with eating a bit.'

Sam laughed politely, although she didn't like the implied criticism. Honestly, where did some people get off? They would never tell some great blubber of a woman to her face that she was too fat, would they? But it was perfectly all right to tell someone she was too thin. Sam always thought that men who said it had a fat wife. Some of them claimed to like it – and maybe they did. Perhaps Pete was a feeder – one of those sinister blokes who deliberately made sure their wife stayed fat, and scuppered all her attempts to diet by cooking everything in butter and stuffing her with chocolate.

Pete said, 'It's not painted yet. Once all the electrics are checked and finished, we'll be in to paint, probably tomorrow or the next day. Is that all right?'

'Yeah, great. Sooner the better. Can I take a look?'

'Help yourself. Just don't be put off by the mess – it'll look spick and span when we're done.'

Sam went off to the kitchen, feeling uplifted. The prospect of a house without builders was wonderful – she couldn't wait to get them all out. It seemed to have taken months, as they'd worked their way through the place, knocking down walls, opening up the space and getting rid of that old-fashioned feel that came from so many passages and doors. They'd installed state-of-the-art electronics throughout, inside the walls. Wires ran everywhere, connecting everything to everything. Ben said they could talk to the house via computer from wherever they were, telling it to turn on the heating, or put on music or even order the shopping. It seemed fantastic.

The builders had begun at the top, adding bathrooms, re-modelling the bedrooms, adding Sam's dressing room, and worked their way down, with the interior decorators following in their wake, stripping, painting and chasing Sam about with colour charts, fabric swatches, catalogues and something called 'mood boards' which, as far as she could see, were just pictures ripped out of magazines and stuck on a bit of cork. She knew what she wanted: it had to be modern, pale and uncluttered. Other than that, she left it to the designers and so far they'd done a great job, sensing exactly what she liked. Her bedroom was a taupe colour with chocolate swirly modern rugs and a honey-coloured leather armchair in the corner. The drawers were all concealed behind panels that sprang open when you touched them. An antique full-length mirror added a touch of class, along with her silver-glass dressing table, which the designer had told her was art deco. She loved it.

The landscapers had promised they'd be finished soon too. The Japanese garden was almost done. But the thing she couldn't wait for was the outdoor Jacuzzi, constructed on a special raised deck and surrounded by rare oriental plants, bamboo and stuff like that; it would be really soothing in the evening when the scented candles were lit. Somewhere for her to meditate and maybe do a bit of yoga if she was in the mood.

The kitchen was, as Pete had said, a mess. Three men in overalls were beavering away surrounded by boxes, plastic sheeting, un-identifiable bits of wood, tool-kits, electric cables and all the detritus of the workshop. The range, ordered from France and made of gleaming stainless steel, was swathed in its protective bubble-wrap but it still looked like something from the Savoy kitchen. Ben would love it. He'd be dying to put on his apron and chef's hat and get cooking. Well, he could wait until the place was finished before he let rip. They'd been cooking and eating in the dining room on a portable electric stove but Ben had been moan-ing for weeks about how useless it was and how he couldn't wait to get back to gas burners. Ben's rooms were the kitchen and his study – he'd been allowed to make all the important choices on those, along with the humidity-controlled wine room he'd had installed in the cellar for his vast collection of bottles – but everything else was Sam's domain and she was really very pleased with it, considering she'd never decorated a house as big as this one before.

When they'd first moved to Rawlston she couldn't understand why Ben had been content with half a house, although he'd told her mysteriously that there was method in his madness and just to wait and see. It was such a strange arrangement: this huge old mansion carefully divided into two halves, with the original owner still living in the other. But now they'd been here for a while, she was glad they didn't have the whole thing. It was big enough as it was, and if you didn't know, you wouldn't guess that it was only part of a larger place. With their big garden, the solid soundproofing and the thick borders of rhododendrons that cut them off from the other side, it was as though they were on their own. Sometimes that did feel a bit spooky, if she was honest. The hamlet was made up of the big house, the lodge half-way down the lane, some farm-workers' cottages and the broken-down old farm, with its rusting equipment and eerie abandoned buildings, now collapsing into piles of rotten wood and crumbling bricks. Apart from that, they were miles from anything. The nearest village was two miles away and the sorry excuse for a town was a ten-mile drive. It was a bit of a change from Cheltenham, and sometimes Sam couldn't help feeling very isolated indeed, as though she were at sea on an empty ship all alone.

She was wondering if she should start getting ready for her tennis lesson when she heard the phone ringing in the study. Ben had a private line there for business and it usually had an answer-machine on it, but now the phone kept shrilling out.

She went to the door, opened it and went in cautiously. There was no real reason for her to be in Ben's study. The cleaning woman, a girl from the cottages called Trudy, dusted and vacuumed, and Ben didn't like his things disturbed. There was a docking bay for his laptop and trays of paper on the large, leather-topped antique desk. Ben liked to joke that it was the kind of desk Napoleon had had: gilt-edged and ornate but heavy and resolutely masculine. There was a large, flat-screen television on the wall for watching sport, and the shelves were messily filled with books and magazines, mostly on fishing, sailing, climbing and computers.

The phone was still ringing, the little silver handset sitting upright in its pod as though begging to be answered. Sam went over and picked it up. 'Hello?'

There was a long pause and the empty air on the line crackled and hissed a little. Finally a voice said, 'Hello, is that Sam?'

'Yes, it is,' said Sam, coldly. 'What do you want, Aileen?'

'I was hoping to talk to Ben,' said the other woman, in the kind of strained voice that meant she was going to be polite no matter how much of an effort it was.

'He's not here.'

'All right.' Another pause. 'Is Emma there?'

'I don't know what sort of time you think it is over here, Aileen, but it's actually only four o'clock. Ben is still at work and Emma isn't back from school.'

Aileen laughed, the sound coming tinnily down the line. It infuriated Sam – she could just imagine Aileen's ugly face splitting into a grin, showing her bad teeth. 'Fine. You stand on your dignity, what there is of it. I want you to tell Ben I called about Emma coming over this summer, but it doesn't matter if you don't because I'll just call him later or email him. Okay? Think you can grasp that?'

'I'll pass on your message,' Sam said stiffly, and pressed the button to cut Aileen off.

Emma arrived back from school at about half past four, her car crunching up the gravel to announce her return. Sam heard it as she lay on the sofa watching a talk show on television, and remained exactly where she was. Emma usually went straight up to her bedroom, not to be seen again until supper-time and as far as Sam was concerned, that was just dandy. She didn't know what on earth she and Emma would have to say to each other anyway – *how was your day at school, dear? Any exciting things happening in the A-level syllabus today?* – so it didn't make much difference if she saw her or not.

Sam heard Emma come through the sitting room to the kitchen, probably after a cup of tea or a bottle of water.

'Hiya,' she sang out, not taking her eyes off the screen, as Emma went by. She liked wrongfooting her.

Emma said a cold hello as she passed and disappeared into the kitchen. Sam followed her with an amused look, catching a glimpse of the girl's back. Now that she was in the last year of school she was allowed to wear her own clothes and Sam felt a bit sorry for her really, as she must be a laughing-stock. She had all that money – Sam knew Ben gave her a healthy allowance – and, instead of wearing anything decent, wandered about in pastel jumpers and long floral skirts like some throwback to the fifties – not the cool fifties, either.

A few minutes later, Emma came back, heading towards the hall, no doubt looking forward to another evening slaving over text-books, revising for her exams.

'Nice day?' enquired Sam sweetly, propping her head up on a hand to look at her.

Emma shot her a cool glance and nodded sharply.

'Your mum called, by the way.'

Emma stopped, looking suspicious. She thought for a moment and then said, 'What did she say?'

'Not much. She wants to talk to you about going to America this summer. You should give her a call.'

'Right. Thanks.' Emma moved off.

'Don't mind us,' called Sam, after her. 'You go to America as soon as you like – and for as long as you like!' She giggled. Emma ignored her and Sam heard her footsteps going up the stairs. She tried to concentrate on the talk show again but it was no good; she'd lost interest. She flipped the television off, got up, sighed and padded outside.

In the garden, she mounted the decking steps up to the Jacuzzi, and sat down beside it, her legs crossed, to smoke a cigarette and contemplate the bamboo. 'Stay calm,' she told herself. 'Visualise something.' But her mind was a blank. Every time Emma was in the house, the whole atmosphere changed. 'I'm too young to be a stepmother,' Sam muttered. And Emma was too old to be her stepdaughter. She was tiring of the constant low-level fight they'd been having ever since they met but the end was in sight. Emma would be leaving home for university soon and Sam knew, that in the long run, she'd win the war.

By the time Ben came home, the builders had tidied up and were gone. She heard his sports car roaring up the driveway and then he burst in, grabbed Sam into a big hug and lifted her off the ground. She loved that feeling: he was so big and strong and tall – a bit paunchy now but he was over forty and a little too fond of his food and wine – and he made her feel all fragile and tiny, like a child.

'Grrrr, hello, gorgeous. How are you?'

She kissed him hard. 'Hi, Benjy, I'm fine. And I've got a surprise for you . . . Look what the builders did today.' She took him by the hand and led him towards the kitchen.

'You know, I don't believe there are any builders,' Ben said, following her. 'I never see them. They arrive after I've gone to work and have vanished when I get home. I think it's really you. When I've gone, you put on your sexy overalls and some gorgeous goggles and a face mask and start plastering.'

'Yeah, *right*,' said Sam. 'Where do you think all the money's going? Come and look at this.'

They stood in the kitchen doorway and looked into the room. It had once been a boot room, and the floor was stone flagged. The tall windows looked out over the lawn and now, in the late-afternoon sunshine, they could see their new and very beautiful kitchen: fine wood cupboards and dressers, all custom-made; a smooth beech worktop that was marble along one side for hot dishes and chopping, bread-making and pastry-rolling; a huge double Belfast sink; plate racks on either side of the window; the fridge, freezer and dishwasher hidden away from sight behind the cupboard doors and, glory of glories, the incredible range in pride of place.

Ben gasped with delight.

'Do you like it?' asked Sam.

'Oh, God, Sam, I love it! I can't wait to use it . . .'

'Pete says not until it's all checked and painted. Can you wait for just a bit longer?'

Ben grabbed her hand and squeezed it. 'It'll be hard but I'll do my best. We'll go out for dinner tonight – I can't bear that bloody stove again – and celebrate the new kitchen. Come on, let's look around.'

While Ben was opening drawers and cupboards and inspecting everything, Sam remembered the call. She said, 'Aileen rang for you.'

'Did she?' Ben seemed more interested in the cutlery drawer than in his ex-wife.

'Something about Emma going to America this summer.'

'Oh, yeah. I think we'd spoken about arranging something.'

'I wish you'd told me, Benjy. I assumed Emma was coming with us to France. I've booked a big place for us all.'

'She probably is. Aileen and I haven't sorted out the dates yet.'

Sam felt herself prickle. The very fact that she felt angry annoyed her. She knew that her marriage would be perfect if it weren't for Ben's first wife and his daughter. They reminded her constantly that she wasn't the first woman in Ben's life, or the only person he cared about. Whenever they talked about Aileen or Emma, it would be like this, terse and clipped, Sam filled with resentment. She hated the very sound of Aileen's name. Ben refused to rise to it. She just wished the ugly old cow would leave them well alone – and take her daughter with her.

Ben came over and wrapped her in his strong arms again. She felt her irritation ease as he kissed her cheek and nuzzled her neck. 'It's a lovely evening. We'll put the roof down and drive over to that wonderful Abbey restaurant near Great Tod. You can get all dressed up.'

'Yeah, and who's going to see me – Old Farmer Brown and his cow?' she said, but she smiled and kissed him back.

Chapter Four

The silence of the place was eerie, Bella decided. Once the bustle of the first morning was over – taking Iain to the station for his train, dropping the children at the village school – and she'd returned to the lodge, the thing she really noticed was the quiet. She walked from room to room, each one still full of the boxes she had yet to unpack, feeling a strange dislocation. What was she doing here? What was this place? She ought to be at work, yet here she was at ten o'clock in the morning on a weekday, drifting around without a soul to talk to.

She went down to the sitting room, turned on the radio and started to unpack. As she put the books on the alcove shelves on either side of the fireplace, she noticed smears of grime and dust at the back, so set about with her cleaning things to give everything a good seeing-to. This made her feel better, but as she sat alone in the kitchen later with her lunch-time sandwich, wondering where on earth she could go to do a big shop, the sense of her isolation came back even more strongly.

Fight it, she told herself firmly. This is day one, for God's sake. Where are your inner resources? There are people just over the road, the Clarke family, Jane Fielding up the lane. You're not on your own in the least.

She spent the afternoon unpacking the boxes in the now-clean sitting room. Every familiar object she pulled out and put in its new place in the room made her feel better. This was her marking of her territory, and it looked much better, though the paint was still terrible . . . She'd paint it, she decided. That would be her project over the next few weeks, doing up this place. She'd find a

DIY shop or go to Oxford and get some colour charts and then . . . she saw herself picking shades and making it all pretty – it would be fun and would keep her busy.

She looked at her watch to see how much time there was before the children had to be collected from school. Her days were going to be framed by these little duties, she could see that: the delivery and collection of her family, leaving her with the hours in between for herself.

A knock at the front door startled her and she looked towards it, almost frightened. Then she gathered herself and went to answer it.

She recognized Jane Fielding at once, even though her face was shadowed by a floppy straw hat.

'Hello.' Her neighbour waved a bunch of flowers as if in explanation. 'I saw that you'd moved in and I was just in the garden when I thought how pretty these ranunculus were, and how you might like them.'

'Thank you,' said Bella, taking them. They were a delicate pink, the rows of petals furled in upon each other to a dark heart. 'They're gorgeous.' She was touched and pleased to have been thought about.

Jane smiled. 'Is this an all-right time to call by, Mrs Balfour?'

'Yes, yes, it's fine. And call me Bella. Please come in.' Bella led the way into the hall, suddenly worried about the state of the place. 'I'm afraid it's a bit of a mess.'

Jane stopped inside and looked about, blinking in surprise. 'Goodness,' she shook her head, 'I'm sorry. It's very different. Even in this short space of time. The last time I was here was not long before the Galloways left – well, Mr Galloway left, after his wife died. The house was very gloomy, lots of dark-wood furniture.'

'When did she die?'

'Just a few months ago, upstairs in bed.' There was a pause. Then Jane said apologetically, 'Oh dear, I hope you're not superstitious.'

Bella laughed, relaxing. 'How fantastically ghoulish. I suppose it was in our bedroom, wasn't it? Don't worry, I'm not bothered.

I've not noticed any ghostly presences – not yet, anyway.' She led the way to the kitchen. 'I'm sorry if it's rather warm in here. We had to light the Rayburn for the hot water. I spent most of last night wrestling with it. Antediluvian, really. Would you like a cup of tea or something?'

'Thank you, that would be lovely. Yes, I'd forgotten about the Rayburn. It is rather a period piece, I suppose. Well, the kitchen looks much better.'

'I've barely done a thing. Just a bit of rearranging. I've got plans for the place. I'll put these in water' – Bella laid the flowers carefully on the bench and collected a vase – 'and we'll have some tea.'

They went through to the sitting room with their tea. Jane had taken off her hat and Bella got a good look at her for the first time. She has a nice face, she thought. It was fine-boned, with good skin. Bella guessed her age at about forty-eight, although she might be older and just looked good on it. Her hair was full with a natural wave and streaks of grey that made her seem even more distinguished. Her eyes were deep-set over high cheekbones and a slightly hooked nose. *Patrician*, thought Bella, that's the word I'm looking for. Jane was dressed in a blue cotton skirt and a white linen shirt, with simple loafers. Plain but dignified. It felt suddenly important to make a good impression and she glanced anxiously about the room – well, it was as good as she could make it in the circumstances. At least it was clean.

Jane looked about with interest. 'It's quite amazing how just emptying a room can completely alter its character. You should have seen it before. It looks much better. It feels like a home already.'

'I feel as though we've barely started, there's such a lot to do. Iain, my husband, is bursting with schemes and plans. It's always been his dream to live in the countryside – he's a city boy born and bred, in case you hadn't guessed. So far, it's living up to the fantasy, but I don't know if he factored a four-hour commute into his boyhood dreams. He never got over reading *The Children of the New Forest* and ever since has yearned to stalk deer, climb trees and shoot Roundheads with muskets.'

'No deer round here, but he's welcome to take a pot at the rabbits. They play havoc in my vegetable garden, and although they look sweet, they're less charming when they've razed everything to the ground.' Jane looked around the room again. 'What a lot of books you've got. I always think they make a room look more cheerful and lived-in.' She got up, went over to the mantel where a pile of framed photographs was waiting to be hung and picked one up. It was Bella and Iain's wedding picture. 'Oh, this is you, isn't it? It's lovely.'

Bella came up beside her and looked at the picture with her. It was a black-and-white shot of the two of them in their wedding clothes: Iain in a dark suit and Bella in a white jacket and long, flowing white skirt. It had seemed so chic when she'd chosen it and now it looked hopelessly dated. It made her realize how long it was that she'd been married.

'Yes, that's us. My husband, Iain.'

'He's very handsome.'

'Is he?' Bella gazed at the picture. He had been handsome, she supposed, with his boyish face, his soft brown hair swooping over his brow, his unlined skin. Was he handsome now? She'd grown so used to him she barely saw him any more. It was hard to tell.

'And now you have children, don't you?'

'Yes. Two. Katie and Christopher. They've just started at the village school. A bit unusual to put them in for the last half term before the summer holidays, but I wanted them to make ·some friends, if they could.'

'Oh, they'll like it there. My two went – I've got a boy and girl as well, Lucy and Alec. Well past primary-school age now.' She frowned. 'They don't get any easier as they grow up, either.'

'And your husband, what does he do?'

'He died fifteen years ago.'

'Oh, God, I'm sorry – how clumsy of me. I do apologize.' Bella felt her face grow scarlet. Jane smiled kindly and put a hand on her arm; immediately she felt calmer and comforted.

'It's all right. It was a long time ago, I'm quite happy talking about it. You haven't upset me, please don't worry. But Theo died when I was a young mother, like you are, and he missed out on so much. He never saw the children grow up. We often used to wonder what would happen to them, how their personalities would develop, and the saddest thing is that he never found out. You may not think it but you are very lucky to have the two of you together, sharing all this.'

'Am I?' She looked again at the wedding photograph and a twist of something bitter rose in her throat; she found she was blinking hard against a sudden heat in her eyes.

'Are you all right?' Jane asked, looking closely at her. 'I'm afraid it's my turn to be embarrassed. I've said something to upset you. I'm sorry – I shouldn't have spoken like that when we've only just met and I know nothing about anything.'

Bella gained control of herself and smiled. 'Please, I'm not upset. Really, I'm fine.'

Jane touched her arm again, the soft, warm touch that Bella had found so oddly comforting. 'If you ever feel in need of company, don't hesitate to come up. I know how lonely it can get round here.'

'I will,' Bella promised. 'I won't forget.'

Sam wished she'd thought to have a tennis court laid when they were designing the garden. It was such a hassle to have to drive into the village where she met her coach on the local courts but she needed to run around three times a week and the nearest gym was probably in Oxford. At least, she hadn't found one closer yet. She turned the Mercedes into the lane and proceeded slowly up, letting the suspension take the strain of the potholes. Ben's little sports car practically bounced up the lane, taking off every time it hit the rim of a hole, but the Mercedes was too regal and smooth for that.

As she was approaching the top of the lane where the farm cottages faced Holly Lodge, she saw a car pull out of its drive and into the lane, obviously heading towards the village. There was no room for them both so the other car pulled up on the grassy verge to let her pass. Sam went by slowly, stopped when she was level and lowered her window. The other woman did the same. She looked to be in her thirties with short dark hair and a face that was too strong to be really pretty.

'Hi,' Sam said, 'you're Bella, aren't you? I'm Sam Clarke. My other half told me all about you. You've just moved in, haven't you?'

'Hello. Yes, I met your husband at the weekend when we arrived.'

'Where are you off to?'

'I'm just going to pick up my children from the village school.'

'I've just come from there,' said Sam. 'Shame, I could've given them a lift.'

'Well, that's kind.' The other woman smiled suddenly. 'Why don't you come down for a coffee when I've got back? I met Mrs Fielding yesterday, so it doesn't seem right that we haven't said hello properly. I'll only be half an hour. If you've got nothing else to do . . .'

'Yeah – yeah, okay. I'll come down later. That'll be nice,' said Sam, and pulled away up the lane with a wave.

Sam changed out of her tennis whites, admiring her brown legs as she did so, and had a short shower, then headed down the lane. It was too early for Emma to be back from school but getting out before she returned was one reason why Sam was eager to be on her way. She always leapt at any opportunity to avoid Emma – she couldn't stand the way the girl moped about, giving her the silent treatment while sending out signals of fierce resentment.

Sam didn't understand it. From the start, before Emma had lived with them, she'd tried to be friendly. She'd had presents for the girl when she came round: cute little handbags or lip-gloss kits, a pricy sarong and matching flip-flops, really lovely things – but Emma had looked at them as if they were offensive and, after a cold thank you, had ignored them. She'd even left the sarong set behind. Sam had tried several times, asking about Emma's school and boyfriends, and offering her some makeup advice, but the girl had never altered her chilly attitude and her polite but clipped replies to Sam's questions. Fine! she'd thought. I've done my best. That girl's obviously not interested. But she's going to be sorry she ever took me on.

They were fighting over Ben, Sam knew that and there was no way Emma could win. If the girl hoped that somehow her hostility would make Sam go away, or convince her father to break up with her, then she was sadly mistaken. In Sam's experience, no husband ever chose his children over his second wife. The children always overestimated their power – they didn't seem to realize that the new arrangement would weaken the old ties and that a smart woman would soon make them appear haranguing, demanding and selfish. She would portray herself as a victim, unfairly treated, not given a chance; she would invoke her husband's position as head of the family, demand he show who was boss. A second wife could always nurture a schism if she wanted, if that was what benefited her. Sam had played on Ben's protective instinct towards her as much as possible. The divorce had been far from amicable and there had been plenty of screaming matches between Aileen and Ben where Sam had been vilified with foul names. Ben was quite ready to believe that Emma's frosty, unbending attitude was because she was being poisoned against Sam by her mother. Sam had listened with gratification when she heard Ben bawling Emma out on one visit, telling her she wouldn't be welcome in his home if she couldn't be nicer to her stepmother.

Meanwhile, Sam was gently easing Ben's daughter out of the picture, cancelling her visits from time to time by booking expensive tickets to shows for the same weekend, slyly removing photos of her from their places. But just when she'd thought it was working, Aileen had decided to take a job in America and Emma had moved in with them, which set back Sam's plans back severely. There was no way Ben was going to tolerate open warfare – he needed to feel that there was harmony in the family despite the upheavals and trauma of divorce – so her campaign had had to go even further underground.

She could tell that Emma blamed her for everything, for the break-up and the divorce. That was just evidence of her pig-headed stupidity – it had been obvious that Ben and Aileen were doomed: Sam had just hurried things on a little. Of course it didn't help that Emma had walked in on Ben and Sam in bed. It was before anyone knew about them, even Aileen, and Ben had sneaked her into his house one afternoon. And, honestly, what kind of idiot walks unannounced into her parents' bedroom when

45

she can hear someone in there? It was one of those uncomfortable memories that Sam tried to push out of her mind as much as possible: the girl – she had been only twelve then – standing at the doorway, eyes huge and face horrified, while Sam lay there with Ben thumping away between her legs. She shuddered whenever she thought about it. It was the most humiliating thing that had ever happened to her – to be seen like that.

She knocked on the door of the lodge and when Bella answered, she said, 'Tanaaaa!' and thrust a bottle of wine from Ben's cellar into her hand. 'Housewarming,' she declared, going into the hall. 'Oh, this is nice,' she said, although she really thought that it was a bit poky. The hall was narrow, with a pile of coats hanging from hooks, and boots and shoes scattered by the door.

'Come in,' said Bella, waving her arm towards the sitting room. 'Can I get you some tea? I've been a real country housewife and made banana bread, if you'd like some.'

'Have you got coffee?'

'Sure. Won't be a moment.' Bella disappeared to the kitchen and Sam sat down on the shabby red sofa and looked around. Now, this is why I have an interior decorator, she thought. It was a mess. She supposed they'd only been there a short time but still . . . she wrinkled her nose at all the books stuffed into the alcoves by the fireplace. If those were her books, they'd be tidied away so as not to disrupt the colour scheme – although, come to think of it, there was no obvious colour scheme here. Nothing seemed to match: the lampshades, the rug, the cushions, the toys coming out of the hamper by the window, that horrid old trunk covered in ancient stickers. She picked up a magazine from the trunk, which obviously served as a table, and leafed through it until Bella came back with a tray.

'Here we are,' she said, and poured Sam a mug of coffee from the cafetiere. 'Milk?'

'Please. Do you have sugar?'

'Sugar? Oh, yes, hold on.' She hurried back to the kitchen and returned with a bag of sugar and a spoon. 'Sorry, I always forget. Now, please have some banana bread.'

Sam thought for a moment. Was bread the same as cake? It looked the same, but in a loaf shape rather than a round one. It sounded healthier, though. 'Go on,' she said. 'I shouldn't but it looks great. Did you really make this?'

'It's not difficult,' said Bella modestly, 'and we always seem to have some bananas turning black in the fruit bowl. I like to use them up.'

Sam took a bite of the bread and ate it slowly, feeling the heavy ball of flour, sugar and butter hit her stomach. She pushed the rest of it to the edge of her plate, and said, 'So, what do you think of Rawlston?'

'Oh, very nice,' Bella said. 'Quiet though.'

Sam laughed. 'It's bloody dead round here! Where'd you come from?'

'London.'

'Really?' She looked closely at Bella. She didn't seem to have the sophistication of the kind of person Sam imagined lived in London. She looked pretty ordinary in her jeans and velvet-edged top. A little on the heavy side, as well. 'You've got kids, haven't you?'

'Yes, two. They're outside playing. All this greenery is a novelty to them after the concrete jungle. Katie and Christopher can't get enough of it.'

'Ah. I expect they're little angels.' Sam eyed the loaf on her plate and felt her tummy rumble round the morsel she'd given it.

'Well . . . sometimes. To be honest, I'm glad to get them out of London. They were maturing too quickly. Katie's only ten but she was nagging me for makeup and high heels because that's what the other girls in her class are wearing. I want them to stay young for as long as they can – there's plenty of time for all that. I've got this rather idealized picture of a country village school but it's probably just as bad as the city.'

Sam looked blank. High heels were fine in her book. A necessity, in fact, and the earlier you got used to them the better.

'You have children, haven't you?' Bella ventured. 'Your husband mentioned a teenager . . .'

Sam shrieked with laughter. 'Oh, God, no! I haven't got any

47

kids. Ben's got one from his last marriage. Unfortunately for me, she didn't go off with her mum in the divorce and I got saddled with her. Bloody unfair.'

'That's . . . unusual, isn't it? The child staying with the father?'

'She started off with Aileen. It wasn't exactly a friendly situation because Ben and I got together kind of before the marriage was officially over, but then Aileen got this job in America so we worked out that it would be better for Emma if she stayed here with Ben.' Sam rolled her eyes. 'If you ask me, Aileen wanted her off her hands and knew that Ben would give her a good life. He can afford it. Nice private school, this big house. Even a bloody Jacuzzi. So she can swan off with a happy conscience, Ben foots the bills, and guess who has to put up with a sulky kid? Muggins, that's who.' She laughed again. Bella blinked and smiled at her.

'It's really nice to have another woman around,' Sam continued, warming to Bella. 'The one next door is a bit of an old bag. Much older than us. But you look like you'd enjoy a shopping trip or two.'

'Yes, I suppose I would.'

'Do you work?'

'Not at the moment – I gave up my job when we came here.'

'Yeah. Me neither. Let's face it, no one wants to work, do they? Everyone does it for the money, and if you don't need it – well . . .' Sam shrugged. 'Ben rakes in plenty – but that's a male thing, isn't it? Part of him proving he's a man. No point in both of us slaving away. I used to work – *hated* it.'

'What did you do?'

'I worked in Ben's company, actually. That's where we met.'

'Oh.'

Sam glanced about her and then said, in a whisper, 'Where's your toilet? Do you mind if I use it?'

'Of course not – it's upstairs, first door on the right.'

'Ooh, thanks.' Sam winked at her, and made her way upstairs. If there was one thing she loved, it was having a peek into other women's bathrooms. It was a sure-fire way to understand them. She resisted the temptation to have a quick snoop in the other rooms and found the bathroom easily enough.

48

Ouch, she thought, looking at the old plastic bathroom suite. This is one room they'll have to get round to decorating fast. There was a carpet on the floor, and carpets in bathrooms made Sam's skin crawl. She liked cool white tiles. The toilet had that low level, slim-line tank that looked like it contained about enough water for a cup of tea, and the bath had the ingrained water marks of years. She supposed the Balfours did have the excuse that they'd only just moved in but still . . . A glass shelf ran above the bath, with a bog-standard selection of shampoos available in every chemist or supermarket — there was even a bottle of own brand. 'Yee-uch,' muttered Sam. A bottle of Radox stood on the shelf, with nothing else to scent bathwater or buff the skin or smooth and tone, unless you counted a plastic razor next to the soap and Sam didn't.

She went to the bathroom cabinet and opened it. Sam liked to see what brands other women used, what creams they had for their faces, eyes, necks, hands and body; what they exfoliated, toned and moisturized with, kept cellulite in check with, smoothed their heels and elbows with. She wanted to see how they plucked and waxed and scented themselves, to see if they had any little secrets she could pick up. She liked to know whether someone preferred Chanel to Lancôme or Doctor Hauschka to Origins. From the evidence in front of her, Bella moisturized with a plain, unscented cream and didn't do much else. There was an untouched tube of Crabtree and Evelyn apricot scrub, a gift set of No. 7 toners, a pot of Body Shop face mask, cotton wool pads and Boots own-brand makeup remover. Sam was astonished. Where was all the other stuff? She had shelves of it, row upon row of enticing-looking packaging in whites, golds, pinks and pale blues; glass bottles, shiny black pots, fluted plastic, frosted and clear. It was normal, wasn't it? Part of what being a girl was about. She closed the cabinet door and stared into the mirror at her own smooth brown face, its high cheekbones emphasized with a light line of shiny powder, and her eyes with their long mascaraed lashes.

She used the toilet and hurried back downstairs. 'This is a great little place,' she said to Bella, coming in. 'You should come up and see ours.'

'Thanks,' said Bella. 'More coffee?'

Sam bounced enthusiastically on the sofa, pleased to have found a friend. 'Better not. But, tell you what, let's go into Oxford one day soon. There're some nice places there.'

'I'd love to see Oxford. I've never been there.'

'It's all right. The shops aren't a patch on Cheltenham. But there's the odd place that's worth a visit.'

'Sounds like fun. I'd love to.'

'And we'll make a date for you and your bloke to come up for dinner. Come and see our new kitchen – it's Ben's pride and joy. Might give you some ideas for when you come to do this place up.' Sam flicked a glance around the room. 'How about next week?'

'I'm absolutely sure we're free,' said Bella. 'More cake?'

Chapter Five

'I don't see what you're so worried about,' said Maggie. 'At least if he was going to get expelled he's done it after he's got most of that very expensive public-school education. He hasn't wasted much money.'

'It's not about the money, you know that.' Jane felt a familiar prickle of irritation. Her sister would always take any opportunity to put in a little criticism of what she considered Jane did wrong in her life: paying for education was, in Maggie's book, a social crime. Living in a large house was irresponsible and immoral. Even having children was a bit dubious – 'As though the world needs more people with over seven billion of us already!' she would say. What Jane couldn't work out was how much Maggie meant, and how much was an elaborate tease. When she sat there over dinner, calculating how many homeless people or battered women could be put up in Rawlston's bedrooms, or how many families the vegetable garden could feed, was she serious? Jane could never quite risk finding out. She added, 'I didn't pay the fees myself anyway.'

'Oh, well, *that*'s all right, then.' Maggie said it so lightly that the sarcasm was almost unnoticeable.

She had driven down from London that morning, her car crunching up to the house at eleven-thirty, and now she and Jane were having coffee in the kitchen, Maggie cutting an exotic figure at the old scrubbed table, with her piled-up curls, velvet top and gold and jade jewellery. Her face was well made-up in the deft, polished way of someone who did it every day. Jane noticed with envy the lightly sparkling pink gloss on Maggie's lips and the long curled eyelashes thick with mascara. If she remembered correctly, there was an old makeup bag upstairs in the bathroom cabinet with some bits and pieces in it, including a lipstick that was going a bit dry and crumbly now. She'd bought it because it was called 'Mary Shelley Red', which had seemed bizarre and funny – naming a lipstick after a nineteenth-century novelist. That was almost the extent of her makeup. But then, Maggie was still young, only in her late thirties, and she lived in a glamorous London world where standards were generally higher.

'Where's the young ne'er-do-well?' asked Maggie, looking about as though she expected Alec to pop out of a cupboard. 'Perhaps he's in the attic, on bread-and-water rations.'

'Yes – this Borstal is so harsh that he's been forcibly kept in bed, snoring his head off, until he feels like getting up and helping himself to breakfast.' Jane felt a bit of retaliatory sarcasm was justified. 'We'll know when he's up. The ceiling starts thumping with that music of his.'

'Ah. Now that *is* criminal.' Maggie grinned and the atmosphere between them lightened. Her eyes grew serious. 'Are you very worried about him?'

Jane ran a finger round the rim of her coffee cup. The ruby in her engagement ring glinted darkly in the sunlight. 'I *am* worried. Not so much about the stupid school—'

'Vile bastion of privilege,' put in Maggie.

Jane ignored her. '—but because Lucy tells me that Alec isn't happy and hasn't been for a long while. And ever since he got back from school, it's been getting worse. He won't speak to me. He hasn't for months – but I put it down to normal teenage reticence – and now I realize that he's actively avoiding me, answering me in grunts, behaving as though I've done something awful to him. But what it is, I can't think.'

'Come on. Let's go out and walk in that ridiculous garden of yours, and see if we can't work it out.'

It was another fine day with a fresh cool breeze that shook the tops of the trees and blew the fruit canes so that the pale green undersides of the raspberry leaves were exposed. Jane and Maggie followed the curve of the lawn towards the weed-choked, muddy old pond that was called, rather grandly, the lake. A dinghy half-submerged in the reeds at the far side showed how long it was since anyone had taken any interest in it. Once, when they'd learnt to swim, the children had spent hours playing with boats and buckets and dams; now only the moorhens were keen on it. Maggie picked her way round the muddy patches in her embroidered shoes and floaty skirt.

She never dresses for the country, thought Jane, amused. 'Did I tell you that I sold the lodge?' she asked.

'I knew you were going to, once the poor old Galloways were got rid of.'

'I didn't get rid of them,' Jane said defensively. 'Mrs Galloway died and the old chap went into a home or something – his family arranged it.'

'I know, I know. So who's bought it?'

'A London couple. I went down and met the wife. She seemed nice but . . . a bit of a lost soul, I thought. The husband is desperate to live in the country but she just seems to have gone along with it.'

'That sounds like trouble,' said Maggie, looking about her. 'I mean, I suppose some people like all this mess and fuss and dirt – give me a nice tidy asphalted road any day.'

Jane smiled and shook her head. The gulf between them was so wide that she sometimes wondered if it would ever be bridged. It was hard to remember that they were sisters – they were such opposites. Perhaps it was the twelve years between them in age, but they had such a fundamental difference in outlook that sometimes it seemed that they were several decades apart.

And she couldn't help feeling that Maggie took pleasure in pointing out their difference. As they turned towards the house, sitting massive and serene at the top of the lawn, Maggie gave a snort and said, 'Your house. Honestly. Why do you stay here? Now that the children have grown up, isn't it time to move to something smaller?'

'I'm sure I'll have to some day but I can't do it yet. Theo

wanted us to stay here as long as we could and anyway, it's only half as big as it used to be.'

'You should sell it,' Maggie said briefly. 'It's not Theo's shrine. It's just a house.'

Jane didn't know what to say. She'd poured everything she had into the house and couldn't begin to think of selling it. All her energies, for the last decade or more, had been focused on keeping it. It was her life now, the link to Theo, to her children and their childhood, to a happier version of herself to which she still occasionally thought back with longing. She had nurtured the house and the garden with the same kind of intense, unquestioning love that she had given her babies – everything was bound up in it. The fact that Maggie saw none of this demonstrated their real remoteness from each other. They saw one another several times a year, and since their parents had died perhaps a bit more often, as though to anchor themselves a little more tightly to each other. But in essence, Maggie hadn't changed since she was a furious toddler, screaming for her own way, or the stroppy teenager telling everyone else they had no idea what she was going through.

Maggie couldn't quite hide the fact that she thought Jane had wasted her life, though she tried to be subtle about it. She'd suggest things brightly, as though they had just occurred to her: wouldn't it be a wonderful idea if Jane went to university? Or did a course? Or learnt Russian? Or travelled? Or turned Rawlston into a school, an hotel, a mission for drug addicts?

Whenever they met, Maggie had a thousand new things to tell Jane about what she'd been doing, where she'd been and what she'd seen, about her life in London, her job at the School of African and Oriental Studies as a lecturer in third-world economics and the movement of refugees. And her friends were like her: Bohemian, intelligent and well read, people who talked easily about art and philosophy and clever books, vibrant people, who had opinions about life and how to live it.

I wouldn't have the first idea, Jane thought. I'm still trying to work out the basics and I'm probably over half-way through my life. Perhaps that was why Maggie's chivvying made her uncomfortable – as though she were saying that there wasn't all that much time left and, really, Jane ought to get a move on if she were going to make anything of herself.

Can't I just *be*? she wondered. Isn't that enough?

Alec was in the kitchen when they got there, a musty, rumpled figure making toast and slurping a cup of coffee. He brightened up when he saw Maggie and the broad, charming smile that Jane saw so rarely now transformed his expression.

'Maggie!' He gave her a hug and a smacking kiss.

'Hello, you young reprobate,' she said, kissing him back. 'What's this I hear about you being expelled from school?'

Alec made a face. 'Yeah. Got the sack.'

'Why?'

'Going out of bounds, drinking. Getting caught. That sort of thing.'

'The horror, the horror. Well, you're probably better off out of it. What are you going to do?'

He shrugged, and sat down heavily at the table. 'Dunno.'

Jane tried not to show how hard she was listening. Maggie had got more out of Alec in a few sentences than she had since he'd got back from school.

'Sixth form college?' Maggie suggested, sitting down opposite him.

He shrugged again.

She looked at him and then said, lightly, 'It all depends if you want to get those A-levels or not.'

Jane couldn't help herself. 'Of course you want to get your A-levels, don't you? You've got to get them if you're going to go on to university – and you've already done a whole year. It would be stupid to waste it.'

Alec seemed to shrink back in to himself, his expression darkened and he looked at his toast as though it had suddenly transformed into something repellent.

Maggie inspected the dark red paint glowing on her nails. 'They aren't the be-all and end-all. Like I said, it all depends, doesn't it?'

55

Jerry called after lunch, sounding rather breathless and excited. 'Janey, I've got a lovely idea. I'm lunching with a couple of undergrads and I thought I might bring them round to you for tea. They're utterly charming, you'd adore them. They'll brighten your whole day.'

'Sounds lovely, darling, but I've got Maggie here.'

Jerry was deflated. 'Oh, yes. I'd forgotten she'd taken some time out from campaigning for the rights of rats, or whatever she does, to blight poor old Rawlston. What a shame.'

'We haven't any plans. We're just chatting. Why don't you come anyway?'

'She might frighten the poor boys.'

'She knows perfectly well how to behave. Now, are you coming or not?'

Jerry sighed. 'They're too divine to keep to myself. All right. We'll motor over at about four.'

Jane told Maggie about Jerry's visit. She was stretched out girlishly on the sitting room rug, reading the papers.

'Oh, God,' she said, turning her eyes to heaven. 'As long as he doesn't lecture me on the divine right of kings, I suppose I can put up with him.'

'He's bringing a couple of undergraduates.'

'As though my life isn't full of enough students, let alone ghastly Oxford ones.'

'I can call and cancel if you like . . .'

'No, don't bother.' Maggie turned back to her paper. 'Worse things happen at sea. I might just stay here, though, nice and quiet, if it's all the same to you.'

Lucy got back from her morning shift at the hotel, and greeted Maggie with a scream of delight and a hug. Perhaps it was because Maggie was so much younger than Jane − she wasn't a typical aunt, with her wild curly hair, glittering clothes and jewellery, and she'd never allowed herself to be called Auntie . . . perhaps that was why the children related to her so well, thought Jane. It was hard to see them so open with Maggie, warm and natural, when they were closed off and furtive with her. It hurt, with a sensation like a needle being poked into her abdomen, and she tried her best to overcome it. Don't be ungenerous, she told herself. Be glad that they get on so well with Maggie. But it felt sometimes as though she were the one left out in the cold, excluded from their warm, lively circle, in which they discussed the details and colour of their lives rather than the bare outlines they sketched for her.

She was in the kitchen, staring at the chocolate cake she'd taken out of the freezer and wondering if it was defrosted in the middle, whether the icing was slimy after its long spell in sub-zero temperatures, when she heard the front door being pounded and the sweet, unfamiliar sound of the old brass bell ringing. Visitors usually came to the kitchen door. Jerry must be showing off.

She wiped her hands on her trouser legs and remembered that she'd meant to change before the guests came but it was too late now. She hurried down the hall, gloomy after the light kitchen, and hauled open the heavy front door. Jerry stood beaming on the step.

'What ho, Jane!' he said bluffly. His plump cheeks were reddened and his eyes bright. 'Here are Ollie and Tom.' He gestured to the young men standing beside him.

Ollie was a tall, eagle-looking man, lolling theatrically against the door frame. His greenish eyes slanted above a slim face and his wide mouth curled into a smile as Jane's gaze landed on him. He was, she saw with surprise, wearing a suit – dark with a faint pin-stripe – and an embroidered waistcoat; in the long bony fingers of one hand he held a cigarette and his long fringe was swept sideways out of his eyes.

'Hello,' he drawled. 'Delighted.'

I ought to have changed, she thought. They look so formal – a suit, in this weather! The type Jerry would be drawn to, I suppose. 'Hello, please come in.'

'What a charming house,' Ollie said. He waved a graceful hand in the direction of the front windows. 'Late Georgian?'

'Yes, I think so. Well, the front is. The back has bits that were added later. The Victorians went at it with their red brick.'

He nodded, and smiled again. 'Those barbarous Victorians!

57

Only joking, of course. I adore them. They can hardly put a foot wrong in my book. Pugin's my utter hero.'

'Tea, boys,' said Jerry, bowling into the hall past Jane, followed by Ollie. 'Are we in the drawing room, Jane?'

'I suppose we are,' she said drily. Like the front door, the drawing room was hardly used – only on special occasions, like Christmas, when it was worth heating the vast, chilly expanse and braving the slippery chintz sofas.

Behind Jerry came the other man, Tom. Like Ollie, he was tall, but where the other was slender and graceful, Tom was squarer in the shoulder and more solidly built. He, too, was oddly formal in a jacket and tie but less colourful and striking than Ollie. He looked older than his friend, with dark curly hair and warm brown eyes behind small round dark-framed spectacles. 'I hope you don't mind the invasion, Mrs Fielding,' he said, stretching out a hand to her. His voice had the faint twang of an accent that she couldn't place. She shook his hand – it was smooth and dry. 'Jerry insisted you wouldn't mind our arriving at such short notice to see the house.'

Jane glanced at Jerry, who had stopped in the hall to point out a picture to Ollie. They were studying it as Jerry talked animatedly. 'You've come to see the house?'

'It's a passion of Ollie's. He's obsessed with architecture and British country houses. We had lunch with Jerry and he said you wouldn't mind showing us Rawlston.'

Tom's gaze was complicit and knowing, as though he were really saying, 'It's so silly, isn't it? You and I are too sensible for all this.'

'Come on, Janey. Let's have tea,' called Jerry. He continued down the hall, chatting away to Ollie.

She took them to the drawing room, wondering if the others would bother to join them. They appeared pleased with the room and immediately started examining everything in it, though Jane hoped they wouldn't look too closely at the dust and the empty vases. She hadn't expected to be showing it, after all.

She left them to it and went to the kitchen to load a tray with the tea things and make a pot of tea. Lucy came in while she was doing it and said, 'Who's in the drawing room?'

58

'Jerry and some Oxford students. They've come to look at the house.'

'This old place? What's so interesting about it?'

'There must be something. Are you going to join us? There's cake. Very old cake.'

'Mmm. Old cake, Jerry and students? Don't tempt me. If Jerry's track record is anything to go by, they're bound to be the gruesome Oxbridge kind. Let me guess – they talk at half speed and wear tweeds. And bow ties.'

'Not exactly. But close. They've got embroidered waistcoats.'

'Oh my God. Grim.' Lucy thought for a moment. 'I might look in,' she conceded.

'Then you can bring the cake.'

The guests had finished their perambulations and retired to the sofas by the time Jane returned with the tea. Ollie, long and lithe, was stretched out along one, his shoes elegantly crossed just over the edge of the chintz. Jerry was in a chair next to him and Tom was leaning against the fireplace, its chilly marble mantel fitting beneath his shoulder-blades. He straightened up as Jane and Lucy came in. 'Can I help?' he asked.

'No, no, thank you. We can manage perfectly.' Jane started to arrange things on the tea-table.

Jerry said, 'Hello, Lucy darling. This is Ollie and Tom, both students at my college.'

'Hi,' said Lucy, a touch breathily. The young men both said a courteous hello, but Ollie turned back quickly to Jerry. Tom asked Lucy if she was a student as well, and they embarked on a conversation as Jane poured the tea.

So that, she thought, is the way the land lies. Jerry was having a flirtation with the seductive Ollie, and the more ordinary Tom was brought along to mask his intentions or to play chaperone. Ollie, with his bony slenderness and drooping eyelids, his air of faint fatigue and aristocratic languor, was just the kind of man Jerry was drawn to. Jane had seen it before. It rarely came to anything, and if it did, it never lasted long.

They drank their tea and ate the cake. Jerry talked quickly and

59

a touch too excitably about the wonders of Rawlston, though Jane felt he was making a lot out of not much. There was little of value in the house; she'd sold anything that was worth the trouble. Perhaps there was the odd piece of furniture or painting that someone somewhere might think valuable but she doubted it. And the house itself, while beautiful to her eyes, was in reality an architectural mishmash of styles with not much to recommend it to the expert.

Ollie had rejected most of his cake in favour of another fragrant, strong-smelling cigarette. He turned to Jane in his languid way. 'I understand you divided the house some time ago?'

She felt immediately defensive, although she didn't know why. 'Yes. Sad, perhaps, but it was a necessity at the time.'

'Jane and I came up with the plan together,' said Jerry.

Jane smiled. 'It was Jerry, really – and very brilliant of him. He saved the house for us.'

After Theo's death, when it became clear that there was no life insurance and only a small pension, Jane had been sure that they would lose Rawlston. She and Theo had lived there since his parents had made over the house to them and gone to live in their villa in Italy, where they had always planned to spend the end of their lives. Of course it had been wonderful to inherit this beautiful golden mansion, tucked away in its Cotswold hamlet, but really it had been too big for them, and too expensive to run. Theo wouldn't think of refusing it, even though it had made them much poorer than they should have been, with Theo still a junior partner in a law firm in Oxford. The problem was that he had never expected to die so young. They'd thought they had years to make everything all right, get the proper provisions sorted out and then . . . *bang*. He was dead.

All these years later, it was hard to remember the dreadfulness of that time. It was like a hazy nightmare now, with moments of sharp colour amid the fug of despair. She could recall little of the funeral – a well-meaning friend had given her Valium to see her through it and it had passed almost without her noticing – except that Alec had kept hiding in her skirts and almost tripping her up.

The things she wanted to forget – finding Theo cold in bed next to her that terrible morning, the ambulance men trying to revive him though it was obvious he was dead, the doctor explaining to her what an aneurysm was, and how it could happen out of the blue – stayed with an unforgiving, hard-edged clarity.

After six months, it was obvious that her financial position was a very bad one. When Jane had confided to Jerry one night over their second bottle of wine that the house would have to go, he'd been horrified. They went through all the options together but it seemed as though selling was the only way.

'Can't you ask Theo's parents?' Jerry had cried. 'They can't want you to sell.'

''They haven't offered and I won't ask. They made us take this bloody place. I'm damned if I'll ever go to them cap in hand, begging for money to keep a roof over their grandchildren's heads. No, I'll sell it. Buy something smaller, closer to a town, and live on the proceeds and whatever I can earn, though goodness knows who'll give me a job.' Nothing seemed to matter all that much now anyway. She wasn't sure how long she'd have to go on existing like this without Theo. If it wasn't for the children, she wouldn't care if it all ended tomorrow.

'Oh, Jane, I can't bear it.' Jerry put his hand over hers. 'This wonderful old house. You simply can't! It's a shame you can't just sell off the odd room here and there. It's not as if you need twelve bedrooms, is it? You could sell half and not even notice.'

That was when it had come to her. The house was so big she could comfortably turn it into two, live in one and sell the other. 'Jerry,' she'd said solemnly, knocking his glass with her own, 'you are a genius. I will not sell Rawlston. I'll sell *some* of it.'

That was what she'd done. She had made her plans, called in an architect, applied for the necessary permission and borrowed the money against the house to get it converted. When it was all settled, months later, she had set about it with an energy she hadn't known since Theo had died. She'd been pulled down into a great dark hole that had sucked all the life from her and numbed her towards everything, only letting her rise to the surface enough to care for the children. It was a constant battle to fight the torpor of grief; some days it was hard even to move her arms and legs. But saving Rawlston had awakened her and given her a reason to get up. She'd helped the builders, learning how to strip walls and mix plaster sand; she'd painted walls and made curtains. When the last brick had gone into place cutting her off from half of her home for ever, Jane had felt a horrible pang of fear. Would Theo have wanted this? But she clung to the thought that he would have understood that she was doing what she had to to keep the place for the children.

It had been remarkably easy to sell the other half of the house, and it had brought her enough money to pay back what she owed and know she had enough to live on for some years. A quiet retired couple had bought it and then, at the start of this year, had sold up and moved to be near their grandchildren. That was when the Clarkes had arrived.

The visitors didn't stay long. Tom and Lucy chattered amiably but it was clear that Ollie was the type who was easily bored, and he began to fidget. 'Is there anything more to see?' he asked, with a weary air. 'Only you did say we'd be dining at the Charlotte tonight, Jerry.'

'Don't let him make you spend all your money on him,' Jane whispered to Jerry, as she said goodbye to them at the front door. She'd seen Jerry infatuated before with greedy undergraduates, who assumed he must be rich and started expecting vintage champagne and to be bought expensive dinners.

'He's divine, isn't he?' breathed Jerry, as he kissed her farewell. 'Didn't I say?'

'Very charming. But watch out.'

Ollie shook her hand politely and said, 'Thanks for the tea,' then sauntered out to stand expectantly by the car.

Tom held out his hand to Jane. 'It's been so nice. Do let us know if you're coming to Oxford and we'll give *you* tea next time.'

When the car had pulled out of the drive, she went to find Maggie to tell her the coast was clear.

'Alec's a wonder – you've got nothing to worry about,' announced

Maggie, coming into the kitchen the next day. She'd risen late and Jane had already been to early morning mass in the village, and got the lunch on. 'Do you know what he just did? He rescued me from the hairiest, most disgusting spider I've ever seen. I was having a heart-attack in the bathroom, I mean, really – shrieking my guts out. He whisked in to my aid like a chivalrous knight.'

'That's very good to know, but how that will help with his A-levels, I'm not altogether sure.' There was no point in trying to explain to Maggie that Alec behaved quite differently when it was just Jane that he had to deal with.

'Don't get so hung up on exams, Jane. I keep trying to tell you, they don't mean everything.'

Jane put the peeled potatoes for lunch into the colander for a rinse. 'It's odd to hear that from an academic.'

'That's the difference between us, I suppose,' said Maggie. 'You haven't passed exams, so you think they must be the gateway to some promised land. I have, and I can tell you that they aren't.'

'Easy for you to say,' Jane replied, 'when you've got them.' Before Maggie could reply, she added quickly, 'Are you going this afternoon?'

'Yes – must get back. Gregor's expecting me for supper and God only knows what the traffic will be like.'

'How is Gregor?' Even after all the time that Maggie and Gregor had lived together, he was still a stranger to Jane, a shadowy half-figure who barely existed. She said his name delicately, like a foreign word.

'He's fine.' Maggie tossed her head, caught hold of her long curls and twisted them up on to the top of her head, securing them with a clip. 'He's talking about going back to Hungary in a few months, for work. He likes to go back every now and then.'

'Will you go with him?'

Maggie put her head on one side. 'Probably not. I can't speak a word of the language. I'm a bit of a dead weight for him.' She glanced up at Jane. 'I'm very busy, actually. There's no way I could think of leaving the country for months on end. I feel as though I've been working hard for as long as I can remember.'

'You must take care of yourself. Don't wear yourself out.' Jane felt the tug of her duty to Maggie; it had been there strong and undeniable throughout their youth, and even now she couldn't stop offering concern to her sister, although it was always pushed away.

'Oh, I can take it. I'm a tough old thing. People have much worse lives than mine, you know.'

'Yes, of course . . . you know you're always welcome here, though, don't you? I mean for a long visit, not just a weekend. I've got so much room, if you ever need some peace and quiet. I wouldn't disturb you . . .'

Maggie shrugged. 'I'll get some quiet when Gregor goes. But – thanks. You never know, I might feel the need of a spell in the nineteenth century.'

Jane laughed. 'Any time.'

Maggie left not long after lunch. They all went out to wave good-bye to her. She drove a Morris Minor – 'I'm a character car person,' she would say. Even though she disapproved of cars altogether and wished she could do without one, she wouldn't change it even when Lucy teased her about how environmentally unfriendly it was, guzzling fuel and pumping out exhaust. 'Second-hand is always environmentally friendly,' Maggie said obstinately.

She'd kissed Jane and said, 'Look after yourself, Sis. Don't worry about Alec. Everything will work itself out. Now you come to me next time. I don't think I can face the weirdness of the country again for a while. I actually saw a bat last night. I was hoping they didn't really exist. Ugh.'

Jane watched her car disappear round the rhododendron bushes, feeling again as though she'd somehow failed to make a connection with her sister. Whenever Maggie left, it was as though a social duty had been fulfilled, but she had a strong sense of incompletion, as though they hadn't talked about the things that mattered to them.

I've got to do it some time, she thought. Or it's going to be too late.

Chapter Six

'Come on, Bella.' Iain knocked on the bathroom door. Bella was soaking in the bath, occasionally tipping warm water over her breasts where they emerged above the surface. 'We're going to be late.'

'What's the time?' she asked.

'It's seven. They said seven-thirty.'

'That doesn't mean seven-thirty. It means between seven-thirty and eight. We won't be eating until eight thirty at the earliest. It's not done to turn up on the dot.'

There was silence as Iain absorbed this. He didn't have a natural social sense and relied on Bella to guide him through such situations but she could tell he was twitchy. An appointment was an appointment as far as he was concerned, as rigid as a train timetable. He couldn't stop his compulsion to be on time and she could sense him frowning behind the bathroom door. 'Look, they said seven-thirty, so just hurry up and get out of the bath.'

She smiled to herself. She'd decided not to get irritated with him tonight, as she so often seemed to. Instead she plunged under the water to soak her hair and wondered what to wear.

In the bedroom, inspecting her wardrobe, she realized she shouldn't even begin to think about competing with Sam's glamour and expensive clothes. She was beautiful, really – or what some people, men mostly, would call beautiful: thin, tanned, long glossy hair, regular features carefully accentuated with makeup. The kind of casual look that actually took hours of work and dedication to achieve and maintain. Bella didn't know how anyone had the time.

65

She picked out one of her favourite standbys: a plum-coloured silk wrap dress with a pointed collar. It flattered her hippy, full-breasted shape, and made her stomach look flatter. Once she had put on her heels and some earrings, she felt glamorous, confident and capable in her own way, although she suspected that it was a different kind of confidence from the kind Sam Clarke had. She'd never met anyone who didn't have to work and was pleased about it. In London, it was a point of pride to everyone that they worked. Even her friends who'd taken a year or two out to bring up children had protested that they'd soon be back, earning their share. Sam was nothing like that. That state of mind was foreign to Bella: how did you define yourself if not through the work you did? She could understand women being fulfilled by their children, but without even that what did Sam strive for? Perhaps, though, there was something liberating about her and the way she was free of the weight of expectation that Bella and everyone she knew laboured under.

I'm surprised by her, she thought, as she wrapped the soft, slippery silk around her and tied it at the waist. Why? She thought hard. It was because the skinny blonde hadn't been what she'd imagined Ben's wife would be like, even at that brief meeting on their moving-in day. He'd seemed more . . . what was the word? *Classy?* No, that was wrong. Still, you could never tell with men and they often seemed entranced by the tacky-looking Barbie doll type. She caught herself: that was mean. Sam had been perfectly friendly. It had been nice of her to invite them to dinner – and in this Godforsaken place, Bella couldn't afford to be choosy about her friends. She'd made a million judgements about Sam from the way she dressed, looked and spoke, and somewhere she'd rationalized Sam's attractiveness by deciding she looked cheap, and undermined her superior wealth and status by deciding she was probably stupid.

Bella inspected herself in the wardrobe mirror. Give her a chance, she rebuked herself. She's probably lovely.

'Good, you're nearly ready,' said Iain, with evident relief, coming into the bedroom. She'd managed to persuade him not to wear his pin-striped work suit and he was looking more relaxed in chino trousers and an open shirt.

'Are you all right about this?' she asked, quickly applying her makeup.

'Yes, yes, fine,' Iain said. But she could tell he was nervous about going up to the big house, and she suspected he was worried about being made to feel inferior in the face of the people who could afford a place like that. He had very low self-confidence, which she felt was due to the influence of his parents who'd idolized their elder son – a doctor, they informed everyone in hushed, awed tones – and failed to find anything to praise about Iain.

'There's nothing to be afraid of. Sam is very nice. They're not grand,' she added, hoping he would get the implication and not wanting to say out loud that she thought Sam was a touch common. 'Not like Jane Fielding.' Iain had been cowed by Jane Fielding: her voice, her confidence, even her open friendliness had scared him. Too upper-crust, he'd said later to Bella. Not his type at all.

'The babysitter's here,' he said.

'What's she like?' Sam Clarke had recommended they ask the girl from the cottages across the road who cleaned for her.

'Fine,' said Iain. 'Come down and meet her. Aren't you ready yet?'

'Just coming,' said Bella, and she slicked some pale gloss across her lips.

The children were already in their pyjamas, fair hair brushed, allowed to stay up and watch television. The babysitter, a stocky girl in her late teens with a round face and glasses, sat on the sofa staring at the television as though she'd never seen such a thing before in her life. Katie perched near her, looking stiff and un-comfortable and somehow old beyond her years despite her flowery nightdress and pink sparkly slippers. Christopher was on the floor cross-legged, watching the comedy and laughing heartily whenever the studio audience did.

'You must be Trudy. Hello,' said Bella, smiling at the girl. 'Very nice to meet you.'

67

'You're all right,' replied the girl, glancing up at her and then back at the screen.

Bella found the reply a bit of a *non sequitur* but said, 'Did Iain show you where the tea, coffee and biscuits are?'

'Yup,' said Trudy, unable to drag her eyes away. Then she said again, 'You're all right.'

'Well, we're on our way then. Goodnight, chilluns. Be good.' Bella kissed them.

'Will you be long?' asked Katie.

'I don't know, darling. We're only up the road, you know. Not far. And Trudy is here to look after you.' Bella hoped she sounded more confident of Trudy's powers than she felt – the girl barely looked able to make a phone call – but babysitters were really there to make the children feel secure. Nothing was likely to go wrong. 'Christopher, bed after this. Katie, you can go at nine. Good night.' Christopher jumped up and ran over to hug her; she smelled his sweet scent of bath and bedtime and savoured the feel of him through his smooth cotton pyjamas.

Katie said, 'You look very nice, Mummy.'

'Thank you, darling.' She smiled at her daughter and wondered if she was growing too serious for her age. She could tell that Katie was not convinced by Trudy and was preparing to take responsibility for the evening in her grave ten-year-old way.

'Come on,' said Iain, anxious to be off. 'Night, kids. Behave for Trudy.'

They walked out into the lane. The sun was dropping behind the woods and the shadows were long and large. Bella picked her way carefully among the stones and dust of the lane, feeling the slight chill of the coming night through the light silk of her dress. 'I hope everything will be all right,' she said.

'Why shouldn't it be?' Iain asked.

'Didn't you think that Trudy's a little . . . odd? Almost a bit . . . backward?'

'Seemed perfectly normal to me.'

She would, thought Bella ironically, both as barmy as each other – then felt instantly guilty for thinking such a thing about her husband. She wasn't sure when she'd started being embarrassed by Iain when they went out but it was something she was ashamed of. A real wife wouldn't feel this way, she told herself sternly. A real wife would stand by her husband, no matter what. She would stand by him tonight, make sure everything went smoothly, protect him, make him shine if she could. She knew she criticized him too much.

They walked on in silence and Bella felt her spirits lift. This was quite something – to be walking up a stony country lane to the big house where they were expected for dinner. They passed the meadow and the old farm and, turning at the top of the lane, approached the mass of shiny-leaved rhododendrons that shielded the house from view. The dense bush had two openings, each leading to a different side of the house. The one furthest up, where the lane ended in thick, dark wood, was the entrance to the Fielding side. The first opening led to the Clarkes' front door, which had once been a less important side door but, with the addition of a stone portico and a gravelled sweep in front of it, was still impressive.

Bella glanced at Iain. He looked rather strained, his face set. 'I'm a bit nervous,' she confided, with a little laugh, to lighten his mood.

He looked at her in surprise. 'Really? I'm not.' But she could see that his knuckles, where he was holding the wine bottle they'd brought, were bloodless and pale.

Sam answered the front door. She looked stunning in a skin-tight, white halter-neck dress that made her skin seem even browner and her eyes even bluer. Her perfectly polished toenails gleamed from high white sandals that had thin leather straps criss-crossed up her ankles, like a Roman's.

'Hiya, come in. Lovely you could make it. You must be Iain.' She leant forward and kissed him loudly on the cheek.

'Either that or I'm his evil twin,' replied Iain, jovially.

Bella winced slightly but Sam shrieked with laughter and said, 'I'm going to have to watch myself with you, aren't I?' Then, kissing Bella, she said, 'You're looking gorgeous, darling. That's a great colour on you. Now come in and meet Himself, if we can drag him out of the kitchen.'

They followed her undulating form down the hallway, a square white corridor with spotlights sunk into the ceiling, seagrass matting, a huge dark oak table with only a large vase of lilies in the middle and, facing a vast mirror, a broad modern canvas of slashes of colour.

'This is lovely,' Bella called after her.

'You're very privileged,' said Sam, flashing them a smile over a bony brown shoulder. 'You're the first people to see it in all its glory. This is the living room.'

She led them into another pale room, this one with polished floorboards, leather and tweed furniture, white mohair cushions and a lot of chrome and glass everywhere. This, thought Bella, must be hell to keep clean.

'It's beautiful,' she said.

'You think so? Ah, that's nice. I like it, anyway. You should have seen it before – all chintz and flowery carpets and wall-paper.' Sam wrinkled her nose and made a face. 'Not our cup of tea at all. And Ben likes all his bells and whistles and boys' toys. He'll show you everything later. Drinks? What do you fancy?'

'G and T, if you've got it,' said Bella.

'Make it two,' said Iain, rubbing his hands and looking about approvingly. 'Yes, this is very nice indeed. Snazzy.'

'Bit of sophistication in the sticks,' said Sam, mixing their drinks expertly. There was even ice in a stainless-steel ice bucket. She handed them their glasses and said, 'Cheers, m'dears.'

'How long has all this taken you?' asked Iain, inspecting the large caramel leather sofa.

'Too bloody long,' said Sam, rolling her eyes. 'I thought the builders were going to end up with squatters' rights.'

Bella left them chatting and walked slowly round the room. It was nothing like any room she'd ever lived in: it was so care-fully assembled, each piece co-ordinating with the rest. The glass shelves were bare, apart from polished wooden sculptures and photos framed in blond wood – careful studio poses of Sam with her husband mostly, and the odd snap on a hot Caribbean beach or glistening white snow slope. She noticed that one photograph frame had slipped behind another so that only Ben's smiling face

70

was visible; deftly, she pulled it out and saw that he was with a girl, brown-eyed and brown-haired, with a skinny sharp face and pale skin. This must be the teenager he had mentioned but it had to be an old photo as she looked young in it. She adjusted the frame so that it sat in line with the others and moved over to the window that gave out on to the front drive and its gravel sweep. The sleek Mercedes and a cheeky-looking sports car sat side by side like a greyhound and a terrier sharing a mat. This is money, Bella thought suddenly. These people are rich – they're different from us. She felt a quick stab of discomfort and quelled it instantly. 'That's no way to think,' she muttered to herself, then turned as the atmosphere in the room changed.

'Here he is,' cried Sam. 'Marco Pierre White himself!'

Ben was standing by a second door leading out of the sitting room, tall, solid and radiating energy. Dressed in baggy linen trousers and a white linen shirt, he should have looked a bit silly – like a Miami tycoon or a man who tries too hard to be young – but his height made him impressive and he carried it off.

He strode straight over to Bella at the window and kissed her cheek, saying, 'Hello there, so lovely to see you . . .' then went to Iain and shook his hand strongly. 'Welcome. We're delighted to see you. I'm so pleased you could make it.'

'Thank you for asking us,' said Bella. 'You have a beautiful home.'

'All down to my beautiful wife,' Ben replied, putting an arm round Sam's slender waist and hugging her while she giggled. 'She did it all herself – just her and five expensive interior decorators.'

'Oy,' protested Sam. 'Someone had to make the final decision.'

'Come and see the kitchen,' said Ben. 'It's the best bit.' They followed him out along a tiled corridor into a large, light room.

'This is amazing,' said Bella, looking about. It was the biggest, most luxurious kitchen she'd ever seen, dominated by a glistening stainless-steel range. She knew it must have cost thousands of pounds; she felt dazed at the thought of being able to spend that on just one room.

'Terrific,' said Iain, who didn't have a clue of how much it

71

would have cost and would probably have passed out in horror if he had. 'You enjoy cooking, do you, Ben?'

'Love it,' said Ben, striding to the stove and plunging a wooden spoon into a saucepan on the hob. A fug of fragrant steam rose from it. 'Never happier than when I'm chopping and stewing and stirring and frying. And I'm a bit of a food evangelist, so watch out if you get me started on that.'

'I'm impressed.' Bella smiled.

He cocked an eye at her. 'All the best chefs are men – everyone knows that.'

'The best *professional* chefs,' she replied. 'All that means is that men demand to be paid for what women are expected to do for free.'

'Not like sex, then,' said Sam, and snorted. 'Do you want a drink, sweetheart?'

'Yes, please.' Ben opened the oven door and inspected the contents. 'It's only another twenty minutes or so and then we're off.'

They left Ben to his cooking and sat chatting in the sitting room. Sam was easy company, interested in everything Iain had to say, and he was evidently more relaxed than when they had arrived. A barked command from the kitchen had her herding them down the corridor to the dining room.

'Only hitch with this place,' she said, showing them in, 'the dining room is miles from the kitchen. But Ben's bought the kind of heated trolley they use in restaurants. Anything for another toy. I call this the Chinese room.'

Bella looked about appreciatively: the walls were a delicate eggshell blue, with faint bamboo stencils climbing them. Framed silk prints of Chinese flowers hung on each wall. Pale curtains printed with little fishermen and birds on blossomed branches finished the effect, with cracked ceramic vases along the surface of the side table.

The table was laid with square white plates, slender glasses and designer cutlery.

'Make mine the chow mein and a number twenty-seven,' said Iain, sitting down.

Sam laughed at him and said, 'You're funny, you are. You're here, Bella,' then moved about pouring white wine into the glasses.

'Dinner is served,' proclaimed Ben, coming through the door pushing an impressive-looking stainless steel trolley. He removed the lid and distributed their starter – a pear, rocket and Gorgonzola salad. 'Tuck in,' he ordered, and sat down.

It was not something Bella had tried before and she loved the combination of the sweet, sharp and mellow flavours. When she praised it, Ben said graciously that it was only an old standby and very easy. 'No carbs,' added Sam from where she was carving into her pear with her fork. Bella ate it slowly, lingering over it.

'You enjoying Rawlston?' Ben asked Iain.

'We love it here,' Iain replied. 'It's just about perfect – apart from the commute. Everything they say about the trains is true. They're a disaster made into full-blown hell with the invention of the mobile phone.' They discussed the problems with the railway – although Ben admitted he always drove everywhere because he hated not being in control – until the plates were empty. Then Ben jumped to his feet, loaded his trolley and disappeared, telling Sam to pour the Saint-Emilion.

'Ben and his wine,' she said, taking a fresh bottle from the sideboard where, Bella now saw, there were rows of bottles, some already open. 'He's a freak about it. I can't tell the difference to be honest – as long as it's white and cold, I'm happy.'

'Don't you like red?' asked Iain.

'Nah. Gives me headaches. I'm sticking to the Chablis.'

Bella sipped the new wine: it was thick and rich and fruity and she could tell it was good, even though she knew little about it. She felt a sudden intoxication at the luxury of the Clarkes' lives. Iain was on a mission to find a bottle of wine for less than £1.99 and sometimes came home with cardboard cartons of something that was supposed to be wine but as the printing was in some obscure Eastern European language, who could tell? There was nothing like that here. Everything was good, the best, even. She was beginning to enjoy an unaccustomed feeling of entitlement.

The main course was a rack of herb-encrusted lamb, cooked to a perfect rosy pinkness inside and served on bed of aubergine – 'it's called a *galette*,' Ben explained when Bella asked – with a thick sauce of fresh tomato and rosemary, with potatoes dauphinoise, creamy and garlicky, to soak up all the juices.

It was delicious. Bella was enchanted with it, exclaiming every few minutes how wonderful it was. It tasted like something she would eat in a restaurant; it had never occurred to her that she could eat this kind of thing at home. Her own cooking was good but simple, and Iain was limited to cheese on toast and pasta, if he was forced to. But this – this was *cooking*. This was the kind of thing that had to be learnt.

'Did you go to cookery school, Ben?' she asked, scooping up some cubes of aubergine.

'No,' said Ben, emphatically. 'I'm self-taught.' Now that the main work of the meal was finished, he'd relaxed, casting off his apron and refilling his glass with the dark red wine. 'I've taught myself everything I've ever learnt. It's the best way.'

'Don't know why you spend a fortune sending your daughter to a private school, then,' said Sam, tartly. She was toying with her food, the creamy potatoes left untouched and curdling at the side of her plate.

'You've got children, Ben?' asked Iain. Bella remembered that she hadn't told him about the teenager: she saw her small pale face again from the photograph in the sitting room.

'One,' said Ben, 'from my first marriage. My daughter Emma. She's upstairs, actually, but she's a bit of a hermit so we probably won't be seeing her.'

'She's lovely,' cut in Sam. 'You'll have to meet her some time.'

'And she's at a private school, you say?' Iain asked, taking another gulp of his wine.

'That's right,' replied Ben.

Sam leant forward, her skin glistening in the candlelight. 'You ought to think about St Mary's for your Katie, Bella. It's really good, apparently. Lots of the girls go to the top universities. Lovely facilities and it's nice and close.'

'She's a bit young yet,' Bella said. 'She's only ten. Besides, I don't know how we'd manage school fees.'

'Oh.' Sam looked taken aback, then recovered herself. 'Maybe she could get a scholarship. I'm sure she's bright enough.'

Iain frowned and shook his head. 'I'm not really in favour of private schools. I find it shocking that this country runs two forms of education, one for the rich and one for the poor. It's not right at all and I don't think I can be a part of it by sending my children to an independent school. The local comprehensive will do us fine.'

'Did you go to a private school, Iain?' Ben asked affably. He'd taken up the bones of his lamb and was gnawing them. Seeing him, Bella picked hers up and did the same, pulling out the last scraps of sweet meat with her teeth.

'No, I went to a grammar.'

'Not a comprehensive, then?'

'No.'

'Ah. And university?'

'I did go to university, yes.'

'Ah,' said Ben again. There was a pause. 'You see, I didn't go to a grammar. Couldn't. I didn't get in. I went to the secondary modern instead. I hated it, left at sixteen and never got any qualifications. They didn't expect any from me – I was already a failure in their eyes. So I didn't go to university. I went to work. I made a success of things, but I'm unusual that way. Most of my classmates aren't living in places like this, enjoying this life. They're living in estates, working in dead-end jobs, if they're working at all. I'm not prepared to let anything like that happen to my kid, and if I can give her the cushion of a good education, something no one can take away from her, then that's what I'll do. I'm not going to change the world by making Emma suffer, or by damaging her chances. I'll change the world with my vote, if I can, and when it's changed to my satisfaction, I'll send my child to a state school. But not until then.'

There was another pause. Iain looked startled, somehow disconcerted, but he said nothing. Ben sat back, expansive, unoffended and unoffending. I'm plain-speaking, he seemed to say, honest and upfront. That's me. There's nothing personal in it. I still like you just as much as I did.

'Bit late for that,' Sam said cheerily, trying to lighten the atmosphere. 'She's leaving in about two weeks! Now, who's for more wine? Ben, you sort everyone out.'

He poured more wine into everybody's glasses and drank from his own. Bella watched him lean back, his eyes glittering. He caught her eye and stared back at her with his intense blue gaze and it was almost as though she could feel the energy of it touching her. It was a tingling, awakening feeling that made her skin prickle like the end of pins and needles.

They returned to the sitting room for coffee and liqueurs. Bella felt fuzzy as they went along the corridor, realizing that she was drunk. How often had her glass been refilled with wine? She could tell that Iain, too, had had a bit to drink; he'd regained his good humour and become entertaining, joky, almost too loud. Over the summer pudding, he'd described his work. Bella had heard it before but Ben and Sam found it amusing. They'd opened another bottle over the cheese.

It was late. Bella knew they ought to be getting back to the babysitter but she didn't want to. She liked the way this place worked, the sense that nothing was too good for them now. She felt replete, luxurious, and she wanted to go on feeling that way. Ben lit a cigar, which made her want to laugh. It was like cooking exquisite food – smoking cigars was something she didn't think people really did. He offered one to Iain, who refused because he'd never smoked and didn't know how to. Bella felt like asking for one of Sam's cigarettes. Ever since the end of the main course – she hadn't had pudding – Sam had been exhaling thick white clouds of smoke, lighting cigarettes one after the other. Bella had smoked occasionally but only when Iain wasn't around. It was usually a reliable indicator that she was drunk, when she looked at that glowing little stick and thought how attractive it was. The cigar smoke wafted fragrant and pungent across the room as Ben poured them brandies; the atmosphere was convivial and relaxed; Bella felt as if she was being reminded of happier, better times even though she was with strangers in a strange place. I'm definitely pissed, she thought.

'We're pleased with this house,' Ben was saying, 'but this is only the start. I've got plans for this place.'

'Plans?' said Iain, accepting his brandy balloon and swilling the liquid round it. He swung his head to look at Ben in the deliberate way of someone not entirely in control of their movements.

Ben gave Bella her glass with a wink and sat down in an armchair, his cigar clamped in his teeth. Sam slid up from the sofa and tottered out of the room. 'Jane Fielding sold half her house,' he announced. 'What she doesn't realize is, that's only a delaying tactic. She'll end up selling the rest eventually, and when she does, I'll be right here and waiting.'

'How can you be so sure?' asked Iain.

Ben shrugged and puffed another cloud of smoke, smacking his lips together with a tiny pop. 'She's not investing. She's spending her capital just running that place. In the end, she'll run out and have to sell because she's got no reserves. These old places – it's extraordinarily expensive to keep them up. You have to make them work for you, if you're not already coining it elsewhere. Look, she's got a farm down that lane – you must have seen it. It's falling apart, mouldering away. She could renovate it, let it, start a business. Boutique farming is where it is at the moment – rare breeds, organic, homemade this, homespun that . . . and as for that wood – my God!' He laughed loudly. 'Don't get me started on the treasure trove she's sitting on. I've got plans for it.'

'Development?' asked Iain, frowning. Bella guessed he was worried that his rural idyll would be spoiled by executive homes.

'Haven't decided. I've got a few options but what appeals to me at the moment is corporate shoots. Very big business. It wouldn't take much to get those started. I want Jane Fielding to come in with me.'

'Have you asked her?'

'No. I will, though.'

Sam came back into the sitting room, unsteady on her high sandals. She was holding a small round mirror with four rough lines of white powder laid out on it. 'Look what I found,' she said, in a baby voice. 'Candy!' She sat down and put the mirror in front of them on the coffee table. 'Who wants some?'

Ben sucked on his cigar impassively and slid his eyes over to Bella.

'What's that?' she asked, although she knew.

'Yummy candy,' said Sam, in the same baby voice. 'Please have some.' She held out a rolled twenty-pound note to Bella.

Iain leant forward heavily and slurred, 'Is that what I think it is?'

Bella took the tight roll of the bank note and bent forward. Iain looked at her, puzzled. She'd done this before but not when he was there: Nicky had shown her once in the loos at her club where she said that everyone did it. She'd said, 'You can't live and not try it – just don't get addicted, that's all.' Ben watched her without expression, his sparkling blue gaze hooded by his eyelids.

She put the note to her nose and bowed over the mirror. She could see her own face looming up at her, her own eyes with the carefully applied makeup faded and the whites slightly bloodshot, and watched herself sniff up the powder. Leaning back, sniffing some more, she handed the note to Sam, who quickly took the second line. She passed the paraphernalia to Iain, who shook his head and gestured to Ben. Sam pushed the mirror towards her husband, who didn't make a move towards it, then got up and shimmied over to the stereo saying, 'Let's have some music!' She stared for a few moments at the CD rack, then swung round and said, 'I know – did you bring your swimming costumes?'

'No,' said Bella, feeling a numbness in her gums and a bitter trickle at the back of her throat.

Sam clapped her hands. 'We can lend you some! Let's go to the Jacuzzi!'

How did I get here? wondered Bella.

The four of them sat in the square pool, up to their chests in a foam of hot water. Around them, beyond the spotlit decking, the woods rose high and dark, occasionally echoing with the shriek or howl of some animal. Clouds of steam wafted upwards and hung above them like vapour over a swamp. The night was cold now but the water was delicious, bubbling below the surface on to their calves and thighs. Only their shoulders could be seen above it, Sam in a white bikini and Bella bursting out of a borrowed polka-dot swimsuit a size or two too small. Iain was next to her, his smooth, pale, lightly freckled body in contrast to Ben's dark hairy chest.

Sam had opened a bottle of champagne and they were all clutching their glasses above the bubbles. She was chattering away madly but Bella couldn't follow anything she was saying. Instead she let her thoughts – fantastically lucid but extremely fast – buzz on, as she gazed around her.

Suddenly Sam shouted, 'Oy! Oy, Emma!'

They all looked up in the direction she was calling. A window at the top of the house was lit and a figure was standing there, silhouetted against the yellow light.

'Come on!' Sam giggled loudly. 'Come and join us, Emma! Let your bloody hair down for once.' She leant over towards Bella and said conspiratorially, 'That's Ben's kid. Uptight little so-and-so. Far too good for us.' She shouted again, 'Come on in, the water's lovely!' then collapsed in more laughter.

Bella stared up at the small figure. It stood still for a moment, then turned and left the window. The light went out.

Chapter Seven

'Alec! Alec,' cried Jane, exasperated. She stood on the landing. From one side came the cheery boppity-bop of pop music, drifting down the attic stairs with Lucy's voice chiming in with the melody. From along the corridor came the more strident thud of rock music, with a wailing guitar and a tortured-sounding lead singer. The noise was awful.

She went to his bedroom door, thumped on it and opened it. The curtains were drawn and the room was dark and gloomy. Alec sat in the darkness, hunched in front of his computer screen, his profile illuminated by its blueish light. He whirled round to face Jane, a scowl on his face.

'What do *you* want?' he asked, although she could barely hear him over the din.

'I'd like you to turn that down a bit, please,' she cried, trying to hold in her temper. 'It's coming through the kitchen ceiling and it's very annoying.'

'What?'

Her temper burst free despite her efforts. 'Alec, just turn it down! I'm not asking you to turn it off, just down. Have some bloody consideration.' She whirled round and slammed the door behind her, breathing hard. A moment later the music was turned down a notch or two, hardly making a difference but at least it was something. She was angry with herself for letting go though; she'd been trying to stay patient, kind and understanding with Alec so that she could break through the wall of silence he'd constructed around himself. It was all very well to waste a month or two playing computer games but soon he was going to have to face the future. What was he going to do with his life? Where was he going to finish his A-levels?

She went down to the kitchen, thinking of their conversation of the night before. They'd been in the sitting room watching some dreadful cop-and-gun movie and when it had finished, Alec had seemed in a relatively good mood. He'd shared a bottle of wine with her, and she'd given him the last glass, then taken the little window of opportunity she saw open to talk to him. Immediately his face had hardened and his body had seemed to close in on itself, as it usually did when she tried to the broach the subject of his future.

'Mum, I dunno, okay? I just don't know.'

'But if you're going to finish your A-levels, you have to think about where you're going to go in September. It may be too late already – the schools will soon be breaking up for the summer, we need to get a move on.'

Alec stared into his glass. After a long pause he said, 'Maybe I don't want to do my A-levels.'

'But . . .' Jane was at a loss. How could he not finish them with a year already under his belt? 'Darling, you know how important qualifications are. You need A-levels to get to university.'

'Look, they're useless, okay? I hate them. They're pointless. I don't even know if I want to go to university anyway.'

Anxiety rose in Jane's chest. She didn't understand what he would do if he didn't follow the normal path; if he had a burning passion in his life – to be a carpenter or an artist or something like that – fine. Perhaps. But . . . 'What do you propose to do instead?' She made an effort not to sound like a barrister cross-examining a criminal. 'You can't just live here playing on your computer for the rest of your life.'

Alec put down his glass. 'Give me a break, okay? You don't know anything about me. You have no idea.' He got up and stamped to the door. Just before he slammed it behind him, he said, 'Get off my fucking case.'

The swearing drenched her like a bucket of water. Alec had never spoken like that to her before. It was as though he had

81

slapped her, and it left her shaken and hurt, unsure of what on earth she should do next.

By the time she reached the kitchen, she was fairly sure that the music was back to its previous level. The sensation of defeat was exhausting. She just didn't think she could battle with Alec every day over every tiny thing, from bringing down his dirty washing and the disgusting mugs with their floating dog-ends, to arriving for meals when everyone else was ready and waiting.

Lucy came in with the post from the hall. 'One for you from Mags,' she said, handing an envelope to Jane. 'You probably don't want to see the rest. Suspiciously computer-generated addresses – bills and circulars.'

'Thanks, Lu. Are you off out?'

'The Carvery calls. I'll have to go in a bit. They're giving me extra hours this week 'cos someone's off. I'm not one to turn it down.'

'You must be earning a bit, then.' Jane looked down at Maggie's familiar curling script on the cream envelope. 'That'll come in useful.'

Lucy poured herself some coffee from the cafetiere cooling on the table. 'Yeah. It'll all help towards September.'

'September? What's happening in September?'

'Oh, didn't I say?' Lucy sat down casually with her mug, pulling the morning paper towards her. 'I'm going Interrailing round Europe with Beth. Thought I'd mentioned it. We're heading off early September for three weeks, to do all the big ones before we go back to uni. You know – France, Italy, a bit of Germany, maybe. I'm keener on Italy but Beth wants to go to Berlin.'

'Sounds lovely. Very exciting.' Jane tried to keep the note of surprise out of her voice. Lucy was an adult now, and perfectly entitled to make plans without consulting her. But she was beginning to wonder if she had failed monumentally, somewhere along the line, when her children seemed to want her in their lives so little. After Theo had died, she'd had the strong sense that the three of them were everything to each other now, that they had to bond together against the world. All that had changed, she didn't know when, and she felt more and more alone as the children pulled away from her.

I never tried to tie them to me, she thought, as Lucy read the paper and drank her coffee. I always gave them freedom. Why are they so desperate to escape?

She couldn't bear the thudding music in the house so she went out to the garden to do some weeding but while the bass was less insistent, she could now hear the whining and wailing of the tunes descending from Alec's bedroom window, so she decided to drive into Oxford and do some shopping, perhaps call on Jerry.

The drive lifted her spirits. She put Mozart on the tape player, opened the windows and let the fresh air of early summer flood into the car as it bowled along the country lanes towards the motorway. It was a bright, blue day with a sky like a freshly painted nursery, and she pushed all thoughts of the children out of her head. Maggie had written a lovely letter thanking her for the weekend and saying she really mustn't worry about Alec too much and that all would be well. It had smoothed her over for the moment, even if she knew her worries would return.

Jane parked the car in the multi-storey and ventured out into the town. The main roads of Oxford thronged with visitors, crowds led by a guide holding an umbrella or stick aloft, or families in backpacks and trainers consulting guidebooks and trying to find their way round the colleges. Exchange students filled the pavements outside the fast-food restaurants, smoking cigarettes and chattering loudly in a babble of languages. The shops were busy and noisy and the golden walls of the colleges seemed even more impenetrable than usual. She decided against shopping and went to Jerry's college instead, hoping he might be in the gallery.

The porter let her through despite the 'No Visitors' board at the college door, and she breathed in the sudden peace and quiet in the main quad with relief. It was so serene, so comfortingly the same. It was blissful to be away from the noise and sheer number of bodies. It made her realize how life at Rawlston had accustomed her to quiet and solitude. I'm like a kind of hermit, she thought. A recluse. The sight of all the people, all the strangers, gave her a rush of horror and a desperate desire to escape back to the familiar peace of the garden. Of course, the contrast was ridiculous: the fury of Oxford in the tourist season was something anybody would want to avoid.

She walked round the quads to the college gallery – it was the kind of luxury that only a rich college could afford, this little series of rooms displaying the art and book treasures accumulated over the centuries. It was open to the public but at such odd hours that hardly anyone, except the really dedicated, managed to visit. Jerry's role, Jane always felt, was undemanding and his hours were flexible, to say the least, so she wasn't surprised when his assistant told her that he had gone out before lunch and wasn't expected back.

'Oh, that's fine. Tell him I called in, will you?' She'd wanted to see him very much earlier in the day, needing his witty frivolity to cheer her, but now she felt better anyway. She took a turn round the pictures instead, admiring again the tiny Raphael Madonna and the pencil cartoons by da Vinci.

Coming out half an hour later into the bright sunshine of the back quad, she was dazzled and stood, getting her bearings and wondering what to do, as her eyes adjusted.

'Mrs Fielding?' said a voice behind her.

She turned and saw, blinking, that it was the student Jerry had brought to the house the other day. Not the effete one – the other – Tom. She found it hard to place him for a second because he was no longer dapper in a jacket and tie but more studenty and young in baggy shorts and a blue T-shirt.

'Hello,' she said. 'How are you?'

'I'm fine.' His voice held the slight twang she'd noticed last time but she still couldn't identify it. 'Were you looking for Jerry?'

'Yes. He's not there, of course. I sometimes wonder what they pay him for.'

Tom smiled. 'He's a bit of butterfly – you never know where he'll be. I have a feeling that he and Ollie have gone on an architecture fest somewhere. They've wangled an invitation to tour a house. The owner has promised to show them over and she's a dowager viscountess, so naturally they're all of a quiver.'

'Well, I wouldn't want to stand in the way of that. Didn't you want to go?'

'Ah – I could take it or leave it this time, to be honest. I had a couple of other things to do.'

They stood for a moment a little awkwardly, Jane wondering how she was going to make her excuses and if she should head for the back gate, which would bring her out on the wrong side of the college. Then Tom said, 'I'm sure I'm no kind of substitute for Jerry, but if you'd like to have some tea with me, I'd be delighted.'

'That's . . . very kind, but . . . won't I be interrupting you? Don't you have work to do? You said you've got some things on.'

'I've done most of what I need to for today. Don't forget, I'm a student,' said Tom, running a hand through his curly hair. 'I work when it suits me – which is a bit less often that it should be, I'm afraid. Besides, term's over. People are hanging about for parties and stuff, but there's nothing much to do. What's more, I read a very boring book for three hours this morning, so I'm feeling very virtuous. I deserve an afternoon off and they've opened a great little tea place along the High – why don't we go and try it?'

'All right.' She was flattered that he wanted to share this exciting new place with her. 'That would be very nice indeed.'

They strolled along the cobbled back-streets, avoiding the crowds trekking along the main road, and chatting easily. Tom asked after Lucy. 'I got the feeling she didn't much approve of us,' he said, with a laugh.

Lucy had indeed been scornful of Jerry's little retinue of time-warp Timmies, as she called them, but she hadn't been as vehement as she might have been. 'No, no,' Jane replied. 'Actually, we don't get many visitors – which is ridiculous with such a big house – so we always appreciate those who turn up.'

'Very diplomatic.' He grinned, showing white, even teeth 'I don't mind if she thought we were idiots. I know that's how we can come across. This is the place.'

Jane was sure that the site had previously been occupied by a shop selling teddy bears emblazoned with the Oxford University crest, like so many that sprang up with offerings for the tourist trade and then vanished. Now it was a pretty, traditional-looking tea room, with a pale green front and little white cane tables. They went in and sat down.

Once they had their little china pots of tea, there was an awkward pause as Jane was struck by the oddness of being here with a virtual stranger, and one not much older than her daughter at that. She struggled for something to say, and remembered the echo of an accent she was picking up. 'You're not British, are you? I can hear something in your voice – are you American?'

'Nope. Most people think it's Australian they can hear. I'm South African, actually. I'm always amazed at how people in England can pick it up. At home, I'm considered to have the perfect British accent.'

'Our ears seem to be peculiarly attuned to voices in this country. I don't know if that's a good thing. But why don't you have a South African accent?'

He shrugged. 'My parents are both British so I didn't pick up the really guttural version. And I did my BA at Southampton, which ironed it out even more. Now that I'm here,' he gestured to the sunlit street, where the University Schools could be seen across the road, grand and imposing, ' well, deliberate or not, I'm losing even more. It's hanging out with Ollie and that slow drawl of his.'

'Your BA? So you're not an undergraduate?'

'Ah, no.' Now that she knew his roots, the African influence in his speech was becoming clearer. His 'ah' had a thick edge to it. 'I'm a post-grad. One of the ancient old things wandering around, being despised by all the eighteen-year-olds.' He laughed. 'Jerry took pity on me at a college drinks where I was loitering at the edges with my Pimm's, trying to find a friendly soul.'

Jane could just imagine how Jerry would pick out a tall, athletic, curly-haired young man who looked in need of companionship. 'He's good that way. Very kind.'

'Yeah, he's great. And a real one-off. If I'm honest, I was hoping I might meet someone like him at Oxford.'

'Oh. I see.' Jane felt rather taken back. She'd assumed Tom was straight and that Jerry's interest lay in the direction of the louche Ollie.

Tom laughed at her expression, throwing back his head and making a hearty sound that startled and rather tickled her. 'Oh, right! I can read what you're thinking. That's funny. I can imagine what it must have sounded like. No – not in that way. I'm afraid I'm very conventional and boring – just your average heterosexual. No, I wanted to meet that . . . you know, that *Brideshead* type. Very English, very old-fashioned, always attending cocktail parties and polo matches. I thought it might be fun to see how the other sort live. That's what they all warned me Oxford would be like. You don't want to go there, they said, it's full of people who think they're in an Evelyn Waugh novel.'

'Is that what you've found?'

'Yes and no. They're here, of course, but they're in the minority. Most of the students are almost aggressively the other way: determinedly modern and cool. Much worse than the tweedy lot are the political types – they're really rabid and nasty, with their eyes on the main prize. They all expect to be in Number Ten by the time they're forty-five. Then there are the would-be journalists, full of self-importance and boasting about how they've already been commissioned by *The Times*. Can't bear them. Following closely are the luvvies – place is packed with them, swooning and declaiming and putting on tights. No one ever mentions that lot, do they? It's always the poor old *Brideshead* types who get it in the neck, and they're virtually an endangered species. I sometimes feel we ought to be protecting them, if anything. None of them have ever been anything but kind and welcoming to me. And Jerry introduced me to Ollie, who took a shine to me and we've been mates ever since. It's a laugh really – all this dressing up, visiting country houses and drinking fine wines as though it's our birthright. Talking to Ollie, what would you imagine he came from? Some kind of well-off landed-gentry family? Well, you'd be wrong.'

'So it's all play-acting?'

Tom shrugged. 'It's fun. It *is* acting. It's a bit of a drama in

87

the most fantastic setting in the world. When you're living in eighteenth-century rooms, with a servant cleaning for you and staff serving you dinner in a fabulous hall every night, well, you can start to believe in it a little. And if it doesn't do any harm – why not? We'll all be tossed out into the big bad world soon enough. I can tell you, there's nothing remotely like it back home.'

Jane laughed. 'That's true enough.' She liked his warm, friendly spirit and his directness.

He gazed at her, his brown eyes solemn. 'Tell you what, when we've finished our tea, let's take a turn round the Botanic Garden. I love it there.'

They walked around the garden until they reached the river and sat down on a bench, watching people wrestling with poles as they tried to manoeuvre long flat punts through the dingy water.

'What did I tell you? Isn't it great here?' Tom looked pleased to have shown her this little treasure, tucked away in the middle of the city.

'It's wonderful. I haven't been here for many years.'

He looked crestfallen. 'So you already know it? Of course, you would. How stupid of me.'

'I used to come here with my husband Theo before we were married, when he was still a student.' She had a sudden vision of them, standing on Magdalen bridge in the cold grey light of a summer dawn in their ball clothes. They'd been so happy just to be together. It cut her through with a desperate sadness that she hadn't felt in a long time. These moments of missing Theo had a raw agony – mild compared to the early days of her grief but still shocking in their power. If she'd known then that she would still be feeling like this so many years later, she would never have been able to carry on.

Tom said softly, 'Jerry mentioned that your husband died. I'm sorry.'

'Please don't be,' she said lightly. 'Don't give it a thought.'

'Have you been on your own ever since?'

She was surprised by the question. Or rather, by his asking it. 'Yes, I suppose I have.'

'That doesn't seem right at all, a woman like you—'

'You sound like Jerry. He's always reprimanding me for not being a social butterfly but, really, I'm perfectly happy as I am. Now – I've taken up far too much of your time already, and I really must be getting back.'

'Have I said the wrong thing?' He looked worried.

'Not at all.' She reached over and patted his hand. 'I really do have to get home. But I've had a lovely time. Thank you.'

He grinned his absurdly young-looking grin. 'That's okay. Any time.'

Driving home, she wondered how on earth he could really have enjoyed it. A young man like him, spending his afternoon with a middle-aged woman old enough to be his mother – he was just extraordinarily well mannered, that was all. He was a little older than she'd imagined; she'd assumed he was Lucy's age but he was a post-graduate so he would be a few years older than that, in his mid rather than early twenties.

Thinking about it, she decided not to tell Jerry. He would jump to all sorts of conclusions and make embarrassing jokes about it. Just because he liked to chase young men around the quads, he'd assume that she was doing the same and she didn't want to be a kind of companion in Jerry's flirtations. It would make her uncomfortable. In fact, whenever Jerry proclaimed that he was trying to find her a lover, she felt uneasy.

She knew that most people must assume that by now, so many years since Theo's death, she must be completely recovered. Over it. But the truth was, she wasn't and she was ashamed of it. People would surely think her weak and stupid if they knew how much she still yearned for him, still missed him. The first few years had been taken up with the terrible, bitter anger she had felt towards him for dying and leaving her, and the guilt for feeling angry, for not saving him when she'd been there with him, in the very room, in the same bed. They had gone to sleep as usual the night before and she'd woken to find him cold and stiff beside her. She'd known at once that he was dead even though she tried frantically to revive him. They told her later that he'd died quickly, probably knowing very little about it, when the vein in his head burst and flooded his brain with blood. Once the initial horror and pain had become more bearable, like a pot of boiling water calming to a simmer, she'd begun to be able to live again but not in the same way as before. Now she felt as though she was living the second-best version of her life. Somewhere there was another Jane Fielding following the ideal path, with her husband at her side, her children happy, her relationships strong and positive. She, though, had to struggle on alone, trying to reach the people around her, but the experience of Theo's death had sent them all spinning into different orbits, so that they could communicate only with difficulty. Nothing had been the same – and she didn't want it to be the same. If she had lived in the right time, she would gladly have worn widow's weeds for the rest of her life, like Queen Victoria, to show the seismic change that had shaken her life apart.

She was hungry for love, that was true. But not the fumbling flirting, the animal sensation of sexual attraction: she craved the deep, loving friendship of a long and happy partnership and that, of course, was impossible. As for sex – she'd been to bed with a handful of men in the last decade; one was the village doctor who'd taken her out on a couple of occasions and obviously decided that his prowess in bed was just the thing to make her feel better. She'd allowed herself to be seduced against her better judgement, hoping that just doing it again would change something, bring her back to life, restore her. It hadn't. It had been a miserable echo of what she'd had with Theo, and afterwards she'd lain in the darkness with hot, silent tears leaking from the corners of her eyes and down into her hair. She'd been glad when, a little while later, he'd moved to another practice.

Friends had persisted in setting her up with their newly divorced male acquaintances and she'd grown to dread those men. They were mostly embittered and unhappy after the failure of their marriages, looking for a woman either to make it better, or to punish. Lots of them were keen, pleasantly surprised when they met her, as though they'd been expecting a monster, a gruesome, dried-up old widow. Some of them had wanted to take her to bed and a couple of times she had said yes, just to remember what it felt like. Once it had been unexpectedly wonderful and the following day she'd been sparkling and alive, feeling somehow regenerated. But that man had never called again and, in her heart, she was glad. She knew that if she didn't love again, she'd never have to risk going through that dreadful loss again either.

Chapter Eight

The drive in the Mercedes was wonderfully smooth. The car purred along as though it ran on honey. Bella had sat back in the leather seat, stroking it surreptitiously with her hand as Sam drove. They talked easily – the dinner party had forged a quick intimacy between them, strengthened by the undiscussed taking of drugs. The fact that Bella had shared in Sam's vice had won the other woman's confidence, and Sam had started calling every day for a chat. Now they were taking their long-discussed trip to Oxford.

They reached the city in no time and Sam headed immediately for her favourite shops, Bella trailing in her wake. She loitered outside changing rooms while Sam stripped off time after time to don tight jeans or tiny frilly tops, white trousers and cashmere vests. Bella found it funny that something so frivolous could be taken so seriously. She liked to dress well and buy things but there had never been the money for her to become a slavish follower of fashion and she'd comforted herself with the thought that, really, it was ridiculous to care too much about clothes.

'Why don't you get something?' Sam said, as they left another boutique loaded with exclusive-looking bags.

'Better not,' said Bella. 'I'm not working. Hard to justify spending that kind of money.'

'Don't you get an allowance?'

Bella laughed. 'Er – no.' An allowance sounded like something a fifties housewife would have, pin money from her hardworking, bowler-hatted husband. 'Why? Do you?'

'Course. How else do you think I could pay for this stuff?'

They stood on the High as crowds strolled by. Bella could see the golden walls of colleges and the high spires of churches, chapels and college entrances. She was surprised to find that Oxford had such a normal town centre, with sandwich bars and coffee chains and clothes shops. Somehow she'd imagined it as interlinking gracious quads with gowned professors and blazered students wafting about.

'Let's get a coffee,' Sam said. 'I'm desperate for a fag. Come on, I know a place.'

She led them to the covered market and they found the café up a dark, narrow staircase, where there was a warm scent of ground coffee and carrot cake. They settled themselves on benches and ordered *caffè lattes*, skinny for Sam, who lit up a cigarette and expelled a long stream of smoke. 'God, that's better. Nothing like spending a great wad of cash to make me desperate for a ciggie. Want one?' She rattled the packet at Bella, who shook her head. Sam opened her wallet and shuffled through the receipts of her purchases. 'Not too bad . . . A bit of a dent in this month's money but I've got enough left to see me through.' She flicked her gaze at Bella. 'Doesn't Iain give you any money, then? How do you manage?'

'I've always worked, I suppose, except when the children were really little, so I've had my own money for all that. We have a joint bank account and put all our money into it but I keep a little aside for my own use. At the moment, Iain puts a certain amount in as housekeeping, and I keep us all going on that.'

Sam frowned. 'Doesn't sound too good. What about the children's clothes?'

'They come out of the housekeeping as well. They don't need much.'

'Holidays? Trips out? Treats?'

Bella was feeling uncomfortable. She had come out with Sam to forget about her own circumstances for a moment, to soak up the other woman's moneyed glamour and have a bit of her credit-card cachet rub off on her. 'We don't exactly plan for those – Iain doesn't think they're really necessary. Once a year we try to get away, usually to Cornwall or Wales, a rented house or something.'

Sam wrinkled her nose in amazement. 'Don't you go abroad? Everyone goes abroad.'

'We've *been* abroad, obviously, but we don't go every year. I actually rather like having our holidays in Britain. You know, a bit different.'

'Yeah,' said Sam, sounding unconvinced. She looked as though she couldn't conceive of life without St Moritz and the South of France.

'Tell me about you and Ben,' Bella said, changing the subject, as the foaming coffee was delivered to them.

'What do you want to know?'

'How did you get together?'

'Oh. Usual way. How does anyone get together? We fancied each other like mad, had a date, fell in love, got married.'

'Right.' Bella felt that this explanation was rather inadequate. Limited though her knowledge was, she was already aware that there was an ex-wife and a stepdaughter in the picture. She said tentatively, 'I thought . . . I thought Ben was married before?'

'Yeah – he was. But what can you do? When you meet the right person, you've got to do something about it, haven't you? Otherwise everyone's miserable all their lives when they don't need to be. I mean, yes, it's painful in the short term for the first wife but she's got to know that something was wrong with the marriage in the first place, or her husband wouldn't have fallen in love with someone else, would he? There wasn't anything we could do about it – our passion was too strong. Aileen did find it a bit difficult, granted, but look at her now. She's got a great job in America, she lives with a dentist, she has a wonderful time. She wouldn't have all that, would she, without me?'

'Oh, I absolutely agree,' said Bella, although she wasn't sure that she did. But the first rule of establishing a friendship meant that she needed to seem on side, no matter what she really thought.

'Besides . . .' Sam looked dreamy, half shutting her china-blue eyes, 'you can see for yourself how sexy Ben is. I fancied him right away. I've always liked big, tall men – really manly. He makes me feel all tiny and womanly. Like a little doll.' She

94

smirked, shooting Bella a glance from under her lids. 'And I can tell you, he delivers. And how. Talk about *fantastic sex*. Ben's the best.'

'That's . . . nice.' Bella felt a little helpless. How did you respond to that? Who was to say what great sex was? She enjoyed it herself and had always felt that her relationship with Iain was healthy and satisfying enough, but when people said they had *fantastic sex*, she felt woefully inadequate, as though they'd been somewhere she'd only read about, or seen pictures of. What was it they did, exactly, that was so different? There were only so many variations on a theme, weren't there? Or was she hopelessly naïve? It always seemed to her that fantastic sex was a relative thing, and based more on the chemistry and the emotion between the parties than a strict practical application of technique. But then, she'd been sleeping with same man since she was twenty-two, so what did she know about it any more?

Sam looked at her. 'He's not your type, though, is he?'

'Isn't he?' said Bella warily. This kind of question could backfire no matter how carefully she answered.

'Well, look at Iain. He's completely different, physically. You obviously like your men a bit girly – ' Sam corrected herself quickly ' – I mean, not *girly*. Just not as macho as someone like Ben. Iain's quite short . . .'

'He's five foot ten,' Bella said quickly.

'Okay, yeah, not *short* but on the short side. And he's not hairy and deep-voiced, is he?'

'He's not a caveman, if that's what you're saying.' Bella felt prickly.

'All I'm saying is that he's not like Ben, so Ben is obviously not your type, is he?' Sam ground out the last centimetre of her cigarette in the ashtray. She picked up her coffee cup and grinned over the top of it. Then she reached out and gave Bella's arm a gentle push. 'Oh, come on. Cheer up. Your Iain's a great bloke and I'm sure he's dynamite in the sack. You just want to get him to loosen the purse strings a bit. Then you'll be all right.'

Bella let herself into the lodge after Sam dropped her off, her one

95

carrier bag clutched tightly in her hand. In the makeup section of a large department store, she had allowed herself to buy a Chanel eye-shadow. The chic black box with its engraved two white Cs somehow allowed her a tiny piece of a better existence. She had bought it slowly and carefully, lingering over the purchase, while Sam had been engrossed in exclusive skincare ranges.

In the kitchen, she took the compact out of its gold and black box and snapped it open. She gazed at the four circles of glittery powder, the white sponge applicators sitting neatly next to them, and stroked her finger over one. It left a pale gold smear of shimmer across her finger tip. I'm so stupid, she thought suddenly. Why did I buy this? It was like a tiny Alice in Wonderland door to another world, one she could never walk into but could press her eye up against and peek through. She was a fool. She was supposed to be clever enough to avoid this kind of insidious manipulation. She snapped the compact shut and put it down.

The day had been meant to make her feel better but somehow she felt lower than before, even more dissatisfied. No matter how friendly Sam appeared to be, everything she said was like a veiled criticism, or a subtle pointing out of how inferior Bella's life was.

She stared out of the kitchen window to the garden stretching away to the fence at the end, and beyond that at the inky green woods against the blue sky. She didn't see it, though: she was seeing Sam and Ben making love, his tall, masculine frame enfolding her slim, lithe one, like a perfect couple in the movies. They were lost in some kind of marvellous ecstasy, their mouths open, eyes closed, panting . . . She shook her head and tried to lose the image. It was replaced with one of herself and Iain, all too human, all too normal – his pale, freckly skin and her fleshy body joined sweatily and quickly on a Sunday morning, all over fast in case the children heard.

She felt a pang of jealousy but quelled it instantly and laughed instead. 'Stop it,' she told herself. 'You don't want to be like Sam. Even if her husband is ridiculously attractive.' She was startled to hear herself say it – she'd barely known she thought it.

When Iain found the eye-shadow on the kitchen table later that evening, he was scornful. 'How much did *this* cost?' he demanded, holding it as though he might catch something from it.

'Not that much.' Bella carried on making the supper, thinking of some way she could distract him. 'It's just a little treat.'

He stared at it suspiciously, then put it down. 'Little treats cost money,' he said pompously. 'And, in case you haven't noticed, you're not working.'

'I know that.' She tried to hide the exasperation in her voice. 'Apart from all the housework, cooking, childcare, cleaning . . .'

'Paid work.'

'Obviously.'

'Did you get a chance to look at the emails I sent through today?'

'Yes, but not thoroughly. To be honest, I'm not sure if they're for me.' Iain was beginning to nag her about working, emailing her job specs from the Internet, or from his own workplace, whether or not they were suitable for her. He'd sent an advert for a vacancy in his company's training department. *Worth thinking about*, he'd written, *good money*. She'd sighed with frustration: yes, good money but she couldn't commute to London with all the hours that would take up and, more importantly, had no desire to work in the same company as Iain, or in any of those big, faceless corporations. Iain wouldn't understand that, though. Jobs were not for enjoyment; they were a means to an end.

'I don't know if you're in a position to be choosy, are you? And if you hang about with your friend from up the road, you're in danger of developing expensive tastes.'

'For God's sake. I'm an adult – I'm perfectly capable of controlling myself. And I need some bloody friends in this place, so don't go telling me who I can and can't see.'

'I'm not doing that.' Iain thought for a moment. 'There's always Trudy from the cottages if you want to have coffee with someone.'

Bella slammed down the saucepan she was holding. She breathed hard, not knowing whether to laugh or explode. His comment seemed to show such an incredible ignorance of who she was and what she was like that it made her question whether Iain had any idea about her at all. 'What on earth would I have in

97

common with an eighteen-year-old girl, who's lived in a cottage in the country her entire life and who is – to be blunt – more than a little backward?'

'She seemed perfectly nice to me.'

'Would *you* have coffee with her?'

'Well, I don't need to.' He cleared his throat in the way he always did when he was about to criticize her. 'I have to spend hours every day commuting and working extremely hard in an office. Perhaps if I had the luxury of whiling away my days at home, I might enjoy spending a bit of time with the locals.'

'You know *sod all*,' muttered Bella, under her breath.

He pretended he hadn't heard her. 'I think we need to draw up a plan of action for you getting back to work.'

'Yeah, yeah,' she said. They always did this when Iain wanted to bully her into doing things his way. In the guise of discussion and co-operation, he would write down everything he thought, then type it up into an official-looking document that somehow became their agreed approach. 'Whatever you say.'

In bed that night, he turned to her and nuzzled her neck. She stiffened for a moment, staring into the blackness, then relented as he sought her mouth and ran a caressing hand over her buttocks. She had been surprised by Iain when they'd first made love: he had been good-looking but somehow unprepossessing – the kind of man she had suspected would be too gentle and too considerate, turning the whole thing into an awkward exercise of politeness. In bed, though, he'd been passionate and his skill and delight in her were part of what had brought and kept them together.

Afterwards she always felt closer to him that at any other time, and right now she needed to feel close to someone, even if it was Iain.

She remembered her image of Sam and Ben together. It sent a tingle of excitement down her, and desire for something of that for herself. She let herself sink into his kiss and pushed her body against his, allowing her mind to set itself free and drift off to wherever it took her.

*

The next day, Bella decided to walk down the lane to meet the children after school. The minibus dropped them at the junction with the main road and they picked up their bikes from a nearby barn and cycled home. She would wait for them at the barn and walk back while they rode their bikes up and down, doubling back to circle round her and shout about what they had been doing.

On the way out, she picked up a thick cream envelope from the door mat. It had been hand-delivered, perhaps while she was in the garden, and she didn't recognize the writing. She took it with her and opened it as she wandered down the lane. It was a card from Jane Fielding, inviting them to the house for drinks and lunch at the weekend, a spidery old-fashioned script in black ink on laid card with the address engraved along the top.

A garden party at the big house, she thought. It seemed smarter than her little coffee mornings with Sam. She was pleased. Life had been taking on a dreamy quality and perhaps this might pull her back into its stream. At first, after the strain of the move and the stress of leaving her job, she had needed the quiet and solitude of the lodge to restore herself. Her initial buzz of energy and schemes to redecorate had dissipated as she'd realized how exhausted she was and how much she needed to sleep. They'd been at Holly Lodge for five weeks now, and she'd almost begun to enjoy the isolation. After a few calls and emails from Nicky, and her other London girlfriends, there had been nothing more. They were working on different time now: her friends' lives were busy and frantic while Bella's was slowing down until she wondered if she would reach a standstill.

Once or twice, she'd driven out to see what lay about. This part of the country was different from any she'd known before, heavy with a lush richness. She imagined medieval farmers fattening their sheep on this claggy, fertile land, producing great bales of thick white wool that made them their fortunes and allowed them to build the golden houses and churches, endow the abbeys and schools, the guilds and halls in all the towns around here. The villages round about had the scent of money in them, with all those wisteria-clad honey-coloured cottages, almost too sweet for a picture book, on their sleepy little high streets, and the larger houses hidden away behind stone walls and high trees, everything neat around the velvet village greens with their dinky cricket pitches. This was commuter land, after all. She began to learn the little maze of villages connected by winding, narrow, hedge-lined roads, and the larger towns with their antiques shops and tea-rooms and tourist trade. She liked to walk into silent, musty village churches, observing the piles of damp hymn books, cork noticeboards testifying to a life there, displays of the Sunday school's paintings, ancient funerary monuments to the local gentry, the war memorial, dusty light coming through diamond-shaped, jewel-coloured glass.

She knew that this strange aloneness and lack of real activity – if you didn't count the usual round of cooking, cleaning, washing, ironing and tidying – couldn't last, and that was part of what made it precious to her. Soon they would need money. Her redundancy payoff was shrinking fast. They had a mortgage, pension contributions to make, bills to pay. The children needed new clothes – the autumn would arrive before they knew it and then there would be new shoes, winter coats . . . But she pushed that out of her mind for now. She wanted to make the most of this unexpected hiatus which allowed her to step outside everything for a time, and breathe.

Sam didn't mind Bella dropping by so often. It was understandable that she would want to escape the poky little lodge and come up here to Sam's large, light, uncluttered rooms, drink wine and smoke the odd cigarette. And, actually, it was nice having a friend nearby. All right, in the normal course of things they probably wouldn't have much in common – Bella was a touch on the mumsy side – but here they were, pushed together in this tiny place, and she couldn't be picky with such a limited choice.

'I see you got one of Jane Fielding's invitations,' Bella said, nodding at the card Sam had pinned on to the corkboard in the kitchen. 'Are you going?'

'Yeah. Ben's very keen. I'm sure he's got something up his sleeve. He was pretty pleased when that landed on the mat.'

'Do you think it's just us?'

'Who else is there?' Sam made a face. 'Apart from Trudy and those people from the cottages.'

'Mmm. Can't wait,' Bella said, and laughed.

'Don't know if I want to socialize with the charlady. It's bad enough that Ben's keen for Emma to come along. He says she should get to know the kids on the other side to stop her being such a recluse. She comes home, shuts herself in her room and that's it. We never see her.' Sam leant forward confidentially. 'I say be grateful for small mercies. But Ben's always on at her to come downstairs and sit with us. I wish he wouldn't. We'll get our fill of Madam when she comes to France with us, though I'm still working on ways that we might be able to avoid that.'

'When are you going?'

'Week after next. I've booked a farmhouse in the Dordogne. You know the kind, old stone, beams, all that antique shit. Ben loves it because there are three Michelin-starred restaurants within a two-mile radius. Right up his street.'

'Goodness, it sounds idyllic.' Bella looked down into her wineglass with a crooked smile. 'I don't know if we're getting away this year. I love France. Lucky you.'

'Yeah. We go most years. To be honest, I prefer a nice fortnight on a hot beach with everything on tap, or somewhere in a city. And now that we're living here – well, it seems a bit mad to go somewhere quiet on holiday. Coals to Newcastle, isn't it? And I have to put up with Miss Sulky Boots, who can't drag up more than one sorry smile a day.' Sam laughed. Then she stopped and frowned. A brilliant idea had floated into her mind that seemed the perfect solution to her problem. 'You know what? I've just had a stroke of genius. Are you ready for this? Okay, so . . . why don't you and Iain and the kids come on holiday with us?'

'The week after next?'

'Yeah, to the Dordogne, to our farmhouse! Think about it! It's perfect! You need a holiday, I could do with human company besides that girl. The kids'll love it!' She felt more and more excited as everything fell into place. 'Well? What do you think?'

Bella wasn't as thrilled as Sam had thought she would be. 'But you won't have room for another four people, will you?'

'There's *loads* of room!' Sam crowed. 'These old farmhouses — you never even find out how many rooms there are. But it definitely sleeps up to nine and there'll still only be seven of us. Oh, come on, Bella, it'll be a great laugh. We can have barbies, go sightseeing. The children will love it — they even have canoeing on the river and stuff like that. There'll be no pressure, honestly. You know us, we're completely laid-back. Mornings we can spend just as we want, whether it's in bed or lazing in the garden. Afternoons we'll go out in a group or do what we want. Evenings, we can all muck in if we cook, or go out for dinner. Go on — it'll be fab to have a bit of adult company. You know you want to.'

'Sam, I'm overwhelmed, I really am. It's a wonderful idea, and so generous. But I'm going to have to ask Iain. He'll have to get time off work, for one thing, and he might feel a bit funny about it. He's no reason to, of course, but he might feel that we're tagging along on your family holiday.' Sam went to protest but Bella stopped her. 'He can be a bit proud, you see, and get a bit prickly if he thinks he's a charity case.'

'Look, it's no skin off our nose. It makes no difference to us money-wise if you come or not — in fact, it'll probably be better for us because we'd share the cost of the groceries and things like that.' Sam put a hand on Bella's arm and said, 'Between you and me, I know you can't afford a break like this at the moment — but there's no need for Iain to know that. And if he feels he wants to give us something towards the house, fine — but you know we don't need it. I just want you to come and have fun with us.'

Bella smiled at her. 'Sam, it sounds great. But what about Ben? You haven't asked him, have you?'

'Don't worry about him. He'll think it's a great idea as well. Leave it to me.'

When Ben came home, he was in a good mood. 'Emma called me — she's out tonight,' he said, after he'd kissed her.

'Oh, yeah?' Sam rubbed her nose on his shirt sleeve, savouring his deep, musky smell. It was as good as a tranquilliser for calming her down, for making her feel safe and looked-after.

'So we're on our own tonight,' he said, squeezing her arm. Then he whispered, 'Shall we make the most of it?'

'Oooh, you naughty Benjy,' she said, jokily reproving. 'You're insatiable, you are.' She wondered when he meant to take her upstairs. Part of her hoped it was going to be later; part of her wanted to get it over with as soon as possible. 'Shall we have a drink?' she suggested.

'We could . . .' said Ben. 'But I'm feeling sticky and dirty after my day. Why don't we go and have a shower?' He turned her round to him and kissed her again. 'Come on,' he said, coaxing. 'Let's go up together.'

'All right,' Sam said, smiling, while inside her head she was telling herself that she would like it, that she always ended up liking it a little, no matter how much she was repelled by the idea beforehand. She followed Ben's broad back up the stairs, letting him lead her by the hand, pushing down her rising sense of dread as best she could.

Afterwards Ben had a shower while Sam lay on the bed, the duvet kicked off on to the floor. When he emerged from the bathroom, a towel round his middle, he came over and lay down next to her, water dripping off him on to the sheet and pillow. She wiped away a few of the trickles on his bare arm with a finger but didn't say anything. It was one of the things he liked about her, she knew, that she never nagged or told him off.

'Are you all right, Sammikins?' he asked, and stroked her face. He was so handsome, she thought. Those blue eyes, that dark hair curling wetly above his ears. It was such anguish to her, really, that she couldn't take the pleasure in it she wanted to. She loved to look at him; it was only when he began to get close that she stiffened up.

'I'm fine, hon,' she replied.

'Did you have a good time?'

'I always have a good time – you know that.'

'Do you?' He looked suddenly boyish and vulnerable. She was

filled with love for him and wrapped her arms round him, pulling him to her and feeling the wet hair on his chest coil against her breasts. He pushed aside her hair and dropped a long slow kiss on the back of her neck.

'Always,' she said, and she believed it absolutely when she said it because she couldn't really admit the truth even to herself. 'Benjy . . .'

'Yes?'

'I've been thinking about France.'

'What about it?'

'I was just thinking . . . maybe we should ask the Balfours to come with us.' She looked at him carefully to gauge his reaction.

'The Balfours?' Ben laughed and rolled on to his back. 'We've known them all of five seconds. Are you serious?'

'Yeah – yeah, I am.' The more she'd thought about it, the more brilliant it seemed. With Bella and Iain there, Emma's power to make her uncomfortable would be defused.

'I don't know. These shared holidays . . . they can go very wrong, especially if you don't know the other people well.'

'It'd be fine,' Sam insisted. 'We had a great time when they came round for dinner, didn't we?'

'It was a nice evening and she's okay but isn't he a bit odd?'

'I thought he was great! On the strange side but in a harmless way. I thought he was an interesting character, actually. Not all like most of the boring blokes you know who only go on about work and football. I think Iain's an intellectual – we could learn a lot from him.'

Ben crossed his hands behind his head and stared at the ceiling. He sighed and said, 'The trouble is, I'm not sure if I want to learn anything on my holiday. I work bloody hard, Sam, you know that and I treasure my time off. If they turned into the holiday couple from hell, I wouldn't be at all happy. One night does not a lifetime's friendship make.'

'But we're not risking anything, really, are we? Chances are they'll be on their best behaviour seeing as they're our guests, and if we don't like them, we've not really lost anything. What we need to do,' she traced a finger through his chest hair, 'is make sure there are some ground rules. You know – certain hours when we have time to ourselves. An outing on our own every other day. That kind of thing. Look, have a think about it, but it'd be fun.'

He turned to look at her. 'Don't you have fun on your own with me and Emma?'

'Course I do,' she said stoutly. 'I mean, she can be a bit difficult . . .' Ben's mouth hardened as it always did when she criticized his daughter and she added hastily, 'in the totally normal way that all teenagers can be. Honestly, she'd probably prefer it if we stopped badgering her to spend time with us and let her get on with her own thing.'

Ben considered what she'd said. She wasn't worried; she was sure she could talk him round to anything she wanted and now that she'd had a chance to think it over, she couldn't see anything but good in the plan. And, she reminded herself, she'd be helping out a family less fortunate than they were.

'I'm not sure, Sam, but if it's what you really want . . . we'll see.'

She kissed his cheek, rough with evening stubble. 'Thanks, darl. I'll tell Bella the good news. You won't regret it. Promise. Now I'm going to get in that shower and then we'll have to think about dinner.' She slid off the bed and padded over to the bathroom, feeling pleased with herself.

Chapter Nine

The garden seemed to vibrate with life. The weeds were springing up overnight, eager to take their share of the rich soil; insects were everywhere and silvery trails showed where slugs and snails had toiled; birds chirped and sang as they stood on the garden wall, watching, then fluttered and dived to snatch at the fruit; the summer vegetables were swelling with such ripeness that Jane wondered if she should make up boxes to distribute among her neighbours – there was no way she could use up so much on her own. The colours in the garden looked injected with acid, they were so vivid: jelly greens and neon pinks flaring vulgarly among blood scarlets and buttercup yellows.

Jane worked hard, perspiration dampening her hair as she picked raspberries to fill her basket. She'd got up early to get this done in the cool of the morning, but it was already hot. The berries would decorate the pavlovas she'd prepared last night for the lunch party today; then she'd get some of those fat strawberries and handfuls of mint leaves for the Pimm's. There was a lot to do before everyone arrived. Lucy was in the kitchen, mixing a batch of Coronation chicken and marinating lamb steaks for the barbecue. The terrace, where Jane planned to put out the long table, laden with plates, cutlery and food, was still bare and she had to get a move on, if she wanted to change before people turned up.

Looking up, she saw Alec drift past the open door of the kitchen garden, his white T-shirt vivid against the green lawn. He must be off on one of the solitary walks that kept him away for hours. He hadn't been much interested in the prospect of the party and hadn't offered any help. Under duress, he'd brought the trestle tables up from the cellar and left them propped up messily against the door, and when Jane had asked if he'd be there to meet the neighbours, he had mumbled something unintelligible so she had no idea whether he would show his face or not.

She took a small ripe berry between her fingers and popped it into her mouth. It was sweet and delicious. When he was little, Alec had loved picking fruit. He and Lucy would rush into the canes with their punnets and earn twenty pence for each one they filled, delivering the fruit to Jane, their mouths stained with juice. It was hard to reconcile that small boy, so eager to please, with this silent, broad-shouldered, unhappy man. That was what really pained her, she thought, his unhappiness. He had so much – he had this wonderful place to live in, the home she had worked so hard to give him – but it meant nothing to him. Perhaps it was losing his father so young – perhaps she had failed him by not being a father as well as a mother. But there was nothing she could do about that. She couldn't simply have magicked up another Theo, much as she would have liked to.

At her own lowest, darkest moments, this place had helped restore her – the garden, Rawlston and all its quiet, crumbling, shabby beauty. It seemed to her that Theo was still here; as a boy running across the garden and down to the lake; as a young man sleeping on the lawn under the papers; as her husband, kissing her on the swing that hung from the oak tree. He was everywhere here, the reason why she could never leave.

'How are we doing?' Jane put the basket of berries on the kitchen dresser.

Lucy looked at her handiwork. Large china dishes filled with food covered the table. 'Pretty good. I'm going to do the salads at the last minute so they don't wilt.'

'Do you think we'll have enough?'

'Plenty. How many people will there be?'

'Well, if they all come . . . Let me see, the Balfours plus children, the Clarkes, the O'Reillys – though I'm not sure if all of them will come – the Pierces. Jerry said he might show his face. I asked

107

a couple of the ladies from the flower committee but only at the last minute. Cathy and Nathan said they might come . . .' Jane stopped trying to count on her fingers. 'How many is that?'

'Hmm, quite a lot. I'm sure we'll manage. There's tons of bread and filler stuff.' Lucy glanced at the kitchen clock. 'Hadn't you better go and get changed?'

'You're right. Knowing our luck, someone will be here bang on twelve thirty.' She went upstairs to run her bath.

Katie and Christopher were over-excited, running about, squealing and refusing to get ready for the party. Bella wanted them well-turned-out and well-mannered, to show that she and her family knew how to behave at this kind of occasion.

'Can't you make them calm down?' Bella said, exasperated, as the children raced by round the corner of the lodge.

Iain flicked down a corner of the paper and said, 'No. Can you?' He was slumped in a garden chair, his legs stretched out in the sunshine, a cup of coffee cooling on the table next to him.

Bella put her hands on her hips and sighed. 'I want them to come in and get ready for this do.'

Iain retreated behind his paper. 'I thought you liked to arrive fashionably late.'

'Well, yes, but that doesn't mean turning up when it's practically finished.' She felt cross. For some reason, she was anxious to get there. 'I'm going upstairs to get dressed. And I want to leave in good time, okay?'

'Okay, okay,' said Iain, in a bored, singsong voice. 'Don't worry about it. The party won't be going anywhere.'

In the event, they weren't very late. The children, promised a delicious lunch and probably fizzy drink, consented to behave and be brushed up to look quite respectable. Bella put on a light summer dress and brought out a straw hat, minty green and floppy with pink silk roses pinned to it, that she'd worn to a wedding, which Iain laughed at and asked if she thought they were going to Ascot or something. He seemed determined not to be overawed by the party.

'It's a barbecue,' he said carelessly, and put on his oldest shorts. Bella was horrified and they compromised on his smartest casual trousers instead, but he insisted on wearing a T-shirt with them.

They went to the huge front door on the Fielding side of the house and knocked as loudly as they could, but when there was no reply, they ventured around the side and came out on to a long, green lawn with a terrace near the house where people were standing about holding drinks. A figure detached itself from the crowd and came forward to greet them.

'Hello!' called Jane, waving as she approached. 'I'm so pleased you could come. Oh, what a lovely dress – and a hat too. Very sensible on a day like this.' She kissed Bella on both cheeks.

'This is Iain – I know you've met before – and Katie and Christopher.' Bella felt oddly breathless and nervous. Jane was very friendly, as kind and calming a presence as she had been before, but nevertheless Bella felt ill at ease. Perhaps I'm overdressed, she thought unhappily, glancing down at the fussy printed sundress. Jane looked wonderfully casual and elegant in a pair of pale linen trousers – uncreased, how on earth did she manage that? – and a pink shirt. The hat suddenly looked out of place and gauche.

'Come and have a drink. We've made a great vat of Pimm's, if that's what you'd like, or there are soft drinks. And wine.' Jane led the way over the lawn towards the terrace and they followed her, subdued by the grandeur and strangeness of the house.

Jane introduced them to the people who'd already arrived, and gave them tall glasses of Pimm's, fruit and mint leaves floating in the yellow foam at the top. Bella made polite conversation with a woman from the village, all the time alert for the arrival of Sam and Ben. From the corner of her eye, she watched Jane moving about among her guests, making sure they had drinks and urging them to help themselves from the loaded trestle tables if they were hungry. The babysitter, Trudy, was standing nearby, moonfaced and vacant-looking, spooning quantities of food into her mouth.

When Bella managed to detach herself from her conversation, she strolled along the edge of the terrace, looking down towards the lake at the bottom of the lawn. Katie and Christopher, with some of the other children, had discovered the rope swing hanging from a thick branch of the oak tree and they were clambering up its old knots. She turned back to look at the house and breathed in at its beauty. The stone had mellowed to a rosy blush, pairs of open french windows stretching the length of the room behind. Sprays of white roses climbed up round them towards the windows above.

What a marvellous house, she thought. How amazing to belong somewhere like this. She was conscious suddenly that she didn't belong anywhere at all – she'd always been on the move, since she'd managed to leave her parents' house, which had never felt like her home. To live somewhere like this, where it was possible to bed in and put down roots, to love it and become a part of it . . . It was extremely seductive. She envied Jane Fielding or perhaps the Fielding children – that pretty girl dishing out salad and the surly-faced boy loitering on the edge of things with a can of beer – for being born to all this and not knowing any different.

'Hello. I'm so glad you made it.' Bella jumped. Jane was standing beside her. She put up a hand to shield her eyes from the sunlight. 'Are you all right here on your own?'

'Oh – yes, I'm fine. I was just admiring your house.'

'Thank you. I'm very lucky. But it's also a burden, a place like this. I wondered how you were getting on at the lodge. I hope you're not bored to death here. There's not much to do, I know, and the people,' she gestured towards the terrace, 'well, they're lovely of course, but probably not as interesting as your London friends.'

'Oh, no, not at all. It's funny, I haven't been bored. I think I needed a break, to be honest. And the woman next door to you, Sam, has been very friendly.'

'I'm glad to hear it. She's coming today, I believe.' Jane smiled. 'How nice that you've made a friend. I've been a bit of a disappointment in that regard, haven't I? If you'd like to, you're very welcome to come up here. Why don't you come next week? I'm usually about.'

'Thank you – I'd love to.'

'I must go and mingle. Don't forget to have some food, will you? There's so much . . .' Jane made her way back towards her other guests, strolling lightly across the grass and waving at a new arrival.

What was it about her, Bella wondered. Something drew her towards Jane and the warmth that surrounded her. It was such a contrast with Sam's self-contained, cool exterior. With Sam, she felt she should watch what she said. With Jane, she wanted to throw herself into her arms, rest her head on that shoulder and confide everything that was wrong.

You idiot, she told herself. You don't even know her.

'What a throng!' said Jerry, in a scandalized voice, gazing at the busy terrace. 'I thought it was the neighbours!'

'It grew a little — you know how these things do.' Jane kissed him hello.

'If I'd known, I wouldn't have brought him . . .'

'Brought who? Ollie?'

Jerry looked mournful. 'Oh, Ollie. Such an angel. A cherub. But also a little fiend. He's gone down for the summer and his parents have whisked him away to somewhere hellishly remote, the rascals. I keep trying to tempt him back, but he's adamant that he has to stay away until at least October. No. I've brought Tom, though.'

'Is he not going home?'

Jerry gave her a look. 'Darling, would *you* want to go back to South Africa when you could stay in Oxford? I know where I'd rather be. He's staying up all summer, to work, he said. College is deserted so I brought the poor thing along. He's sitting in the car waiting for the yea or nay. I thought you wouldn't mind because it was only going to be small.'

Jane laughed. 'Oh, goodness, one more won't make any difference. Go and rescue him — I'm sure he's longing for a drink.'

He darted in and kissed her cheek. 'You're an angel, have I ever told you that?'

'All the time. Now I've got to go and say hello to the vicar's wife.'

It was much later when Sam and Ben finally arrived. Bella was feeling comfortably woozy after a couple of glasses of Pimm's and had been talking to an elderly man from the farm cottages. Apart from his habit of spitting food while he talked, he had been surprisingly good company. She was making her way back to the drinks table when she felt two arms snake round her waist. Turning, she saw Sam's laughing face.

'Hiya! We're here!'

'Where've you been?' Bella smiled, relieved to see her.

'Couldn't decide what to wear, and Ben had some work to finish. But what do you think?' She spun round on her high sandals, showing her slim figure in a tight white off-the-shoulder top and girlish, gypsy skirt. Her blonde hair was long and sleek round her face. As usual, she looked as though she'd stepped from a different, polished universe into the normal, scruffy world to show everyone else how it should be done.

'You look terrific,' said Bella sincerely, trying not to think about her pale fleshy arms and the mosquito bites on her ankle.

'Oh, thanks, love, so do you. Great hat. Very posh.'

Bella wished she'd never thought of the hat. Only the vicar's wife and one or two elderly ladies were wearing them. 'Where's Ben?'

'Over there.' Sam jerked her head to where her husband, looking cool and expensively dressed, was pressing a bottle of champagne on to a politely protesting Jane. 'Vintage Bolly,' confided Sam. 'Very pricy. So, what do you think of this place?'

'Lovely.'

'Mmm. Old, though, isn't it? Bit shabby?'

'Well, it's not as gorgeous as your side,' Bella said, seeing at once what she ought to say.

'Nah.' Sam wrinkled her nose. 'She wants a designer in, that's what. Come on, let's go and get a drink.'

Sam resisted the food table and lit a cigarette instead. When they were settled she said, 'So, don't keep me hanging on! What does Iain say? Can you come?'

Bella smiled at her. 'Iain says thank you very much, and we'd love to come.'

Sam clapped her hands gleefully. 'Oh, great! That's fantastic.'

'And what does Ben say?'

'Yeah, he says the same as me. That we'll have a really good time. We must talk about all the arrangements. Oh, I'm really, really excited now!'

'Me too.'

They'd been at the party too long, Bella thought. She was feeling hot and had stopped drinking the innocuous-tasting Pimm's. Sam and Ben were talking to Jane Fielding and she loitered on the edge of the party, trying not to feel left out. Iain was enjoying himself hugely, locked in animated conversation with a couple, waving his glass of wine as he talked. He was not a great drinker and she could tell he was a little drunk.

Do I really want to go to France with the Clarkes? she thought, and imagined a stone farmhouse in a French village, long warm evenings with the local vintage on hand, the sophistication and glamour of Sam and Ben to add a bit of spice. Who was she kidding? It was a marvellous idea. She couldn't deny the children this opportunity, either. They'd never been to France. Come to think of it, they'd never been abroad full stop. Air tickets for the four of them were an impossible expense, even with the budget airlines. Iain always wanted to travel by coach but the idea of hours of hell on a dirty bus, with disgusting loos and hemmed-in children was too appalling to contemplate; so they always ended up going to Wales to stay in a caravan park not far from Bella's family, or to a rented flat in a Cornish village by the sea. It wasn't bad, and the children always enjoyed it, but the idea of a holiday in the Dordogne was almost irresistible. Bella had been grape-picking as a student and had adored France; she had memories of long hot days and frivolous evenings getting drunk and kissing handsome local boys.

When she'd suggested the holiday to Iain, he'd been won over very quickly. He could see that they would never be able to do such a thing on their own, especially this year. The offer of a virtually free holiday in France was not something he was inclined to turn down. His only real reservation was that he didn't like Sam's dabbling in drugs but Bella had assured him that, as far as she could tell, it had been a one-off. There wouldn't be anything like that in France. After that, Iain was perfectly happy and, once he'd arranged his holiday with work, enthusiastic about the trip.

Why, then, did she have these doubts? Bella looked over at the Clarkes, Ben so tall and handsome with his petite, girlish, glamorous wife at his side. She was torn by wanting to be like them and having a weird desire to run away as fast as she could. There was something simultaneously attractive and repellent about them, like a wicked temptation. Perhaps I'm jealous, she thought. Sam's life seemed so delightfully carefree and luxurious, so focused entirely and shamelessly on herself. Perhaps I want a little of that, Bella thought. Is that so bad?

We'll go, and we'll enjoy it, she decided firmly, pushing uncomfortable thoughts out of her mind. I like Sam – there's nothing more to it than that. It would be madness to say no. They didn't have to ask us, they obviously think it will work. In fact, the more Bella thought about it, the more it seemed impossible to refuse.

She was sitting on the lawn watching the children play, her legs tucked under her, the heel of her hand in the cool grass when Ben came up to her.

'Hello – all alone?'

She looked up. He towered above her, silhouetted against the sky. Blinking, she smiled at him. 'Just taking some time out.'

'Sam's gone home.' He crouched down beside her and leant forward to kiss her cheek. She felt it as a cool buzz on her skin. 'I haven't had a chance to talk to you until now. Sam tells me you're coming to France.'

'It's very kind of you to invite us,' Bella said.

Ben shrugged. 'It'd be fun. More company for Emma.'

'Is she here?'

'No. Refused to come. You know – teenagers.' Ben sat down properly and stretched out his legs, looking across the lawn to the lake. 'I wanted to come and scout this place out. Magnificent, isn't it? Imagine what it would be worth if it was all one house – with today's markets, you're looking at seven figures, easily. I just told Jane Fielding that. Even with half the house she's sitting on a valuable asset, and if you factor in the land, she could sell up for quite a pretty penny. Nice, cosy, comfortable retirement some-where small.'

'What did she say to that?'

Ben made a face and slid his blue gaze round to her. 'Oh, you know these landed-gentry types. She looked like I'd just suggested she eat her own vomit or something.' He put on an affected posh voice. 'Oh, I don't want to sell – that's the point. I want to live here.' He laughed. 'But she can't afford to live here. And I'm ready and waiting.'

'Do you want to buy this whole place?' Bella couldn't see why he would need it.

'Bit by bit. The land first, then the house.'

Bella glanced back over her shoulder at the rambling old place, with its air of comfortable shabbiness. She imagined it polished up and redesigned, like the other side. White walls, spotlights, beach stones on blond wood shelves. It seemed sad, really, something to be regretted, as though the colour was being leached out of the world. But there was something about Ben's energy and con-fidence that was hard to resist.

Her attention was drawn by a movement. A wasp was crawling slowly along Ben's white trouser leg. 'Oh, look,' she said, 'I'll get it.' Leaning forward, she brushed it lightly away, sending it off into the grass, but lost her balance as she did so and fell forward, putting her hand on the firm flesh of his thigh to right herself. 'Oh, I'm sorry . . .' She pushed herself away, feeling her face flush with embarrassment.

Ben grinned. 'No need to apologize.'

They stared at each other for an instant, then Bella dropped her eyes and pretended to brush something away from her skirt.

Jane said goodbye to the Balfours – the husband was clearly drunk with a flushed face and a loud voice, and Bella keen to get him home – and thought that on the whole the party had been a success. It had been a little bigger than she'd planned, not quite the intimate neighbourly gathering she'd originally envisaged, but it had still served its purpose which was to offer a welcome to the new arrivals.

She began to walk about absent-mindedly, collecting up dirty glasses and plates from where they had been abandoned on the terrace. There were still knots of people standing about or sitting on the lawn.

'Let me help.'

She turned to see Tom grinning at her, holding a pile of dirty plates. He looked cool and summery in a pair of baggy chinos and a blue linen shirt. 'Where should I take these?' he asked.

'Hello! How nice to see you. I'm sorry I've not said hello before now,' she said breathlessly. 'Very bad of me. You shouldn't be doing that – you're a guest.'

'Too late. Come on, I want to help. Let me earn my share of that delicious food. It's the least I can do when you didn't even know I was coming.'

'Well, you don't have to. But . . . follow me then.'

'Lead on, Macduff.'

They went through the french windows into the dining room, then along the passage to the kitchen. It was a relief to be away from the sunshine and the heat of the terrace in the cool dimness of inside. They put the plates on the kitchen table where there was already a vast array of washing-up.

'Wow, what a great kitchen.' Tom looked about.

Jane followed his gaze and saw only old cupboards, a tatty armoire, a mixture of china and dishes collected in bits and pieces over the years, and her trusty old Aga in the chimney breast. It looked old fashioned and overused to her.

'It's a bit of a period piece,' she said uncertainly.

'Oh, no. It's fantastic, large but cosy. A family place. A lived-in place. It's beautiful. I mean it.'

'Goodness. No one's ever reacted quite so enthusiastically to my kitchen before.'

He laughed, and she remembered as she saw them again how white and even his teeth were. 'Ah, excuse me. I can't help myself when I see something I love. It's because I'm such an Anglophile. And in South Africa our house is very modern. The kitchen is big but it's all Formica and stainless steel. A bit too wipe-clean and soulless for my taste.'

'And does your mother cook?'

'She does not,' he said. 'We've got staff for that.'

'Staff! Now it's my turn to be impressed. You must be rich.'

He shrugged. 'No. It's not such a big deal over there. There's so much poverty, people will work cheaply. Now,' he changed the subject decisively, rubbing his hands together, 'shall we get started on this lot?'

'Oh, no, no. Lucy's already loaded the dishwasher. And I mustn't be away from the guests for too long. We'll do it tonight when everyone's gone.'

'If you're sure.' He looked regretful. 'Shame. I was hoping to get you to myself for a bit.'

She laughed to hide her slight discomfort. He was flattering her, and she couldn't think why. He didn't need to be nice to her, and she was sure he was far too young to find her interesting. So what was it? The house? Men had liked her for the place before now — one divorcé a friend had brought round had seen pound signs when he'd laid eyes on Rawlston and spent an evening crawling to her in the most obvious and off-putting way. But Tom didn't seem like that sort.

'Don't be silly,' she said. 'Come on, we'd better get back. Shall we see if we can find Lucy?' she asked, over her shoulder, as they went back into the corridor. Surely her daughter would be of much more interest than she was.

'If you like,' Tom replied carelessly, looking about as he followed her. He stopped suddenly in front of a picture and said, 'Hello, what's this?'

She went back to see what he was talking about and saw that he was looking at an old pastel sketch of her, done twenty years ago by a friend of Theo. It showed her sitting in a chair in the drawing room, rather elegant in a pale green cardigan with a string of pearls. She looked unbearably young in it, with wide eyes and unlined skin, her hair in a short bob as it was now, but dark and without its streak of grey.

'Oh, that old thing. It's just an amateur sketch. I don't think it's too bad, though,'

Tom was staring at it, his hands thrust into his pockets. He said at last, 'It's beautiful. You look amazing.'

'I think the artist was particularly kind.'

He frowned. 'I wish you wouldn't put yourself down so much. It's just like you. I knew it was you at once. It has your expression, that clear-eyed goodness and your quality of innocence.'

'Well . . . I don't know what to say.' She looked again at the soft lines of the drawing. Her younger self gazed back, oblivious of everything that was to come.

He glanced down at her with a smile. 'You think I'm a silly young thing, don't you? You think I should be interested in drink and teenage girls.'

'No, no, of course not . . .'

'Yes, you do. Come on, how old do you think I am?'

'Well – twenty-three, twenty-four?' It was hard to guess these things. He looked young to her, and that meant around Lucy's age. But as he was a post-graduate, she had added a year or two.

He laughed. 'I'm closer to thirty than I am to twenty-four. I'm almost twenty-nine.'

'Really?' He must have started his studies late, she thought.

'Yes. So, you see, I'm not quite the babe in arms you assumed.'

Tom was standing disturbingly close to her and his presence made her feel breathless and flighty. She smelt the light fragrance of a scent that made her heart jump with its familiarity – it was almost, but not quite, the same as the old Penhaligon scent that Theo used to wear. She had the feeling of being pulled back through time by her senses, and gasped lightly.

'Are you all right?' he asked, concerned. His face was near hers, and she could see the soft pink curve of his lips, the smoothness of his complexion, his finely shaped brown eyes. The air around her seemed to buzz.

'We should go back outside,' she said quickly, thinking that she must escape before she gave away how odd he was making her feel.

He said in a low voice, 'Can't we stay here? I like talking to you like this.'

Confusion was muddling her mind. What was he saying? What could he mean? She stumbled for something to say that would bring the conversation back on to normal, everyday, predictable lines, away from this talk that felt underscored with meaning. The shrill ring of the telephone in the corridor broke into her struggle.

'The phone,' she said, with relief, drawing away from him. 'You must excuse me.' She hurried to the hall table where the phone was. Tom did not follow her. 'Hello?' Her voice sounded as though she had run up a flight of stairs.

'Is that Jane?' The voice was thick with an accent and it was hard to distinguish the words. 'It is Gregor here.'

'Yes, this is Jane.' She recognized the voice now, and could see the tall, skinny, hook-nosed man in her mind's eye. 'Is everything all right?'

'Jane. You must come at once. Maggie is in the hospital.'

Chapter Ten

The Mercedes slipped gracefully in and out of view. They seemed to have been catching glimpses of its elegant tail for hours. As they rounded a bend in the motorway, it would be soaring away ahead, sliding from lane to lane. There was no point in trying to keep up. The engine roar was giving Bella a headache, the children were tetchy and bored in the back seat, and Iain was clutching the steering-wheel with white-knuckled determination. He was nervous of the French traffic and kept the car firmly in the middle of the motorway, watching for the car up ahead.

The journey felt interminable but it was only that morning, at dawn, that they had pulled out of Rawlston in their small convoy, the Clarkes' car taking the lead for the drive to the Eurotunnel. Once the cars were loaded on to the train, they got out in the carriages to stretch their legs and take the children to the loo. Ben and Sam joined them but Emma, whose pale face and hunched form Bella could make out through the Mercedes windows, didn't emerge. The train journey was smooth and swift and it was barely any time before they were out of the other side and disembarking at Calais. The tension in the car rocketed as Iain grappled with driving on the right, reading the foreign road signs and keeping the Clarkes in constant sight. Things were easier on the long stretch of the motorway, except for the dullness of the landscape. Bella stared out of the window at the flat fields punctuated by occasional buildings or lines of poplars; as the miles slid by, the view remained exactly the same.

'It's not like this in the Dordogne,' she told the children. 'It's lovely there.'

Three hours later, the Mercedes signalled that it was pulling off and they followed it away from the tedium of the motorway and on to winding narrow roads. They stopped outside a charming restaurant, with a sloping mossy roof and tubs of bright flowers outside its low bay windows.

'What do you think? Lovely, eh? We found it last time,' said Ben, once he had parked his car and come over to the Balfours. 'It's quite reasonable too.'

'Actually, Ben, if it's all the same to you, we'll just stay outside and have our sandwiches. We packed a picnic and it seems a shame to waste it,' Iain said, from the driving seat.

Ben smiled. 'Fine with me. You'll be missing some of the best onion soup in France, but up to you.'

'Too hot for soup,' said Bella, leaning over from her seat. 'We're saving ourselves for the holiday proper.'

'Aren't you coming in?' shouted Sam, looking impossibly cool despite the heat in her white T-shirt and jeans; her blonde hair was twisted up on her head, dark sunglasses obscuring her eyes.

The Merc must have bloody good air-conditioning, thought Bella, trying not to feel envious. She had endured a steady stream of cold motorway air, sometimes carrying tiny stunned bugs in it, blasted on to her chin by the vent. 'No, we're staying out here. You go in, though. We'll be fine.'

The Clarkes vanished into the restaurant while the Balfours laid a rug on the grass verge and opened clingfilmed parcels of ham and cheese sandwiches, drank tepid water from a bottle and passed apples around. The children ate hungrily, regained some energy and played quietly while Bella read and Iain napped.

It was an hour or more before Ben, Sam and Emma emerged. Bella had a chance to look at Ben's daughter now, a thin girl with brown hair brushed back into a ponytail and an unsmiling face. She climbed immediately into the car without acknowledging the Balfours.

They repacked and set off again, back on to the motorway and down through France towards their destination.

They reached their village in the late afternoon and Bella felt her spirits rise as they approached it. The scenery had become lush and green, with picture-book villages and pretty farms tucked away in it.

'This is more like it,' she said to Iain.

'Yes – it's nice.' He nodded.

They followed the larger car around narrow bends and through a silent, apparently deserted village until they reached a drive-way, and turned off to reach, at last, their holiday home.

The grey stone house, with small windows dotted randomly about its broad walls, each with brown shutters, sat large and warm-looking in a raggedy orchard. The doors were low and wooden, and a rickety staircase led up the side of the house to a loft window. Greenery climbed up the sides and flourished along the walls, softening the flat lines and giving it a romantic air of semi-desertion.

'Oh, it's gorgeous,' breathed Bella. It was better than she'd hoped. She'd expected a manicured conversion, with paved ter-races and a lurid blue, sun-loungered swimming-pool. But there was a delicate wilderness around the old house, with weathered wooden chairs grouped around a table in the orchard, near a homemade brick barbecue. The children scrambled out of the car, delighted to be at the end of their long drive. 'Be careful,' Bella cautioned. 'We haven't had time to check everything yet.'

Emma watched them but stayed loitering by the car as Ben hauled luggage from the boot. Sam came over, picking her way across the stony drive in her high heels. 'Well, what do you think?' she called.

'It's beautiful,' said Bella, climbing out and breathing in the soft sweet air. 'I can't quite believe it.'

'No pool, I'm afraid, but there's a swimming area in the river if we want it. Shall we go inside?'

The rooms were cool and plain, the bedrooms sparsely furni-shed. By unspoken consent, Ben and Sam took the largest with the en-suite shower room and the vast bolstered bed. Emma dis-appeared up the stairs to the furthest reaches of the house to find the attic rooms, while Bella discovered one with bunk beds for Katie and Christopher and a nearby double, dark and cool, for her and Iain. Once the rooms had been allocated and the luggage moved, they all met in the kitchen for cold drinks and a rest.

'First things first,' said Iain, in a businesslike voice. 'We need to find a supermarket and stock up on supplies. Let's make a list, plan some menus. We brought a box of staples – salt, pepper, tea, squash and so forth.'

'It's pretty well supplied here for basics, actually. The owners provide a welcome hamper.' Ben gestured over to a box on the bench, already opened. Bottles of wine and a packet of coffee sat next to it.

'Oh. Well. We'll need some other things, won't we?'

'Look at this,' Sam said, bringing over a bulging file. 'It's a guide to the house and area. I don't think there's a supermarket nearby, not a big one anyway. There seems to be a small one in the town but we're expected to get most of our stuff from the market. It's on three days a week, according to this. Otherwise there's a baker in the village for bread and milk.'

'That sounds all right,' said Iain, cheerfully. The idea of a market obviously appealed to him. 'We can establish a rota of shopping and cooking and start a kitty for shared basics and perhaps even a cost limit per meal so that we keep a lid on our expenses and make sure we spend the same amount. Now, what shall we do tonight? Shall we go and find this little supermarket? If so, we ought to get moving – it's already getting late.'

Bella looked at him from under her lashes, willing him to be quiet. She was used to his zeal for organization and schemes. They never came to much – he was always unable to stick to his own rules and his mind was more chaotic than his talk suggested – but the Clarkes wouldn't know that. Iain was putting himself forward as a leader and she felt that, in the circumstances, they should hold back and follow the others. Ben's expression was unreadable and Sam appeared to be lost in the house file. I hope they're not regretting it already, she thought. Why does Iain have to act like this? Can't he see the effect it has on other people when he starts laying down the law? It wouldn't matter if it weren't so bloody obvious – he's behaving as though no one has ever had to buy food before.

Ben leant back. 'Don't know about you, Iain, but I'm worn out after that drive. Why don't we take it easy on ourselves tonight and go out? Is there anywhere nearby, Sam?'

'There's a bistro in the village, according to this.'

Iain looked uncertain. Bella knew what he was thinking: he would only expect to eat out once or twice in the holiday, and when he did it had to be planned, anticipated and treated as a special occasion. It went against his economical nature simply to wander out for a meal because he didn't feel like cooking. He would consider it a waste to go out for dinner on their first night. She knew he would be remembering that the Clarkes had already had lunch in a restaurant and worrying that he would be pressured into spending more money than he wanted to, which in turn would mean he would dig in his heels and they'd be lucky to see the inside of a café, let alone a restaurant, for the whole holiday.

Why did we come? she thought, suddenly desperate. It's bound to be a disaster. We're not like these people at all. It's all horribly, horribly embarrassing. It's like being naked in front of strangers, exposing ourselves and the way we live in front of them. She said, 'Come on, darling, let's not cook tonight. We deserve to relax a bit. We can stock up tomorrow and have a lovely barbecue in the evening.'

He frowned. 'Well . . .'

Ben said, 'Look, we can decide about the restaurant later. I'm sure there's enough here in the hamper to provide a decent supper for us. Bread and cheese will be fine.'

'Best meal in the world, actually,' put in Iain.

'Absolutely. So, let's relax and take things easy. I don't know about you lot, but I could do with a nap.'

Sam and Ben disappeared to their room. Iain went upstairs to read and sleep for an hour while Bella went out to explore the garden and check on the children. She skirted the back of the house and saw the hunched figure of Emma, sitting and rocking to something she was listening to through headphones. She left the girl alone and picked her way round the house, past the loft staircase, where a window was now open showing which room Emma had bagged, and saw two flashes of bright colour moving about in the long grasses at the end of the orchard. Katie and Christopher were absorbed in the stream at the far end. When she reached them, Bella saw that it was overgrown with weeds and full of stones and rubbish. They were crouching over it, carefully shifting the stones into a pile on the bank and pulling back the foliage.

'We're making a dam,' explained Katie.

'So that we can have a swimming-pool,' added Christopher, scooping away small stones from below the surface of the water.

'Won't it be a little bit small for a swimming-pool?' Bella asked. 'Perhaps your toes can go for a swim.'

'Not for us, silly. For Rose and Elizabeth.' Christopher shook his head at her ignorance. 'They want to have a swim too, you know.'

The dolls were propped up on a stone, she saw now, staring out over the proceedings from their perch, already in their swimming costumes. They were cheaper versions of Barbie dolls and had come with a wardrobe of lurid clothes – the children loved them.

'Oh, yes, of course Rose and Elizabeth must have a swim,' she said gravely. 'Are they enjoying France?'

'They're a little confused,' said Katie, 'because they don't speak French.' It always surprised Bella when Katie entered into the doll world. On the whole, she preferred her books and puzzles to dolls, whose unchanging plastic forms bored her. But Christopher loved them so wholeheartedly that he could lead Katie into his fantasy without her questioning it.

'They want to go shopping,' said Christopher, 'because they need some new clothes. Can we go and buy them some?'

'We'll see,' said Bella. 'I don't know if the shops here will sell the right ones for them, but we'll find out when we go into town.' The children didn't reply. They knew too well what 'we'll see' meant. She watched them for a few minutes more as they worked methodically, then said, 'Be careful. Don't get too wet,' and she went back slowly through the orchard towards the house.

'Mmm, Sammy, Sammy.' Ben's voice buzzed in her ear, tickling uncomfortably, but the bolster was crammed against one side of her head, making it impossible to move. His weight pinned her to the bed, which sank underneath her in strange places. She hated new beds. She hated holiday beds, where countless strangers had pounded away just like this. She concentrated hard on it all being over, and panted encouragingly to Ben with the small high gasp he liked.

'Oh, Benjy . . . yes, ye-es,' she whimpered, while she thought, who on earth wants to have sex after driving for seven hours? It was something about being away from home – Ben was always desperate for it whenever they went away. God, I hope no one can hear us. The Balfours' bedroom was on the other side of the house and the walls were thick so it was unlikely. Emma? She was somewhere upstairs and, anyway, it wouldn't do her any harm to be reminded that Ben was still all over Sam.

Come *on*, she thought crossly. How long was this going to take? She shifted her hips to change Ben's sensations and he grunted appreciatively in response. He gathered speed, and then thrust his mouth on hers and kissed her fiercely before he finally reached his climax with a long, soft moan. He slumped over her shoulder, panting, until she pushed him and he rolled off.

'Did I leave you high and dry, Sammikins?' he asked, concerned.

'I'm fine,' she said. 'You know I don't need it every time.' She climbed off the bed. 'This thing is bloody uncomfortable. You'd think they could replace the mattress when it's obviously had it. I'm gonna take a shower.'

When she was clean, she changed into one of her outfits especially chosen for the evenings: slinky, sexy and clinging. It was like an act of defiance; the less she enjoyed the experience of sex, the more she felt compelled to advertise her attractiveness, to look as though she revelled in it when really, most of the time, she could take it or leave it. Not that that bothered most men. Even Ben had no idea of how little she felt: as long as she made the right noises and the right moves, it was fine. She'd learned to do everything she was supposed to and could perform a successful blow-job as expertly as she could fake an orgasm. And she didn't always need to fake it. Every now and then when something, she didn't know what, went right, she could experience a tiny peak that she felt must be something like other women had: a quick, muted electric sensation that made her limbs tingle and something in her relax. It was bitter-sweet, though, leaving her with a vague sadness that this faint echo was all she would have of whatever it was that happened to other people.

The only other time she enjoyed sex was when she was high, preferably on her favourite cocaine, which filled with her a giddy sense of power. It numbed her to physical sensation, so there was no way she'd ever climb to her little summit, but that didn't matter. It made it better really, as she didn't feel that rising anger at the physical invasion that she did when she was sober. Instead she felt strong and sexy and in control, and willing to writhe, bounce, gasp and put on the show of her life. But Ben didn't like it, and he always seemed to know when she'd been at it, so she kept it for special occasions when it seemed as though she took drugs to have fun, rather than equip her for sex. For the rest of the time, she just got on with it.

She looked at herself in the dressing-table mirror. The sleeveless black jersey dress clung all the way down her body, over her flat stomach and long thighs, round her tight bottom. She brushed out her hair so that it was sleek and golden, and slicked fresh gloss over her lips. She knew she looked beautiful. Ben was snoring quietly on the bed after his exertion, and she left him sleeping.

Downstairs, the Balfours were sitting at the kitchen table, the contents of the welcome hamper spread out in front of them. Iain stared at her appreciatively, while Bella said, 'Goodness, Sam, you look wonderful. I didn't know we were going to be so dressy in the evenings. I haven't brought anything like that.' She was wearing a printed blouse and some pale cropped trousers and sandals.

Sam hadn't worried about Bella being competition for her – she'd known her long enough to realise that it was not an issue – but it was still a relief to see how dowdy she was. 'Don't worry, love, it doesn't matter at all,' she said, with honesty. 'I'm a bit of a glamour addict – anything to dress up. Ignore me. You're much more sensibly dressed.'

'Well, yes, I suppose so,' Bella said. She looked down at the table and gestured to the food. 'There's some wonderful stuff here. We'll be fine for tonight. Look – *foie gras* pâté. So luxurious.'

'Yeah, lovely,' said Sam carelessly. 'Anyone for a drink?'

The following day, they went to discover the market in the nearby town. It was a bright warm day with a fresh breeze and everyone's spirits lifted now that the journey was behind them and the holiday stretched ahead. Even Emma looked a little less sulky than usual, Bella thought. She'd been a quiet, hunched presence at dinner the night before, and when the others had loosened up with a few glasses of wine, she'd slunk away to her room.

The town centre was lively with crowds exploring what was on offer, a mixture of determined locals with baskets and loud voices, and curious tourists poking through the fresh produce. The market square and surrounding streets were filled with stalls of meat, fish, cheese, oils and piles of vegetables, and they had wandered about buying whatever took their fancy, even Iain, who was delighted by the prices. 'You couldn't get stuff of this quality at the same price in England,' he kept saying.

Ben was firmly in charge and he could barely conceal his delight at the bounty everywhere he looked. 'My God, look at these cheeses,' he exclaimed over a table of huge waxed rounds and dripping ripe soft wheels, and Sam had to restrain him from buying up a whole stall. It was obvious why France appealed to him. Bella and Iain followed behind, happy to let him exercise his expertise and his French – 'It's terrible, all self taught, but I get by,' he said – while they breathed in the sights and sounds of the market.

Bella found herself standing next to Emma while they lingered near a bread stall. She really was incredibly thin, Bella thought, staring at her wrists, which had the thickness of a bam-boo pole. She concealed it under a long skirt and a baggy top, but it was obvious that she was far too tiny. Eating disorder? Bella wondered. I wouldn't be surprised. Living with Sam would be enough to send any girl over the edge, especially a Sam who can't stand you. I wonder if Ben's noticed . . .

Emma turned suddenly and looked her directly in the face.

Bella smiled in a friendly way to defuse the confrontation — Emma had clearly registered that she'd been staring. 'This is great, isn't it? We haven't really had a chance to say hello before now, have we?'

'Yeah.' Emma flicked her gaze about the busy market. 'Dad loves this kind of thing.'

'And what do you think?' God, how should I talk to an eighteen-year-old? Bella thought. I'm only used to ten-year-olds. What was it like being eighteen? She could barely remember.

Emma shrugged. ''Sokay.'

'I don't know about you, but I can't understand a word. And I did French at A-level. Disgraceful, isn't it?'

Emma smiled, her thin face lighting up unexpectedly. 'Yeah, well, you forget everything the minute you walk out of the exam room. I've just taken my A-levels. Cram, cram, cram — and then, pouf, all gone.'

'How did they go?'

'All right. I worked pretty hard. I was quite pleased with them but I've got to do well. I've got a two As and a B offer from Edinburgh.'

'That's brilliant. Congratulations. I'll keep my fingers crossed for you.' Bella smiled at her warmly as Katie pulled her away to look at a stall selling birds in little wicker cages.

Not long afterwards, they headed home and, after a long lunch in the orchard, walked down to the river where the children begged to swim, and sat for a couple of hours outside the local bar with coffees and then with light beer. A delicious holiday sensation settled over them, as the long sunny hours drifted away in making plans for expeditions, and letting the stresses of home melt away.

Perhaps, Bella thought, things were going to be better than she'd expected when they first arrived. Perhaps it was going to be all right.

*

The holiday seemed harmonious enough. There were some strains, it was true. Sam and Emma barely glanced at each other, let alone spoke. Sam would address her loudly in the third person, with a forced cheery tone that dripped with irony. Instead of offering her something, Sam would say merrily, 'Emma doesn't like bread, does she? I expect she won't want any of this!' or 'I'm sure Emma won't want to come to the river with us. We're far too old and boring for her!' It seemed to send the girl even deeper into herself.

Why doesn't Ben see it? Bella wondered. He ought to stop Sam treating her like that.

Emma relaxed if Sam wasn't in the room and became almost happy, even giggling at some of Iain's terrible jokes. She joined in the general spoiling of Katie and Christopher who were, apart from a couple of ugly squabbles, good-humoured and charming. Ben insisted on buying ice-cream and Coke and, in the local supermarket, he stocked up on a plastic cricket set – obviously aimed at the British holidaymakers – some tennis rackets and balls, as well as a rubber dinghy and toys to play with down at the river. Then he cajoled everyone into joining in the games. Bella sat in the orchard watching as he tried to explain the rules of cricket to Christopher, showing him how to face the ball and encouraging him to run along the wicket and back to the stumps. 'Come on, Chris, my man!' Ben roared. 'It's a bye – you can get a run off that!' Christopher, who didn't have a clue what he was supposed to do, ran shrieking down the patch of grass while Iain lumbered off to retrieve the ball and Bella laughed to see her son's skinny legs as he careered about.

The children were wide-eyed around Ben, as though he were some kind of fairy godfather; Bella had to admit to herself that they rarely received so many gifts even at Christmas. The children leapt about, their hair turning golden and their skins brown in the summer sun – even Sam, who was fairly immune to children, couldn't help stroking their heads or beckoning them to sit by her at dinner.

The holiday began to slip away and soon there were more days behind them than ahead before they would have to go back to Rawlston.

Sam got out of bed. Everybody was asleep but her. She thought it must be two a.m. They'd finished dinner after midnight, a long, boozy barbecue but, despite all the wine, she couldn't sleep – the bed was so damn uncomfortable and Ben had curled his massive form round her, making her too hot. She padded out of the room, found her way downstairs slowly in the darkness and let herself out of the kitchen door into the garden. Even though it was so late, the sky wasn't really dark. A bright moon shone overhead, illuminating the orchard with pale, cold light.

She breathed in the fresh air deeply, wondering why she felt so ill at ease at the moment. The table was still covered with the detritus of their evening meal – they hadn't bothered to clear it up before they went to bed. She wandered over, sat down, and took her cigarettes out of her pocket. Blowing a stream of smoke out over the dirty plates, she felt herself relax a little. What is it? she thought. Something was bothering her. There was the usual annoyance of Emma, but having the Balfours around was . . . What? It was going all right. The kids were charming and not the burden she'd feared they might be. But somehow, off her own territory, the balance of power had shifted. In Rawlston, she felt completely in control, secure in the knowledge of Bella's envy of her home and her life and her looks and everything about her. Here . . . it felt as though Bella had lost some of her wide-eyed admiration. She didn't seem quite so impressed. And she was getting on Sam's nerves by speaking French to the locals, chattering away about medieval this and historical event that, making jokes, holding everyone's attention. Showing off, basically. Sam had even seen her talking to Emma sometimes, and Bella knew how she felt about that.

Sam sat for a while, staring at the garden and puffing at her cigarette. Then a small sound disturbed her, a high whimper. She stiffened and looked about for where it had come from: was it an animal? Some kind of rodent? The noise came again, longer this time, but still a high, almost childish, moan. Sam listened carefully and got up. As it sounded again, she realized it was coming down to her from above and walked back towards the house. A window on the first floor was open and as she approached, it came more loudly, a shaking, throaty sound that she knew now was human. She stood beneath the Balfours' open window, her feet chilling on the stones and grass, and listened to the little cries until, finally, there was silence.

After days of fine weather and outings to local caves, surrounding châteaux and vineyards for *dégustation* and wine-buying, the weather turned on them. One morning they woke to dark grey skies and a chill in the air. By midday, heavy drops of rain had begun to fall, a thick roll of thunder sounded overhead and a magnificent storm began, with crackling, flashing lightning and a tumultuous downpour. The children pressed their noses against the windows and counted the seconds between flashes and rumbles.

They all stayed in the kitchen, making coffee and hot chocolate. Bella discovered an ancient compendium of games in the dresser drawer so she, Katie, Christopher and Sam sat down to play Ludo while the men read and Emma laid out games of Patience on a side table.

Bella played with one eye to stopping any squabbles that might develop. Sam played with unexpected ferocity, glancing up with gleeful triumph whenever she landed on Bella's counter, sending it firmly back to the start. She was taking no prisoners and when she'd won, she got up and left the others to play out for second, third and fourth place, Bella making silly mistakes to give Christopher a chance to catch up.

She watched Sam's slim form saunter off while she shook the dice in their canister. Sam was beginning to puzzle her. Their previous camaraderie had disappeared, for what reason Bella couldn't think. She'd become cool and distant and now and then, Bella caught her staring at her with something like defiance.

Why would she do that? wondered Bella. There was nothing she could think of to explain the sudden chill in relations. In fact, if anyone should be feeling disgruntled, it was her. It was getting her down, the way Sam looked so polished and glossy all the time.

Bella had assumed that on holiday they wouldn't be making an effort and had packed only comfortable old things, but Sam had taken everything up a notch or two. She was permanently perfectly made up, and dressed in clothes that wouldn't have looked out of place in a nightclub. For Bella, tramping around in her shabby holiday clothes next to a fashion plate was depressing. It wasn't just the clothes either. Perhaps she was being paranoid, but whenever she looked up during a meal, Sam was pushing something away from her, or picking half-heartedly at a salad. Bella had been looking forward to steak *frites* with mayonnaise, to soft white baguettes smeared with pâté, and rich glasses of red wine with Camembert and biscuits – wasn't that what a holiday was all about? – but the sight of Sam renouncing all this turned food to ashes in her mouth. It felt unwomanly to eat so much, to eat like the children and the men, but she couldn't bear to deny herself the delicious food that was everywhere.

I won't be so shallow, she scolded herself. I mustn't let myself be influenced like this. I'm never going to look like her, even if I never eat another morsel, so I may as well just get on with things and enjoy myself. And if she wants to be distant – well, it's not as though we were best friends to start with. I'm not really losing anything.

'Who wants to go to market?' demanded Ben, striding into the kitchen where the Balfours were having breakfast. The rainstorms had disappeared and the calm blue radiance they were accustomed to had been restored.

'We want to go swimming!' said Katie quickly, looking anxiously at her parents. 'You said we could go swimming.' The charms of the market had worn off for the children and instead they were obsessed with the slide on the riverbank, which they climbed up endlessly to swoop down and plunge into the water.

'It'll be cold in the morning,' said Bella. 'Much better to wait until the afternoon when the sun has warmed it up a bit.'

'*Pleeease*,' begged Christopher.

'Shouldn't make all that much difference,' said Iain. 'The water warms up over the summer and chills in the winter. Not much changes overnight. If the kids want to go down to the river, I don't mind taking them.'

The children let flood a chorus of pleading and Bella agreed that they could go swimming this morning if they wanted. 'I'll come to the market,' she said to Ben. She liked his enthusiasm for the local food, his insistence on buying the best and the way he charmed the stallholders with his terrible French. 'Is Sam coming?'

'Still in bed,' Ben said briefly. 'Come on, then. Much better to go early, get the best bargains and beat the crowd.'

It was always a little treat to travel in the Mercedes. If anything emphasized the difference between the two families, it was the moment when they climbed into their respective cars for a trip somewhere, the Balfours into their hot, noisy little thing and the Clarkes their sleek, cool one. Bella despised herself for caring about it, but she couldn't help it.

They pulled out of the driveway and along the route towards the town, Bella still disconcerted by being on the wrong side of the road – it meant that she was on the inside where the steering-wheel should be, and she was bitten by tiny attacks of panic that she wasn't in control of the car, or feeling that she was lopsided.

'So,' said Ben, after they had driven along in silence for a while, 'are you enjoying yourself?'

'Oh, yes, very much.' Bella turned to look at his strong profile. There was something very safe about Ben Clarke, as though he was always on top of any situation. She always felt drawn to him. He was handsome, of course, but it wasn't just that. There was something magnetic about him. 'It's wonderful – thank you so much for asking us.'

'It wasn't me. It was Sam.'

'Yes, I know. I hope you don't feel we're crashing your holiday.'

'Oh, not at all. I admit I had my doubts but I'm enjoying it. You've got a couple of good kids there – Katie and Christopher are top notch.'

'They are, aren't they?' she said, proud. 'But it's luck really, you never know how the mix is going to turn out. I think they're people-pleasers, they like to be good. Lucky for me, really.'

'You should take some credit. It's not that easy to produce happy children.'

'Well, you've made them *very* happy, with all the lovely presents. I can't think when they've had so much fun. It's very kind.' There was a pause and she added a bit weakly, 'Emma's a lovely girl, too.'

Ben's eyes were shaded by his sunglasses so she couldn't read his expression, and he continued to stare straight ahead at the road. Then, ignoring her comment about Emma, he said, 'Just say if you think I've overstepped the mark. I don't want to offend you and Iain, you know.'

'You haven't!' protested Bella. 'And, really, the presents are for everyone, aren't they? Everyone can have a go if they like.'

'They can.' Ben smiled his crooked half-smile. 'But I don't recommend you put on those waterwings and get into that dinghy. You might risk losing your dignity.'

Bella laughed. 'I meant the tennis and cricket. Though, I must say, my dignity is just as likely to be dented trying my hand at those. Have you seen me try to hit a ball?'

They spent an hour browsing among the stalls. Some of the owners recognized Ben and welcomed him, bringing out baskets of vegetables or fine meats that they claimed they had been keeping back for someone of his taste and discernment.

'What shall we eat tonight?' Ben asked, as they pushed their way through the crowds among the colourful stalls, following a delicious smell to giant paella pans full of yellow rice, prawns and mussels. 'This is putting me in the mood for fish.'

He led her over to one of the many fish stands, and bargained for a dozen fresh mackerel, some crabs and a bag of juicy-looking langoustines. 'Fish feast tonight,' he said to Bella, handing her the bag. 'Now, shall we get a drink? This is thirsty work. Then some fresh bread and we'll go.'

They crossed the market square, which was noisy with the crowd and the music blaring out of loudspeakers mounted on the

135

town-hall walls – 'A crazy French idea to try and cheer us up, I assume,' said Ben. 'What a bloody din' – then they went along one of the cool dark passages and out into another light square, quieter than the main one, where cafés and bars lined each side. They found one with little wicker tables shaded under a red and white striped awning, and sat down. When the waiter came, Ben ordered two beers.

'I was going to have coffee,' said Bella.

'In this heat? Beer is best, with a mineral water to follow.'

'All right,' Bella said, smiling. She wondered if the waiter thought they were a couple. She was sure he would – why would he think anything else? She rather liked the idea that she seemed an obvious match for Ben, with that grey-flecked dark hair, his sunglasses and his expensive linen clothes. His hat ought to look stupid on him but instead he looked quietly impressive. It was a change from being with Iain, who would, no doubt, have ordered clumsily and been uncomfortable talking to the waiter. Ben had complete mastery of himself and every situation. The two families had been living together for well over a week now, but Bella still felt he was a stranger to her: enigmatic, self-contained, perhaps even exciting.

'I think crab and langoustines to start,' he said to Bella, break-ing into her thoughts. 'Nothing fancy – just the good shellfish with lemon, pepper and mayonnaise for dipping. Have your chil-dren had langoustines before?'

'I can honestly say they haven't.'

'They'll love them. Kids find them gruesome at first, with the eyes and long antennae and things, but the minute you show them how to rip it all off and take out the meat, they get very excited. Meanwhile, I'll stuff the mackerel with herbs, then barbecue them with oil, a bit of wine, maybe some lemon. Dee-licious.'

The waiter returned and put down glasses of golden beer in front of them. Ben paid him and they sat sipping their drinks, observing the people passing by in the square. Bella felt a little awkward, as though she were with an important person whom she ought to impress but who made her feel like an inexperienced teenager.

'You know, Bella, we really don't know much about each other, do we? And that seems a bit odd, considering we live next door to each other and here we are on holiday with our families. I suggest we remedy that. I want you to tell me five things about yourself, right now, without thinking.'

'Oh – God, all right. Er, my real name is Annabella and I hate it. That's one. Number two . . . I grew up in Wales but lost my accent when I went to university—'

'Did you like Wales?' Ben interrupted.

'It wasn't Wales I didn't like. My family life wasn't exactly a picnic – nothing spectacular, I just didn't get on with my parents – and I knew I didn't want to stay in our town. I couldn't wait to get out, actually.'

'All right. Next thing.'

'Um – let's see. I married when I was twenty-two, which was far too young and we didn't really need to. I think we were both rather conservative and it seemed like the proper thing to do. I think I'd tried so hard to get away from my own family, it seemed right to start a whole new unit as quickly as possible.'

'It's got to be fast – don't linger.'

'How many is that? Three? I'm a computer-training manager and I'm good at it. I'm good at teaching people things and I've always liked knowing how things work. It's my bossy, know-it-all side. Number five . . . Oh dear, I can't think.'

'Anything. Your favourite food, your shoe size?'

'Um, last thing, last thing is . . . I miss my work. There. That's it.' She was rather surprised to hear herself say it. She'd been considering her favourite flavour of ice-cream when the admission slipped out. She laughed. 'I don't know if that's contributed much of an insight into me. Now, what about you?'

'No, no, this is my game. I'm interested in *you*. We can do me another time, if you like. Now I'll ask you some more questions. I want to know about your work. Why do you miss it?'

'I took voluntary redundancy when we left London, and the money helped us buy Holly Lodge. I don't know what I was thinking but I expected something else to come along and instead I've hit a kind of wall, both internally and externally. I love it at

Rawlston but it's shutting me off from the real world and all the things I expect of myself – *want* from myself. I've taken the local papers and checked the Internet for jobs but I can't see the kind of thing I can do anywhere.'

'There must be computer training companies in Oxford, mustn't there?'

'You'd think so, but I can't find any. Or not what I'm used to, anyway.'

'Mmm.' Ben looked down into his beer. Then he looked back up at her and took off his sunglasses, revealing his startling blue gaze.

What is it about those eyes? she wondered. Whenever Ben looked directly at her, she felt uncomfortable and wanted to shift in her seat or shake herself. It was unnerving, the directness in the way he looked at her and, now she thought about it, the way his eyes roamed over her. Not in a slimy, staring-at-your-chest way but as though there was something interesting and unusual about her, something worth looking at. And when she spoke, he watched at her mouth. 'Well, we'll have to do something about that, won't we? I don't want you going quietly bonkers down the road. Have you thought about starting your own business? It must be possible to freelance what you do, and there should be a lot of young companies needing computer training for their employees. I know I need it for my lot.'

'I don't know . . .' Bella said. She frowned. 'I've never thought of it.'

'It's an idea. You won't need much in the way of start-up as you work on-site. Just some marketing and advertising to get some clients. A bit of cold-calling, perhaps.'

'I wonder if I could.' She began to feel excited. Perhaps this was the answer – why had it not occurred to her? She could work from home, travel to clients, run a website. Work for herself, earn her own money. 'It's a very good idea. I shall have to think about it.'

'I've had some experience in the area,' Ben said. 'Let me know if I can be of any help. Now, Annabella, shall we go and get some bread?'

On their last night, they decided to stay in and cook. They'd been out a few times to local restaurants and Bella suspected that Ben's tact had had something to do with the fact that they had avoided Michelin-starred places and instead had gone to cosy bistros with *prix fixe* menus or special tourist prices.

Ben cooked, as usual, and they ate outside in the orchard, and toasted the holiday in white wine and the local peach liqueur, then moved on to some of the red that Ben had bought at a nearby vineyard. As darkness fell, the dying fire providing their light, Bella realized they were all very drunk. The children had been sent to bed, but Emma was still there sipping her wine with increasingly bleary eyes.

'Why don't we play a game?' suggested Bella.

'Oh, yes, let's play a game,' Sam exclaimed, clapping her hands.

'Ludo?' asked Iain.

'No.' Sam laughed. 'Not Ludo!'

'Monopoly, then.'

'God, I don't know. What are you like? No, let's play a proper game, like Winking Murder, or something.'

Bella said, 'It's too dark for Winking Murder. We won't be able to see each other.'

'All right, not that. I know! Hide and Seek.'

'Too boring,' said Iain. 'I know what's better than that. Sardines.'

Sam frowned, her head swaying gently. 'What?'

'Sardines – haven't you ever played it?'

Sam shook her head. Iain leaned forward. 'It's like Hide and Seek in reverse. Instead of everyone hiding, and one person seeking, in Sardines one person hides and all the others look for them. But when you find them, you squeeze into the hiding-place with them until all of you have found them. And the last one to find the others is . . . I don't know, the sardine or something.'

'The hiders are the sardines,' corrected Ben. 'The last one is just the loser.'

'All right, yes, that's it. What do you think?'

'Sounds all right,' said Sam. 'Do you wanna play?'

'I don't,' Emma said firmly, from her end of the table. 'My room's out of bounds if you're going to play stupid games.' She stood up, picked up the half-empty wine bottle and headed inside.

'Well, that's an improvement for a start,' slurred Sam. 'Come on, then, let's play. How do we begin?'

Bella got the short strip of napkin from the drooping pieces that Ben tore up and held out in his large fist. She left the others counting obediently with their eyes shut and slowly circled the house, picking her way through the long grass. It was a diversionary tactic, in case the others were peeking, as she knew where she was going to hide. She moved round the house until she reached the front, then darted round the corner and in through the open kitchen door; she went straight to the cellar and down the steps. They didn't use the cellar but had all been down there to inspect the dusty floor and low ceiling lit only by a bare bulb; Bella, on another nose around on her own, had discovered that, almost invisible behind the stairs, a narrow passage led into another room, also dirty and empty and much smaller than the main one, barely big enough for a person to turn in. She went carefully down the stairs in the dark, aware that her reflexes were numb from the wine, and crept into the small second room. She pushed her back against the wall, slid down it, sat on the dirty stone floor and prepared to wait.

She heard them as soon as they started their search: they made a racket opening doors and thumping about the house, shouting to each other. She wondered if the children would be woken up and, worse, if the seekers would start searching Katie and Christopher's bedroom. She should have made that out of bounds before they started.

A series of knocks and bangs alerted her to someone searching the kitchen. Then she heard the cellar door open and the flash of yellow light from the other room as the bulb was switched on. She'd assumed that the cellar would be an obvious place so she kept her nerve as loud footsteps stomped down the wooden stairs.

'Bella, are you in here?' It was Iain. He reached the bottom of the stairs and scanned the dusty, empty corners of the room. 'Bella?'

There was a pause and she guessed he was looking around. This was the danger point. She was banking on no one noticing the passageway, lost in the shadow behind the staircase. Her heart raced and her mouth dried. It must be some kind of primitive instinct, she thought. My senses don't understand it's only a game. A crawling fear was in her stomach. Then she relaxed as she heard him making his way back up the stairs. In the kitchen he shouted, 'She's not in the cellar – I've checked. It's clean.'

Long minutes went by and no one came back. She began to be bored – had she been too clever? Would it be any fun if no one found her? When should she show her face? The darkness was soft and cool, and she drifted off in a dream. She was almost asleep when the light in the cellar flashed on again. Someone came quietly and easily down the steps and reached the bottom. Bella jerked alert, stared towards the garish light in the passage and waited, but there was only an almost eerie silence as whoever it was circled the cellar. Then, unexpectedly, the light was blocked out by a shape and she felt someone approaching her.

Stay very still, she told herself. They won't be able to see after the light in the cellar. Her heart was beating violently again and she tried to control her breathing, which was suddenly loud and fast. The shape moved towards her and then she felt something press against her feet – they had found her. A hand brushed against Bella's face as she looked upwards into blackness.

'Well, hello,' said Ben's voice, as soft as the darkness. 'I think I've found a sardine in the cellar.'

Once he'd gone back to switch off the light, then sat down next her, they were jammed together against the stone wall, their feet tucked under them, knees bent up to their chins. She could feel the heat of Ben's skin through the thin cotton of his shirt.

'This is a very clever place,' Ben whispered. 'Did you find it tonight?'

'No, I spotted it the other day. How did you discover me?'

'I've looked everywhere. I had a feeling you were in the house and I've been in every room except the children's. It had to be down here.'

'Do you think the others will find it?'

'It's hard to say. How long shall we wait?'

'I don't know. I don't know how long I've been here already. It feels like ages. I was on the point of coming up to find you all and declare myself the winner.'

'You might still be able to. Well, we can be joint winners.'

They sat for a little longer in silence, their eyes becoming accustomed to the gloom but still seeing little.

What am I doing sitting in a cellar in France next to a strange man? Bella thought, and was struck by the oddness and the curling excitement of it. There was a sense of complete isolation, as though the others would never find them, as though, in fact, the others had gone far, far away and she and Ben would be like this, pressed together, for ever. A tingling tickle made her want to shake her shoulders and head to be free of it but she stayed still, riding a wave of excitement. Why am I feeling like this? she wondered, and then she saw, with sudden clarity, that for the whole week she had been wanting to get close to Ben and had been reaching out to him, sending him minute messages. Without even being conscious of it, she'd been feeling her way towards him and now here they were, in a delicately and cleverly engineered fashion, alone together, almost as close as they could be.

But what do I want? she wondered. Why do I want to be near him? She was experiencing the kind of sensation she'd had as a teenager, when she'd hero-worshipped some boy and done anything to be near him. Bella hadn't thought she was susceptible to that unbearable compulsion any more. Instead, these days she felt attraction, its poorer relation, in a cool, almost detached way when she observed that some man was good-looking, had an attractive smile, or warm eyes.

So was this just lust? Was all this tingling and stomach-swooping just the last flicker of adolescent fire, now without its idealism and romance and revealed for what it really was? She hoped not. She wanted to control herself, to rein herself in, but she could feel herself taking steps in the wrong direction at every

142

moment. If she could control herself, if she could have some mastery over her unconscious desires, then what was she doing here, in the dark, with the man she'd been watching from under her lashes all week while his wife and her husband looked for them? And what was he thinking?

'I don't think they're going to find us,' Ben said quietly. 'Perhaps we should go up.'

'Sam hasn't been down yet,' whispered Bella. 'Should we wait for her? She's bound to come down. She might find us.'

'Iain claims to have checked the cellar. She might not bother.'

'Shall we wait just a little while longer?' She didn't want this odd black warmth to be over yet, or lose this delicate intimacy.

'Well . . .' His voice was low. He must have turned his head towards her because it whirred in her ear and his breath moved a strand of her hair with almost unbearable lightness over her neck. 'How long do you want to wait?'

'I don't know.'

'Should we stay? I can't hear them moving around.'

'Would it spoil the game if we went upstairs?'

'That depends. They might not be playing the game any more. Perhaps they want us to come upstairs.'

'Do you want to?'

There was a long pause. 'I think we should go upstairs.'

They emerged into the night air which felt clear and clean after the musty cellar, and bright with moonlight. Sam and Iain were sitting at the old orchard table, a bottle of wine open between them, talking. They turned and saw Bella and Ben coming towards them.

'Where've you two been?' demanded Sam, indignant. 'Where were you hiding?'

'We looked everywhere,' added Iain, 'and then we gave up because it wasn't fun any more.'

'We're not telling,' said Ben, as they came up to the table, 'in case we play again. It's a rather brilliant hiding-place so I'm not going to give it away.'

'Were you in the car?' asked Iain sulkily. 'I bet you were. I knew you must have broken the rules.'

'It's our secret,' said Ben.

Chapter Eleven

It had been late by the time Jane reached London after a long, anxious drive. She went straight to the hospital, a grey collection of large, dirty buildings on a busy road. When she had found somewhere to park, she ran back to the entrance and immediately found herself in a foreign, bustling, impersonal world. Patients in grubby dressing-gowns loitered about the entrance, some in wheelchairs, some with friends, some smoking alone. In the foyer, fluorescent strip lighting gave even the healthy faces a tinge of sickly green.

The hospital reception sent her to another wing, then up in a long lift, big enough for a trolley bed, to the tenth floor, through more wide corridors and endless swing doors, past striding nurses and doctors to Maggie's ward.

She was lying in a curtained-off bed half-way down, her eyes closed and her face shockingly pale. Jane felt her stomach turn over with sickening anxiety at the sight of her; Maggie looked like a consumptive pre-Raphaelite model with her thick curls strewn round her on the pillow and her eyelids tinged with lilac, the only colour in her face. She sank down in the chair next to the bed, and put her hand on her sister's. 'Maggie,' she whispered. 'Are you awake?'

Maggie's eyes opened slowly and focused on Jane's face. The corners of her white lips curled up in a half-smile. 'Ah. You came.'

'Of course I did. I came as soon as Gregor called me.'

'It's kind of you, I know how you hate London.'

Jane winced. 'Oh, Maggie, it's not kind. You know nothing would have stopped me coming, no matter where you were.' Her eyes burned but she was determined to keep control of herself. Even lying here in hospital, Maggie was not going to drop her sardonic tone and her well-honed way of making Jane feel guilty. 'How are you?' A metal stand next to her dangled a bag of clear liquid with a tube that snaked downwards and into Maggie's hand.

Maggie sighed, and a veil of sadness fell over her face. 'I'm all right. I'll be fine. That is – I'll live, even if nothing else will.'

'I'm so sorry, darling. Do you want to tell me what happened?'

'What happened?' Maggie looked almost blank and then she seemed to remember why she was there. Her lips twitched. 'It's all changed so quickly, I can't quite believe it. Isn't it strange how things change so quickly? This morning I was eight weeks' pregnant and everything was fine. I was counting how many weeks it would be until the baby came, until I gave up work, until we could have a scan and see it . . . Well, we ended up having the scan rather sooner than we expected. And now there's no baby and no pregnancy and only one Fallopian tube left.'

'They took it out?' Jane echoed the anguish she heard in Maggie's voice.

'They had to. It was an ectopic pregnancy and it had all gone too far. It was too stretched, almost to bursting point. If it had got any worse, I would have died as well. So they gave me a . . . now, what did they call it? A salpingectomy, I think that's right. Where they just snip it all out and fix you up again.'

It was like Maggie to want to get the term just right, to use the right definition. She would want the doctors to know she was capable of understanding what was happening. Jane tightened her grip round her sister's hand. 'I'm so sorry. I didn't even know you were pregnant.'

'I'd only just found out myself. I was two weeks' late before I bothered to check. The whole thing seemed such a remote possibility and we hadn't planned to do it. But when it was positive . . .' Maggie blinked slowly, her mouth sinking downwards '. . . we . . . we were so happy. And I was glad that the decision had been taken out my hands, that we could just get on with it and not have to sit down and discuss money and timing and drawbacks and all that. It was a done deal. And once I saw that second blue line in the little window . . . I felt my stomach lurch and I was filled with – with real *happiness*. When you haven't felt it for a while, you forget what it's like, that giddy rush. I realized that I wanted to have a baby and I'd never known that before.' Her voice wavered at the end, wrenching at Jane's heart. 'Then, this afternoon, I started to ache on my right side and it got worse and worse, so quickly I couldn't believe it. I went to the loo and blood was seeping down my leg and it all hurt so much, I knew something awful was happening. I thought it was a miscarriage, and I could hardly bear that, but now . . .'

'Did Gregor bring you here?'

'He called for an ambulance.' Her smile twisted again. 'Very dramatic, I'm told, though I don't really remember it. Straight in here and off to have the operation. They think I'll be out tomorrow. It doesn't count as a big procedure.'

They were silent. Jane tried to sort out her thoughts: Maggie had been pregnant, going to have a baby – but the poor little thing had been doomed from the start, trying to root in before it reached the womb, developing in a tiny passageway where it could never hope to survive. And now Maggie had only one Fallopian tube.

She said hesitantly, 'Can you try again?'

'Opinion seems to be divided on the subject. They tell me different things in such gloomy voices that I'm not optimistic, to be honest. I can't . . . I can't think about it right now.' A tear rolled out from under Maggie's lashes and hung there, but she made no other sign that she was crying. 'I thought I was going to have a baby and now it's gone. It's all I can begin to understand at the moment.'

Jane sat with her for an hour or more, the sounds of the hospital muted behind the curtain. They talked quietly, Jane trying to offer what comfort she could before she had to leave. 'I'll come back tomorrow,' she promised.

'They're chucking me out then. Where're you staying?'

'At your place. Gregor and I will come first thing and take you home.'

'All right.' Maggie smiled at her weakly. 'Thank you for coming, Jane. I mean it.'

'You don't have to thank me. You know that.'

Maggie's flat was on the second floor of an early Victorian house with a white stucco front, a shabbier, grimier version of the kind of glistening family home to be found up the road in Islington. Here, in Hackney, all the houses were divided up and had the same air of neglect, with crumbling plaster, peeling paintwork and litter jammed in their front iron railings.

Jane found the area depressing but, she supposed, it must be possible to get used to it after a while. Maggie had lived there for years, after all, and seemed happy enough. But she found it chilling and alien, and hated breathing the air thick with dust and dirt. It was so concrete. She glanced down at the pavement, the kerbstones and the Tarmac; it seemed as though the earth had been coated with a thick, impenetrable armour, to keep it from interfering with the needs of city life. It felt bleak and arid: the only signs of greenery were the dry, yellowy leaves of the plane trees planted at intervals along the road, the wilting geraniums in occasional window boxes, and the strands of weed pushing up between the cracks in the paving-stones.

When she buzzed the flat, Gregor let her in. The hallway of the building was grimy and badly lit, the carpet littered with junk mail, mostly shiny squares with pictures of pizza on them, and Indian-restaurant menus. Climbing the stairs, she saw Gregor standing in the doorway, grey-faced and thinner than she remembered.

'Jane. Hello. Welcome. Thank you so much for coming.'

Inside, the flat was all the more welcoming and beautiful for the contrast with the dirt and colourlessness outside. It was bright with pictures, rugs and Indian throws; soft lamplight illuminated the full bookshelves and the large red squashy sofa was covered with embroidered cushions. Gregor brought her a glass of red wine and she sat down, exhausted. It was almost dark outside.

Gregor sat down opposite her, folding his long frame into an armchair, clasping his hands round his bony knees. He had a sallow face that sank under his high cheekbones, making shadowy hollows.

'Maggie,' he said. His accent was still strong despite the years he'd spent in London. 'How was she when you left?'

'She seemed . . . all right. But I think that this is only the beginning. She's only just starting to realize what happened to her.'

'I know.' Gregor stared unhappily at the rug and knitted his fingers together. 'This . . . we were so happy and now . . . I can't believe this has happened. It was so terrible.'

'Maggie is still alive. She's going to be all right. That is the most important thing,' Jane said softly. 'But I know your loss must be awful.'

He rocked back and forth, his face creasing in unexpected places. She thought he was going to cry but instead he burst out angrily, 'We have lost a child, yes. I am struck with grief about it! But the terrible thing is that this is not the one child – we have lost all the children we might have had. This is the real loss. All the future is gone.'

'Is that true? Can there be no more children?'

'Well, what do you think? They have removed one of her tubes, how can we have a child now?'

'But surely it's still possible with one tube. Maggie said . . .'

'They will tell her anything at the moment because they can see her heart is broken. But I have been researching since I got back from the hospital and they say that half of women who have this condition—'

'Ectopic pregnancy.'

'—yes, that is it – and have a fallopian removed, half of them are left infertile and many will have much trouble conceiving again. All of them are told to consider the prospect of IVF. We are not young, Jane. We are not a fresh couple in our twenties with years ahead of us to try. We knew that this baby was maybe our last chance and when it happened so easily it was such a relief for us, even though we'd never spoken about it, because in secret we'd both feared that we'd left it too late. Now it has all been destroyed and we have to face this fact: that really we did want

149

the baby very much. And that now there might never be a baby at all.' He passed a thin hand over his eyes, as if to hide them from her.

Jane reached out to him and clasped his other hand. 'But there *might* be. You could be the lucky ones. It might happen again just as naturally as the first time.'

'But now we know, do you see? The spell is broken. Now we know how much it matters to us and that is what I cannot bear . . . the months ahead, the waiting, the trying, perhaps the disappointments. Oh – I don't know how we can do it. And all this terrible pain. I don't know how Maggie will cope with it.'

They cooked supper together in the tiny galley kitchen and ate it on their knees in the sitting room, trying to talk of other things, but it was an awkward affair. It was brought home to Jane again how little she knew her sister's partner, even though Maggie and he had been together more than ten years. Her path had crossed his only occasionally and even then they hadn't made any real connection with each other. She found him intimidating and un-smiling, with his height, thick accent and air of academic intens-ity. Apart from general politeness, she'd said very little to him at all. Now it was only the subject of Maggie that could animate their conversation.

'It is good you are here,' Gregor said bluntly, as they finished their meal. 'Even though you are not close, Maggie needs you.'

Not close? Jane blinked at the hurt the words caused her. It was something she could admit to herself but hard to hear from Gregor, and in the way he spoke of it as an accepted fact, casual, established and understood. Why weren't they close? Who else did they have but each other? Some sets of cousins in far parts of the country they never saw. Each of them was the only link to the other's past and yet they were not close. It seemed like a terrible waste.

'Tomorrow we go and get Maggie and bring her home,' he said. 'I'm glad you are with me. I hate that place. I hate to think that she is there tonight.'

'It's not good,' Jane agreed. 'I didn't like to leave her there either. Have you spoken to her work? Told them she won't be in?'

'I cannot do that until Monday.'

'Of course not. Stupid of me to forget. But she will need some time to recuperate, to get better. She mustn't go to work.'

'It is the summer holidays. There are no students, just summer-school seminars and some other things. There will be no problem. Maggie is owed much time anyway – she works far too hard.

'Good. I can stay as long as you want.'

Gregor looked uncomfortable. 'That is kind, Jane. We don't have much room here . . .' He looked about the small sitting room. 'There is the spare bed in the study for you, but it is not a bedroom, it is an office. It isn't . . . hospitable for you.'

'Don't worry about that. I can manage perfectly well.'

He seemed to consider, then smiled at her. 'You are good. Thank you.'

In the morning, she woke confused about where she was. Sunlight was falling between the slats of Venetian blinds, painting bright gold stripes on the opposite wall. Then she remembered: she was curled up on a sofa-bed in the tiny study at Maggie's flat. The night before, she'd been so tired that sleep had come immediately, despite the thin foam mattress on the hard bedframe. She heard Gregor moving about in the kitchen, so she got up and went to the bathroom.

He had made coffee and put out toast and cereal for her when she came into the kitchen later. 'I don't know how you like to break-fast,' he said politely. 'There is also fruit or ham, if you prefer.'

'This is lovely, thank you. More than I need.'

He glanced at the clock. 'I have called the hospital. We can collect Maggie this morning so, as soon as you are finished we will go.'

They left twenty minutes later, Gregor anxious to be off. Jane felt the same – she wanted Maggie out of that place as soon as possible. They had saved her life there, of course, and that was something to be grateful for, but the hospital was not a place of recovery: it was there to deal quickly and efficiently with

151

emergencies, to patch up what was immediately wrong and shift the patient on to recuperate elsewhere – at least, that was the feeling Jane got in those heaving, noisy wards.

Maggie was waiting for them on her bed, dressed and ready to go. She was still pale and her face had swollen in the night. They saw her before she noticed them, a hunched figure on the bed, swinging one leg and gazing aimlessly out of the window. When she turned and saw them, her expression transformed and she smiled broadly. The familiar faces of loved ones must be like manna from heaven in this place, Jane thought.

They made their way out of the hospital as quickly as possible. No one wanted to linger. Maggie walked slowly, leaning heavily on Gregor's arm. 'Look at this,' she joked, as they progressed slowly along the corridors. 'Little old ladies on zimmer frames are racing by.'

'Would you like a wheelchair?' Gregor asked, concerned.

Maggie shook her head. 'No, no. I'll be fine.' And she carried on in her slow but persistent way.

It was a relief to be home. Outside the flat, the air seemed so dense that it left her breathless. The urge to get away was almost irresistible but Jane pushed it down and tried to put it out of her head. Even in the flat she felt the closeness of the walls and the lack of outside space. The windows in the sitting room opened on to a tiny balcony space, barely big enough for some flower-pots. The back windows looked down on to a dry, dusty patch of green that belonged to the basement flat, whose owners didn't seem to care much for it. Jane felt boxed in and almost panicked when she thought of how these little rooms were all there was, that there was nowhere else to go.

I'm spoiled, she thought. I've got used to Rawlston. I mustn't forget how lucky I am.

She and Gregor bustled about Maggie, making her comfortable and fussing over her, bringing her cups of tea and asking every few minutes if there was anything she wanted. Maggie let them, with an air of bemusement, as though she was indulging them, and she probably was. There was little they could really do to make her better.

When Gregor went out to do some shopping for the evening meal, Maggie said, 'When do you go back to Rawlston?'

'I can stay as long as you need me,' Jane replied firmly. Maggie was lying full length on the sofa, a light blanket draped over her. She turned her head to Jane and gazed at her solemnly. Then she said slowly, 'You don't really need to stay at all, you know. It was lovely of you to come here, and I appreciate it more than I can say. But I'm fine now. Gregor will look after me. You're needed at home.'

'Lucy and Alec are perfectly all right,' Jane protested but Maggie cut her off.

'No – really. I think we should get back to normal as soon as we can, and I won't feel normal as long as you're clucking round me like a mother hen, much as I'm grateful to you for looking after me. But, really, I just want to put it behind me.'

There was a pause. Jane looked down at the swirling pattern of the throw on the armchair where she sat: burgundy Paisley teardrops interlinked and spun away from each other in an endless dance. She traced one with a fingertip, her chest feeling odd and light. When she looked up, Maggie was still gazing at her, the light from the windows gilding the dark hair on the top of her head, her eyes direct and clear. Finally she said, 'I can quite see you want to get back to normal. I'll head back tonight.'

Maggie shifted uncomfortably. 'You don't have to go tonight. Stay for dinner with us and go tomorrow.' She smiled. 'There's no hurry – I didn't mean to imply I was chucking you out.'

'I don't want to be in the way.' Jane hated the tone of self-pity that crept into her voice, but she *did* feel rejected and unwanted. Her urge was to be with Maggie, to look after her and do whatever she could to help – but what good was that if Maggie didn't want her?

'Oh, you're *not* in the way, don't be so stupid. I just don't need to be fussed over. I want to get back to my normal life as fast as I can. Is that so strange?' She sighed irritably. 'For God's sake, stay tonight. Gregor's planning to show off to you with his goulash. It'd be a shame to miss that.'

153

'All right.' Jane smiled weakly. 'But I'll leave first thing in the morning.'

Despite her intentions, she didn't go until mid-morning on the Monday. It was hard to leave Maggie, still pale and bloated around her face and in obvious pain, but she insisted that she was fine, so Jane kissed her goodbye and made her promise to call at once if there was anything she needed.

The traffic was horrible. She'd forgotten what it was like to drive in London, in the fits and starts of the traffic signals, surging forward with the throng only to jerk to a halt a few metres later. Aggressive drivers pulled out in front of her, sometimes with a flicking light and a flash of arm through a window to warn her, at others without notice; buses lumbered unstoppably along the street, determinedly oblivious of everyone else; motorcycle couriers roared up frighteningly at her side, then dodged forward among the static cars and trucks ahead. It took an age as her car crawled timidly among all this pushiness.

The high street was a messy collection of fast-food outlets, newsagents, hairdressers with bleached glamour posters in the windows, and small supermarkets offering cheap beer, phone cards, foreign calls and, outside on the pavement, a selection of dusty vegetables on plastic carpets of fake grass. There seemed to be so many people, sauntering or rushing, pushing children in buggies or chatting on mobiles, leaning lazily outside shops, arguing on the roadside while they waited for the crossing signal. It filled her with a kind of exhilarated fear: this was the city, dense and active, and so different from what she knew. She felt like a child here, not knowing how to behave, completely without the confidence and self-possession of the people she could see, who were at home on these hard, dirty streets, oblivious to the noise and rush, following their own paths.

The road took her into the middle of London, towards the tourist postcard bits. The streets broadened, she saw parks, fountains, an elegant swirl of traffic on a huge roundabout with a monument to a Regency general in the middle. The shops became smarter, offered cashmere and suits, shoes and bags. She passed restaurants and hotels, bookshops and bars, tour buses and travel agents before she was out again on the other side, taking her place in the stream of cars heading west, through Hammersmith and on to the motorway. When the road broadened into three lanes and the office blocks, trading estates and sprawling suburbs were behind her, she felt at last as though she could breathe again.

I'll stop in Oxford, she decided. The day was gloomy after the blazing blue of the weekend, with overhanging dirty white clouds and a heavy closeness. She would go to that café on St Aldate's where they served wholesome health food, pulses and vegetables hot and stringy with melted cheese. It was comfort she needed, to fight the depression that was sinking over her.

The café was crowded, mostly with young mothers and local workers. Jane bought a plate of lentil bake at the counter and found a table where she could read a paper while she ate, but found it hard to concentrate on the news: she read the same sentence over and over again without making sense of it. Instead she heard snatches of the conversation around her. A man said jovially, 'Did I tell you I finally fired my assistant? Can't tell you how great it feels.'

A woman nearby said, 'Of course, I was shocked when I heard the news. I didn't know what to think,' and her friend replied, 'Mmmm. I've finally taken that wallpaper down in the lounge.'

When she glanced up, she saw a woman's broad back in a blue stripy top, and over her shoulder a baby stared directly at Jane, supporting itself with its chubby hands as it balanced precariously on its mother's lap. It was a boy, she guessed, and about seven months old, plump, peachy-skinned and golden haired, with wide blue eyes. She and the baby looked at each other for a few moments, the baby's fat little mouth hanging open as he concentrated on standing upright. Then, as he gazed at her from those bright saucers of blue, a huge grin spread across his face, lifting his cheeks into round cushions and exposing soft pink gums and he said, 'Daaa-aaah', starting on a high fluting note and sliding down to the last low 'aaah'.

It came upon her so suddenly that she was taken by surprise – a huge wave of sadness. A flood of tears burst into her eyes and gushed down her face, bypassing the usual tingling nose and burning lids and taking her into full, weeping grief in an instant. Almost blinded, she dropped her fork and picked up her bag. Without looking back at the cooing child, she dashed for the door, pushing through the queue, where people drew back quickly when they saw the tears on her face.

On the street, she fumbled in her bag for a tissue as she made her way round the corner of the café and into a nearby doorway off the main road. Stop it, she ordered herself. Stop it this instant. Everyone will see you! But the tears refused to obey her and she stood sobbing into her tissue, her back to the street and her shoulders shaking.

I can't stay here, she thought, after a few minutes. The tears were still coming, but with less power than before. Where can I go? I'll find Jerry, she thought. He'll be at the gallery. I'll go there.

'I'm terribly sorry,' said the assistant nervously. 'He's not here.' She was trying to ignore the signs of crying on Jane's face. 'He's out for the whole day.'

'Never mind. Thanks for your help.' Jane turned back to the quad outside, thinking, Blast that man – where is he when I need him? She stopped outside on the gravel and remembered the last time she had been here, when Tom had appeared unexpectedly and taken her to tea. Her need for companionship was overwhelming and she was seized by a desire to find him, to go for tea with him again, perhaps back to the Botanic Garden . . . but the chance of him appearing again was slim. I must find him, she decided. On her previous visit, Tom had pointed out the windows of his room as they passed through the college. 'I'm lucky,' he'd said, 'most post-grads go into the new buildings up the road. But I got a college room. Call it luck, or call it a bloody long evening buying sherry for the junior censor and dropping heavy hints.' It had been a tiny window, tucked under eaves at the top of the square of buildings.

The route back to the gates led her into the quad she remembered as his. She stood and gazed round at the identical staircase doorways and the regular pattern of windows stretching upwards. How on earth would she know which was Tom's? Walking the square of the quad, she saw nothing that jolted her memory: each doorway seemed the same as the last, except for the variations in chalk annotations around each one, proclaiming some kind of result in what she assumed were rowing competitions. I'll just have to climb each set of stairs and try my luck, she thought. The more unlikely the success of her search became, the more determined she was to undertake it. Then she noticed that, inside each doorway, a painted board listed each room, the initial and surname of the occupant. That was a start. But she didn't know Tom's surname . . .

Another circuit of the quad told her that there were five occupants of top-floor rooms whose first names began with T. I'll start at the beginning and work my way round. A small voice told her she was wasting her time – she probably wouldn't even know if she found the right room, as he was unlikely to be there anyway – but she pressed on. It took her mind off her sore eyes and heavy nose.

The first two rooms she tried were empty or, at least, no one answered the door. But, she reminded herself, it was hardly surprising. It was the summer vacation, after all. There was probably no one there. The third time, a cross-looking girl with stringy hair answered with, 'Yeah?'

'I'm looking for Tom,' ventured Jane.

'Don't know any Toms,' was the reply, along with a slammed door.

She climbed the fourth set of stairs slowly. After this, there was only one more name she could try and then she would have to face the fact that she wouldn't find him. She stopped outside the door and waited for a moment, then knocked. When it opened and revealed Tom, her Tom, she could hardly believe it and just smiled at him with relief.

'Jane?' He looked astonished to see her. 'What are you doing here?'

'Oh . . . I just . . . I was just . . . I . . .' The tide of tears was too strong for her again and, to her horror, she felt her chin wobble, her mouth distort, and the crying overwhelmed her.

He was very kind about finding a weeping woman on his doorstep and hustled her inside, sat her down and made instant coffee, while she apologized and sniffed into her tissue. She calmed down quickly and looked about while Tom went about boiling the kettle and locating the coffee jar.

Was this a typical student room? Things had changed since Theo's day: Jane remembered his room as rather grand, furnished with antiques and pretty much unchanged since the nineteenth century. This was freshly done up, with pale wood furniture and built-in shelves. On the desk, tucked under the window, was a computer and a telephone, along with a pile of books, an open notepad and a futuristic chrome lamp. Apart from two armchairs, a cupboard, a chest of drawers, a small coffee-table and a heater, there was nothing more in the room except the single bed against the far wall. It was neat and tidy and the overflowing ashtrays, dirty cups and abandoned plates that she might have expected were nowhere in sight.

'Here.' Tom handed her a cup of coffee, the undissolved granules floating on the top like little lumps of chocolate. He sat down opposite her, looking too large for the small chair. 'How are you feeling?'

'Fine. I'm fine, really. Goodness, that was embarrassing. You must forgive me.' In the first rush of tears, when he'd opened the door to her, she had gabbled out an explanation.

He looked at her sympathetically. 'So, let me see if I got this right. You saw a baby in a coffee shop?'

'Yes, such a gorgeous little thing . . .'

'And your sister has just suffered a bad pregnancy.'

'Ectopic.' Jane warmed her hands round her coffee cup and stared at the liquid inside. Despite the summer day, she felt cold. 'She might never be able to have a baby now. The thing is, I never even knew she wanted one, or that she was pregnant, or . . . It just seemed to illustrate the terrible space between us, that I know so little about her. And when I saw that child . . . well, it seemed to be so many things to me all at once. It was Maggie's baby, the one she wanted and that nearly killed her. And it was my babies – I remembered at once, and so vividly, what it had been like to love that smell, the sensation, the closeness of my baby. And now they're grown-up and Alec and I are so far apart . . .' She stopped, feeling a warning thickness in her voice. Blinking hard, she regained her composure and took a deep breath. 'Oh dear. I'm a bit emotional today.'

'It's fine,' said Tom, leaning towards her. He wasn't wearing his glasses and she could see flecks of hazel in his brown eyes.

'And it was Maggie herself, Maggie as a baby. I remembered when she used to smile at me like that, before all this distance came between us. Before I went and ruined it all somehow.'

'I don't think you should blame yourself for everything. It's rare that one person in a relationship is responsible for everything that goes wrong in it. Maggie has to carry some of the can as well.'

'Perhaps. But I'm the older one, I was the grown-up. I must have done something wrong to drive such a wedge between us. Perhaps I should have been there more for her. I was so much older, you see. By the time she was a young girl, I was already almost an adult, absorbed in my own life and my own affairs. I didn't really have much time for a little sister.'

'That's normal.'

'Is it?'

'Of course. You can't expect more of yourself than is reasonable. It's not your fault there was such a large age gap between you.'

Jane plucked at a fresh tissue, tearing the fibres apart and trying not to feel wretched. 'I can't help it. I feel responsible. And now that I want to help her, now that she needs me, she's pushing me away. It hurts me more than I can say.'

Tom gazed at her thoughtfully. 'What does *she* give you?'

Jane blinked. 'What do you mean?'

'I mean, these things are two-way streets. You need to get as well give back. And I'm guessing that you don't get much from her for yourself, do you? Does she praise you? Admire you? Love you? Call to see how you're feeling?'

Jane laughed weakly. 'Praise me? She despises my life, I know that. I'm not clever and educated like she is. She thinks I'm dreaming my life away weeding and cleaning. She thinks I've locked myself away at Rawlston like some kind of nun, in perpetual mourning for Theo.'

'And have you?' he asked gently.

'Perhaps . . . perhaps I have. But she doesn't know what it's been like.'

'So if she can't understand you and you can't understand her, what are you going to do?'

'I don't know,' Jane answered unhappily.

'You obviously care deeply about it.'

'I do — I do care. It's dreadful. We're all we've got. We're sisters! And, you see, you're wrong about the two-way street. I can't just say, if she doesn't love me back, I won't love her. It doesn't work like that. I have to love her anyway, no matter how much or how little I receive in return — it's like being a mother. It's unconditional.'

'Even now, when she's an adult?'

'Even now. And always.'

Chapter Twelve

Coming back to Rawlston from France marked a change, Bella thought. It was as though they'd all been picked up and shaken and put down, each one subtly different. She hadn't seen Sam since they'd got back; although there was no reason for it, she felt a prick of discomfort when she thought of her. The holiday had pressed them unnaturally close together, far closer than their brief friendship had readied them for, and she wasn't sure where it had left them. Now the kind of intimacy they had shared, of having seen each other in the heart of their families, pulled them apart, like a couple who had had a one-night stand on the first date and could now no longer look at each other.

Perhaps it was natural, she thought, to have a break from each other. And the hot height of summer had definitely passed: there was a chill in the air, the scent of the coming autumn. The children would soon be going back to school. She needed to get on with things.

Bella went about the routine of settling back: unpacking the suitcases, shopping for groceries to fill the bare cupboards, thinking about winter clothes and shoes for the children. In Oxford, she found them two plastic macs, one in fire-engine red for Katie and a smaller one in canary yellow for Christopher.

'You look like Christopher Robin,' she told him, as he stood proudly in the shop, the coat buttoned tightly to his chin and skimming his bony knees. 'Remember? On rainy days when he goes out to look in puddles.'

'I'm Christopher Robin,' he declared. 'That's my name from now on.'

'Come on then, Christopher Robin, let's go and get a milkshake. I'll take the macs,' she said to the shopgirl.

She took the children to the coffee shop above the market that she and Sam had visited: Katie had hot chocolate and Christopher a banana milkshake. Bella even bought them a flapjack each. She liked to treat the children sometimes – it was easier when Iain wasn't around to make everyone feel guilty for daring to buy a drink out that they could make more cheaply at home. After all, the evenings would darken soon and there would be no more playing in the garden until bedtime. They deserved something, really.

The truth was that when Bella was happy, and in a good mood, she indulged the children. It was a reflection of how she was feeling about herself when she bought them things. Why am I happy? she wondered. Nothing has changed. I'm stuck out in the country without a job and without my friends. But she *was* happy – she wanted to hug herself sometimes, and danced round the kitchen singing 'la-la-la-la' in no recognisable tune. It was ever since France, though why that should make her so jolly she couldn't think. On the whole, the holiday had been a success. Iain's worries about drugs and having to spend too much money had not been realized, and Bella was grateful for the Clarkes' sensitivity. They must have got Iain's number early on and changed their own habits to accommodate him. It was good of them.

That was what it was, of course, although she hardly admitted it even to herself. When she thought of Ben Clarke there was a small but delicious fizz in the pit of her stomach, and she thought of him often, enjoying the tiny somersaults in her belly.

Nothing, absolutely nothing, had happened. But after that night in the cellar she'd felt that things between them were subtly different. The following day, when he'd walked into the room or come near her, her skin had tingled again, and she'd sensed him looking at her when she was otherwise occupied. They avoided each other's gaze and stopped talking to each other directly – the classic signs of a nascent attraction. But she refused to make any more of it than that, putting a self-imposed ban on following through any of her thoughts. All it meant was that she dipped her toe into the delightful warm waters of her recollections, but went no further.

'Come on, kids,' she said, as they tried diligently to get the last banana foam and chocolaty cream from the bottom of their mugs. 'One more stop and then we'll go home.'

They walked down the back-streets where there were chi-chi shops with delightfully frivolous things inside them, exclusive boutiques with so few clothes that Bella wondered how they kept going. She'd seen an interesting-looking place she wanted to explore, but once they were inside she didn't see anything she liked. Instead, they went into a children's clothing shop next door, full of the kind of beautiful, well-made clothes that Bella imagined children of the rich in the 1940s had worn: smocked pinafores, flared dresses, white leather Mary Janes, knitted tank tops and cardigans. Katie was in raptures and they all spent a happy half-hour trying on the lovely things.

Katie came out of the changing room wearing a beautiful dress like something from *Ballet Shoes*: a delicate pink and white check in fine wool, with velvet collar and cuffs, and little pink buttons all the way up the front.

'Mummy, I *love* it,' Katie breathed, turning beseeching eyes on her mother. 'Can I have it, please?'

'She does look an angel,' said the shop assistant. 'Doesn't it suit her? Pink always looks good on blondes.'

'It is nice – but when would you wear it?' Bella said. There was no denying the dress was gorgeous and Katie looked beautiful in it.

'For very best,' Katie said, stroking a sleeve, 'for birthdays and Christmas and parties . . .'

'But you're growing so fast, you won't get more than a year or two at the most out of it. I don't know . . .'

'*Please*, Mummy.' Katie twirled in front of the mirror, enchanted by her reflection.

What the hell? Bella thought. Why can't we afford pretty things once in a while? What has the world come to if we can't get a bloody dress for our daughter? 'All right,' she said, to her daughter's excited shrieks, 'you can have it. But you'd better be perfect for the next six months *at least*. Understand?'

Bella was struggling to keep calm but she was losing the battle. 'I can't *believe* I'm fucking hearing this,' she said, her voice rising in volume.

Iain was white-faced, his hands shaking as they always did when he fought. 'Don't use that kind of filthy language,' he said shortly. 'You know how much I dislike it.'

'Bugger you!' she screamed. She could feel her temper taking over and the last vestiges of control disappearing. In a way, it was a relief to surrender to her anger and scream at him. As she yelled, she realized she'd wanted to for a long time. 'I'll talk the way I fucking want.'

Iain's voice rose as well. 'Control yourself, for goodness' sake.'

They were heading down the road towards a full-out fight. She knew the signs. Iain slammed the receipts on to the table in front of her. 'Just explain to me what this means.'

They faced each other over the kitchen table, Iain with his palms flat upon it, Bella gripping the top of one of the chairs.

'It means what it says,' she said defiantly.

'Are you telling me – are you actually trying to tell me – that you've just spent two hundred pounds on clothes?' His voice had dropped menacingly low.

'They're not for me, for Christ's sake, they're for the children!'

'How many clothes do children need? It seems to me that they had plenty already.'

Bella rolled her eyes in frustration. 'What you don't understand is that they are *growing* children. They grow out of clothes, they need more – so I buy them new clothes. Christopher can't wear Katie's cast-offs because he's a boy. Katie is ten years old – I can't stuff her into the dresses she was wearing last year. Things are expensive these days, it's just a reality. I didn't go mad. You know I don't spend money for the hell of it. I got good things at a good price. It was worth it.'

'Worth it? You said yourself that they're growing children. How can this much money be worth it when they'll only be able to wear these things for a few months? Did you try the second-hand shops?'

Bella laughed hollowly. 'Oh, yes, we've been to the charity shops. We always go to the charity shops. But they can't wear cast-offs all the time, you know. There's no reason why they can't have something nice and new once in a bloody while!'

'Bella,' he was starting to shout again, 'perhaps you don't understand that we have just bought a new house at huge expense, we have paid thousands in fees and stamp duty and you don't even have a damn job. How do you think we can afford these things? Whose money are you spending?'

'Well, I thought I was spending *our* money, there for the welfare of our family.' Her tone was lengthening into a sarcastic drawl. 'Oh – am I wrong? Am I mistaken? Silly me, I forgot. It's *your* money, isn't it? Although I seem to remember that when I work, that money is our money and you're perfectly happy for me to spend every last penny of it on the children.'

'You've spent fifty pounds on a dress!'

'That's how much it cost!' Bella screamed. 'You've got no idea! When did you last go into a shop and buy something? You've no idea what it costs to clothe a child. It's not as though I'm shopping on Bond Street, buying them Ralph Lauren outfits, for Christ's sake.'

'She doesn't need it,' Iain spat.

'According to you, she doesn't need anything! We can feed them on bread and cheese and make them toys out of garden waste and clothe them in hand-me-downs. Iain, you're living in a dream world. This isn't the bloody *Good Life* – they're normal children and once in a while they ought to know what it's like to live in the real world. You won't do them any favours by turning them into freaks!'

The kitchen door opened and Katie put her head round it. Her face was white and her grey eyes huge. 'Mummy and Daddy, please don't fight,' she quavered. 'I don't mind if we take the dress back. I can wear my old one—'

'Katie, go away,' snapped Bella. She took a breath and said in a calmer voice, 'We're not fighting, darling, we're talking.' She remembered Katie twirling delightedly in the dress and she wasn't going to let the child sacrifice it now. It would undermine everything. Of course, she knew that climbing down and suggesting she take the dress back was the way to placate Iain, give him room to forgive her and allow the dress to stay, but she couldn't bring herself to do it. Why should she have to engage in these ridiculous power struggles for something so simple as a party dress? Why *couldn't* they have it? They weren't on the breadline, whatever Iain might say.

Katie lingered in the doorway and Bella turned to her. 'You heard me – *go away*.' Katie's face creased, her eyes welled and she slid away from the door.

'What kind of a mother are you?' Iain hissed, his grey eyes icy.

'What kind of husband are you?' she demanded. 'I won't tolerate you searching my things. That's how you found the receipt, isn't it – by looking in my bag?'

Iain chuckled flatly to himself, as though Bella's line of attack was precisely the kind of stupidity he expected from her. 'If you didn't have nasty, expensive little secrets, I wouldn't need to search.'

She felt her head fill with pounding blood, her eyes hot and stinging. She couldn't bear the feeling of powerlessness – all she had was what she could scream at him. 'Well, *fuck you*!' She strode to the back door, opened it and went out, slamming it behind her.

Outside she gasped for breath, fighting with herself for control. Tears of anger poured down her cheeks. It was absolutely unbearable – did anyone else have to live with that kind of behaviour? She knew his attitude to money was all part of his need to control her, and that was part of some kind of bigger fear of the world – but she couldn't be bothered with it any more. She'd spent years trying to work him out, trying to make him see that he didn't have to be frightened of her, that she loved him – but nothing she did changed him even a tiny amount. She couldn't understand it. They were supposed to be in partnership, to trust each other. Did he see nothing shameful in searching her bag, or hiding her

chequebook? Didn't he ever question his own behaviour? Did
he think this made her fonder of him, more likely to fall into line?
How could he be so . . . destructive and not see it? The ridiculous
thing was that he forced her into doing the things he feared:
hiding things, paying for them in cash so that he couldn't trace it
– even something so harmless as taking the children to a café –
lying to him. What kind of a marriage was that?

She set off up the lane, not seeing anything but the muddy,
stone-encrusted surface beneath her feet. Anger and indignation
bubbled inside her. She knew she didn't deserve to be treated like
this – she was an adult who should be respected, not a naughty
child to be told off. She resented the way he would never let her
win an argument, never even concede a point to her. Instead his
superior attitude and cold disdain drove her to fury and frustration and she always lost because she couldn't stay calm in the face
of his patronizing, unfair attitude to her. Just thinking about it
made her hands tremble. This wasn't what she had signed up for
fourteen years ago – she hadn't relinquished the ability to make
her own choices and do what she thought was right. She hadn't
given away all power over herself. But Iain behaved as though she
had. It worried her more and more that he appeared to think that
she was his possession, that their marriage was indissoluble, no
matter what he might do or how she might feel.

She could hardly bring herself to think about it most of the
time, the fact that she felt so wrong. It had crept up gradually. At
first they'd felt fused, a team, united against the world, defined by
each other and by being together. Then, slowly, Bella had felt
herself pull away, wanting to distance herself from things about
him, trying to reclaim her own identity. She'd married him
because she loved him. But they were different people now: was
it right that they should be together?

She rounded the curve in the lane that led up to Rawlston
House. As usual, there was an air of lazy quiet around it. Walking
towards it was like walking towards a different world – it was
hard to imagine stress and strife within the rhododendron bound-
aries and the honey-stone walls. She wondered if she should go
and see Sam, then decided against it: she was pent-up and would

want to talk about the row, and she didn't want Sam to hear the things she would no doubt say. Besides, would Sam be that interested? She always seemed to have a look of distraction when Bella talked about her problems, as though she couldn't wait to get the conversation back to herself. She would wait until Bella drew breath and then break in quickly with 'Yeah, that's just like when I . . .' and the focus would be pulled back to her.

Bella stopped on the grassy verge and wondered what to do. She could make out the house between the thick glossy leaves of the hedge. How much did it cost? she wondered. She knew that she and Iain could never dream of living in such a place. She'd been rather proud of that when she was young, as though by choosing a husband who wasn't rich or determined to be so she'd made a statement about herself: *I don't care about money – my mind is on higher things.* But she hadn't understood then how much difference it made, how much conflict arose from lack of money – though, of course, they weren't poor, she reminded herself hastily, not in any real sense. Certainly not like a huge number of people. The problem was that they had middle-class aspirations and were without the income to indulge them. When she saw Nicky getting her hair done every few weeks, going on shopping trips to cheer herself up and thinking nothing of eating out three times a week, she felt a sense of thwarted entitlement, as though she was supposed to have those things too but something, somewhere had unaccountably gone wrong.

What would it be like to be married to a rich man? What was it like to be Sam, with nothing to do but amuse herself with her credit card? She felt a sneaking shame in thinking it – she'd always been proud of being able to provide for herself, to keep up her end of the bargain by working and contributing to the family. It was naughty – no, *wrong* – to start imagining being kept by someone else, being given money, having no responsibility, being idle . . . Her imagination roamed over the deliciously enticing fantasy. Shopping, holidays abroad, Paris, a car, pampering. Someone to clean and cook. Fine food, vintage wine. No skimping or getting by.

She shook her head. This wouldn't do. It wasn't a reality for her, even if it was for some privileged others. She'd chosen a marriage of equality, where both partners paid their way. She could never be kept . . . except, when she thought about it, her marriage wasn't equal, was it? She wasn't accorded her rights.

'Bella!'

The shout made her jump. She looked round and saw Ben coming down the drive towards her, his mobile in his hand, smiling.

'Hello,' she said, feeling suddenly on edge. 'How are you?'

'Fine. You?'

'Yes – fine. I didn't think anyone was at home.'

'Oh. Casing the joint, were you?'

'No . . . no.' She laughed, realizing she must look rather odd, standing staring at the house. 'Just out walking.'

He reached her and stopped a pace away. 'Haven't seen you since France. Everything all right?'

'Yes.'

He stared at her. 'Have you been crying?'

Her hand went involuntarily to her cheek. She'd forgotten about the argument and the tears. Then she felt embarrassed: crying always left her with puffy, swollen, lavender-lidded eyes and a shiny nose. She didn't answer.

'Don't say if you'd rather not.' He looked down at the phone in his hand. 'I was talking to work. I always wander out here when I'm on the phone – the reception's better. I start off in the office, and when I've finished, I look up and find myself outside in the garden, chatting to some rosebush or on the edge of the Jacuzzi. Funny, really.' He weighed the phone in his hand, and gazed at the ground. Then he glanced up, his eyes serious. 'Sam's not in, I'm afraid, but why don't you come in for a drink? You don't have to talk about anything private, but I've got a very nice Italian prosecco chilling that I've been meaning to pop. Would you like some?'

Bella thought, Why not? She imagined Iain at home and knew she didn't want to return there yet. 'Thanks. That'd be nice.'

They walked together down the driveway and into the house. Ben showed her into the sitting room, which was as immaculate as she remembered – pale, delicate and clean – while he collected the wine from the kitchen. She sat down and looked about her. Had she meant this to happen? Had she come walking up the lane from Iain, looking for Ben? It hadn't been a conscious thought but here she was. She remembered the cellar in France and the unbearable tingling of her nerves that she had felt sitting next to him. She had barely dared admit to herself that she found Ben attractive – he was so different from her normal type for one thing, the slim boyish model that Iain embodied, with his size and solidity, those dark good looks. She ran a hand through her hair and over her face.

Ben returned with the bottle and they settled down with large glasses of the fizzing wine.

'This is very civilized – thank you,' Bella said.

'Nice to be out of the house, is it?'

His voice, she noticed, was deep with a warm buzz at the base of it. His accent was neutral, giving away nothing about where he came from. She leant back in the soft leather armchair. 'You've probably guessed that Iain and I have had a fight. It doesn't happen all that often, but when it does it isn't pretty.'

Ben looked into his drink. 'I don't want to pry.'

'I know. That's why I don't mind telling you. Sometimes it's easier to tell a man. You don't jump to all the conclusions that women do. You're not as judgemental. I think it's probably because you're not as interested. Women are always desperate to find out every detail of each other's lives so that they can compare it to their own and see how they're doing – am I happier than she is? Cleverer, prettier? Is my husband more caring? We're always wanting to solve everything for each other. It can be a bit tiring, really.'

'Men don't think about other people's relationships, they just accept them. They hardly think about their own, to be honest, once everything's done and dusted.'

'Really? Well, then, Iain must be the exception. He doesn't seem to think about anything else.'

'I didn't notice it when we were on holiday. Except in as much as you seem like a close family, a family that likes to do things together.'

Bella laughed. 'You've got that much right. Iain hates being on his own. He's no good at it at all. He wants us all to be together all the time. That's what I mean, I suppose. I just wonder if it's normal for a man to be so wrapped up in his family, to find it so . . . what's the word? *Protecting*. It's like we're his safety blanket. That's partly why I'm dreading when the children get older. I think we're going to have big problems with them finding their independence. He's all or nothing. There's no half-way house with Iain – you're either with him or against him.'

'It sounds as though you've analysed it pretty thoroughly,' Ben said, with a crooked smile. 'You seem to know what the problem is.'

'I've had a lot more time to think about it lately – coming out here to the country. You know, I didn't really want to come at all. My friends are all in London, my career – such as it is, career's just a word for job these days – was in London. I've felt so uprooted and isolated here. Lonely, really. I hadn't noticed how far apart Iain and I have grown over the years and now here I am, looking after the family in a house in the middle of nowhere and the spotlight's been thrown hot and strong on my marriage. It's supposed to be your base, isn't it? The place you start out from. But I'm beginning to feel as though it's a prison . . .' She shook her head. 'I don't know why I'm telling you this. I shouldn't.'

Ben shrugged. 'Tell away. I'm not going to pass it on, if that's what you're worried about.'

'I've talked to Sam about it anyway – well, not all of it. Hardly any, actually.'

Ben smiled. 'I shan't breathe a word.'

'I'm sorry to offload it all on to you.'

'Don't be.'

They sat in silence for a moment and then Ben said, 'Have you thought any more about your work – starting a company?'

Bella looked up eagerly. 'Yes, I have, and I think what you suggested is a really good idea. I'm going to follow it up and see what I can do.'

'I said it before and I meant it – if I can be of any help, I'd be delighted.'

'Would you mind? I hate to trouble you – you've already been so kind.'

'Don't be silly. I've offered.'

There was another heavy pause. What's he thinking? Bella thought. Ben said suddenly, 'I know what you mean about being lonely in marriage.'

'Do you?' she said slowly, thinking, *I knew it. I knew Sam wasn't enough for him. It's obvious.*

'Yes. My first marriage ended because of it. We were both working hard, I was setting up my business, and it got to the point where we were barely exchanging five sentences at the end of the day. All Aileen could talk about was Emma. We stopped being interested in each other. We were sharing a bed but we'd become strangers. Then I met Sam and she brought the sparkle back into my life. I knew I couldn't spend the rest of my life without it, living this dreary half-existence with someone who appeared able to tolerate me when she wasn't actively disliking me. It's sad – and it's not meant to happen. No one gets married thinking, Well, this should last about eight years – but sometimes it does and the best thing is to admit it, and get out. Aileen's married again, living in the States, and about a million times happier than she was before, even if she'd die before she confessed it.'

Bella scuffed her shoe over the rug, watching the white fringe shift over the floorboards. 'What about the children?' she asked at last. 'That's the problem, isn't it?' She remembered the looks of hatred she'd seen Emma shoot at Sam in France, the way the girl would avert her gaze whenever her stepmother entered a room, and leave as soon as she could. Anyone could feel the power of Emma's loathing for Sam, even if Sam put up a good show of pretending not to notice. All that hate was obviously the result of something more than just poor Sam, however annoying she might be. It was clear that Emma's youth had been blotted and stained by the pain of her parents' divorce, and however happy her mother and father might now be, her unhappiness and its fallout would be with her for years.

Ben nodded. 'That is the problem. But you can't stay together for their sakes — it just doesn't work. They know when something's rotten. The best thing you can do is end it gracefully. It's not the divorce that's the issue, it's the way it's done. You have to manage it in such a way that the children know they're cared for.'

'Is that what happened with you and Aileen?' asked Bella, disingenuously. She knew very well that it hadn't been at all graceful, if Sam's stories were anything to go by.

Ben looked uncomfortable. 'I tried my best, but it wasn't easy. Children are very sensitive. Emma never seemed to take to Sam — I don't think she gave her a chance. There's still time, though.' He stared into his wine again, thoughtful, and it was as though a shutter came down, closing the subject away. 'Come on, let's drink this up and go into the office. We'll do some research on your new company.'

They sat side by side at Ben's enormous desk, Ben surfing the net, Bella making notes as they talked and read. The bottle of prosecco was soon empty so Ben fetched another from the kitchen and they made inroads into that, as the office grew murky in the evening light, the screen glowing in the gloom. Ben talked enormous sense — about set-up costs, competition, marketing and business plans. He made it sound do-able, achievable, as though it were within her grasp to set up a business and turn it into a profitable organization.

'You might want to think about staff at some point, but start simple. As long as you don't have to pay someone else, don't. It's worth doing it yourself.' He clicked off another web page. 'And don't forget to steal as many good ideas as you can. That's the real key.'

She smiled. 'I won't. I'm taking plenty of yours, aren't I?'

'Those aren't stolen. They're given,' he said gently, and turned to look at her. 'It's always a pleasure to be a help to a beautiful woman.'

He said it smoothly and without a leer but . . . Is he flirting? she wondered. Or mocking me? How can he think I'm beautiful when there's Sam, so slim and gorgeous? But she knew he wasn't mocking her; the air suddenly prickled with tension and she felt a tingle climb her arm where it was almost touching him. Why has this happened? she thought, and then saw he was staring directly at her mouth, as he had done in France.

'That's very sweet of you,' she said, compelled to say something. 'I mean it, you've really boosted my confidence.' He didn't take his steady blue gaze off her lips. It was disturbing: harmless and yet loaded at the same time. It was also, she realized, very sexy – far more sexy than having her breasts or legs assessed. Does he know he's doing it? she asked herself – but it was almost more powerful if he didn't. She smiled. His eyes flicked back to hers and he smiled back.

'You shouldn't need your confidence boosted,' he said, in a low voice. 'You've got so much going for you.'

They stared at each other for a long moment, and then he leant over very fast and kissed her, strongly, on the mouth. He pulled away before she could respond and said, 'I'm sorry. I don't know what I'm doing.'

She was breathless, her heart racing. 'It's okay,' she said, in a whisper. 'I don't mind.' It was true – the only thing she did mind was that he might not kiss her again and she suddenly, desperately, wanted him to, wanted to feel his lips again and, this time, to open her mouth to him.

He glanced downwards and breathed heavily. 'We can't,' he said shortly. 'Not because I don't want to. I do, and I have since France, since you made me sit next to you in that bloody hole in the ground. But if I kiss you again, I won't be able to stop myself and that's not right – it's not the right place or time and you're upset with your husband and it's all wrong.'

They sat in silence, Bella agonized by the awakened desire buzzing through her, fresh and strong.

'Perhaps . . . perhaps I'd better go,' she ventured.

He nodded. 'Sam'll be back soon. It'd be best.'

'Okay.' She got up. 'Thanks for the wine. I'll let myself out.'

She felt as though she were floating as she went back down the lane in the darkness. A vigorous breeze was blowing but she felt nothing at all because she was marvelling at what had happened.

He kissed me, she thought, as enraptured as a teenager. She didn't want to think of anything but the dizzy pleasure of it and how delicious it had made her feel.

She reached the lodge sooner than she wanted, and let herself into the kitchen. It was in darkness, even though it was only about nine-thirty. She remembered that hours ago, it felt like days, she and Iain had had a fight in here. He had probably sent the children up early, then gone to bed himself in a post-fight sulk. No doubt he would have his back firmly turned towards her side of the bed, not that she minded about that . . . then, suddenly, she saw him emerge from the shadows.

'Where have you been?' he asked, his voice trembling. His eyes glinted in the residual light and she saw that he was furious. She felt a flash of fear, a sort of animal panic that told her she was in danger.

'I was up at the big house—'

'Who with? *Sam*?' He said it with a sneer.

'No, she wasn't there,' Bella said, and heard her mistake as the words left her mouth.

Iain's face contorted. 'With him?' he spat. 'With Clarke?'

'Yes, Ben was there. He was very friendly.' She tried to sound calm, to defuse his anger. She could tell he'd been working himself up for hours, turning his jealousy and possessiveness into a ripe, rolling fury. 'We had a drink and talked about me finding a job. He had lots of ideas I want to tell you about.' Her knees were weak but her entire effort was in trying to sound casual, in trying to block out the picture of Ben kissing her. She had to believe in her own innocence if she was to convince Iain – and she *was* innocent. What had they done? A brief kiss on the lips? It was nothing!

'Was that all? Chat?' he asked.

What does he know? she thought, panicked. Did he notice something in France? Has he guessed? 'Yes, of course that was all. What on earth did you think?'

'Did you *fuck* him?' The obscenity was unexpectedly vicious.

Bella gasped, shocked, almost laughed, then stuttered, 'What?' Then her instinct for self-preservation kicked in and she said, 'Of course I didn't! Don't be so stupid – of course not! There was no – no *question* of that. You're being ridiculous. It was just a friendly drink.'

'You went there after our row and you thought you would teach me a lesson by fucking him. Didn't you?' His voice was low and acid with rage.

'No, I . . . of course not! I . . . we just had some wine . . . talked . . .'

'Don't treat me like an idiot.'

'I'm not, honestly, nothing happened—'

He suddenly rushed at her and began clawing at the button of her jeans, wrenching away at it with intense single-mindedness.

'Iain, what—what are you doing? Stop it, get off me, I didn't sleep with Ben, for God's sake. Iain, stop it!' She tried to push him off but she was ineffectual, her hands beating lightly at his iron grip. He pulled the button apart, forced down the zip, then dropped to his knees, pulling her jeans downwards with him. She staggered as her legs became trapped by the trousers bunching round them. What's he doing? she thought, confused. Does he want sex? And then she realized with horror what he was doing as he pushed his face towards her crotch, forcing his nose into the white triangle of her knickers. My God! He's *smelling* me! She choked as she tried to speak. 'Iain, my God – stop it. I told you—'

He rose slowly from his knees and stared at her. She couldn't read his expression.

'All right.' The fury had vanished and was replaced by blankness. 'Then come to bed.' He turned and walked out of the kitchen. Bella was overtaken by a fit of trembling as she fumbled to pull up her jeans with shaking hands, listening to Iain going slowly up the stairs to their bedroom.

Chapter Thirteen

Sam loved the feel of the car under her feet: the pedal moved with imperceptible smoothness, the engine obediently increased its hum and the needle on the speedometer lifted upwards. She loved speeding past men in their cars on the motorway, tossing her hair and throwing them a provocative look as they gazed at her, not knowing which they wanted more: the sleek Mercedes or the equally sleek woman inside it.

It had been a girls' day with Becky. It was supposed to be 'the girls', the gang Sam counted herself a member of, but in the event it was only her and Becky, having a sedate game of tennis on the indoor court at Becky's health club, then a light lunch in the restaurant. Sam didn't mind much that the others hadn't turned up. If she was honest, it was only Becky she really got on with. The other girls were threatened by her – it was the obvious explanation for the way they kept their distance and didn't seem to want to get cosy with her.

She didn't mind: girlfriends were overrated. They almost always had agendas to follow, Sam thought. They were judgemental and critical, and even if they didn't say anything, you could see it in their eyes: envy. Envy because Sam was thin and beautiful and married to a rich man who gave her anything she wanted. Envy because she didn't have a lot of brats pulling her down and taking up her every waking minute and because men couldn't help looking at her wherever she went. Of course she was a threat to other women: she understood that and understood why. It meant that she had to be careful whom she trusted, whom she allowed into her world. Becky was fine – Sam had never seen a flicker of jealousy in Becky. Admiration, yes, and a sense of comradeship, because they'd both gone out and used their skill and determination and nature's gifts to get what they wanted. It was true, Sam allowed, that Becky wasn't the sharpest knife in the drawer, but she had a heart of gold, and that was what counted.

Bella . . . Now, she was different but Sam couldn't quite work out why. She'd thought, when the Balfours first arrived, that Bella would be a good foil for her. The other woman had obviously been a bit starry-eyed round the Clarkes, and who wouldn't be? It was natural to look at their home, their life, and be a bit over-whelmed by it, if you didn't have it yourself and never would. She thought Bella would be just the kind of friend she wanted: nowhere near as glamorous as herself, admiring, unquestioning – a kind of disciple. That was why she'd felt able to relax with her, share a bit, open up more than she was able to with the Chelten-ham girls. And Bella had a touch of London about her, something a bit different and sophisticated that made her a worthy friend.

She had to admit it – taking the Balfours to France had been a mistake. It hadn't worked the way she'd expected. Somehow the balance of power had imperceptibly changed and Bella Balfour had become an unexpected challenge. But how? Sam stopped singing and considered. Nothing had happened – nothing she could put her finger on, anyway. But the tightness of the little family – perhaps it was the charm of those kids, who had certainly won everyone over – had thrown something about the Clarkes into contrast. It wouldn't have been so bad if Emma hadn't been there. Sam couldn't help feeling that Bella and Iain were watching and judging – as if they had any idea of how sodding difficult it was to deal with that awful girl all the time – and she'd felt as though somehow she'd been found wanting, even though she knew she'd done nothing wrong.

Then there was Bella herself. From the start, Sam had assessed her carefully, everything about her. She'd thought she was ordin-ary, a typical middle-class English woman who might have read the classics but who didn't have the first idea how to look after herself. She was carrying at least a stone too much weight, she didn't take care of her skin and her hair cried out for a decent cut and style. There was no way she could compete with Sam: for God's sake, her nose was too big, her mouth too wide and her eyes too close together. And yet . . .

She wrinkled her nose, thinking hard, trying to analyse what was disturbing her. In France, she had looked at Bella differently. She'd been surprised by the way Bella made the others laugh, by the odd and interesting things she said. Sam didn't understand that at all, and she couldn't do it. While that didn't bother her much, what did bother her was how the things Bella said made her seem *physically* more attractive. How did that happen? All right, she wasn't a monster or anything – certainly nothing like frumpy old Aileen – but she was nothing special either. Then, at the dinner table, or round the barbecue, Bella would have a sort of vibration about her, a kind of sparkle in her eyes that made her more interesting to look at.

That was annoying and it was worrying because it wasn't the kind of thing Sam knew how to replicate. She could copy makeup techniques, change her hair colour, use a different perfume. But she didn't know how to turn that – that *thing* on that Bella seemed to have, and it made her angry and suspicious.

Sam saw the turn-off for the village approaching in the murky gloom of the approaching night, and puffed air through her teeth to vent her irritation. She was overreacting. It was all in her mind. Come on, now, she chided herself. Do you seriously imagine Bella's a threat to you? Don't be stupid – *you're* the threat to her! Now just keep your distance for a bit, remind her who's boss, and it'll all be fine.

The lights of Rawlston House glowed yellow and homely as Sam pulled up and parked in the driveway. She'd liked the house when they'd viewed it, and she liked it better now that they'd had all the work done to it, but she didn't love it. It wasn't what she would have chosen – particularly as it was only half a house. Ben had been saying lately that since the house was finished they ought to have people over, their old friends from Cheltenham, for dinner parties and so on, but Sam wasn't keen on that idea. There was something about the place she felt vaguely ashamed of.

She breezed into the hall, dropping her gym kit by the table so that Trudy would take it to the laundry the next morning, and followed the lights into the sitting room.

'Hello, honey!' she called, as she went in, but Ben wasn't there. Instead there was an empty wine bottle and some sticky rings on the glass table that showed where wine glasses had stood. 'Ben?'

She went to his study and opened the door, but the room was empty. There were two wine glasses on the desk, both with dregs in them.

She found him in the kitchen, bent over the stove, where a casserole was boiling away with savoury steam coming off it. 'Hiya, darling,' she said, going over to him.

Ben jumped and turned round quickly, then smiled to see her and kissed her warmly. 'Hi, sweetie, how was your day out? Did you have a good time with Becky?'

'Yeah, it was great, thanks.' Sam leant back against the granite worktop, propping herself on her thin elbows. 'What've you been up to?'

'Oh, not much. Some work. I spent a long time in the office.'

'What're you making?'

'Chicken stock,' he said. 'We're running low so I got those carcasses out of the deep freeze and thought I'd boil them.'

She looked at him thoughtfully. Ben turned to cooking when he was ill at ease or out of sorts, and he made vats of chicken stock whenever there was a cold snap or someone came down with flu, or when he craved home comfort. 'So who was your visitor?'

Ben turned back to his casserole and stirred it. 'Visitor? This needs another hour or two, I think . . .'

'Yes, someone's been round. Who?'

'Oh – yes, Bella popped round. You know I told you she was interested in starting her own business? She came up for a bit of advice.'

She watched his broad back as he moved about the stove, milling some pepper into the stock and tidying up some vegetable cuttings. 'Was she well?'

'Fine. She didn't stay long. She was sorry to find you weren't here, of course.'

'Of course,' said Sam, still watching his back intently. 'Of course she was.' Her good mood evaporated instantly. She didn't like Bella coming round here when she wasn't there: it set alarm bells ringing and gave her a sensation of alertness, like an animal wary of predators.

'There's something else,' Ben said. 'I've had a call from Aileen – she's not going to be able to have Emma over after all. Something's come up – some conference that her husband has to go on somewhere glamorous, and she's going as well because it's a chance of a lifetime et cetera. She'll take Emma at Christmas instead.'

'You mean Emma's staying here all summer?'

'Until she goes to Edinburgh, unless she comes up with an alternative.'

Sam's good humour had long vanished but now she felt a flash of anger and her mood turned evil. Everything was conspiring against her. First Bella had become a thorn in her side and was sneaking round here when she, Sam, was out; now the thing she'd been looking forward to for weeks – Emma's departure for America – had been ripped away, just like that. *Why* was everything going so wrong? She felt like hitting someone.

'Are you all right?' Ben asked, turning to look at her at last. 'You've gone quiet.'

'Fine,' she snapped. 'Just bloody fine. I'm going upstairs.'

Dinner was even more miserable than usual. The last few nights Sam had been quite happy, secure in the knowledge that Emma was going to be leaving at the end of the week. Now the sight of the girl, so skinny and pallid and boring, picking at her food at the other end of the table, infuriated her, irritation bubbling up inside her and threatening to burst free.

'Bad news about America, Emma,' she said, unable to bear the silence that hung over the three of them.

Emma flicked a cool gaze at her, then away. 'Yeah. But Mum didn't really have much of a choice.'

'Didn't she? Not much of a choice between seeing her only daughter, and going on holiday? Hmm, no, I can see that's a toughie. Well, the comfort is you'll see her at Christmas and that's only . . . well, four months? Or is it five?'

Emma stared at her plate and bit her lip. Then she muttered, 'It's work.'

'Not *her* work, though, is it? Isn't it that funny boyfriend of hers? Some kind of dental conference, isn't it? Sounds like a barrel of laughs. Don't like to say it, Emma, but if your mum prefers a hundred dentists talking about fillings or false teeth or whatever they talk about to you, you'd better do some work on your conversational skills before you get to Edinburgh.'

'Sam,' Ben said warningly.

'I'm just saying,' Sam protested, as if affronted. 'Just saying, that's all. You want to make friends in a place like university or you're going to be a bit miserable, aren't you?'

'It's not Emma's fault that her mother can't take her.'

'I don't want to stay here!' Emma burst out furiously. Her cheeks were tinged with pink where they were usually pale and sallow. 'The last thing I want is to be here with you. I'm going to find somewhere else to go.'

'Where would that be?' Sam asked sweetly. 'Off to stay with one of your many friends? You must have friends from that school of yours, surely, even if we've never seen any of them here. Or perhaps you'll go and stay with your boyfriend – oh, I'm sorry. Touchy subject. You don't have a boyfriend.'

Ben sighed heavily and muttered, 'Sam, please . . .' under his breath.

'I'm sure that'll change when you get to university,' she continued. It was helping her feel better to talk like this, like scratching an itch. All the crossness and thwarting she'd felt that afternoon was coming out, and she was enjoying the release. 'There'll be lots of blokes up there and it's so bloody cold in Scotland they won't be picky. Anything to warm them up at night.'

'Dad!' Emma's face was growing scarlet. 'Dad, stop her.'

'Sam,' said Ben again, with a note of helplessness in his voice.

'And when they do ask to shack up with you,' Sam went on, unable to stop, 'don't worry about it. You'll get the hang of it quick enough even if you are a beginner – and don't forget you can always ring home. Your dad and me will always be happy to talk about sex with you and tell you how it should be done.' She smirked. 'After all, we're experts.'

Emma leapt to her feet. 'Shut up, you vile bitch!' she screamed. 'You love it, don't you? You love making me feel awful. What have I ever, ever done to you? Why do you hate me so much? It was my family you destroyed, it was my mum you sent to America and my dad you stole from me. You got everything and left me with nothing. Haven't you had enough? Don't you think I feel bad enough that I won't be seeing my mum this summer without you humiliating me? No – no, you just want to poison *everything*, don't you? God – I hate you!' Her voice rose as she shouted until she ended on a scream, and ran from the room.

There was a nasty silence. Sam looked at Ben with an injured air. 'What was all that about?' she said innocently. 'I was just having a joke with her.'

Ben's eyes were cold and steely, the blue turned to ice. 'That was despicable.'

'Oh, take her side. You don't have to see how she treats me when you're not around.'

'She's eighteen!' Ben shouted. The unexpected roar in his voice made her jump. 'Have some fucking charity!' She said nothing. He looked down at his plate. 'I don't know what's wrong with you lately.'

'There's nothing wrong with me. It would just help if you took my side once in a while, that's all.'

'Sam—'

Suddenly she was filled with fury. She pushed away her untouched plate and got up. 'Oh, fuck off. I've had enough.' She stalked out of the room, leaving Ben alone.

It's a long time since I've prepared a dinner as carefully as this one, Jane thought. She couldn't explain why she was taking so much trouble. When Jerry came over, she would bung any old thing in the oven and know he'd be perfectly happy with it. Why she should take more trouble over Tom she had no idea.

She'd made a chicken-liver pâté to start with, and was surprised to find herself carefully clarifying the butter for the top, and decorating it with sage leaves. It was an absurd effort to make but something in her wanted Tom to be impressed. She had the feeling that he would enjoy it, that he would certainly notice it, and that it would appeal to him. The pleasure he took in the little details of life was one of the things she liked about him. When she'd left his college room the other day, insisting she wouldn't take up more of his study time, even though he protested that he had hours to spare, she'd invited him on impulse to come over for dinner and he'd accepted at once with evident pleasure.

It's just politeness, she told herself firmly. A thank-you for his chivalry when he found me behaving like a puddle outside his room. When her thoughts strayed back to the moment in the corridor as they'd stood in front of her picture, she reined them in at once. That was nothing. He was a kind young man, far from home, alone. If she invited him over for dinner, it was out of friendship, nothing more, and it was ridiculous even to consider anything else.

She glanced up at the clock for the twentieth time and saw that there was still half an hour before Tom was due. He was taking a train and then a taxi, so she could pretty much predict when he would arrive. Lucy was working and Alec, in a bit of unexpected serendipity, had decided to meet friends in Oxford that evening. She hadn't allowed herself to pick a night when the children were out, and that they were going to absent themselves was entirely unforeseen. Her conscience was clear.

The phone broke into her thoughts with its shrill ring. Wiping her hands on her apron, she answered it. It was Gregor.

'Is everything all right? Is it Maggie?' She was instantly panicked, planning at once to cancel dinner, to rush to London if she was needed.

'Don't worry, Jane,' Gregor said. He was obviously on a mobile outside and traffic sounded loudly behind him. 'It is not an emergency. Maggie is all right. But I wanted to talk to you because she is not herself and I must go away and I am worried about leaving her.'

'Your trip to Hungary.' Jane remembered Maggie speaking of it before.

'Yes. I must go and she is not well enough to come too. Also, she is still having tests at the clinic to make sure she is recovering appropriately. But, Jane, she is very low. She is not happy. I am worried. What can we do?'

Jane took a deep breath. As soon as he spoke, the thoughts that had been dimly in her mind ever since she'd returned from London crystallized. She said firmly, 'She must come here.'

'To stay with you? I don't know if she would agree . . .'

'We must make her agree. The dusty, dirty city is no place for her. It's no wonder she's depressed. Gregor, it's the obvious thing. You said yourself she was owed time off. This is the place for her.'

Traffic horns hooted in the background and a siren wailed past as Gregor considered what she had said. 'You are right,' he said at last. 'It is the obvious thing. Now I must convince her – and you know that will not be easy.'

'You can do it.' A weight lifted from her and she smiled down the phone. 'It is the right thing. We both know that.'

Tom was prompt but not too prompt, which meant that when he rang the front-door bell, she was ready. She had to admit, even to herself, that she looked good: her hair was shiny, its streak of white curling into the dark of the rest. The trusty old makeup had been dusted off, and now a swoop of mascara had widened her green eyes while a shimmer of peach above them had brought out their sparkle. The powder she'd applied had given her cheeks a soft mattness and her lips, which she considered too thin, were plumper with a slick of Mary Shelley.

'You look beautiful,' Tom said earnestly, when she opened the front door to him. He handed her a bouquet of velvety red roses.

'Thank you! These are lovely. My goodness . . .' She had been about to say, 'It's so long since anyone gave me flowers,' but stopped herself. That sounded too much as though this was a date, and it most certainly wasn't that.

He complimented her dress with easy charm, and his relaxed air put her at ease. He must have been perfectly aware of the casual

185

nature of the evening, and had come looking smart but informal in dark trousers and a shirt that showed the broad squareness of his shoulders. They walked past the chilly drawing room to the more comfortable sitting room at the far end of the passage; Jane went to put the flowers in water while he moved about the room, inspecting the bookcases and the family photographs. She returned with a bottle of champagne in a bucket.

'What a treat,' Tom said, smiling. 'Is this in my honour?'

'A guest at my garden party gave it to me. It will only gather dust if we don't drink it, or my greedy children will gulp it down. So I thought, why not have it tonight?'

Tom did the honours and opened it and made her clink glasses with him.

She looked at the golden bubbling liquid and said, 'I suppose it's also a celebration in way. My sister – you remember . . .'

'Of course. I hope she's feeling better.'

'She's not feeling that much better, but the good thing is, she's going to come here to recuperate. I feel as though it's a chance for us. You know, a door opening.'

'Jane, that's wonderful.' He smiled at her with real pleasure. 'I could see how much it meant to you.'

They drank the champagne – 'Bollinger,' said Tom with satisfaction. 'Very nice' – and then went into the kitchen for dinner. Jane had considered eating in the dining room but the idea of the two of them in that enormous room, watched through the gloom by the oil portraits of dour old men, had seemed ludicrous. Tom had clearly liked the kitchen, and with the candles lit and the lights off, there was quite an effect of a little bistro, or so Jane hoped.

They talked easily. Tom was a good listener and it was only when she began that Jane realized how little she had confided in anyone for a long time. Suddenly it seemed that a dam had been broken and she had to keep checking herself or she would have talked on and on. Every question he asked led to more and more explanations, but he never seemed less than interested in everything and pressed her to tell more when she said she should stop doing all the talking and let him have a chance.

By the time she was cutting the strawberry tart and scooping soft vanilla ice-cream over it, she'd told him all about her worries for Alec and the fact that he still hadn't come to any decision about what he was going to do in life.

'It's getting so late in the year,' she said, sitting down with her pudding. 'I don't know if anywhere will take him now and that means a year out, in the middle of his A-levels. It seems crazy. All the work he's already done will be wasted, he'll have to start again. He'll be years behind everyone else.'

'If it's any comfort, I was a late starter.' Tom looked appreciatively at the tart in front of him.

'You were?'

'Oh, yes. I hated school. I loved sport — I wanted to be a professional sportsman. Rugby was my game. But I wasn't good enough. I got to represent my school and went even further than that, but there was no way I was an international. It took me a couple of years to grasp it but luckily by that time I'd matured a bit, gained some other interests and realized that life, with all its options, was still open to me. It was difficult because all my friends were finished university by then, and were starting their jobs and their city lives. Some had been travelling, done their year or two abroad, and come back. You can imagine I felt like I was a million miles behind them. But it didn't matter — what I learnt was that our lives don't have to be dictated to us by our age, the year we were born, or by what our peer group does. I think we're all too susceptible to sheep-like behaviour. We can do what we want when we want. And it's never too late.'

Jane stared at him, feeling that he was making a point to her. His expression was unreadable but his face was gentle in the candlelight.

'I'm just saying,' he continued, 'that your boy can take a year out, start again, or take another direction. Don't be frightened if he wants to be different. Think how many years he has ahead of him.'

She blinked. 'You're right.'

'Of course I'm right. Now, did you make this amazing tart yourself?'

After dinner they went back to the sitting room and finished their wine there. Tom told her funny stories about life at his college and made her laugh.

'It must seem so ridiculous to you, coming from outside,' she said, feeling lightheaded from giggling. 'So archaic! If that's like that now, you can imagine what it used to be like.'

'I can't. It's crazy enough as it is. But I love it.'

'Tell me more about your life in South Africa.'

'Ah – you don't want to hear about that. It's boring. There's nothing interesting to tell.'

'Come on, there must be. What about your family? Do you have brothers and sisters?' She sipped her wine. They'd opened a second bottle and a pleasant warmth was melting her inhibitions.

'Hmm. You're not going to let it drop, are you? I've got two older brothers, and they are very average guys. They work in offices and have blonde wives and a couple of kids each. I can't say I have much in common with them.'

She waited for more and when he didn't continue, protested, 'Well, that's not enough! What about your childhood? Your school days?' She paused and added, 'Girlfriends?'

'Ah. Girlfriends. Yep, I've had a few girlfriends. No one recently. My last was when I was at Southampton. Nice enough, but not serious.' He gazed across at her. 'Are you interested in whether I have a girlfriend?'

'Oh, no . . .' She laughed, embarrassed. 'Of course not! No, I'm just interested in your life in general.'

'And I'm interested in yours,' he replied slowly. Then he said, 'It's warm in here, isn't it? Why don't we go outside on to the terrace?'

'If you'd like to.'

'I would.'

She led the way to the dark dining room, through the french windows and outside. The urge to laugh was gone now and instead she became acutely conscious of him. They walked across the cool stone and sat on the balustrade that ran the length of the terrace. Above them the sky was dark blue and scattered with milky stars. The air was touched by chilliness but it was still warm enough to be there. Noises of night animals came from the woods, loud in the still air. In the distance, the dark shape of a fox slunk along the lawn.

'This is an amazing place,' Tom said, looking out over the garden. 'I can't believe I found you and it.'

'It is. It is amazing.' The soft breeze played through her hair and across her skin. Under her leg, the stone of the balustrade was prickly and rough. She rubbed against it, experiencing the sensation. Everything seemed loaded with meaning and all her senses were alert. Tom put down his glass on the stone, and turned towards her. He was wearing his glasses again, and they hid the expression in his eyes. His hand lay on the balustrade beside her, and she examined it: it was square, solid and masculine, with blunt-ended fingers and short but unbitten nails. It looked strong and capable.

'Do you know what I want to do now?' he asked gently.

She shook her head, unable to trust herself to speak.

'I want to kiss you. Are you going to let me do that?'

Her voice felt strangled but she managed to say, 'No, no . . .'

'Why not?'

'It's not right, Tom. I'm so much older than you.'

'I've already told you what I think of that. I don't let things like that bother me.'

'You can't possibly really want to—'

His hand came up and touched hers. 'Do you think I'm lying to you about that? That I'm pretending or leading you on? Why would I do that? I'm only telling you the truth, that I want to kiss you. If you don't want me to, then I shall accept it gracefully and withdraw, even if it will drive me mad tonight. Don't you want me to?'

She shivered. 'I . . . I *do* want you to.'

'Then how can there be a problem?'

'I don't know . . . I'm afraid that if . . . I'm worried that . . .'

'You worry too much.' He slid towards her and put his hand through her hair. Despite the strong, labouring look in his hands, his touch was so tender that she felt her stomach swoop and her skin tingle. He leant forward at last and pressed his lips on hers. The sensation was so extraordinarily sweet that, after a few moments, she lost her breath and had to pull away.

'That bad?' he said with a grin.

'No, oh, no . . .' She took a deep breath and put a hand to her chest. 'Very good,' she managed to say, smiling.

'Excellent. Then I think we should do it again.'

At each step, he persisted gently and thoroughly until she couldn't do anything other than accord. The sweet kisses led inexorably to strong, passionate, deep kisses, and then to caresses, and then they led upstairs to Jane's bedroom.

On the bed, slowly but determinedly, he asked permission at every step, which at first she would deny, protesting that really they shouldn't, until his gentle persistence and her own awakened senses changed her mind. They kissed for a long while; he stroked her, undressed her slowly and tenderly, allowing her to be happy at every stage before he continued. He took off his shirt, revealing the brawny arms of an ex-rugby player – 'You're so young!' she breathed, with something like awe, as she ran a hand over his stomach – and then, finally, he forbade any more talking or protests and made love to her.

Chapter Fourteen

Iain came home from work the following Monday with a bunch of flowers, the kind sold at a station kiosk — thick-stalked, weedy things that would die in a few days — but still a bunch of flowers.

He laid them carefully on the kitchen table like an offering. Bella looked at them briefly and turned back to the stove where she was preparing supper.

'These are for you,' he volunteered, in case she hadn't guessed. 'I wanted to say . . . I'm sorry about the other night, about our row.'

'I'm sorry about it, too,' said Bella. 'But there's a difference in being sorry a thing happened, and sorry for making it happen.'

He considered this while Bella waited, interested. This would usually be the moment when Iain would take her on, unable to resist trying to beat her down and score victories over her. He said finally, 'You're right. I was in the wrong. I don't know what came over me. I shouldn't have done . . . that thing.'

'What thing?' She turned round to look at him full in the face. He stared downwards, his face wretched.

'When I took your jeans down,' he said haltingly. 'I wasn't in control. I was jealous and I know it was wrong. I . . . I'm sorry.'

He looked drained by the little speech. Bella knew how much it had cost him to say it. His pride is such a stupid burden to him, she thought. His life would be so much easier if he could only let go of it sometimes, stop fighting everything.

'Apology accepted,' she said.

His face lightened immediately and he gestured down at the sorry bunch of flowers. 'Do you like them?'

'They're lovely.' She turned back to the saucepan she'd been stirring. 'I'll put them in water in just a moment.'

Nothing more was said about the children's clothes, or returning Katie's dress. It was another gracious gesture of part-apology, part-forgiveness. *I shouldn't have done what I did*, he was telling her, *and so Katie can have her dress.*

Bella regarded the whole thing with curious detachment. In a way, she was grateful to Iain. His horrible behaviour was her way out, her excuse, even if he had apologised for it. It made whatever she was going to do defensible because she hadn't started it unprovoked. And she had an idea of what she was going to do, though, as yet, she had refused to admit it to herself. But when she'd taken Iain to the station, and the children were occupied downstairs, she'd go up to the little box room where the computer was and, with a racing heart, boot up the machine so that she could access her email. Her excitement was enjoyable in itself – a kind of luxurious feeling with little shots of adrenaline sparking it up from time to time. For the first few days after the evening with Ben there was nothing, but something had to happen, she knew it. It was impossible that there would be no outcome, that they would forget the kiss and the way it had felt. It wasn't possible for one person to feel that electricity, that extraordinary excitement. It was a reciprocal thing: to exist, it had to feed off what the other person was feeling.

Her inbox was empty, except for some junk, a short, cheerful hello from Nicky and an irritatingly large attachment from some distant relative who insisted on sending photos of her children to everyone in her address book. On the third day, she gave in and wrote a message to him:

Hi!
Just to say thanks for Saturday, I really enjoyed it! You had some excellent ideas and I'm going to find them really useful. Hope we can do it again some time, if you don't mind me picking your brains.
Love
Bellaxxxx

She stared at it for several minutes, reading it over and over. Then she deleted it and wrote:

Ben,
I don't think either of us can deny what happened on Saturday. I know it's wrong but I also know that I don't think I can resist it so please let me know what you feel because I'm going mad down here. Let me know if you want to see me again.
Bella

It was a relief to write it down. She read and reread it, trying to summon up the courage to send it. Then she scrubbed it again, and wrote:

Hi, Ben
Thanks for Saturday. Your ideas were very helpful and I've been feeling excited about what I can achieve. I hope we can talk again some time.
Bella x

She pushed 'send' before she could start going over every word, and let out a long, tremulous breath. By emailing him, she'd gone against every word of advice she'd ever offered to friends, but it was too hard to sit there, impotent, waiting, watching her inbox sit empty, obsessing over what he might be thinking. Now she had opened the proceedings and it was up to him to make the next move.

To stop herself clicking obsessively on her inbox, and in some way to connect with Ben, Bella worked hard at researching her business. There seemed to be a gap in the market for what she could offer, and she felt more and more positive that she could make a go of it. There were plenty of companies in and around Oxford – small independents or offshoots of larger parent firms – who would need staff training on-site but couldn't maintain a large IT department to provide it. Bella would be perfect, able to tailor courses to exactly what was needed and train either one-to-one or groups. She wrote up ideas of what she could offer, how much she would charge and how she would market herself.

I can do it, she thought. *I'm sure I can make a job for myself, a career.* The more she thought of it, the more capable she felt. It was almost as though she was getting back in touch with a younger version of herself, the one who'd believed that all things were possible, that she could go as far as she wanted in life; the one who was proud to tell people who she was and what she did. She began to see herself as an entrepreneur, a self starter. In her wilder moments, she saw herself in a Jaguar, hair whipped in the wind, soaring to her company headquarters, a sexy, powerful businesswoman.

She was absorbed in her work when the phone rang, making her jump. She looked at it almost fearfully. Her heart started to pound and her mouth puckered with sudden dryness. She reached out a hand and picked up the receiver. 'Hello?'

'Hi, it's Sam. I wondered what you're up to today.'

'Oh . . . hi, Sam.' Her heart rate slowed but her hands felt clammy. She concentrated on swallowing and sounding natural. 'What am I up to? Well . . . not much. I'm doing some research and drawing up ideas for getting some freelance work but I'm nearly out of inspiration, actually.'

'I'm at a bit of a loose end,' Sam said. 'It's raining. There's no tennis today. Do you fancy going to the hotel near the station for coffee?'

'Um – yeah. That'd be nice.'

'Great. I'll pick you up in ten.' Sam hung up.

How odd, Bella thought. Why is she calling me? Sam had gone cold on her since France and now here she was, suggesting coffee, as though nothing had changed. Well, fine. If she'd decided to warm up a little, that was okay by Bella. She pushed all thoughts of anything to do with Ben firmly out of her mind – she simply wouldn't think about that.

By local standards, the hotel café was smart. It offered *lattes* and mochas and herbal teas made with real mint or camomile. It was still unmistakably small town, though, with the piped music, the stiff pink linen and laminated menus. Sam and Bella found a table near the window that looked over the drizzly countryside cut through by the railway line. Grubby trains, silenced by the double glazing, went by every few minutes.

'Yeah – a skinny *latte* for me, thanks,' Sam said to the pretty waitress who came to take the order.

'One skimmed milk *latte*,' the girl said, scribbling on her pad. She turned warm eyes on Bella. 'And for you?'

'I'd like tea, please. Darjeeling.'

'Okay.' The waitress wrote it down and then made her way back through the tables to the kitchen.

'You know who that is, don't you?' Sam said, lighting a cigarette and nodding after the departing figure.

'She looks familiar.'

'That's Jane Fielding's daughter. She was at the garden party – didn't you see her? I think she's got some kind of holiday job here. Doesn't seem like the kind of thing a girl like her would do full-time, anyway, does it? Posh boarding-school type and all that. How are you, then?' Sam sat back and regarded her through the plumes of smoke from her cigarette.

'Oh, fine. Good. Determined to get going with my work.'

'Good on you, if that's what you want. I mean, I suppose you don't have a lot of choice in it, do you? You've got to work.'

'Absolutely. And I enjoy it. I can't really imagine a life of leisure. I'd always want to be doing something.'

'Yeah.' Sam sucked a long pull on her cigarette. 'I can't do that. Ben would hate it. He wanted me to give up work as soon as we got together because he knew that there wasn't any point. It's not as though I'm going to be businesswoman of the year, or anything. He hates women who want to compete for the sake of it.'

'Does he?' said Bella, surprised. 'He seemed supportive when I mentioned my business plan.'

'Oh, yeah, for *you*,' Sam said, with a touch of disdain, 'because, like I said, you don't have the choice. But Ben thinks that women in the workplace who don't really need to be there are making things worse for the rest of society.'

'What?' said Bella. She laughed. 'No one seriously thinks like that, these days. He must have been having you on.' The waitress came up with their drinks and put them carefully on the table. Bella said, 'Thanks,' and smiled at her.

'No – think about it. It makes sense,' Sam insisted. 'Overcrowding in higher education – why? Because as many women as men want to get a degree. Competition in the job market increases male feelings of inferiority, halves the jobs available for men who have families to support, and means that, overall, families get poorer.'

'What? How? Now, that can't be right. There isn't a finite amount of opportunity in the world and surely more competition means standards get higher. And two-income families are richer, aren't they?'

'That's the lie, though, isn't it? You might have more money coming in, but the end result is more money going out. Life becomes more expensive for everybody. Ben explained it to me. House prices are forced up because, first, single women are buying on their own and, second, two incomes make a family more likely to want a bigger home and the market responds by pushing up the prices accordingly. It gets so that you have to have two incomes to be able to afford a decent house to raise a family in, whereas previously, with just one earner, homes were more affordable.'

'Well . . .' Bella was bemused. 'I suppose there's a kind of twisted logic in there somewhere.'

'And then the women have to go to work, farm their kids out to childminders or pay extortionate wages to a nanny, and it becomes a vicious circle. Have to work to pay for the nanny to look after the children while the mother goes out to work. It's crazy. And you're getting this highly privileged upper-middle class, intermarrying and making themselves a more select unit. It's why the rich are getting richer and the poor poorer.'

'I had no idea you felt so strongly about these things,' Bella said drily.

'Me? I don't give a monkey's. It's Ben who told me all this, and I think it makes sense. What's the point in me slaving my guts out when I don't have to, taking a job away from someone who needs it? I'm not political, I don't care about all that. But I've got the sense to see that much.'

Bella was silent. She poured her tea thoughtfully. She was astonished by what Sam had just come out with: she honestly hadn't thought that in this day and age people could still question a woman's right to be in the work place, but if it were just Sam, fine – obviously she had to justify her life of leisure to herself somehow.

'I didn't have Ben down as the kind of man who thought that way, that's all,' she said at last, and sipped her tea.

'Yeah, well. He shows his best face in company, of course. He says what he knows people like to hear. Anyway, enough about him. I want to talk about you.'

'Really?' Bella was startled. Sam never wanted to talk about her.

'How are you?'

'Fine.'

Sam stared at her. She looked immaculate as usual, her blonde hair glistening with good condition and her skin satin smooth. Her lashes stood out spiky with mascara and her lips were coated with juicy gloss, but her china-doll eyes were hard and without any sign of feeling in them. She seemed to be considering Bella's response. At last she said, 'And that husband of yours, how's old Iain?'

'He's fine too. We're both . . . fine.' Wondering what Sam was getting at, she added, 'We're both a lot more relaxed since the holiday – it was a terrific idea.'

Sam didn't answer at first but smoked out her cigarette. 'He's a great guy. You wanna hold on to that one. A really brilliant father, anyone could see that. Your kids adore him, don't they?'

'I suppose so.'

'Ah, come on. They can't get enough of him. You're very lucky. Happy little family.'

When did Sam become a champion of the traditional family unit, with Mum at home doing the baking? wondered Bella. Before or after she broke up Ben's first marriage? 'That's very nice of you to say so. To tell you the truth . . .' She hesitated, considering whether she should go down this particular path. 'I've been wondering if everything's all right between you and me. I thought things went a bit chilly in France and I haven't really heard from you since.'

Sam frowned. 'Of course it's all right. What do you think? We're here now, aren't we?'

'Yes.'

'I'm asking you how you are, aren't I?'

'Yes, and that's lovely of you—'

'Well, then.' Sam spread her hands as if to show how self-evident it was that she was a caring friend. 'I don't understand what you're saying.'

'Good – that's good,' Bella said heartily. 'We're friends again.'

That was very odd, Bella thought, after Sam dropped her back at the lodge. Katie and Christopher had taken advantage of her absence to put on their favourite video and they were sitting through it attentively for the hundredth time. Bella looked in on them briefly and then made her way upstairs to the computer and switched it on.

She waited for it to warm up, thinking over what Sam had said. Despite her protests, she'd been chillier than an iceberg, and all that guff about Ben disapproving of working women – well, it simply hadn't rung true. He'd never said a word along those lines; why on earth should Sam make it all up?

She clicked on to the Internet connection, then to her inbox and saw that a message from Ben was waiting for her. She caught her breath and her hands trembled. He'd replied, at last. She clicked quickly on the message.

Dear Bella

It was lovely to see you on Saturday. I enjoyed every moment. Of course I want to see you again. To be honest, I've thought about nothing else. I've got a surprise for you. Call me on the mobile when you can – office hours are best.

Can't wait.

Ben

She stared at it with a racing heart. This was it. She was standing on the brink. This whole thing could go forward, or she could stop it now and put everything back as it had been. It seemed as though there was a fork in the road, one path leading to something unknown but exciting, the other promising only the straightforward trudge she'd known for so long. She knew that, really, there was no choice.

'Bella, that's excellent,' Iain said excitedly, when she told him. 'Really – terrific news.'

'It is, isn't it?'

'It's a real start. I wasn't sure at first, you know. It's a risk going out on your own. I veer on the side of playing it safe, getting your pay packet and all that.'

I know you do, thought Bella scornfully. You'd never take a chance. That's why you'll always be what you are. Small-time.

He continued, oblivious, 'But if this comes off, it could be a success. You don't have to have much capital so you're not risking much. Yes . . . it could really work. You know what we should do?'

We? 'No.'

'We need to start looking at tax issues, small-business grants, that kind of thing. A name for the company, some headed stationery. Business cards.'

'Calm down,' she said, with a laugh. 'It's only a meeting.'

When she'd called Ben, her voice high and breathless, he'd told her his surprise. He'd arranged a meeting for her with the head of human resources in his own company. 'I told you we needed training. I've explained to Paula what you do – I haven't said we're friends, so she won't be biased towards you – and I've asked her to assess our needs and have a frank discussion with you. If the budget looks right, we might be able to hire you – but I'm going to leave that decision to her.'

'It sounds a little like pulling strings to me,' Bella said. 'I want to get this going through my own efforts.'

'Don't knock contacts,' Ben advised. 'It's the way the world works. Look, it's a possible foot in the door, nothing more.

Getting your first client is always the hardest bit. After that, you have a recommendation. Besides . . .' His voice dropped, became low and intimate. 'I was hoping you'd let me take you out for lunch afterwards.'

Her hands shook and her throat dried. So that was what this was really about. She managed to say, 'Of course.'

Ben had laughed, a low rumble over the phone. 'Good. That's settled. I'll give her your number to arrange a day.'

Now, with Iain all a-flutter about her meeting – she hadn't mentioned that Ben had set it up but let Iain believe it was the result of the cold-calling she'd been doing – she hugged her secret to her. Let him start sticking his oar in now that it looked as though it might work. He could be as irritating as he liked, she didn't care. She had *this* – she didn't name it, she didn't want to do anything that might make her have to consider what it actually was – to dream of, and think of in private, far from where Iain could sully it.

When he turned to her that night and ran a hand over her hip and breast, she rolled away and buried her head in her pillow, muttering that she was too tired and wanted to sleep.

Emma had taken to going out for long hours each day; God only knew what she was doing, but Sam wasn't complaining. She liked the peace that settled on the house when she knew Emma wasn't in it, and she was looking forward to the time when that was a permanent state of affairs.

But in truth, it was difficult to find any kind of peace at the moment, even with the quiet. She drifted through the house in her white drawstring trousers and little vest, which made her feel as if she were fresh from the yoga mat although she'd only gone to one class in her life and not enjoyed it. The instructor had spent ages making them sit in silence, breathing and visualising – how this was meant to make her fit Sam did not know. And then there was a bit of strenuous stretching: she'd had to put her legs in the air and prop her hips up on her elbows, which had been bad enough, but then the instructor had come along and pushed her legs down backwards over her head so that suddenly she was looking into her own groin. She hadn't enjoyed it at all. Still, someone must be getting something out of it – it was so popular.

Ben was at work and she was in the house alone again. When they'd first come to this place she'd missed Cheltenham like mad. She still did, if she thought about it hard enough, but in some ways she'd got used to this house where she could pad from room to room. She could spend hours stretched out on the sofa, flicking the television from channel to channel, roaming over the daytime schedules and lunch-time movies. She liked to go into Ben's office and look around: she could scan his email account – he used the same password for everything – and see what was up, have a quick browse through his things, the letters, the bank statements, the scribbled notes to himself. It was as well to keep on top of things. If Ben really wanted to hide something, he'd make sure she couldn't find it – so all this was fair game and, besides, she didn't mean anything bad by it. She was just interested. There were always messages from Aileen that Ben forgot to tell her about and it was reassuring to see that they were as terse and unfriendly as usual.

She went into the office and turned on the light. She wondered why she'd ever been threatened by Aileen. It was obvious that any power she'd had over Ben had disappeared long ago. The only thing that still tied them together in any way at all was Emma. No – Sam knew she'd been stupid. It wasn't the past she had to fear, it was the future. She'd thought she'd built enough defences against the unknown, by being beautiful and stylish and sexy, but it seemed now that she'd have to use her other weapons: her cunning and her intelligence. They had always served her well in the past – she'd always got exactly what she wanted, shedding friends and boyfriends along the way to her goal. And Ben had been what she'd wanted.

She switched on Ben's computer and loaded his settings. She opened his email and scanned down quickly over the last entries. Ben got hundreds of emails every day, from the unsolicited junk that everyone got to updates from his favourite sites and companies: the sailing-boat enthusiasts, mountaineering societies, and all the other activities that he had to enjoy vicariously because he never had time to go out and do them. The business mail took up most space – he was copied in to every email circulated at his company along with the thousands intended for him alone. And he never seemed to delete anything.

There were seven unopened messages at the top of the inbox but she knew who all the senders were so she didn't waste time wondering what they said. Instead she scrolled down the opened messages, scanning every sender, passing back over the last few days. Then she saw it. *BellaB276*.

'Shit,' she swore. 'I *knew* it.'

She clicked on the message and read it. It was innocuous enough, thanking Ben for his advice. Well – big deal. She knew about that visit. There was nothing in it she didn't already know. She closed it impatiently, and saw that the little arrow at the bottom of Bella's address showed that it been replied to. She clicked quickly on the sent mail folder and scanned for the reply. There was nothing. She looked over and over, checking the date Bella had sent her message and then where she guessed a sent mail ought to be. Nothing at all.

He's deleted it, she thought, a nasty coldness creeping over her. And why would he want to do that, unless he had something to hide?

Jane spent a whole morning clearing out the spare room for Maggie.

'Gregor's going in the middle of the week,' Maggie had said. 'I'll come down after that.'

At first she had complained that she'd been ambushed by the two of them, Gregor and Jane. 'You're forcing me into this! You're making me feel like some kind of invalid, sent away to convalesce. I've lost a baby, for God's sake, not caught measles. It happens to hundreds of women every day. It's better if I just get on with my life.'

Jane had explained gently and firmly that, just now, she had no interest in what happened to hundreds of other women, only in what happened to Maggie and that it was obvious a stay at Rawlston would help her. 'Do you have any reason to stay in

London?' She couldn't help thinking, with a shudder of horror, of that dirty street and the confined flat. The whole place struck her as unhealthy, as though it were still tainted with Victorian smog and the hollow coughs of consumptives.

'I ought to be near the doctor,' Maggie said.

'Why? Are you still having treatment?'

'No,' she conceded. 'They've stopped monitoring my HCG level. It's back to normal. I've got some medication but I suppose that will last me.'

'We have doctors in the countryside, you know. It's not the back of beyond.'

'I know, I know.' Maggie had sighed. 'All right, I give in. You can mother me for a little while, and when you've had your fill, I'm coming right back home. Okay?'

'Anything you say.'

Jane threw open the windows to let light and air into the spare room. There was a grand guest room that had stayed the same since Theo's parents' day, with an embroidered counterpane on the bed, oil paintings on the walls and damask curtains sweeping past the tall windows that gave on to the front of the house, but Maggie preferred the less formal spare room. It was next to the old nursery and must have once been the nanny's room, white-painted and cosy, with a black iron bedstead, sprigged curtains tied back to reveal the garden, and a small bookshelf full of battered old favourites of the kind Jane liked to curl up with when she was ill. She was putting a bunch of garden flowers into a vase on the bedside table when she heard a distant sound of a car engine coming closer and closer. With a burst of relief, she rushed along the corridor and down the stairs. Throwing open the front door, she saw the Morris Minor drawing to a halt. She ran across to it and pulled open the driver's door, saying excitedly, 'Oh, you're here! I'm so glad.'

'Calm down, for crying out loud,' said Maggie, getting out. 'Yes, I haven't been abducted or ambushed along the way. They say travel is quite safe these days. The highwaymen have all given up since the horses found it so hard to keep up with the traffic.'

Jane stepped back to assess her sister. Maggie looked better than she had in London but there was no way she was restored to the colourful woman of before the pregnancy. The bloating was gone now and she had lost weight. She hadn't adorned herself with her jewellery and lipstick as she usually did, and her embroidered, sequined clothes were replaced by a sombre dark jumper and plain skirt.

The sparkle, thought Jane. The sparkle is gone. 'How are you, darling?' she asked, putting a hand on her arm.

'Fine, fine,' Maggie said, with a shrug. 'Gregor went this morning, which was pretty upsetting. He's been wonderful to me the last week or so, you wouldn't believe it. Well, *you* wouldn't. I know you don't like him very much.' She pulled her suitcase and bag from the back of the car.

'That's not true.' Jane was indignant. 'I like him a lot – I just don't know him very well.'

'If you say so.' Maggie sounded weary and Jane felt instantly guilty. She's not herself, she thought. I mustn't rise to her – it's unhappiness talking. Maggie put her cases on the gravel. 'Well? Are you going to show me to my room?'

'Of course. Let me take those.' Jane picked up the luggage and led the way in through the front door. 'How was your journey?'

'As dreadful as you'd expect. There are too many cars in this country. Too much moving around. People should stay put. Well, well' – Maggie looked about her – 'we don't come this way very often.'

' I know.' The main hall had a musty, dark feel, with its brown carpet, dusty rugs and old brass chandelier hanging from the ceiling, like a big tarnished spider on the end of its web. 'I never thought it was a nice way to meet the house, coming in here, but recently I've start opening the front door a little more often. Perhaps I should think about sprucing up this hallway. It hasn't been touched in generations, I'd guess.'

'I wouldn't waste your money,' Maggie said.

She went downstairs feeling tired already, with Maggie there only ten minutes. The kitchen calmed her, as it always did. A few of her cookbooks lay open on the table: she had been wondering about preserving the last of the summer fruit in jams and pickles. A bag of currants in the freezer was calling out to be cooked down and jellied, to eat with cold lamb or smeared over a runny, smelly cheese, or sweet on a hot scone. She thought suddenly of Christmas. Already summer was feeling stale; soon it would be autumn and she would start to think about making a pudding and a cake, boiling up mixed fruit and brandy for mincemeat.

Lucy came in, humming to herself. 'Did I hear Maggie arrive?'

'You did. She's just settling into the spare room. I told her to take her time – she was a bit zonked from that journey.' Jane had told the children what had happened to Maggie, and they had been solemn and sympathetic.

'Where's Alec?'

'In his room, I expect. He's given special dispensation to Maggie: he won't play his music at top volume as long as she's in the house.'

'Result.' Lucy looked satisfied. 'If anyone can handle him, it's Maggie.'

'Hmm – just think what it'll be like when you're both gone and I'm here on my own with him. At this rate, Alec will be here for the foreseeable future.'

'Well . . . don't think about that now. You never know what's going to happen. It'll be nice for you to have Maggie here – it's been so long since anyone stayed.'

'Yes,' said Jane, staring hard at a cookbook. She flicked a quick glance at her daughter's face but it was serene and innocent, without a touch of sarcasm.

She hadn't been sure that Tom had left unobserved after his night with her but she supposed he must have. That morning she had woken early and been surprised by the rumpled state of the bedclothes, then remembered everything with a jolt and glanced over her shoulder to see Tom's broad, brown back curving away from her, his dark curly head on the pillow. As she'd turned, he sighed, disturbed by her movement, rolled on to his back and stretched his arms over his head.

'Good morning,' he said, with a sleepy smile, opening his eyes lazily.

'Good morning,' she replied, sounding prim and formal because she was in an agony of embarrassment. What was she doing waking up in bed with a twenty-eight-year-old South African rugby player? The whole idea was ridiculous! And when she thought back to what they had done the night before, to his slow, insistent lovemaking, she wanted to curl up into a ball and hide at the bottom of the bed.

'How are you this morning?' He rolled towards her and reached out for her.

'Very well, thank you,' she answered, stiffening.

He pulled back a little, raising his eyebrows. She tried not to look at his wide smooth chest; she tried to look anywhere but at him.

'I see we've made backward progress in the night.' He grinned. 'There's no need to be embarrassed.'

'I'm not.'

'I had a wonderful time. *You* were wonderful.'

'Oh . . . well . . . that's nice.' It sounded so horribly lame. What was wrong with her? 'I'm just a bit worried about my children seeing you. They would have come in late, you see, and while they're not early risers, I wouldn't want them to stumble on us. I don't really make a habit of having men over . . .'

'I quite understand.' He leaned his head over winningly, looking up at her boyishly from his soft brown eyes. 'Why don't you and I wake ourselves up with some gentle exercise and then I'll be on my discreet way? Look, I'm more than ready for you . . .' He caught her hand and began to pull it downwards to where she could see an obvious lump under the covers. She snatched it away, flushing. He laughed, looking a little hurt. 'What's wrong?'

'I . . . can't.' She wanted to explain that there was a difference between being seduced gently and expertly under the stars, after a luxurious meal and champagne, and leaping on to him cold-bloodedly first thing in the morning. She didn't work that way.

'Why not? Are you regretting it?'

She turned over and stared at her bedside table: the little pile of books, the lamp, the clock, the water glass. Did she regret it? She didn't think so. Her body felt as though it had been switched back on after a long dormancy.

'I see,' he said, taking her silence as assent. 'I can't tell you how sorry I am that you feel that way. I don't see what there is to regret. We're both consenting adults, and there was nothing we did that we didn't want to do – at least, there wasn't on my side.'

Jane stayed silent, unable to reply. Tom's voice had become as formal as her own. She felt him lift the sheet and climb out of the bed.

'I'll get dressed and be on my way.'

She lifted her head but couldn't bring herself to look at his nakedness. 'Would you like me to drive you to the station?'

'Actually,' he said, 'I feel like walking. I know the way from last night. I'll be fine.'

'All right,' she said, thinking that she should stop him, be braver. But she let him get dressed and pad out of the bedroom. A little while later, she heard the back door close behind him, and sighed.

Chapter Fifteen

Bella came out of the office feeling pleased with herself. She stopped outside in the fluorescent-lit corridor, adjusted her wrinkled suit skirt and took a deep breath. She'd got on well with Paula, the head of human resources in Ben's company, and she knew she'd come across as professional, articulate and skilful. It had been odd at first to be back in an office environment with its artificial chill, muffled atmosphere and the static air full of electricity. Paula had said that it all sounded very good and that she'd be back in touch after some internal discussions.

She took the lift down to the ground floor and loitered by the waiting area in the impersonal glass-and-potted-plants reception, wondering whether to pick up the lonely copy of *The Economist* that sat on a side table, and checking her watch every five minutes. Her high heels – how long had it been since she'd last put them on? – clicked on the tiled floor as she paced nervously up and down the lobby, watched by the receptionist, and wishing she had a mirror so she could check her appearance.

Then the lift chimed again, and the doors slid open. Suited office workers came out, heading briskly for the front door, and then behind them, the tall, casual figure of Ben. He strolled out, looking unconcerned – certainly nowhere near as nervous as she felt – smiled when he saw Bella and came over.

'Well, Mrs Balfour, hello. How nice to see you. Did your meeting go well?'

'Very well, thank you.' She plucked nervously at her skirt.

He looked at her appreciatively and said quietly, 'You look fantastic. Shall we go?'

They went out through the glass doors and into the car park. Ben led her to his car in its private parking space, and opened the door for her. Wordlessly she climbed in, and stilled her trembling hands by clutching the underside of the seat. Ben got in on the other side, fired up the engine, and they pulled away from the office building, still without speaking.

They raced along the country roads, leaving the trading estate far behind them. The roar of the engine excused them from speaking and they continued in silence until Ben suddenly pulled off into the car park of a long low Cotswold stone inn, a hotel with a pub attached. He stopped the car in an empty space. 'Come on. This is it.'

She followed him in, tottering in her tight skirt and high heels, feeling painfully shy. He led her into a deserted lounge bar and asked for two whiskies from the waiter, while Bella sat down, stiff and awkward, on the velvet sofa by the fire.

'I've ordered some sandwiches,' Ben said when he returned. 'I hope that's okay.'

'It's fine. I'm not very hungry.' She couldn't imagine eating a bite. Her mouth felt far too dry to cope with food.

'Nor am I,' he said softly. 'It's not quite the romantic lunch, though, is it, some sandwiches in a basket? I hope you're not disappointed.'

She shook her head. The waiter came up and put their drinks in front of them. She took a grateful sip of the burning liquid as Ben clutched his glass and raised it to his mouth. His hands, she noticed, had a tiny tremor in them; something in her relaxed and warmed towards him. What are we doing here? she wondered, half amazed to find the two of them alone together. Is this really going to happen? Am I really about to embark on this?

She had slept with no one but Iain for fourteen years and the prospect of revealing herself to Ben was terrifying; she felt hopelessly inadequate. And after Sam, with her slim litheness and unashamed sexuality – how could she, Bella, be anything but lumpen and disappointing? Suddenly she felt that she couldn't possibly expose herself to such humiliation, to the disappointment in Ben's eyes when she revealed herself to him, or the flatness afterwards when she'd failed to live up to expectations. It was better to live with the fantasy than experience that. She twitched nervously. She had to go, right now. This was ridiculous. What was she thinking of?

'Are you all right?' Ben frowned, aware of her discomfort.

'I don't know what we're doing here. I think I ought to go.'

He put down his whisky glass, looking grave, and said, 'If that's what you want, we can go right away.' He glanced around for the waiter, who was nowhere in sight. He turned back to her, and she was struck again by his handsome features: the long straight nose and the curling full lips. 'I can't ask you to do this,' he added, 'not if you feel in any way against it.'

'It's not *me*,' she protested. 'I just feel . . . Sam . . .' She'd been going to say that Sam was a hard act to follow but she stopped herself in case it sounded as though she were fishing for compliments.

'Sam. Of course we ought to talk about Sam. You're her friend, after all.'

'Oh no,' Bella said hastily. 'That is . . .' She felt caught: if she was not Sam's friend, why did she behave as though she were? But what friend would be with another woman's husband, clearly intent on betraying her? 'It's complicated,' she ended weakly.

Ben smiled. 'You don't have to tell me that. I know Sam's difficult. I knew from the start you and she weren't going to be soulmates, for the simple reason that she doesn't have soulmates. Not among other women, anyway. She finds them too much of a threat.'

'How can she feel under threat when she's so beautiful and desirable? Most of us spend our lives trying to look a fraction as good as Sam does.'

'But that's part of the problem – yes, she's beautiful and polished and perfect looking but, no matter how hard she tries, she's never satisfied. She never feels as though she's safe. God knows why, God knows what made her this way. There's nothing she's ever told me and now I think she was simply born like this. I'm only just beginning to realize the extent of it, how worthless and threatened she feels all the time. But she can't recognize it, and her response is to be aggressive, to attack and scare people off. Look at the way she treats Emma.'

'I wasn't sure you'd noticed.'

'Of course I have. But I don't want to see it and half the time, I close my eyes to it. I know I do – I'm not proud of it. She's threatened even by a teenager, if she suspects she might get in the way or turn me against her. So she lashes out and thinks she'll win that way. She doesn't trust anyone and that's partly because she's not trustworthy herself. God . . .' Ben laughed cynically to himself. 'Here I am, talking about my wife being trustworthy. Look at me, for goodness' sake . . .'

'Do you love her?' Bella asked softly. She was feeling better. It made the world a more just place, somehow, if someone beautiful like Sam suffered for it in other ways.

Ben stared into his drink again. 'I did once,' he said at last. 'Or I thought I did. Perhaps it was because I thought she adored me, and that's very seductive, you know. And I appreciated her charms, of course – who wouldn't? But she can't love – she's dead inside, Bella. I'm only realizing it now, as I talk to you, that I've known for ages there's nothing really between us. I couldn't face it before, not after all the pain we all went through to get here – the divorce, Emma, everything. But she's hollow. She's empty. I can't love that. No one can. Not even Sam can love herself. It's so desperately sad.' His eyes were agonized. 'That's why, when I met you, I was afraid. I had to keep my distance from you because your life force is like a magnet to me. You're a full person, a whole person, a *real* person, and for me that's like a thirsty man being shown a glass of water. I'm desperate for some bloody *life*. I'm like a vampire.' His voice rose with emotion. 'I don't think you're happy either. Is it so wrong if we find some comfort with each other?'

Bella buried her face in her hands. 'I don't know!' she cried, from behind them. 'Of course it's wrong. But if it's what we both want, I don't know how we can fight it.'

'We can't,' Ben said briefly. 'It's obvious now, isn't it?'

Relief lightened her. He'd made his decision – she only had to concur, if she wanted. For an instant, everything seemed to hover in the air, vibrating; she was hanging between two lives, the old and the new. She could choose safety or adventure.

'Yes,' she whispered.

Ben went to the reception desk and booked a room for them. Bella didn't go with him. She was sure that something in the eyes of the receptionist would ruin everything – one glimpse of sordid amusement or disapproval and the whole thing would collapse. She waited in the bar, her stomach churning with a painful excitement, watching her knuckles turn white as she clenched her fist against her skirt until he came and beckoned to her. She followed him out of the bar and up the carved wooden staircase to the carpeted corridor. He led the way to the room, saying, 'I don't think this is their busy season. I got this one with no trouble.'

Inside the hotel room a four-poster bed was covered with a tapestry counterpane and plump pillows. Hunting prints and oils of flowers hung on the walls, illuminated by brass picture lights. Two green armchairs faced each other over a walnut table by the window.

'Very smart. This can't have been cheap. Do they rent by the hour?' said Bella, trying to relieve her nervousness with a joke, her voice higher than usual. Ben didn't answer. He strode over to the window and pulled the curtains shut, so that the room was instantly lowered into gloom. He turned, a dark figure against the curtains, then walked slowly towards her. Bella resisted the urge to clutch her stomach, which was somersaulting painfully. She longed for him to kiss her just to quench this terrible, painful desire that had been building up with every step as she'd followed him from the bar.

He stopped in front her, towering over her. He reached out and stroked her hair. 'God, it's soft,' he whispered. 'Real hair.'

Bella started to tremble. She felt like a teenager, awkward, longing, nervous. 'For Christ's sake, Ben,' she whispered, 'please . . .'

He lowered his mouth to hers and kissed her gently, before she was possessed by all the yearning and passion that had been building up in her for weeks and responded to him with a violence that left her spinning somewhere far away, in beautiful darkness.

Kissing, Bella thought, is so important. She remembered the boys she'd kissed as a teenager, with their over-wet mouths and thrashing tongues. She'd wondered what all the fuss was about until she'd been kissed properly and she'd experienced that moment when two mouths fitted together as though custom-made, when there was no awkwardness or clashing or dribble but the endless, delicious rightness of the perfect kiss.

Ben's mouth is like that, she thought, watching him snooze on the pillow beside her. Perfect for mine. His lips were slightly open, their pirate's curve softened to a gentle Cupid's bow, like a child's. She couldn't imagine ever tiring of that mouth or the taste of it. Kissing him had felt like taking off, like flying through a velvety night. Her fears of his revulsion had not been realized: he'd adored every inch of her. She giggled and clutched herself. When did I last feel so . . . wonderful? I thought there would be guilt, I thought I'd feel rotten but I feel like I've been effervesced. I feel like I'm walking on air!

Ben's eyes opened. He blinked slowly at her. 'Are you laughing?' he said.

'Yes.' She laughed again. 'I'm laughing at how happy I am.'

He grinned at her. 'It was rather marvellous, wasn't it?'

'Marvellous?' She bent her head and buried her nose in his chest hair, inhaling the scent of him. 'It was like nothing on earth,' she said, muffled. Then she came up to look him in the eyes, close to his face. 'It was *fantastic*. You are a wonderful lover, Ben Clarke!' She kissed his mouth. 'I haven't been . . . done like that for a long time.'

'Done? What kind of a word is *done*, woman?'

'Well, I don't know how to put it politely . . .'

'You could say just about anything else and it would be an improvement. Now come here, because I'm going to *do* you again . . .' His arms came up around her and pulled her to him, crushing her breasts against his chest and they began to kiss with more ardour. She heard his breathing quicken and a faint growl at the back of his throat; it excited her unbearably and she surrendered herself to it.

Bella drove back late. Iain might even be home by now – she'd have to think of something convincing to tell him about why her lunch-time meeting had ended much later than expected. She'd have to do something about the sparkle in her eyes as well, find some way to damp it down. Flicking down the visor mirror, she inspected her face: her skin was glowing.

'Iain won't notice,' she said to herself, indicating to turn off. 'He never notices a bloody thing. I could walk in half naked with a bed sheet hanging off me and he still wouldn't twig.'

She knew that she ought to feel appalled at herself, low and decadent. What was she now? A scarlet woman? An adulteress? But how could she help it if instead she felt as though she'd been injected with some kind of extraordinary drug that made her vibrate with life and sensuality? God, he was amazing. She shivered at the memory, then sang out loud to herself and laughed.

I must put on a cap on this! she thought, reproaching herself. What if my husband sees me giggling and gambolling like this?

She felt solemn again. My husband. Iain. Bella and Iain Balfour. Iain and Bella. That was how it had been for years now. Once Iain had made her feel like this, although she couldn't believe it had ever been as exciting as the new feeling. Years ago, she'd thought they would always be like that. She hadn't been a total fool: she'd expected love to change and calm down after the heady early days. The first five years of marriage had been wonderful – not without their troubles, of course, but full of the excitement of all the new experiences they had had together: first flat, first sofa, first car, first baby. She remembered the intensity of Katie's arrival, her plump, fair, gorgeous daughter. She hadn't known it was possible to feel so much at once; she'd thought then that they had a chance to be a perfect family. But gradually there stopped being firsts and it became just more and more of the same. If she thought about it now, it seemed that something had been missing from the start; even so, she had held out hope that it would get

better and it had never occurred her to that it might end altogether and, if it did, not like this.

Will I have to leave him? she wondered. The idea was simultaneously exciting and terrifying. Where would I go? To Nicky?
Could the children come too . . . ?

She saw an enticing glimpse of a life where she and Ben and the
children lived together in the big house. It would be a good life, a
happy life, with Sam and Iain painlessly erased.

'Listen to me,' she said aloud. 'One afternoon of steamy passion
and suddenly I'm packing my bags. I must calm down. I'm going
right back to my ordinary life. I'll probably never see Ben again.
I ought to cherish it as a lovely thing that happened quite unexpectedly and put it behind me.'

But she knew in her heart that it would happen again. It was
impossible for it not to. Before they had parted, Ben had told her
that he would see her and that she was not to think of avoiding
him. 'I'm not letting that happen,' he'd said, stroking her face
with a tenderness that almost made tears come into her eyes.
'Here.' He handed her a piece of card with an email address on it.
'If you want to get in touch, use this address, not my normal one.
It's the one I used to contact you before.'

'A secret email account?' she said.

'It's as well to be careful,' he'd said. 'The best way to be
reckless is cautiously.'

'Hello, love, how did it go?' said Iain, when Bella came into the
kitchen. The children were already at the table eating scrambled
eggs on toast. 'You're back late.'

'Yes – it ran on a bit and then I stopped off in town on the way
back to look at mobile phones. I might need a new one now that
the business looks like taking off.' Where did that lie come from?
she wondered. She hadn't planned it. It was rather good.

Iain came over from the stove. An apron was tied roughly over
his suit trousers and his loosened tie dangled over it. He kissed
her cheek. 'I made the kids their tea. Do you want something?'

'I'll have something later,' she said, sitting down at the table,
thinking that she might never be hungry again.

215

'You can have some of my strangled egg,' Christopher said graciously. 'If you want some.'

'No, thank you, darling, but that's very sweet of you.'

Iain came and sat down. 'So, what did they say? Did they make any promises?'

'No, you know how it goes. They listened attentively and they're going to let me know. But it all seemed very positive. They were impressed, I thought.'

'Love, that's terrific,' Iain said, smiling.

Please don't, thought Bella. Don't be nice and kind and reasonable and empathetic. Not now.

'I'm proud of you,' he said, took her hand and squeezed it. 'This could be the start of something really big.'

'Yes – it could be,' Bella replied, feeling weak. 'It really could be.'

Sam paced from room to room. It would be possible to go mad here, she thought. She could go bonkers in this huge place, miles from civilization and everything that made life worth living, where she seemed to be losing the previously iron grip she'd had over her life. There was nothing concrete she could hang her fears on, just a desperate feeling that things were going wrong. And here it was, well after six o'clock, and Ben wasn't home.

All right, that wasn't unusual. Demands at work often meant that he was late. But she needed him right now! Couldn't he tell? She needed reassurance. She needed him to come home and growl, 'Sammy, Sammy' in her ear as he did when he wanted to hustle her up the stairs to the bedroom. Just for him to come in and sweep her up in a bear-hug would be enough. She was feeling vulnerable, needy – and it was bloody selfish of him not to see that.

In her bedroom, she went to her silver-glass dressing-table and drew out from the back of her jewellery drawer the small plastic bag that Becky had given her at the gym the other day. Now that she was out here in the sticks, she had to rely on her friend – her *good* friend Becky, she thought self-pityingly, who never let her down – to get the little pouches of powder that kept her going when things were rough. And they were rough now, for God's sake. No one could blame her if she needed a pick-me-up, could they?

She poured a little white heap on to the surface of the dressing-table – one of the advantages of having a glass one, she thought, clever, clever me – took her slim metal nail file and used the edge to chop her way through it, milling it down to an even finer powder. Then she drew it into two thick lines, gazing at them with anticipation mixed with greed. Yummy, she thought. Swee-ties, all for me. Rolling a note from her pocket, she sniffed them up quickly, first one nostril, then the other, threw back her head to inhale again and make sure all the little bits had gone in, then wiped away the residue on her nose with a finger and rubbed it on her upper gum. There. Bliss.

It's not like I'm an addict, she thought to herself, clearing away the detritus. I don't need this stuff every day and I'm not going to lose bits of my face or anything. But today I deserve it.

She went downstairs feeling happier and more confident, look-ing forward to the buzz cutting in and lifting her even higher. She went to Ben's wine cupboard in the cellar, took out a bottle of vintage Veuve Clicquot and, in the kitchen, popped it open with a flourish.

'What's the point of being able to afford this stuff,' she said, pouring a foaming glass, 'if I can't bloody well drink it when I want?' Cocaine always brought out her taste for the high life and she loved the way she could drink and not feel drunk after she'd taken a line or two. 'I need it,' she said, raising her glass to the empty kitchen. 'Cheers, m'dears!' And she gulped down a mouth-ful of the fizzing liquid.

When Ben came back, she was dancing to MTV in the sitting room. The wide-screen television was on full blast, pumping out the latest hits, and Sam bounced and writhed along with them, a glass in one hand and a cigarette in the other. She joined in breathlessly when she knew the words and sang 'yeah, yeah, oooh . . .' when she didn't. The thumping bass was so loud that she didn't hear the sports car arrive, or the front door open. She didn't even hear Ben calling to her. She only noticed he was back when he strode past her, grabbed the remote and pushed the mute button. There was sudden silence leaving only a faint buzzing, which, Sam thought, might be inside her head.

'Aagh – what d'you do that for?' she said. 'I was enjoying that!'

'I don't think the rest of the village were, though. I could hear it coming up the drive.'

'Bit of life here can't hurt, can it? Bit of bloody lifeblood? It's what this place needs!' She sucked at her cigarette and puffed out a thick cloud of smoke. 'Where've you been anyway?' She stared at him defiantly. 'I'm here on my own. Your bloody daughter's out amusing herself. Can't I have a bit of fun?'

He looked at her with an unreadable expression. 'I've been at work,' he said quietly. 'Where do you think?'

'Oh, Benjy.' She put on her baby voice, widened her eyes and shimmied towards him. 'I've missed you. I've been lonely today. I wanted you to come home.'

'Did you?' he said, almost sadly. Sam felt a wave of powerful attraction to him; good old candy, she could always rely on it. He was so tall and handsome, standing there in his smart Italian trousers and pale checked shirt – the nearest Ben ever got to a suit. He embodied everything to her, everything she had ever wanted for herself: power, success, pride, money . . . God, she loved him and he was hers – all hers.

She put down her glass, propped the cigarette in the ashtray on the coffee-table and wrapped her arms round him. 'Come on, Benjy,' she purred. 'Don't you want to make me feel less lonely? Huh? Haven't you got a little present for your Sammikins? Or do I mean a *big* present? A lovely big *hot* present for Sam? Hmmm?'

He gazed down at her, his eyes intense. Then he unwrapped her arms and held them by the wrists. 'Sam,' he said, 'you must think I'm an idiot if I can't see what condition you're in.' His eyes flicked over the room. 'You've been up to your old tricks, haven't you? The champagne, the dancing . . . how much have you taken?'

Sam blinked at him, innocent and winsome as a child. 'I don't know what you mean,' she protested. 'I've just had a drink.

We've got thousands of bottles of the stuff – why can't I drink any when I'm feeling all alone?'

'Come on.' He wiped his hands over his face as though he were exhausted. 'Look at you. You can't stop chewing your lip. You're clearly high.' He sat down in a chair and looked up at her help-lessly. 'You know I hate that stuff. You know how much I hate you using it. Why do you think I want to make love to a woman whose head is on another planet?'

'Benjy!' She fell to her knees in front of him and clutched at the fronds of the white-fringed rug. 'I only took a little bit, just a teensy-weensy bit, because I was on my own.'

'That stupid bitch Becky gave it to you, didn't she?' He sighed. 'I can't blame her, I suppose. You'd find another way if she didn't.'

Sam rubbed her hands over his knees and along his thighs. She put her head on one side and blinked at him. 'I'm sorry. I won't do it again, I promise. This was the very last time. I mean it. Now . . . please can we go upstairs, Benjy? I need to feel that you still love me.'

For a moment she thought she'd won. He put out a hand to-wards her, then patted the side of her head. He shook his head. 'No, Sam, not today.'

Her mood changed instantly. 'Why not?' she shouted, her face contorting. 'Why the fuck not? All the fucking times I have to put up with it when *you* want it. All the times I have to lie there fucking suffering while you hump away, getting all the fun you need. And just one little time when I want something back it's no, Sam, not today. Well, why the hell not, Ben? That's what I want to know. Why the hell not?' She wanted to scream out, *are you planning to fuck someone else, you traitorous shit? I know you are!* But even her current recklessness wouldn't let her. She knew that if she said that aloud, it might make it real and she wasn't strong enough to face it yet.

There was a long pause. Her shouting seemed to hang in the air, vibrating there.

'I'm sorry you feel like that,' Ben said quietly, at last. 'I don't know what's wrong with you. You're a bitch to Emma and now you're a bitch to me.' He got up and walked out of the room, leaving her kneeling on the carpet, looking helplessly after him.

Chapter Sixteen

'You're a naughty girl, aren't you?' chided Jerry, when he called.

'Am I?' Fear clutched at Jane – Tom had told him. How could he?

'Fancy not telling me. You *are* wicked . . .'

'Well, I—'

'You usually warn me when Maggie comes to stay.'

Relief washed over her. Tom hadn't said. There was no way Jerry would have been able to stop himself mentioning it.

'This is rather odd,' he continued. 'She was down earlier in the summer and now she's back. Most out of character. I usually assume the coast will be clear for at least six months after she's been around and now I'm going to have to avoid poor old Rawlston until she's gone. When is she off?'

'Jerry, darling, she's been very ill . . .'

Instantly he was all solicitude. 'Poor dear! What's wrong? Can you say? Nothing serious, I hope. Oh, poor Maggie. Well, she's in the right place, you'll look after her. I can't think of anyone better—'

He has a good heart, Jane thought, when she put the phone down at last. Though he pretended to be brittle and shallow, he was not at all. He had suggested that she and Maggie come over for dinner in his little cottage but Jane had invited him to lunch instead, partly because she didn't think Maggie would want to go out, and partly because she feared he might invite Tom as well, and she didn't know how she would face him.

A few mornings after their dinner together, a polite but cool letter arrived from him, crisply written in a clear, neat hand, thanking her for a most enjoyable evening. He said nothing else beyond that he looked forward to seeing her again at some point in the future.

She spent a long time staring at it, imagining those square, workman-like hands holding a pen and producing this neat, compact writing. The black-inked letters seemed to hold in them the power and the delicacy she remembered.

What had made him so knowledgeable? she wondered. How many other women had he slept with? Who had taught him what he clearly knew so well?

'Love letters, Jane?' asked Maggie carelessly, coming into the kitchen, wrapping her long hair round her head with one hand.

Jane flushed and folded it away. 'Of course not. How are you?' Maggie's first days in the house had been characterized by her absence. She'd stayed in her room for hours on end, reading and sleeping. At dinner she still looked dozy and by the end would be yawning gigantically. 'I can't understand it,' she would say. 'I've never been so tired yet I'm sleeping all the time.'

It was, Jane hoped, part of the healing process, but it bothered her that Maggie's eyes were still dull and her sparkle had not returned, although she was physically well, showing no more effects of her operation that Jane could see. She wondered what she could do to amuse her, to stimulate her, but Maggie didn't seem in the least interested in getting away from Rawlston. Instead, she had taken to sitting with Alec in his room where they played computer games together – Jane could hear the electronic gunfire and explosions and the occasional whoop of triumph from one of them – or strolling out on walks.

'I'm fine,' she said. She pulled out a kitchen chair, sat down and put her face in her hands. Looking up, she was bleary-eyed. 'How long have I been asleep?' she said, yawning. She was wearing a soft green dress with a cherry-coloured cardigan over her shoulders. 'It's so hard to know what time it is here.'

'It's getting on,' said Jane, going the sink to wash salad, tucking her letter away in her pocket, 'but that's all right. I want you to rest. You need it.'

'It has been a hard term,' admitted Maggie. She poured herself a mug of coffee from the cafetière on the table. 'It gets harder every year – more admin, more marking, more pressure to get the students through.'

'But you still enjoy it, don't you?'

'Mmm.' Maggie sipped at her coffee.

Jane stood at the sink, her back to her sister, stripping stalks off spinach. 'Have you heard from Gregor at all?'

'Of course. He's fine, though so incredibly busy he's emailing me in the middle of the night, which is the only time he's got a free moment. Thank goodness for Alec's Internet connection. It keeps me in touch with the real world.'

Jane said nothing. Her world seemed real enough to her, but she didn't want to start Maggie off on a tirade. Instead she said, 'Jerry's coming for lunch.'

'Christ, is he? I might be out.'

'Come on, Maggie, give him a chance, he's not as bad as you think. He was genuinely upset to hear that you're not well.'

'What did you tell him?' demanded Maggie quickly. 'Did you tell him about the baby?'

'Of course not—'

'Good. Because I don't want anyone to know. I can't bear the sympathy and the sorrowful eyes and the gentle hugs.' Her voice was fierce.

'All right, all right . . . it's fine, I haven't told him. Only the children know.'

'Okay, then.' Maggie's temper subsided and she pulled the newspaper towards her to read.

Jane could see now that when she'd invited Maggie down it was with rosy visions of the two of them talking about things together as they walked through the woods, their minds in harmony for the first time, perhaps, in their lives. She'd thought of some kind of reconciliation, as though Maggie's broken heart had opened up, letting her in.

Of course, it hadn't happened. It was so hard for them to get close to each other, perhaps because they didn't have a reserve of shared memories. When Maggie was born, Jane was already at boarding school and they saw each other only in the holidays.

Jane could remember the curly-headed child eyeing her warily when she came into the house, taking a few days to get used to her, never really settling down with her. And the force of Maggie's personality meant that everything tended to revolve around her; their parents, startled by their unexpected late child, delighted in her and the starchy, rather strict childhood that Jane remembered was not what Maggie had. Their mother was a different person with each of them. No wonder they found it hard to bond.

But still, here she was, at Rawlston. And that, somehow, was progress.

Jerry came at twelve thirty, looking immaculate in a blazer, pressed shirt, perfectly creased trousers and a vivid orange and white silk scarf tucked about his neck.

'Hello, darling – goodness, you look like you're off to Henley,' Jane said. 'It's only casual – Maggie won't be dressing up.' She doubted Maggie would make any effort at all. 'Is that a cravat?'

'Not strictly. It's a gorgeous Hermès scarf I picked up for a song. I adore it so much I have to wear it whenever I can. Don't you love it?' Jerry held out a silken corner for her to admire.

'Beautiful. Now come into the kitchen and have a drink. Maggie's outside. Here's Lucy – she's helping me with lunch.'

'Slaving away as usual,' Lucy said, peeling potatoes.

'For a contribution to your Interrailing fund,' Jane reminded her. She hadn't wanted to leave Jerry and Maggie together while she cooked, so roping Lucy in seemed the obvious answer.

'Are you going travelling, Lulu?' Jerry asked, perching on the table while Jane poured him a gin and tonic.

'Yup. I'm off quite soon, actually. God, I can't wait. If I have to spend much more time at the Station Hotel, I'll go utterly barmy. Time to get some culture in, I'm such a barbarian. So it's off to Rome and Florence and Pisa and all that.'

'Ah! *La bell' Italia*!' Jerry cried. 'Oh, lucky, lucky you, to see it all for the first time. It's heaven, utter heaven. We must sit down and I'll tell you all the best places to go. I know some divine little galleries and one of the curators at the Uffizi is a special friend of mine – I'll talk to him and I'm sure he'll be delighted to give you a tour. There's no one in the world who knows more about the magnificent Titian. And there are so many lovely restaurants, you'll eat till you burst!'

'On ten pounds a day, I'm not so sure,' said Lucy. 'We're roughing it.'

'A few pounds in Italy can buy you a feast. Forget ghastly English food – overpriced rubbish. Think of fresh pasta, glowing tomatoes, a slab of matured Parmesan – what more do you need?' Jerry looked up to heaven with rapture.

'You obviously like Italy,' Lucy said drily and then, as Jerry took another breath to launch into a new rhapsody, 'You must tell me all about it *after* lunch.'

'Yes, let's go out and join Maggie,' Jane said, passing him a tall glass, a piece of lemon bobbing in the fizzing drink. 'We mustn't leave her alone too long.'

Maggie was on the terrace, gazing at the lawn. She'd let her long hair down, and was pulling her fingers idly through her curls.

'Ahoy!' called Jerry, as he approached her. 'Hello there, Maggie. How lovely to see you!'

Maggie turned to him, bemused. Her eyelids fluttered as Jerry bent to kiss her, as though his nearness made her want to flinch and she was concealing it with an effort. 'Hello, Jerry,' she said, and, to Jane's relief, smiled. 'How are you?'

'Super, super! Nothing much has changed with me – still worshipping at the shrine of earthly beauty in the form of my gallery.'

'Of course you are. How nice.'

They sat down in the other chairs. Maggie had pulled her feet up underneath her and was nestling back into hers, the wrought iron looking rather cold and unforgiving against her rounded form. Despite the warmth of the day she had wrapped her cardigan tightly about her. Long strands of her hair lay caught in the fuzzy wool fibres. 'Did you bring any more wine out, Jane?' Maggie gestured to her empty glass.

'Oh no, I didn't. Shall I go and get some?'

'That would be so kind.'

Jane went back into the kitchen where Lucy was roasting peppers under the grill. 'How's it going?' she asked, as her mother came in.

'Hum – not sure. Somehow I scent danger. No matter how charming Jerry tries to be, he's going to wind her up, I know it. I think this may have been a bad idea.' She collected the wine bottle from the fridge. 'Now, back to the fray . . .'

Lucy glanced up from watching the skins of her peppers turning brown under the gas jets and grinned. 'Good luck, Colonel. See you back in Blighty . . .'

But it seemed to be going quite well when Jane emerged back on to the terrace. Maggie and Jerry were chatting in low voices, and when she got closer, she was relieved to hear that it was the uncontentious subject of the garden. They were both admiring it – or, at least, Jerry was and Maggie was agreeing with him, as far as Jane could hear.

'What's so nice is to have some peace to enjoy it in,' Jerry exclaimed. 'Now, Jane,' he said, as she approached, 'let me take that wine. I'm just about ready to move on from the gin.'

It seemed that Jerry's good humour was having the opposite effect to the one he intended. No matter how chirpy he was, Maggie responded by sinking even deeper into herself and becoming more and more ferocious in her response to him. By the time they were ready to eat, and Alec and Lucy had joined them, even the most innocuous subject was ripe for conflict. Complimenting Lucy on the meal led to a discussion of food and how it was grown and sold – and while Maggie tried to begin political debates, Jerry would infuriate her by airily saying things like, 'Well, I'm sure the farmers are perfect darlings!' or 'I do adore peaches – I don't mind if they come from Israel on a plane. Lucky us, I say.'

Jane tried to steer the conversation into safe waters whenever she could but she could see that Maggie was spoiling for a fight. She wanted to argue and she was going to take the diametrically opposed position to Jerry's every time. And, of course, that wasn't hard because Jerry delighted in his frivolous, unabashedly conservative line. Lucy, following Jane's lead, tried to lighten the atmosphere, while Alec ate quickly and silently, then slipped away.

The weather was darkening and Maggie huddled even deeper into her cardigan, clutching her glass to her with both hands as though it was warming her somehow. She seemed pale and fragile and, when she wasn't talking, frowned to herself.

'Are you all right?' Jane asked. As far as she knew Maggie wasn't a great drinker but she was sloshing it back.

'I'm fine,' Maggie said, in a low voice. 'Just a bit of a headache, that's all. Really – nothing to worry about.'

'Now this is perfect,' Jerry said, oblivious to the women. 'That was delicious, Lucy. And here we are, enjoying a lovely day at this very fine house.' He looked up at Rawlston, looming above them, its windows reflecting blue-grey in the light. 'I think we should raise a toast to this wonderful place.' He lifted his glass. 'To Rawlston and Jane, and may she and all the other Fieldings, children, grandchildren *et al, ad infinitum*, et cetera, et cetera, live here happily for ever!' He swung his glass with a flourish, then took a large swig.

Maggie leant forward, her eyes suddenly alive. 'That's bloody typical! I can't believe I have to sit here and listen to it. I hate all this,' she said furiously, almost spitting. 'Why do we have to dig ourselves in so much? Why is it so necessary to make things comfortable and less frightening? It's ridiculous that we invest so much in stones and surnames. We should do away with it all – tribes and names and addresses and divisions, and all the bloody crap that comes with it, and just be who we are.'

Jerry blinked and said, in a tone of faint surprise, 'Oh. Well.'

'It makes me sick, that's all, seeing you here, celebrating your good fortune and delighting in shutting everyone else out – *planning* to keep everyone else out for good, if you can. Can't you see how wrong it is, how everything you believe in is for the good of the few and sod everyone else? Oh, I'm sure you think you're very holy as you go smugly off to your church and pray for the poor and sick and ill – just as long as they're kept out of your bloody way.'

Jane said, 'I think that's a bit harsh . . .'

Maggie turned on her swiftly. 'You're as bad as this sad excuse for a man – don't pretend you aren't.'

'What do you mean?'

'You stand for everything that's wrong with this society. Selfishness, division and privilege.'

'That's not fair – how can you say that? You don't know the first thing about my life!' Jane cried. 'Everything you say is based on your idea of how I live – you've never bothered to find out the reality. You're as bad, as prejudiced as anyone. You wouldn't dream of judging anyone else but me in the way you do, and you think you're allowed to because somehow the fact that I live in this house gives you permission to treat me and my friends like rubbish.'

'Oh, give me a break,' Maggie sneered. 'My heart bleeds for you. I can't bear another minute of listening to you both twittering about how gorgeous everything is. You know nothing about the real world, nothing about sadness, deprivation or *grief*.'

Jane gasped. She felt as though she'd been slapped in the face. Lucy stared at her aunt, her face grim. 'How can you say that, Mags?'

Maggie leapt to her feet, pushing her iron chair back across the terrace and, said almost hysterically, 'All of you can go to hell!' She turned on her heel and ran back into the house, leaving them watching after her.

Jerry left not long afterwards. The mood of the day was too altered for them to be able to continue. Everyone was shocked by Maggie's outburst, Jerry more than the others because he didn't know anything of the circumstances. 'How dare she?' he whispered, indignant on Jane's behalf, as he kissed her goodbye. 'What has *she* got to complain about? That's what I'd like to know.'

Jane said nothing and, after he'd gone, she went and sat for a long time in the kitchen garden, perching on an upturned box by the glass-house. She took Tom's letter out of her pocket and looked at it again. The experience she'd had with him that night haunted her. She'd been unable to think about it at first but now it was humming through her mind almost constantly. It had been so different from anything she'd experienced since Theo; the delight, all the sweeter for being so unexpected, had awakened her skin somehow. It affected the way she moved, the way she walked, the way she brushed her hair; everything bristled with an electrical charge that, instead of diminishing as she'd expected, was growing stronger.

When Maggie had said she didn't know anything about grief, Jane had felt deeply wounded, bitter with the injustice, and yet, now, looking about the garden and up at the house, breathing in the cool air, she suddenly felt that her sister was right – perhaps not completely right, but that she had pointed out something with an element of truth in it. Maggie was in the turmoil of fresh pain but she, Jane, had come through all that a long time ago. Her grief still existed and always would, but it was old now, ready to be let go. She'd never felt she could do it before it was the centre of her existence, the meaning of her life – but now her body was throbbing with something that she was beginning to remember and recognize. It was telling her that she was alive and that she must seize life at once, while she had the chance.

She decided, quite calmly and coolly, that she would go to Oxford and find Tom.

Bella could barely wait for Iain to be at work and the children at school so that she could boot up the computer and check her emails. There were no new messages but she tried not to be too disappointed. She mustn't rush things. She must take advantage of this breathing space to examine what she was doing and think everything through. After all, she thought, I'm not a giddy teenager. I'm a grown woman, married and with children. I can't afford to do anything stupid – much as I'd like to.

Instead she tried to concentrate on her work, doing some more cold-calling and researching more companies she could try to sell herself to. Then, on impulse, she dialled Nicky's office number. They hadn't spoken in ages. They'd meant to, of course, but time had drifted past. None of her friends had managed more than the occasional brisk, bouncy email, explaining that they were frantically busy but would be in touch soon for a real catch-up, that they couldn't wait to see her and they must arrange something. It never happened, of course.

'Nicky Morrison,' said a clipped, businesslike voice, when the phone was answered.

'Nicky, it's Bella. Is this a good time?'

Nicky's voice relaxed. 'Bells! How lovely. How are you? How's life in Ambridge?' Then she became contrite. 'I'm so sorry I haven't been down to see you. I really want to, it's just – well, time goes by and life is such a dash.'

'I know, I know. It's fine. Actually, I thought I might come to see you.'

'Really? That would be wonderful! When?'

'I'm not sure about dates, but quite soon. Can I confirm with you when I have a better idea?'

'Of course you can, darling. You know I'd cancel anything for you. Now, tell me about the house and the children and everything . . .'

When it came through, Ben's message was everything she'd hoped for, sending delightful shivers up her back and recalling their fierce intimacy. He was desperate to see her again, he wrote. When could she get away? She sent a reply at once.

God, it was all that and more. We must meet again as soon as possible. I think I can arrange a trip to London this week/next week. Could you do that? Just let me know what would suit you. Bxxxx

Off it went, winging its way to Ben's secret email account, digging her further in to this impossible, irresistible mess. Am I really sitting here, sending messages to my lover, arranging secret liaisons with him? It's awful! She didn't want to think like that. She didn't want to stand back and observe herself and start judging it all. Instead, it was far pleasanter to wallow in it, to push her reservations to the back of her mind, out of sight, and allow herself to enjoy it. I only have one life! she thought. Why shouldn't I grab what I can from it?

'I'm planning to go to London to see Nicky for an evening,' she said casually, after supper, to Iain. They were sitting under soft lamplight, music on the stereo, reading their books in companionable silence, the children upstairs in bed. It took an enormous effort to break into the quiet with her lie and it hung in the air, infecting the cosy domestic scene with its light poison.

Iain looked up. 'Are you, love? That sounds nice. You haven't seen her for a while, have you? When were you thinking?'

'Next week. Wednesday,' she said. It had been the night Ben had suggested. He had said he could get away then, that it would fit well with his work. 'I want to leave at about lunch-time, so I can look about before I meet Nicky. I'll stay the night, I should think. I can arrange for Trudy to come in and look after the children till you get home from work.'

'Fine,' said Iain. He looked benign and affable. 'It'll be nice for you to get away for a bit.'

She smiled at him, secretly disappointed. She'd hoped for some resistance for her to fight against, to get her blood up. His unwitting complicity in her betrayal was a nasty little worm crawling in her stomach. 'Yes,' she said, sadly.

'Don't go mad with the credit card,' he added. Which helped a little.

It was all arranged with very little effort. Perhaps she was good at this. Perhaps it was her real vocation – conducting a secret love affair, or perhaps, she corrected herself, she should call it her sexual liaison. But that sounded too cold and didn't encapsulate the fizzing warmth she felt when she thought about it.

The days crawled by but she didn't mind existing in her heightened state, enjoying the anticipation of the night with Ben that approached steadily, if slowly. She walked the children down the lane every day, their primary-coloured coats bright and incongruous against the dull greens and browns of the hedgerows and the fields. They were back at school now, and the summer colours were fading, replaced by the unmistakable signs of autumn. Along the lane, the brambles held dark blackberries among the thorns and the ground was thick with fallen leaves.

She took them down on the Monday morning, striding along with a walking stick Iain had made from a branch he found in the woods, as Katie and Christopher pedalled away on their bikes, pausing every now and then for her to catch up when they had something to shout or a new curiosity to show her.

'Car!' she called, as she heard an engine behind her. The children pulled in to the side of the lane and stopped. She climbed up on the muddy verge – the weekend had been cold and wet and there were oily, khaki puddles all the way down the lane. The grass was bedraggled, showing the dirt beneath like a bald patch under thinning hair. The Mini went slowly past, negotiating the slippery surface of the lane and the waterlogged potholes with care. Bella could see through the window that it was Emma Clarke. She waved and received a smile and a tight little wave in return. Then the car had passed the children, continuing its slow progress towards the main road.

I wonder where she's going, she thought. Poor girl. 'Come on, you two, we'd better get a move on,' she called to the children. 'You'll miss that bus.'

'I'm planning a treat for Emma when she gets back,' Ben said to Sam over supper. He had thawed towards her since their argument, unlike Emma, who had refused to speak to Sam at all after the dinner-table outburst and who had left that morning to stay with a friend in Cornwall. Sam hadn't been sorry to see her go. She didn't have time for a sulky girl when there were more pressing problems at hand. 'A treat, for her results.'

'Yeah?' said Sam, pushing a piece of calf's liver round and round her plate. 'Great.' Actually, Emma wasn't inspiring her with the kind of annoyance she would once have felt.

'Can you think of anything she'd enjoy? I'd like to do something special for her.'

'Um . . . not really. Don't have any idea what she'd like. A night at the opera? I dunno.' Emma's A-Level results – God, she'd never hear the end of them. What was all the fuss about? Every-

232

one knew that all the kids these days got As, and after the amount her education had cost, she had to do well. Thank goodness she was going a couple of hundred miles to Edinburgh, that's all. Moscow would have been better but Edinburgh would do.

'The opera. That's not a bad idea. She'd like that – something at the Royal Opera House, a night in London, a meal out.'

'Lovely,' said Sam, thinking how terrible it sounded. But she bit her tongue – she was still trying to mend fences with Ben. He was normal enough, but every time he looked at her, she felt as if she was being reprimanded for the other night and the champagne and the dancing and whatever it was she'd said, which obviously had been in the heat of the moment and not meant to be taken seriously. It was just – she couldn't mention it, couldn't say she hadn't really meant it, without reminding him of it all and she wanted him to forget it. Didn't he owe her that? She barely asked anything of him. Was it so bad to ask this?

'I meant to say, I'm away on Wednesday,' Ben said lightly.

Instantly, she was on the alert. 'Oh, yeah? Where?'

'London. I've got a meeting there in the afternoon and it'll probably go on late and end in a boozy dinner. That's what usually happens with the people at Janssen's.'

'Oh, right.' She looked down at the congealing sauce on the cold liver. Then said brightly, 'Why don't I come too? I need some things in London. We can have a nice time together.'

Ben's eyes were hooded and unreadable. 'If you want to, but you won't have much fun. I'm not going to be anywhere fancy – a Holiday Inn probably. Having me rolling in drunk at one-thirty isn't going to be much of a treat for you. I'd feel better if I didn't think you were waiting up for me. I might not even stay in a hotel. I might kip on a friend's floor.'

'Oh. Okay,' said Sam, something turning to steel inside her. It was exactly as she'd expected. All right, she thought grimly, if you want to play games, that's fine. Just fine.

The next day, she called the lodge. Bella answered quickly on the third ring.

'Hiya, how are ya?' Sam said cheerily. 'Listen, Ben's going away

233

this week and I'm going to be all on my own. Why don't you come up for a girly night on Wednesday? We can have some wine and watch a movie and do our nails or something.'

'That sounds lovely,' said Bella. 'It's just . . . I can't on Wednesday. I'm seeing my friend Nicky – did I tell you about her? Otherwise I'd love to. Can we make it another time?'

'Oh, yeah, yeah, of course. If you're already busy,' Sam said smoothly. 'I'll take a long bath and get an early night, then.'

I bet you're busy, she thought grimly, as she put the phone down. She sat, staring at it, a nasty, bitter taste in her mouth. Bella should have thought twice before she took Sam on. This wasn't going to be the walkover she so obviously expected. In the distance, the vacuum cleaner hummed irritatingly. That Trudy girl better not even try to talk to her today. She had a lot to think about.

Chapter Seventeen

Once she'd made the decision to go, Jane didn't stop to talk to anyone. She went straight to her room, picked up some things and walked out of the house. It was unlike her – she usually made sure everyone knew where she was going and when she'd be back – but some little thread in her had snapped and suddenly she didn't care about any of them, not at this moment.

She drove to Oxford on autopilot, hardly seeing the countryside, deposited the car in the stinking gloom of the multi-storey car park and marched through the meandering crowds on Queen Street to Tom's college. Would he be there? she wondered, as she approached the golden walls with their forbidding battlements, and the tiny gate guarded by a bowler-hatted porter. Her luck couldn't hold, could it? First, he'd found her in the quad that day, then he'd been in his little garret when she'd come knocking. It was too much to hope that he'd be in this time, wasn't it?

She passed the porter unchallenged, her confident stride convincing him she was no tourist but a legitimate visitor, and went directly to Tom's room.

Of course, of course, she thought, when she knocked and there was no reply. She wondered what she should do. She didn't want to lose this reckless mood of liberation and was worried that it would fade away, and with it her courage, but who could tell how long Tom would be away and when he would return?

She left the college, slipping out by the back gate, and walked into town. She went to the Ashmolean and spent an hour among the pictures, then went into the same tea room on the High where she and Tom had gone that afternoon, almost as though she hoped to find him there, but there was no sign of him among the shoppers enjoying their afternoon tea. She paid, went outside and headed back to the college, her breath short when she imagined him answering his door. How would he feel at seeing her again? Would he be angry with her behaviour that morning? It had been bad, of course, but she'd been shocked and confused by what had happened, thrown into a state of disarray. She hoped he'd forgive her.

His door remained resolutely unanswered when she knocked again, breathless from the climb up the narrow wooden staircase. There was nothing for it. She sat down to wait.

Pounding footsteps coming up the stairs made Jane leap to her feet, suddenly nervous. A moment later, Tom appeared at the top, looking unbearably fresh and young in jeans and a red shirt. He stopped short when he saw her and stared, unsmiling.

'Hello,' she said. 'I'm sorry. About the other morning. It was terrible of me. I've regretted it ever since.' She stopped short, unsure what more to add or if there was any point before she knew whether or not he had forgiven her.

There was a long pause before he said, 'You'd better come in.'

'I can't pretend I wasn't hurt,' he said, as he made her coffee. She didn't really want any but it seemed rude to refuse. 'You were very cold.'

'I know. I didn't mean to be cold – I didn't *feel* cold – but I can see how it came across that way.'

Tom sat down opposite and leant forward towards her earnestly. 'Didn't it mean anything to you at all?'

'Oh, Tom . . . that was the problem. I don't know how to explain it you – it meant too much in a way. I wasn't at all prepared for it and you must understand that my life has been very . . . *quiet* for a long time. It was a shock to my system.'

'So why are you here now?'

'I've had a chance to think about things. And to feel things. Realize them. I don't know what I want but I'm beginning to understand that I can't be afraid of things happening. Do you see what I mean? I've resisted change and the outside world for so long, it's difficult for me to start accepting it. But I want to, I do.'

'Am I part of that?'

She reddened. 'I'm not sure what this is. We're such different people, so far apart in so many ways. It's probably quicker to list what's similar about us than what's different. But I do know that I liked what happened between us . . .' It was an effort to get the words out. 'Very much. I liked it very much.' She had stared at the carpet as she said the last bit, but now she risked a glance upwards to see how he'd responded. His face was still impassive. She wasn't sure if he was about to spit with fury and order her out, or burst out laughing at her nerve.

She felt foolish. Why would he be interested in what she had to say? He'd probably been off with pretty undergraduates all day, enjoying the company of women his own age without all the wrinkles, grey hair, sulky children and baggage that she had. She was about to get up and go when he said, 'Well, then, if you liked it and I liked it . . . what's standing in our way?'

A single bed! she thought, in mock horror. When had she last made love in a single bed? Some time in the late seventies, perhaps? She was crushed against the cool plaster of the wall on one side, and the damp heat of Tom's body on the other, but it wasn't uncomfortable. In fact, she liked it, the way their bodies were pushed so tightly together. From the window over the desk she could see the opposite roof of the quad silhouetted against the night sky. Tom was nestling into her neck, a hand moving lazily up and down her arm, smoothing her skin.

'It's late,' she said. 'I ought to go home.'

'Why?' he said, his voice muffled.

'Why? Because I have to. They'll be wondering where I am.'

'They're all grown-up, aren't they?' She could see every hair in his brows, the dark dotting of stubble coming through on his cheeks, the glint of light along the ridge of his nose. 'Why do you have to go back?'

She digested this for a moment, and tried to imagine them all at home: Alec was probably slumped in front of the television with a can of beer; Lucy heading off on another shift or in her room. Maggie . . . well, she couldn't imagine. Sleeping, perhaps. Spoiling for a fight. Walking about, hating everything. Poor Maggie, she thought. Her own luxurious, sensuous happiness made her feel a fresh wave of sorrow for her sister. She, Jane, had so much and Maggie was afraid that she'd never have that most primitive, basic, natural experience of being a parent. No wonder she was angry and bitter and lashing out.

'I suppose I ought to make dinner,' she said lamely.

Tom burst out laughing, his chest shaking against hers.

'Make dinner?' His tone was scandalized. 'Oh, please. Let them make their own dinner, for God's sake. Do you really want to leave me here and go and make spaghetti for some thankless kids?'

'You're right.'

He nuzzled into her ear and kissed it. 'Stay here with me,' he murmured. 'Stay the night.'

'I can't do that . . . I must phone home at least.'

'Jane.' He pulled back and looked at her solemnly. 'Stop it. Stop thinking about them. Think about yourself. We can call later, if you like. But let's just forget about them right now, okay? I want you all to myself . . .'

They got up at eleven and went out for dinner, staying as late as the waiters would let them, talking and drinking. Then they went back to Tom's room and slept wrapped round each other in the tiny bed. The next morning was bright and clear and Jane felt ebullient with energy and possibility as she showered in the little bathroom shared by three rooms along Tom's corridor.

'You're staying with me today, aren't you?' said Tom, anxiously. 'Don't go home yet. Let's go and get breakfast together instead.'

They went to the Queen's Lane Coffee House, then walked to the Botanic Garden, talking all the time. There was so much to say to each other. The only thing that stopped them was when Tom pulled her under the willow by the river and kissed her hard and long. Then they hurried back to his room in case they disgraced themselves in public. The afternoon melted away in the quiet, passionate privacy of his room, and it was evening again before they thought about rousing themselves.

'This is very seductive,' Jane said, tucking the sheet round her chest.

'Why, thank you.'

'Oh! You, of course, you're very seductive . . . but I mean this life. It's so careless. There's nothing you have to do.'

He shrugged. 'This is being a student who doesn't have to work in the vacation. I do enough studying to get by and the rest of my time is my own.'

'It's wonderful,' Jane said. She reached out a hand and ran it through his hair. 'But I can't stay in this dreamland for ever. I have to get home – they haven't heard from me since yesterday.'

'Call them.' He gestured towards the phone. 'Call them and stay here.'

'No.' She didn't want to tarnish this place that contained just the two of them by bringing home into it in any way. 'No. I must go.' He protested, but she reached for her clothes anyway.

She pulled the car to a stop in the darkness and sat looking up at the house. It was so familiar to her but she was seeing it through new eyes, this huge, beautiful place with its graceful windows. *Do I really live here? How did I come to live in such a place?* It was a path her life had taken, leading to this house. For a long time it had felt like the end of the road. Now she wondered if something lay beyond it, after it. *It was never really mine, after all. It never will be mine, no matter how much I want it to be. We're always just passing through these places and leaving them to the future.*

The front door swung open suddenly, making a patch of gold on the drive where the hall light glowed. A figure came running out and she saw it was Maggie, coming swiftly over the gravel towards her. She opened the car door as Maggie reached her. Her pale face looked in. 'Jane! You're back, thank God! We've been so worried.'

'Have you?'

'Of course! Why didn't you ring us?'

'Is that Mum?' It was Lucy calling from the hall and then she, too, was coming across the gravel. 'Mum, where the hell were you?'

Jane got out of the car as her sister and daughter stared at her with a mixture of accusation and concern. 'I'm touched by my reception, I must say.'

'We had no idea where you were.' Lucy's voice rose indignantly. 'You could have said you were leaving!'

They went in, Jane refusing to answer their questions, remaining firmly silent under the barrage of interrogation. In the kitchen, she filled the kettle to make herself some tea. Alec came in and joined in the general chorus of demanding to know where she had been.

Jane sat down and looked their faces. Behind the insistence and the noise, she could see something else, something that looked like fear. In her children's eyes there was a kind of bewildered anxiety that their mother, their touchstone, the one who was always there providing for them, caring for them, could take off and leave with no explanation. And in Maggie's face she saw something like guilt.

'I needed to get away, that's all. You're all adults. You can all take care of yourselves. I don't stop any of you doing what you want, so I don't see why you can't accord me the same privilege.' She sounded insouciant. It made her laugh inside to remember her nervousness in Tom's room, her insistence that she ought to get home to cook dinner. She was hiding all that very well now.

'You could have told us,' Lucy burst out. 'We always let you know when we're staying away.'

'Where were you, Mum?' Alec asked. He was knotting his fingers together. 'Where did you go?'

'I stayed with a friend,' she announced. That was all she was going to tell them.

'Well, it wasn't Jerry,' Maggie said. 'We called him at once. He was very worried too. You've had us all in a state.'

Jane gave her a hard, direct stare. Maggie dropped her eyes. Jane said, 'It's nice to know I was so missed. I had no idea you'd all be so concerned.'

They were all rather cowed by this unexpected Jane, this self-possessed, cool, unrepentant Jane, who had a firm idea of herself and an aura of energy around her.

Lucy made a late supper and they sat together in the kitchen and ate it, talking mutedly and avoiding the subject of Jane's absence. At eleven o'clock Jane excused herself and went up to bed, leaving the others in the kitchen to make what they could of her odd behaviour.

Her bed felt too large and cold after Tom's narrow single. She took a pillow from other side and clutched it to her, holding it tightly as she went to sleep.

She was first up as usual. She liked that: the peace of the kitchen in the earliest part of the morning when there was time to think and still so many possibilities in the day. There was no sign of anyone else coming downstairs when she heard a knock at the kitchen door. When she answered it, she found Bella Balfour, rosy cheeked and bright-eyed, on her doorstep.

'Hello! I hope you don't my coming round so early. I've just walked down the lane with the children and I thought I'd call on you, as I was out and about.'

'Not at all.' Jane stepped aside to allow her into the kitchen. 'There's some fresh coffee if you'd like some.'

'Lovely.' Bella took her coat off. 'It's really turning to autumn now, isn't it? I've not noticed it for so long, but you can't help it, living here, can you?' She sat down where Jane gestured. 'How are you?'

'I'm fine. My sister is staying at the moment. You might meet her if she comes down. And Lucy, my daughter – did you see her at the party? Goodness, that seems a long time ago, doesn't it? She's about to go Interrailing. My son is here too. So I'm keeping busy.'

'Oh. Well, perhaps you're too busy for this . . . It's just, I was going to ask a favour . . .' Bella frowned.

'What favour is that?'

'I'm going to London tomorrow for the night – to see a friend – and I thought that Trudy O'Reilly would be able to babysit. But she says she can't so I wondered if you'd mind having the children up here for a couple of hours after school, just till Iain gets home. They won't be any trouble, I promise.'

Jane smiled. 'It would be a pleasure. We'd love to have them.'

A wave of relief passed over Bella's face and she grinned broadly. Her eyes seemed to sparkle even more. 'That's fantastic, thank you so much.'

'Just tell them to come up when they get back from school. I'll be here. Would they like biscuits, do you think? Silly question, of course they would.' She poured out some coffee and pushed the cup towards Bella with the milk jug. 'But tell me how you are. You look very well.' In fact, the other woman looked transformed from the miserable creature who'd opened the door of the lodge to her all those weeks ago. 'Perhaps country life agrees with you after all – or is it the prospect of getting back to London?'

'No, no . . . I like it here. I never thought I would. But I do.'

'It helps having a friend, I suppose.' Bella looked puzzled so Jane added, 'Mrs Clarke.'

Bella's gaze moved away. 'Oh. Yes. Sam.'

Jane said nothing but wondered why her tone sounded less than enthusiastic.

'I really appreciate you looking after the children,' Bella said, her voice lively again. 'They won't be any trouble. I promise.'

She stayed chatting for half an hour, then she said she had to be going. Jane was sorry: she was good company, animated and funny. She had a tendency to talk too fast and say too much but was mostly amusing, so it didn't matter.

'You must come again,' Jane said, as Bella took her leave. 'I mean it.' She felt that they could be friends, if they had time to learn each other.

'I will. And thank you again,' said Bella, then headed off down the steps and strode round the house to the lane.

'Who was that?' Maggie asked, coming in to see Jane shutting the back door.

'Bella Balfour. She lives in the lodge.'

'Bella Balfour? She sounds like a heroine in Sir Walter Scott.' Maggie went to the Aga and leant against the warm rail, wrapping her fingers round it. 'Jane . . . there's something I want to ask you.'

'Yes?' Jane sat down.

Maggie stared at her feet, then took a breath and looked up. 'Was it me? Did you go away because of what I said?' There was a pause, and then she added in a rush, 'Because I know it was dreadful of me, unforgivable. I can't believe I said such an awful thing, that you didn't know what grief was, as if you hadn't suffered a million times more than me when Theo died. I don't know how I could have said it.'

'It's all right. Really.'

'No. It's not all right.' Maggie's expression was anguished. 'I'm not such a fool that I don't know what I've been like. And I know very well that I've refused to let you have any feelings at all. I've always brushed them aside. Made fun of them, in a way. Because I knew you would always let me, and not complain.' She began to pace back and forth along the short length of the Aga rail. 'I've always been testing you, I suppose, seeing how long you'd stick around, punishing you for not being there when I was little. In a way, I was trying to see what would make you turn round and say, Go to hell. And I think I got there. I think you went away because of me. And I feel absolutely bloody about it.'

She stood still and looked Jane straight in the eye. 'I want to say sorry. That's all.'

Jane was silenced. Never in their lives before had Maggie apologized to her. Did I leave because of Maggie? she wondered. Did I fly off to Tom because of her? She realized that, in a way, she had. Maggie had given her permission, set her free, when she had said that poisonous thing – it had been a release.

Maggie sat down. She spoke again, more quietly now. 'I don't know why I've always felt so angry with you. Perhaps it was because life seemed so easy for you. You seemed to forge on ahead as though you knew exactly where you were going, getting through everything with no trouble at all, as though you were in possession of some secret of success that I couldn't share. You seemed to take all the luck in the world and leave none for me.'

'But you . . .' Jane was baffled. Her mind was flooded with memories. 'You're so clever, you went to university, you had ambitions, you did exciting things . . .'

Maggie smiled. 'It's strange what we see when we look at other people's lives, isn't it? They always seem to know something we don't, to have some recipe for living that's a little better than our own. I've envied so much about you, from your children to your cooking. When Theo died, it was so awful. I wanted to come to you then and offer you comfort, but I didn't know how to. I thought I wouldn't have anything to give you. You'd tried to mother me a little when we were growing up and I'd hated it – you remember how vicious I was. So how could I try to mother you? Besides, I thought we were too different. I came to believe that we were almost of different tribes.' She laughed, a little bitterly. 'And then widowhood seemed to suit you so well! Suffering and saintly, with your good works and your village committees and your garden. It was the kind of image of womanhood I'd worked so hard to change. You became my anathema, my opposite. If you liked something I didn't, and vice versa.' She paused, and glanced up at her sister with something almost like timidity. 'So that's why I've come to say sorry. Because I've been foul to you, and it's all been about myself and my own inadequacies and nothing to do with you at all. Can you forgive me?'

'Oh, Maggie.' Jane got unsteadily to her feet and went to her. Maggie stood up and they embraced, properly, hugging each other tightly. 'Of course . . . of course.'

Bella spent the whole morning in the bathroom, taking her time. First, a long, luxurious bath in scented water – she had bought some rose and geranium oil specially – with a face mask and a hair treatment. Then she scrubbed every inch of her body, soaped all over and shaved her legs and underarms. After she was thoroughly clean and rinsed, she dried herself, applied soft white lotion all over and rubbed it in.

It was a bit silly, getting ready like this when she wouldn't see him for ten or more hours, but she wanted to do it. It was part of the pleasure, these elaborate preparations. When had she last done this for Iain? When had he last cared?

She drove to the station. Iain would pick up the car this evening and drive himself to the station in the morning and it would be here waiting for her again tomorrow. Who would she be tomorrow? Someone entirely different?

The train journey into Paddington was smooth and stress-free. She had a seat and a book, and when she was too excited to follow the words she stared out of the window at the scenery rolling by, imagining. The train disgorged all its passengers and she was carried along in the spillage as they headed for the underground. It was only early afternoon – she had hours before she met Nicky at her club. She took the tube to Oxford Street and walked down it, looking in the shops. She'd barely been away from London for half a year, but already it felt as though it had moved on without her. Had it always been so frantic, so busy? So obsessed with selling things to the hordes of people wandering up and down outside the shopfronts? Perhaps I'm really a country bumpkin now, she thought. But actually she felt apart from all of it, from the office workers dashing out to shop, tourists staring and house-wives going to John Lewis. I'm going to meet my lover. We're going to make love, she thought. Have you done that? she mentally asked a passing woman, who hurried by with a set expression. Or you? to a slinky Italian girl. Or any of you? Today I'm special. Today, you should all want to be lucky me.

She went into Selfridges, lingered in the food hall, inspected lipsticks in the cosmetics department and browsed the leather goods. She felt bigger than all this, where usually she felt small and poor and cheap. It was what Ben did for her, she assumed: he must give her spirit and courage. The escalator took her up to the lingerie department and she spent a long time looking – something she never usually did: she usually dashed in to find the plain white cotton and dashed out – then bought an outrageously expensive matching set of bra and knickers called 'Boudoir Chic'. Then, satisfied, she walked to Soho to meet Nicky.

'You look different, darling. This country air must agree with you.' Nicky lit a cigarette and gazed at her appraisingly. 'You're really . . . glowy.'

'Am I?' Bella said, pleased.

'Yes, you bloody are. Makes me sick.' Nicky poured her some

wine. 'Now, what's the plan for tonight? Where shall we go, what shall we do? I've made up the sofa-bed for you, the world's our oyster.'

'Ah. Well. I didn't exactly tell you everything on the phone. I'm sorry to put you to the trouble of making up the sofa-bed but I won't be needing it. I'm staying somewhere else. In fact, I'm heading off at ten.'

Nicky blinked, surprised. 'Oh. Ten? Are you going home?'

'Um . . . no.'

'Then where? Who are you meeting?' demanded Nicky. 'Have you got a better friend lined up?'

'Not a friend, exactly . . .'

Nicky gasped. 'Ooh – are you a dirty stopout? Are you? Is there something you're not telling me? There is, isn't there? What is it?'

'All right, I'll tell.'

When she'd finished, Nicky's eyes were wide and her expression startled. 'You're having an affair?' she said disbelievingly.

'Well, if you can call one afternoon and then tonight an affair . . .'

'Bloody hell, Bella, do you know what you're doing?'

'I . . .' She was surprised and taken aback. She'd imagined that Nicky would be thrilled by her spicy gossip, giggly and complicit.

'Because you're playing with fire, that's all. And I hope you know what you're getting in to.'

'I didn't think you liked Iain – I thought you'd be pleased.'

Nicky sat back and took a slug of her wine. 'There's a difference between thinking that you and Iain are not the ideal couple and egging you on to sleep with some other woman's husband.'

'But he . . . she and he . . .'

'Not going well, is it? They don't understand each other? Of course not. Look – what you do is your own business and I'm not going to criticize. I'm your friend. But I have to tell you that, in my experience, getting yourself involved in two complicated situations at the same time is bad. You want to leave Iain? Leave him. Then have the affair. But your judgement is all skewed by this fantastic sex you're having. You don't know what you're doing. You might make the wrong choices. Look, I may be wrong.

246

I hope I am. Maybe it's a lovely little interlude for both of you, and you'll end up going back to your marriages refreshed and sorted out and all the happier for it. And no one will be any the wiser.' Nicky sighed. 'God, I'm not exactly the voice of wisdom. And I don't know why I'm bothering – you'll go ahead and do what you want anyway. You won't be able to help yourself. I've been there, darling.' She shook her head.

'I – I want to do the right thing,' said Bella, faltering, feeling stupid.

'Yeah. We all do. Look, let's settle back and have a good old natter. I bet you're dying to talk about it – it must have been all bottling up down there in Arcadia. What's the wife like?'

Bella left Nicky at a quarter to ten. She felt better. Nicky had let her talk obsessively about the whole situation for three hours, never looking less than fascinated, asking all the right questions, saying what Bella wanted to hear. She understood the duties of a friend. When they came to part, she kissed Bella's cheek and said, 'Have a good time, darling. You deserve a bit of fun in your life. Just watch out, all right? Adultery is like murder – very hard to commit well and very hard to hide.'

Bella smiled, kissed her back and left her at the entrance to the underground. She took a taxi, feeling urbane and sophisticated as she flagged it down and gave the name of Ben's hotel. In the cab, she watched the sodium-lit city pass by, the familiar landmarks bleached white by beams of light trained on them. She rubbed her nylon legs together and felt the scratch of her unfamiliar lace underwear which she'd changed into in the ladies'.

She paid the cabbie at the door, which a uniformed doorman opened for her, and went to the desk of the bright reception area where people milled with bags, arriving and leaving.

'Ben Clarke, please. He's expecting me,' she said smoothly, trying to sound calm.

'Ah, yes, madam. Room six nine two.' The receptionist barely looked at her. 'The lifts are through the lobby. Floor six.'

'Thank you.' She walked carefully across clacking tiles to the lifts. Inside, the walls were mirrors and she could see her face, now looking a little frightened in the tinted glass, as the lift whisked her to the sixth floor. She found the door easily and stood outside, nerves tingling all over, stomach churning with excitement. Then she knocked and heard a gruff 'Yes?'.

'Ben, it's me,' she said, in a low voice, as though someone were about to hear her.

'Come in.'

She opened the heavy door slowly to darkness. Blinking, she tried to make out what lay beyond the little hallway. 'Are you there?' she said, into the blackness.

'Come in.' His voice was soft and low.

She stepped inside and let the door close behind her. Advancing into the dark, she put one hand against the wall to steady herself. 'Ben,' she said, with a laugh, 'come on . . . where are you?'

There was no reply. She thought she could hear his breathing but perhaps it was only her own. She took several steps forward, wondering if she was in the room proper yet. 'Ben . . . where are you?'

Suddenly she sensed him very close, then a hand touched her shoulder and she was pulled into his warm body, feeling his heat through his clothes. She gasped but her mouth was stopped by a kiss. Disoriented by the dark, she was dizzy and heady with excitement, by the displacement of having this invisible, strong man invading her so intensely with his kiss and his hands. He pulled at her jacket, forced it over her arms and discarded it. She felt as though she might fall over and that it was only his embrace that kept her upright. Then he was moving her, pushing her legs with his as though they were in an untidy waltz, and she felt the edge of the bed at her knees. His mouth left hers, and his face moved to her chest, burying itself in the softness of her top, in the valley between her breasts. His fingers were on the buttons, busy tweaking at them, opening them until her shirt was pulled apart. She could feel her breasts exposed, the new bra pushing them upwards so that half globes emerged ripely from the lace and silk cups. As he kissed them, he groaned so yearningly that her stomach somersaulted with desire.

He pushed her back on to the bed and lay on top of her, crushing her with his massive frame, and they kissed wildly. She didn't know how long it lasted, only that she couldn't wait any longer for him. She could feel him hard against her thigh and tried to fumble with his belt while the other hand pulled his head tightly to hers so that she wouldn't lose an instant of his mouth. He pushed her hand away and deftly undid the belt himself.

Dark is good, she thought with sudden clarity. It hid all those clumsy moments as clothes came off, shirts were unbuttoned, trousers shuffled down legs or tights rolled away. Ben moved to one side and for a moment was gone, then she felt the delicious softness of his skin and the delicate roughness of his chest hair. It took her breath away.

It felt as though it were impossible to be too close to each other; she wanted to absorb him and be absorbed by him. She wanted them to be one thing. When – it felt so long and yet they must have been together only a few minutes – he finally entered her, the sensation was so incredible that she cried out. She had forgotten that sex could feel like this, that it could lift someone out of themselves and into another place of extended, extraordinary pleasure. He moved inside her and it felt as though at last they had found each other, two pieces made to fit exactly together. She could think of nothing but the delight in each sensation until, finally, it built up to such a pitch that she couldn't bear it any more and it was over in a finish so intense that, for a moment, she felt as though she'd vanished.

They got up and put on the white towelling robes from the bathroom. Ben suggested that they order some food, and Bella realized she was starving. He phoned for some dinner, then opened the bottle of champagne he found in the mini bar. Now that the lights were on, Bella could see that they were in a typical town hotel room: insulated, luxurious, characterless. The bed was a mess, with covers and pillows everywhere, and their clothes were scattered about it on the floor.

'Look at us,' Bella said, her champagne in one hand. 'Just what you'd expect an adulterers' hotel room to look like.'

'Or anyone who's got some excitement in their lives,' Ben said, coming out of the bathroom.

A waiter brought them a trolley of food and set it out on the table, ignoring their state of undress and the messy bed. Ben tipped him a note as he left. Then, ravenous, they fell on the food. It was standard hotel fare but the appetite they'd worked up made it delicious. Then they lay on the bed eating chocolate raisins, also from the minibar, and sipping the champagne.

'Is Iain likely to phone Nicky to see if you're there?' Ben asked idly.

Bella shook her head. 'He doesn't much like the phone. And he's never called Nicky in his life – they don't really get on. I imagine he's in bed by now. How about Sam? Does she know where you are?'

'No. I told her I was at a hotel but not which one.'

'Would she try to find out?'

He looked uncomfortable. 'She might. She's what you'd call a bit paranoid. She likes to check up on me. And she takes the odd look round my office, I think. Sometimes I find a hair on my computer keyboard, or a pile of paper moved to the other side of the desk. I think she needs to keep tabs on what's going on.'

'God,' said Bella, fascinated. 'Doesn't it bother you?'

Ben shrugged. 'I know how to keep things secret if I need to.'

'It's a strange state for a marriage to be in.'

'I don't think either of us has the ideal relationship, do we?'

'You could be right.' She smiled at him. 'I didn't want to go to Rawlston at first, you know. I really didn't want to leave London, my life here, everything I knew. But now I'm glad I did. Now I feel like it happened for a reason.'

'Maybe,' he said.

She rolled on to her back and stared up at the ceiling. 'What do you think will happen to us?'

'What do you mean?'

'Here we are, having sex in hotel rooms, deceiving our wife and husband so we can be together. It should be seedy. I should feel ashamed. But I love it. I want to do it again and I can't imagine *not* wanting to do it again.' She looked at him. He was propped on an

250

elbow, regarding at her. 'What about you? Don't you want to do it again?'

He didn't say anything for a moment and then sighed. 'Of course I do. And I don't let anything stand in the way of what I want. But I can't make any promises at this point, Bella. You're starry-eyed.' He held up his hand as she started to protest. 'I only say that because I am too. I could hardly wait for tonight. You could probably tell – I've had a hard-on all day, for Christ's sake. But a lot of people are involved and I want to be careful. I don't intend to give up on my marriage quite yet and I don't think you do either. I know it's wonderful to think we've found the answer to all our problems in each other but I have to say I'm an old hand at this, with one divorce behind me already, and I can tell you that we haven't. We've just found something to take our minds off them – but it's quite possibly the way to a whole raft of unpleasant new ones. All I'm saying is, don't fall in love with me yet, Bella Balfour. Hold back a little. Let's give each other breathing space.'

'Of course,' she said, staring back at the ceiling. She ought to feel affronted, she thought, but she didn't. They had to go through this – the wary stage where they seemed to hold back – but she felt sure, in her heart, that this was something special. That kind of love-making didn't come along every day – perhaps once or twice in a lifetime for the lucky ones. It meant something, *signified* something. She couldn't imagine giving it up and knew she would choose it over almost anything else in her life. Except the children, of course.

Ben lay down next to her. 'We've finished the booze. Do you want some more?'

'Yes,' she said. 'More. I want to get drunk with you.'

He sighed. 'We'll have to hide this. Do you think you can do that? If we have to meet socially, as two families?'

'I know I can.'

'Sam's smart,' he warned. 'Sharper than you'd give her credit for.'

Bella grinned. 'I'm smarter.'

He laughed. 'Okay. I believe you. To be honest, I don't think we have a choice.'

They drank more wine and talked and laughed until some late hour, then made slow, agonizingly delicious love that didn't end until a shaft of grey daylight came through the curtains and they fell finally into a deep sleep.

Bella woke with one of Ben's arms heavy across her. When she'd wakened him, they were both bleary-eyed with lack of sleep but still vibrant with the charge that being together gave them. They had breakfast downstairs in the hotel dining room – Ben collected her fruit, yoghurt and muesli from the buffet with some strong coffee – and read the papers together. When it was time to leave, he walked her to the lobby and kissed her softly on the lips. 'Have a good trip home,' he said gently. 'I'll call you soon.' He turned to go.

'Ben . . .' she called. He turned and she had the mad impulse to say, 'I love you' but she quelled it and said instead, 'Thanks.'

He grinned. 'You are *very* welcome.'

''Bye.'

''Bye, Annabella.'

Chapter Eighteen

Sam was woken in the most revolting way possible, with a slavering tongue all over her face and meaty breath blasted into her nose. 'What the fuck?' she said, pushing away whatever it was.

'Sorry. Get down, Jason!' said Trudy's voice.

Sam opened her eyes and saw the girl looking down at her through her thick bottle-glass lenses. Her dog stood panting right on the same level as Sam's face, a long pink tongue hanging from the side of its mouth.

'You all right, Mrs Clarke?' she asked.

'I'm fine. Just get the bloody dog away from me.' She rubbed at the drool on her cheeks. 'What's he doing in here anyway? I told you he stays outside.'

'You look like you've been sleeping here on the sofa.' Trudy looked down significantly at the empty bottle, the stained wineglass, an overflowing ashtray, the bits of drug residue that would probably mean nothing to her.

'So what if I have? It's my house, isn't it?' she said irritably. She pulled herself upright and blinked. Her eyes felt dry and gritty.

'Mr Clarke not here?'

'No, Mr Clarke is not here,' she snapped. 'For all that it's your business.' She knew Trudy was thick but sometimes she got the uncomfortable feeling that the girl was laughing at her. 'Haven't you got work to be getting on with?'

'I was going to ask you if you wanted the bedrooms doing,' said Trudy, unperturbed. 'Is your daughter coming back?'

'She's not my bloody daughter, and I don't know. I think she's back tomorrow or something. Oh, look, just do the kitchen and the bathrooms. Wait! On second thoughts, clean the bedrooms too. Okay?' Even the simplest decisions were complex and difficult.

'Right you are, Mrs Clarke. What about this stuff?' She gestured at the detritus of Sam's night.

'Forget it. Leave it. I'll do it.'

Sam took the dirty things through to the kitchen. She could hear Trudy climbing the stairs slowly and heavily, hauling the vacuum cleaner after her. It had been a difficult night. She'd felt so impotent. Ben had been away before – lots of times – and perhaps the fact that Bella was away too was just a coincidence, but Ben's phone had been off all night. She'd tried it last at three o'clock in the morning – surely he would be back from his dinner by then – but it had clicked straight to his answer machine and she'd heard it with a slump of depression. At some time, she'd gone to sleep. Without making it upstairs.

She put the things in the dishwasher. It was full of clean crockery but, sod it, Trudy could sort it out. Let her earn her money. Running the tap at the sink, she splashed her face with cold water and stood dripping, staring out over the garden. What was she going to do now? Something in her felt defeated, but she wasn't going to let that happen. What would she do? What would she do if Ben really was being unfaithful to her? More than anything, she wanted to be wrong about it. She wanted to run to him and tell him her fears and have him laugh and tell her not to be so stupid.

The truth was, she was frightened and that wasn't a feeling she was used to. But if Ben was cheating on her, it meant her spell was broken and she couldn't understand why that should be. She was still thin, still beautiful, still perfect-looking. She was available to him whenever he wanted. What more could she do, for God's sake? And if he was going to choose that other woman over her – the fatter, plainer, unpolished woman – how could she even begin to understand it? It didn't make sense! It broke the rules. It wasn't fair.

I won't be frightened, Sam told herself sternly. I won't. I'll be angry. I've got every damn right. I'm his *wife*. He can't do this to me.

She went quickly to Ben's study and opened his email. Still nothing. There was only one explanation: he had another email account. How on earth could she find it? He would be sure to have out-thought her. She slammed her fist on the desk and swore loudly. To her relief, she felt a roll of anger in her gut. She understood anger – it wasn't like fear. If she got angry she would be powerful. Come on, she urged herself.

She got up, put on her coat and went outside to walk up and down the garden, puffing at a cigarette.

Why did I ever trust her? She's a fucking Judas. But how am I going to see them together? How am I going to catch them? And what will I do then?

There was no point in stalking Ben. He'd spot her a mile off. It would mean hiring a car, wearing a wig, lurking in lanes. No, that was stupid. And as for calling him to check up – he always had a million excuses why he couldn't be contacted, most of them valid. His secretary would tell her he was in a meeting and he probably was, damn it. As for checking pockets and credit-card bills – she did, of course, but never found anything. Ben was far too smart for that. She knew because he'd been the same when they were trying to conceal their activities from Aileen. If it had been up to Ben, his wife would never have found out about the affair. They'd probably still be married, and Sam still his bit on the side in that poky flat in Cheltenham. It had taken some proactive initiative from Sam to get things moving; some clues left carefully to point Aileen in the right direction; a few phone calls dropped with a little gasp of horror when the wife answered. That sort of thing.

So she knew the way he worked and he was a pro. When he came home in the evenings, you'd never guess that he was playing around. He was still making love to her. Not quite as often as usual but regularly and with, as far she could tell, his usual enthusiasm. No – she wasn't going to find out just like that. She'd have to be smart about it and use the eyes of others instead, if she was going to have a chance of making certain of her suspicions.

Bella had entered a new realm of existence, she felt, where all that mattered was herself and Ben. All that occupied her was how often they could see each other and where. She found it hard to leave the computer in case an email came through from him, and he sent several messages every day. They had worked out that Ben could spare two lunchtimes a week away from the office and that Bella could drive to meet him at a hotel on the outskirts of Oxford. They practised their theory on the first day possible and it worked beautifully. It was hard to see how anyone could be the wiser.

The sex with Ben was lending a golden glow to her life. She couldn't remember being so happy and contented. All her movements seemed smoother and more graceful because her body felt so well looked-after; her daily life had taken on a meaning it had lacked before, because of the intensity at the heart of it. Simple things, like making tea or washing up, gave her a kind of pleasure because she could imagine Ben watching her, murmuring sweet things into her ear as she did it. Sometimes she thought vaguely of Sam, but she was like a distant object, far removed from the centre of things. If she did think about her for more than a few minutes, she couldn't help concluding that there was some kind of karmic justice in the situation. Sam had stolen Ben from his wife: it was not surprising that she should lose him in the same way.

Iain had noticed nothing, of course. He went through his daily routine of leaving for the office, Bella driving him to the station, then returning in the evening, drained and exhausted by the commute, for Bella to take him home again. His attention when he was at home was firmly fixed on his plans for the garden and he spent hours with his nose in a book or outside prodding at the thick dark earth. Nothing had yet materialized in the garden but Iain was still deciding what he wanted to grow and how, and whether he ought to keep chickens or even a goat.

Bella let him ramble on, nodding and agreeing where necessary, but lost in a dream most of the time. She was imagining different futures, and different outcomes but she couldn't conceive of giving up this rare thing she had found. Nor could she imagine Iain ever knowing about it, though she realized it was impossible to reconcile all her fantasies. At some point surely, Iain must know? She couldn't bear to think of his reaction so she shut it out and refused to face it.

'Does this feel like home to you?' Iain asked. It was a Sunday afternoon, and they'd decided to walk off their lunch by tramping down the lane and circling back round the fields, along the wood and home again. The sky was grey and the air damp; it had been raining heavily the day before and the countryside, Bella had noticed, took longer to dry out than the city. They wore gumboots that were soon shiny with wet. The children took pleasure in jumping in the largest potholes, sending sprays of dirty water up their bright coats and boots. They called out for their parents to come and look at things of interest – plants, burrows, mud casts left by worms summoned to the surface by the pounding rain – and ate blackberries plucked from brambles as they passed.

'Home?' echoed Bella. The landscape was already familiar to her. She knew the surface of the lane well, where to avoid the largest pitfalls and the way it curved round to the right before they hit the main road. She thought of the house, now well worn in. Pretty Holly Lodge, full of the Balfour junk but comfortable and cosy. It hadn't taken long to spread out in it, and to appreciate the larger space, and it was hard to imagine now going back to the small dimensions of their London house. She thought of the Rayburn, and the way keeping it alight was second nature now. As the weather got colder, she liked to sit next to it with her coffee and a book, soaking up the radiating warmth. The view to the old farm cottages, with the broken-down old car outside, hardly bothered her. The isolation, which had seemed so spooky when they'd first arrived, had become normal, and now the sound of a car bumping along the lane made her a little uneasy. Dirt and mud and stones and grass were becoming part of the fabric of her life. The urban existence that her Sunday supplements were obsessed with was becoming more remote and dreamlike, a Brave New World way of life, sheltered and artificial, at odds with the reality beyond it.

'Yes,' she said at last. 'It does feel like home.'

Iain looked pleased. 'I knew it – I told you you'd like it.'

'You were right.'

He looked satisfied.

'It's not perfect. I still don't know whether my work is going to take off . . .'

'But you've had a good response, haven't you? Didn't you get a training booking last week?'

She had. She'd been pleased: a booking for four days' work next month, training four groups of six. Before Ben, she'd have been ecstatic. Now she felt contented by her success. 'Yes. But one booking doesn't make a successful business.'

'It's a start. Didn't someone say a journey of a thousand miles starts with a single step?'

'I'm sure they did.'

Katie came running up. 'Mummy, Mummy, can we go to the stream?'

Bella frowned and said, 'You shouldn't go there in this weather. It'll be very muddy and slippery. It was just a trickle in the summer but with all this rain, it'll be much deeper and fast-flowing. I don't want you going there.'

'We're all right,' Katie said obstinately. 'We're not stupid. We know where the slippery bits are.'

'I fell down it last week,' said Christopher proudly, coming up with a handful of sticks he had carefully collected.

'You slid down the bank?' Bella asked, concerned.

'He only got his boot full of water,' Katie said carelessly. 'And a muddy *bum*.'

'*You*'re a muddy bum,' burst out Christopher.

'No, *you*'re a muddy bum.'

'All right, all right.' Bella stopped what was obviously a well-rehearsed routine. 'I don't want you down there alone, kids. Okay?'

The children stomped along in silence, unwilling to agree.

'Kids,' Iain said warningly. 'Answer your mother.'

'O-*kaaaay*,' they said, with reluctance, then ran away up the lane to show their disapproval.

'What are we going to do with Katie next year?' Iain asked.

'What do you mean?'

'She'll be leaving the primary school, won't she? I'm just wondering what we should do.'

'She'll go to the comprehensive, like all the other kids.' They'd never planned anything else.

'I suppose so. It might be worth looking at St Mary's. I mean, if she can win a scholarship, we might as well.'

'What about Chrissie? What if he can't win a scholarship? We can't send one private and not the other.'

'All right, all right. I'm just thinking aloud, that's all. We need to make plans.'

Bella watched her boots splash through the mud. She didn't want to make any plans at all. She didn't want to think about the future: the here and now was fine for her.

Maggie threw away the newspaper in disgust. It landed, rustling and awkward, on the sitting-room floor. 'This is so boring. Sometimes it all seems like so much yatter, doesn't it? Yak, yak, yak. Filling space for the sake of it. And they're so London-centric! I hadn't realized it before, but it's all they talk about.'

Jane looked up from her book. It was the quiet, full-bellied period after Sunday lunch and before the clearing up had to be done, a time she usually enjoyed but today it had a less cosy feeling. Lucy had left a few days before, bent under the weight of her giant backpack, to go on her Interrailing trip and the house seemed emptier without her. 'I thought you loved London.'

'I do, I do love London. Not everything about it, of course.' She thought for the moment. 'I hate the Underground. My life would be significantly improved if I never had to travel on it again.'

'The Underground,' echoed Alec. He was playing cricket on his Playstation with the sound turned down, cross-legged on the carpet in front of the television screen.

'It may seem glamorous now, all part of life in the big city,' said Maggie, 'but wait until you've endured it every working day for fifteen years. You'll loathe it with a passion, I promise.'

'Don't want to live in London,' was the gruff reply.

Jane raised her eyebrows at his hunched back. For Alec to express any view on what he did or didn't want to do was unexpected. She said casually, so as not to frighten him back into silence, 'Don't you? Where do you want to live?'

He carried on staring at the screen, his thumbs working away at the levers and buttons on his console. It's like getting a wild animal to trust you, Jane thought. Then he said, 'I don't want to live in London, that's for sure. I prefer the country. More room. More air.'

'Goodness. Well, that's good.' Jane sat up straight, rather excited. This was progress. Suddenly she saw Alec running a small law practice in a county town, or being a country doctor or a vet . . . something prosperous, comfortable and safe.

Alec swung round with a scowl. 'I expect you can't wait to pack me off to the city. You're always on at me to go away: off to school, off to A-level crammer, off to college, then off and away to London to work.'

Jane gaped at him, then stuttered, 'That's not true at all.'

Maggie said, 'Now, Alec, we've talked about this. You're not being fair on your mother. You know very well she'll support you in whatever you want to do. Right?'

Jane was even more stunned by this, and stared at her sister, speechless. What on earth had happened? Was Maggie defending her to Alec? She'd sensed a change in relations between them since the unprecedented apology the other day; not a huge shift – Maggie still had a biting tongue and a careless manner with her – but there was a subtle relaxation, as though hidden tensions had been eased away. Maggie seemed lighter in herself, less burdened by her sadness, and the bond between her and Alec had strengthened. Jane had often seen them walking out towards the woods together, deep in conversation, and felt that familiar pang of being left out. But she had given up trying to force Alec to talk to her, and now that she had her own secret to hide away she felt a little better, as though the balance had been redressed.

Alec shrugged and turned back to his game.

'Maggie's right,' Jane said at last. 'I don't want to send you away – I only want you to do what will make you happy. My worry is that you find *something* to do.'

Maggie shook her head quickly, but with a complicit smile that took the sting out of it. Let it be, she seemed to be saying. I'm working on it.

Jane pulled out of the driveway and into the lane, and saw the small blond figures of the Balfour children trudging towards the house. Ever since Bella had left them with her for the afternoon, Katie and Christopher had taken to wandering up after school, poking their heads round the kitchen door and seeing who was there. Jane suspected it was the hot Ribena and cake that tempted them, but they also played for hours on the rope swing, or tramped round the lake under strict orders not to go near the water, or sat in respectful silence and watched Alec on his Play-Station, always hopeful that he might hand it over for them to have a go.

At first their presence had bothered Jane. She'd worried that young children might depress Maggie, like having two little ghosts of the future in the place making her dwell on what she had lost, but as soon as she saw that they actively cheered her sister up, she stopped worrying. It was good to have children around in this huge old house: it was really what huge old houses were made for. She certainly didn't mind them racing about and enjoying it, and Bella didn't seem to either – at least, she never said anything. She'd wander up the lane herself and drop in for coffee and conversation under the guise of picking up the children and taking them home for dinner, but as often as not would stay chatting until Jane was getting anxious about her own supper. She never mentioned the woman next door except once when, after Jane had enquired, she'd said lightly, 'Oh, I don't really see Sam much any more,' and left it at that.

Jane tooted her horn and waved at the children as she went by. They waved back furiously from the roadside, and then she watched their backs in the rear-view mirror as they toiled on up the lane. She liked Bella Balfour, she'd decided, and if her children were part of the index of a woman, she couldn't be all that bad.

The drive to Oxford was familiar, but now it was loaded with a secret and delicious meaning. Every mile took her closer to Tom, waiting for her in the small room tucked under the college eaves. No one asked her where she was going any more, or when she would be back. They'd had to learn to trust that she'd return. This was, she felt, one of the small steps she was taking every day towards liberation. She wasn't sure where she was coming from, or going to, but this new sense that she was on a journey of some kind was, in itself, elating.

The college was unusually busy when she arrived, with people strolling up and down the quads.

'A conference,' Tom explained. 'They often have them in the holidays to get the cash in. This'll be the last one, though, with term so close to starting. I've got special dispensation to stay up. The other students all have to leave over the summer so that the delegates have somewhere pretty to stay.'

'That's sad,' Jane said. They were lying on his bed and her head was on his chest. She could hear the slow, rhythmic pounding of his heart through his clothes.

'Yeah, well, I guess it has benefits in other ways. It makes the college richer, which helps us all. That's the theory anyway.'

'I didn't mean that. I mean it's sad that you stay here all on your own, with all the other students off at home, or travelling and working. Don't you want to go home?'

He shifted a little under her arm. 'No. I'm happy here. SA is a long way away, you know? I haven't got anything to go back for.'

'No friends? What about your family? Don't you want to see your brothers, or your nephews and nieces?'

Looking down at her, he frowned although with a smile. 'Well, well, what a lot of questions. I thought we agreed we'd stay off all this.'

They had agreed that, she supposed, though not in so many words. There was a mutual lack of questioning about the past and the future, as though it were delicate ground they preferred not to tread. It would make the present so much more loaded, and neither of them wanted that. At the moment, they were content to just be as they were, assuming nothing and taking each meeting as it came. Nevertheless, he was still a stranger to her in many ways.

262

She sat up. 'There's so much I don't know about you.'

'You don't have to be in a hurry to find it all out at once, you know. You've been so much more relaxed lately. You won't spoil it, will you?' He dropped a kiss on to the tip of her nose.

'Of course not,' she replied, and settled back on to the comfort of his chest.

She returned from Tom, feeling refreshed as she always did. Was it because it was a secret? If I had to tell anyone, something would be lost. They'd ask what I wanted to happen, they'd ask why a young man like him wanted an old woman like me, they'd make me question his motives. It would spoil the magic. It would ruin it.

What Tom could gain from it was a mystery to her, unless it was what she got from him: happiness and the comfort that came from skin pressed against skin, and arms wrapped round each other.

Jane knew for certain that things were improved with Maggie when she came downstairs, her usually sombre dress lightened with the addition of plum lipstick and a chunky amber and silver necklace. Colour crept along her cheekbones and her hair was well brushed.

'You look perky,' Jane commented. She was cleaning the silver at the kitchen table, burnishing photograph frames to a gleaming shine.

'I feel good, actually.' Maggie sat down, took up a rag, spread cleaner on to a ladle and rubbed it in idly. 'I'm a reformed character.' She looked up mischievously. 'And I owe you an apology.'

'Another?' cried Jane, ironically. 'The floodgates are opened. What for this time?'

'For being so down on this place. I expected to feel trapped here, but it's been . . .' Maggie grasped for the right word. 'It's been very *healthy*. I don't know what it is or why. I can understand now why Alec can't bear to live anywhere else.'

'Well, I'm delighted. Delighted. Does that mean that there's an end to your carping about my house?'

'Not completely. I still think it's crazy to have two people living in this place all alone.'

'Two? Three, you mean. You, me and Alec.'

'Ah. Well. I'm going home, you see. Back to the smoke.'

Jane put down her picture frame and her cloth, dismayed. 'You are? Why?'

'I can't stay here for ever, Jane. I've got work. I have a life. Gregor's coming home and I need to be with him.'

'Of course you have. It was . . . silly to think you didn't have to go back. And are you feeling better about . . . the baby?' She hardly dared venture it but she had to ask.

Maggie's eyes darkened. 'Of course I can't feel better about it, not yet, but I'm coming to terms with it. More importantly, I'm beginning to admit to myself that I want children in my life. Having those little Balfour creatures running about is making me more sure of that than ever.' She grinned. 'They've made me see that I've just about had enough of cynical, lazy students slouching about. It's so refreshing to see some eagerness, some innocence, for a change. So I think that, after I've talked to Gregor, we'll come to some decisions about what we're going to do, whether it's keep trying for our own baby, start thinking about IVF or—'

There was a knock at the door and they turned to look at it, as though they might be able to see who it was through the wood. Jane made a face and went over to answer it. On the doorstep stood a slim figure, its back to the door, looking down towards the lake, its hands thrust deep into the pockets of a pink fleece.

On hearing the door open, Sam Clarke spun round, her china-blue eyes wide. Her blonde hair was in pigtails, with a white ribbon carefully tied at the end of each one.

'Hiya,' she said brightly. 'Is this a good time?'

'Hello – yes, it's fine. Please come in. This is my sister Maggie. Maggie, this is Mrs Clarke.'

'Sam.'

Maggie smiled. 'Hello. Nice to meet you.' She turned back to the ladle she was polishing, gracefully allowing the other two women to talk.

After offering the usual coffee, which was refused with a quick shake of the head, Jane gestured to her visitor to sit down.

'I'll stand, thanks.'

'How can I help you . . . Sam?' The use of her Christian name implied an intimacy with this woman that Jane didn't feel they shared, and she was quite sure of her impression that they never would. Bella Balfour had something human and approachable about her, but Sam . . . she'd rarely felt such a chill coming off another person. All that icy whiteness, from the too-blonde hair to the bleached teeth, made her want to shiver.

Sam had an air of carelessness that Jane could tell was assumed. 'Yeah, I was just passing, really, and I thought I'd pop and in and say hi. You know, be neighbourly.'

'Well, that's nice . . .'

'Yeah. How are things? This is great.' Sam nodded round at the kitchen. 'Cosy. I was just wondering . . . I couldn't help noticing you've had those kids from down the lane up here. Katie and Christopher.'

'Bella's children?' Jane raised her eyebrows. She hadn't been expecting Sam to take that line. 'Yes, they come up sometimes to play. I think their garden is quite small and it definitely doesn't have an old pond, like ours. You know how children can't resist water.'

'Yeah.' Sam's gaze shifted about, sometimes meeting her eyes, then skittering about, focusing on nothing in particular. 'Nice little things, aren't they? They came on holiday with us earlier in the summer, to France. Actually, I noticed that Bella, their mother . . . I noticed that she's been popping round a bit as well.'

'Yes,' Jane said slowly, feeling that they were coming to the point.

Sam's hands burrowed down again into her pockets and her shoulders hunched. 'I just wondered if you'd noticed anything strange about her. Anything a bit . . . odd?'

'Odd?' Jane repeated. 'How do you mean?'

'Oh, I dunno. I thought we were pretty good friends for a while – I invited her and her family on holiday and everything. But she's gone all cold on me. I never see her. And I wondered if she might have said anything to you about it. She just . . .' Sam breathed in deeply, then exhaled slowly. 'Personally I think she's a bit peculiar and I just wanted to make sure you were keeping an eye on things. You know, the way she treats those children or, rather, doesn't treat them. She barely seems to notice they exist, she's so wrapped up in herself. She leaves them on their own in the house as well, if that's what she feels like. Seems to live in a dream world half the time. So I thought that if you were keeping an eye on her too, we could make sure everything was all right.'

'Well.' Jane considered this. 'I'm sorry to hear you've fallen out with Mrs Balfour. I must say though, that she seems fairly normal to me.'

Sam flared up at once, her eyes angry. 'She's *not* normal, believe me. I'm telling you, there's something wrong there.'

'All right.' Jane kept her voice calm and her expression neutral. 'If you think there's cause for concern, I'll keep my eyes open and let you know if I think there's a problem.'

The other woman appeared mollified by this. She nodded. 'All right. Just thought you ought to know, that's all. I've gotta get going now.' She went to the door, opened it, looked back over her shoulder and said, 'Thanks. I feel a lot better knowing you're on the look-out as well,' then closed it behind her.

Jane turned to her sister with a quizzical expression. Maggie put her tongue out and crossed her eyes, then shrugged her shoulders and said, 'Weird.'

Chapter Nineteen

Are we on for today? Must see you ASAP. Have been desperate for you.
Bxxx

Bella sent the message and clicked on to her solitaire computer game. It helped her to pass the time while she was waiting for him to reply. She listened to the radio absentmindedly while lining up red card on black card, queen on king, four on five, working automatically, unaware of what she was doing. Then, another click, the screen would change in front of her, and there it would be: a fresh message in her inbox waiting for her like an unwrapped present.

The answer came back quickly.

Of course. Same time, same place. Can't wait to taste you. X

She shivered slightly and said, 'Wheeee' under her breath. Excellent – now there was a point to her day. She shut down the solitaire and went to run her bath in preparation for Ben's attentions.

She arrived at the hotel almost exactly on time. She had the distance down pat now, and knew just how long it would take her to get there. Pulling into the car park, she wished they could have found somewhere slightly more glamorous for their affair. This place was more like a motel – low, single-storeyed, brown. A place for businessmen, commercial travellers and less discerning tourists. It ran a restaurant called La Brasserie that was only really a notch or two above a service station but aimed at a much more genteel atmosphere with its 'Please wait to be seated' sign.

Bella knew that in Oxford there were much grander places: the Randolph, for one, with its imposing Victorian Gothic style, and the quainter boutique hotels in old stone and with beamed ceilings. But they had to be practical and anonymous, and for that this place was perfect.

Ben was waiting for her in the bar and, after a discreet few minutes, they made their way along a corridor to their room. As they went, Bella noticed the barman staring after them. He'd seen them a couple of times now. Perhaps he was wondering if she was a prostitute. It made her want to laugh. Let him wonder! He had no idea.

In the bland little room, Ben pulled the curtains and, in the gloom, they made love quickly and fiercely. They had only an hour or so, but that didn't really matter. Their accumulated hunger for each other was so strong that they wouldn't have been able to hold back even if they'd wanted to. What Bella regretted was that they couldn't spend the afternoon in bed together, getting their fill of each other slowly and lingeringly, learning each other more tenderly. It wasn't possible this way.

'How are you? Okay?' Ben asked, as they lay together afterwards. This bit was so sweet, Bella thought, tangling a finger in his hair, so bitterly, yearningly sweet.

'Fine,' she said. 'You?'

'Not so bad. How's your work coming along? Did my people talk to your people?'

'They did. I've got two bookings now – your company wants me in just before Christmas.'

'That's great! Really – I didn't have a hand in it. I promise.' He grinned down at her, and squeezed her tightly.

'I know you didn't. I know I got it on merit. That's nice. But you . . .' She stroked his neck. 'I thought you didn't approve of women in the workplace. Barefoot in the kitchen, I thought that was how you wanted womankind to spend their time.'

'What are you talking about? I don't think any such thing.'

'Well, that's what Sam told me. Apparently the working woman is the cause of all of modern life's ills, from the cost of housing to youngsters demanding Nike trainers.'

'That's what she told you?' Ben looked puzzled, and then he groaned. 'Oh, God, that's not me. She's quoting her friend Becky's ludicrous husband. Those are all his ideas. He's a nightmare. Why did she tell you all that?'

'I've no idea.'

They lay in silence, both solemn. After a while, Ben said, 'That's bad, you know. She was warning you off me, that's what she was doing. Trying to head you off at the pass. The thing is, that means she must have reason to suspect. She's got an idea that you and I might be attracted to each other. It's not good.'

'How can she know?' Bella asked. She didn't want any hint that they might have to end it. There must be no clouds on the horizon. 'She can't possibly. You said yourself she's paranoid. She'd probably be suspicious of any woman. Does she have many girl-friends?'

'No.'

'There you are. She's a woman who hates other women. They're the very worst kind. Now, come on. I'm hungry. Can we go to the bar and get one of their sandwiches? You can spare twenty minutes more, can't you?' she pleaded.

He stared at her for a moment, then said, 'I can't resist you. Come on, then.'

Jane was on the ring road heading out of Oxford, still in a warm glow from an afternoon spent with Tom, when she noticed that the petrol gauge on the car showed a worryingly small amount of fuel in the tank. She had driven so much more than usual lately, with her trips to see Tom, that she had lost a sense of what she had been using. I'll stop at a service station, she told herself, and kept her eyes open for one. She soon spotted a place and pulled off the road to fill up the car. As she stood under the station awning, breathing in dense fumes, the pump nozzle hooked into the car, she realized she was hungry. Across the way was a hotel, the kind that would have a restaurant for travellers, so she bought a paper when she paid for her fuel and drove over to the car park. She would stop for ten minutes and have something to eat before she headed home. As she collected her bag and coat from the passenger seat, her eye was caught by movement in the rear-view mirror. She saw, quite plainly, Bella Balfour walking across the car park towards her car. How odd, she thought, what is she doing here? Shall I say hello?

Then she saw another figure a few yards behind her, going to a different car and paying no attention to the woman. But that was odd because it was Ben Clarke and he knew Bella, so why didn't he say hello to her? Surely he must be able to see her – they were really quite close. And how strange that they should be in the same car park at the same hotel at the same time, she thought. And then: Oh. Oh dear. Well, that explains it.

Emma's good mood was driving Sam round the bend. Ever since she'd got back from her holiday, Emma had been far more in evidence than ever before, floating about the house with a supercilious smile on her face and dropping into every conversation the fact that she would soon be off to Edinburgh. Dinner drove her wild: how many more times would she have to sit through Ben and Emma yattering on about student accommodation and lectures and societies and all that crap?

The thing was that Ben was so normal. It was hard to believe that he was fucking Bella Balfour. Occasionally, as she watched him while he and Emma chattered away, she found herself hoping against hope that it wasn't true, that she was just going mad, driven to ridiculous conclusions through jealousy. But then she would remember little things that seemed to point conclusively to the fact that he was cheating: why did he never mention Bella? Why was it so hard to reach him on his mobile? Why did she have that gut instinct that something bad was going on?

The latest thing was that he was thinking of buying Emma a flat in Edinburgh. When this had been discussed at dinner, Sam had smiled sweetly and said what a lovely idea, but inside she'd seethed with furious rage that he could give Emma so much when he gave her absolutely nothing.

She couldn't stand it much longer, she decided. She couldn't think about anything but Ben. Sometimes she was on the point of storming down to Holly Lodge and confronting Bella, or rushing up to Ben and scratching his face, demanding to know the truth. But something stopped her. She longed for it all to go away, to get back to normal. Sometimes she fantasized about Ben taking her in his arms and kissing her and crooning in her ear. I don't want her, she imagined him saying, she's nothing to me. You're everything, little Sammikins, the most beautiful woman in the world. You're the one I want.

She couldn't give up on that quite yet.

By the time Jane got home it was raining. The sky was heavy and low, and the windscreen wipers had to fight against the force of the raindrops pelting down from the black clouds. It was late afternoon but already almost dark. The autumn was well upon them now.

She let herself into the light warm kitchen, shaking herself free, like a cat, of all the raindrops in her hair and lashes and clothes. Home. It came into its own when winter arrived. There were parts of the house she abandoned to the cold and dankness but the kitchen, sitting room and bedrooms were always warm. It felt different now, though, without Maggie. She'd packed her suitcase and climbed into her Morris Minor the day before and headed for London, waving and shouting that'd she'd be back soon, she promised. Jane was missing her more than she wanted to admit to herself.

She was making a cup of tea when Alec came in, holding a sheaf of papers. 'Mum,' he said briskly, 'I want to show you something.' He sat down at the table and shuffled his papers into different piles. 'Maggie's just sent me all this through on the email.'

'What is it, darling?'

'Prospectuses. Information about courses. And ideas of people to approach for work experience.' He grinned. 'We've been sorting it all out, and I've decided what I want to do.'

'Yes?' She tried to keep the apprehension out of her voice.

He looked triumphant. 'I'm going to go to agricultural college!

I'm going to learn how to manage land, run a farm, and I'm going to get this place going again. Make it pay for us, so we don't have to think about moving or losing the house again. That's what.'

'Really?' She absorbed what he had said. For a moment, it was hard to make sense of it, and then she understood. 'That's wonderful,' she said sincerely. It was as though a door had opened and she could look through it. Alec's future had been entirely closed to her and now she could see opportunity and possibility. 'But . . . won't you need A-levels for that?'

'Yes, yes,' he said brusquely, as though she was being very slow indeed. 'I'll need two. But Maggie thinks that won't be a problem as I'm already half-way through three. She thinks I'll be able to get accepted late into a sixth-form college, or else I can take a year to do some work experience on farms and estates – that's this pile, these are possibles I can approach – then do my exams next year and go to college the year after that. But,' he wrinkled his nose and frowned, 'I'm kind of thinking that I want to get on and go to college next autumn. Get started, you know. So I'm going to contact possible places, even though their terms have already started. We might be able to fix something if I promise to work hard and catch up the few weeks I've missed.'

'Alec, this is wonderful,' she said excitedly. 'What a brilliant idea! It makes complete sense. I don't know why we didn't think of it before.' She jumped to her feet and stretched across the table to hug him. 'You clever thing.'

He allowed her to embrace him and patted her arm. 'It was Maggie, really. She helped me.'

'Helped you see what you already knew. Oh, it's so exciting! I'm very, very proud of you, do you know that?'

'Aw, shucks. I'm just an ornery kid,' he said. 'I was a bit worried you'd be disappointed I wasn't going to go to Oxford and become a lawyer like Dad.'

'Never,' she said vehemently. 'I don't want you to be Dad. I want you to be you. Most of all, I want you to be happy.' He mimed playing a violin and they both laughed. 'Wicked child! Mocking your poor old mother . . .'

*

When Alec had gone, she thought for a while, then rang Bella, who answered immediately in her breathless way.

'Miserable day, isn't it?' Jane said, looking out at the rain. 'I wondered if you'd like to come up for tea – or I can come down to you.'

'Oh, well . . . that's very kind but I'm a bit tied up—'

'It's quite important. It's about lunch-time.'

'Lunch-time?'

'Yes. Lunch-time today.'

There was a pause. 'I'll be right up.'

When Bella arrived, Jane had brought out a bottle of wine rather than tea. It seemed more appropriate. Bella came in, shaking off the rain, and one look at Jane's face was enough. She sat down at the table and took the wine Jane gave her, saying brightly, 'So. How did you find out?'

Jane sat down opposite her. 'There's no point in beating about the bush, is there? We may as well be candid. I was coming back from Oxford today and I happened to stop at a hotel place on the ring road. I saw you and Ben Clarke together. I don't have to be Miss Marple to make the obvious deduction.'

'I suppose not.' Bella didn't look in the least bit guilty or nervous. Instead she smiled broadly. 'Caught in the act!'

'It explains a lot, I suppose. Your glow, your cessation of relations with Mrs Clarke.'

Bella laughed, with a touch of embarrassment. 'Oh, yes. Well, there are limits, even for me.'

'But that's the thing.' Jane looked at her earnestly. 'That's the worry. If I saw you, it's perfectly possible that someone else might, someone who might not keep it to themselves. I'm not making moral judgements – you're both adults and what you do is your own concern – but it's very hard to do these things successfully. I just want to warn you. I stumbled on you accidentally – and what are the chances that I should decide to go to that particular hotel on that particular day? If it can happen with me, it can happen with anyone.'

'We are careful.'

273

'I'm sure you are. But I would hate to see all this explode in your faces. Stop me if you think I'm being too interfering.'

'No. No, you're not. It's just . . .' Bella sighed. 'I can't end it. Not just like that. I need it too much. It's all that keeps me going.'

Jane understood only too well; it was like an addiction. 'The thing is,' she said slowly, 'I think Mrs Clarke might be suspicious of you. She came round here the other day, and said some very odd things.' She outlined Sam's visit.

'She can't possibly know,' Bella said airily. 'We've been very careful. Besides, she's too self-obsessed to notice. She's more interested in the latest highlight colours than in Ben.'

'I wouldn't bank on it. I really wouldn't. I'm saying – be careful.'

'Message received,' said Bella lightly.

'My goodness, it's pouring out there, isn't it?' Iain tweaked the curtain shut on the wet darkness outside. 'Brrr. Makes me glad we're safe and warm in here.'

'Mmm,' said Bella. She was still feeling luxurious from lunch, even if Jane's warning had put anxiety into the pit of her stomach. But she pushed the uncomfortable thoughts out of her mind. Now Christopher was curled up next to her, his head in her lap while she stroked his soft fair hair and they watched television. It was nearly his bedtime and he was tired. Katie sat at her feet, her back propped against the sofa, reading a book.

'This place is a good old house,' Iain said, looking about. 'Good, solid. We're all right here.'

'We're fine,' Bella said absently.

He stared at the ceiling for a while, then nodded and said, 'Yep. It's a good old house.'

'How was your day, dear?' Sam said, with a sickly sweet smile when Ben got home.

'Fine, good.' He kissed her lips and squeezed her arm briefly. 'How was yours?'

'All right. That stupid Trudy brought her bloody dog in again.

Muddy paws all over the kitchen. I think she's feeding him from our fridge. I'm sure that lasagne you made has disappeared.'

'She's a good cleaner, though, isn't she?' Ben went to pour himself a drink.

'I suppose so. It's all she's good for, anyway.' Sam sat on the sofa and curled her legs up under her. 'Get me one of those, will you, honey? A nice strong one. Stronger the better.'

'Whatever you say.' He poured her a large dose of Tanqueray and topped it up with tonic. 'What have you been up to here all on your own? I've been worried about you.'

'Have you, sweetie?' Sam said, with a touch of sarcasm. 'Ah, you're so lovely to me.'

'You haven't been to see Becky for ages. How is she?' Ben sat down casually opposite her and took a sip of his drink.

Sam felt herself tensing, her lips tightening and her eyes hardening. *Keep it in*, she thought. 'She's fine, as far as I know. Do you think I should see her?'

Ben shrugged. 'Well, you know. You like going off for a girls' day out every once in a while, don't you? You haven't been to Cheltenham for ages. I don't want you getting bored and miserable here on your own.'

'Yeah. Yeah, I do like seeing Becky. Perhaps I'll give her a call, see if she's busy. I'll do it after dinner.'

'You deserve a treat.'

'I do, don't I?'

Whenever Bella answered the telephone, she couldn't help injecting a note of breathless excitement into her voice in case it was Ben who called. When it was him, her voice sank at once to a low, seductive tone, heavy with promise.

He called a few days later in the afternoon. 'Guess where I am.'

'Hmm, let's see. The office? Too obvious. The stationery cupboard with your secretary? Or somewhere more exotic? The top of the Duomo in Florence?'

'No. I'm at home. What are you doing?'

'Some emailing, some housework, some Internet surfing. Boring stuff. Why are you at home?'

'Sam's gone to Cheltenham. I'm working in my study, but d'you know what? I can't get a thing done because I keep thinking of you and all the delicious things you do to me.' She giggled. 'Do you want to come up here?'

'What?' She was vaguely scandalized. 'Have sex in your house? What about Emma?'

'She's gone down to the village. And she's walking so she'll be gone for hours. Come on . . . let's be daring.'

Bella thought uncomfortably of what Jane had said to her. 'No. I don't think it's right. It's too risky.'

'Let me come to you then,' wheedled Ben.

'No, I don't want that. Not in our house. I couldn't . . .'

'For God's sake, Bella, you're driving me wild. How about we meet in the old farm? You know, you must pass it all the time. There's an old barn there, one of the few buildings with a bit of roof left on. Meet me there.'

She was tickled by the idea. 'All right. Shall I see you there in ten minutes?'

It was no longer raining but the ground was still damp. The clouds had cleared, though, and a pale golden sunshine was touching everything with colour. Bella went up the lane and took the turning down towards the old farm where the mellowed old buildings were quite picturesque in their slide into ruin. The red brick was crumbling away and the slates were slowly descending through the wooden frames to the ground. It looked as though only the carpet of moss was holding the last few in place. Everything was overgrown, and among the long grass lay piles of rusting farm machinery, built for long-forgotten purposes and now left here as relics: curious implements with hooks or blades or raked fingers, broken saddles and metal wheels.

Bella picked her way through the wet grass, past the old stables, now open to the elements, and some dingy outbuildings towards the barn. She wondered what it had once been used for: perhaps animals, to shut them away from the bitter winter weather in warm, hay-filled darkness. It was certainly the sturdiest structure, the only one left that provided any real shelter. As she approached, Ben stepped out from the shadowy interior.

'Halloo,' she said, smiling to see him. His height, the blue of his jumper, the grey streaks in his freshly washed hair — everything about him was pleasing to her, and just the sight of him sent a pleasant surge through her. He reached out a hand and she took it, saying, 'You must have left quickly to get here so soon,' when he pulled her swiftly into the barn. Inside it felt damp in the darkness and she wondered if they were going to lie down, but Ben didn't give her any time to think. Instead he pushed his mouth against hers with force, shutting off anything further she had to say. She wrapped her arms round his neck but he took them strongly in his hands and pulled them down. She tried to pull away from his embrace a little, wanting to ask him to slow down, but he was insistent, following each movement of her twisting head with his own, covering her whole mouth with his, breathing hard as he did so. He pushed her back against the wall. She felt the rough surface of the brick through her jacket, then a rush of cool air on her stomach as Ben yanked up her top and grasped her breast. It was happening so fast, she thought. Why was he in such a rush? They had time today: they weren't in the hotel room with a lunch-hour limit.

His hand reached down and pulled up her skirt, letting the chill breeze move round her thighs. She felt herself respond now, his excitement leaping to her like an electric charge. They pulled apart from their kiss and Bella reached down to her knickers, pushing them as far down as she could while Ben fumbled with his trousers. A moment later he lifted one of her thighs, and wrapped it round his waist as he found her. He pushed upwards into her, his mouth tense and his eyes fierce. She drew breath sharply and her jacket rasped against the brickwork as he moved her with him, faster and faster. She threw back her head, not heeding the wall behind her, and closed her eyes, gasping with each strong movement.

'Oh, my . . . oh, my God,' she whispered, burying her face in his heaving shoulder. 'Oh, my God . . .'

*

277

Ben didn't speak until they'd been recovering for some minutes, their clothes now restored to their rightful places. They sank down in the afterglow, not minding the damp earth, and now sat languid, looking out at the farm building opposite.

He turned to Bella and said, 'I believe that was what they call a bucolic bonk.'

'A rustic romp.' She grinned at him.

'Rural rumpy-pumpy.'

'Pastoral pleasures.'

He thought for a moment. 'You win, I'm all out.'

'Arcadian amorousness,' she said.

'Show-off.' He punched her arm lightly.

'An idyll,' she whispered, and kissed him. 'That was quite Hardyesque. I felt like Tess of the d'Urbervilles or something.'

'I'm sure you did – whoever she is.' They sat quietly for a few more minutes, then Ben said, 'I'd better be getting back.'

'So should I. What's the time? The children will be home soon. Come on.' They got to their feet and stepped outside into the long grass at the front of the barn. A trail of crushed stems showed where they had been before. Ben bowed to her ironically, and she curtsied back. 'Thank you, my fine lady,' he said gravely.

'The pleasure was all mine, my good sir.'

He kissed her deeply, as though to take one last long savour of her mouth. 'Mmmm. You taste so good. 'Bye, my Bella. See you soon.'

' See you soon,' she replied, and they made their separate ways home.

Chapter Twenty

'My D. Phil ends next year, did I tell you that?' Tom said casually, as they walked in the woods near the house. He had come to her this time, as Alec was out visiting a college, and the house was all Jane's for the day.

She shook her head. They'd never discussed anything so far as a week away, let alone a year. It was an unspoken condition of what they were doing: by never discussing the future, they were tacitly acknowledging that there was no future for them, that this was just a delightful interlude on their way to different places.

'I don't know what I'll do after that. I suppose I'll have to become a sensible grown-up and get a job. I'll probably go back to South Africa.' He kicked his feet through the crackling carpet of red leaves.

'Is that what you want?' She sniffed the air. It was rich with the hint of a bonfire.

'Don't know what I want. I might be deathly sick of this country by then. I might be craving some warmth.' He shivered. 'I can never get used to the weather.'

'This is only autumn! It's still warm!'

'I know only too well. I didn't go to Cambridge because I was warned about the winters there. I can hardly imagine it. Brrr.'

She laughed. 'You really are a South African!'

Tom grabbed her hand and squeezed it. He tucked it with his own into his pocket. 'Have you ever thought of going there?' he asked.

'What? To South Africa? No. I can honestly say that I never have.'

'Maybe you should.'

She stopped walking and stared at him. 'With you?'

He flushed. 'Perhaps. Is that so weird?'

Frowning, she looked down at the woodland floor. A row of damp little mushrooms was growing among the mouldy leaves at her feet. 'It is quite weird. You're talking about next year. You're talking about this . . . lasting.'

'Well, why shouldn't it?' He looked young and vulnerable. 'Don't give me that rubbish about your age. You know it doesn't matter to me.'

She pulled her hand free from his pocket, turned back to the path and started walking. 'It's not rubbish, Tom. It's a reality. We're not just a little bit apart, we're a lot apart, not just in age but in everything. I've got two grown-up children for a start. This is a wonderful thing, extraordinarily precious to me – because you are very special and because I know it can't last. Not just that it can't last – but that it shouldn't last. It's a mystery to me why you feel about me the way you do, but I do believe in it. I believe in it, and I'm very grateful for it – but that doesn't mean I believe you're going to feel the same way for ever.'

'I'm not a child.' His voice rose with anger, his accent becoming more pronounced. 'You treat me like I'm seventeen. I'm nearly thirty – plenty of people have made their life choices by now. Why are you so convinced that I'm in the grip of a passing in-fatuation? I don't fall in love with women because of their age or their hair colour. I fall in love with them because of who they are.'

Jane was silent. Neither of them had used the word 'love' – and the more dramatic 'fall in love' put a whole different slant on what was happening between them. It meant that this wasn't simply a sweet and careless interlude in their lives, but a pact, with responsibilities to be assumed. She had kept the idea of all that far away; she didn't want to examine what was happening, or have to start making choices and decisions.

'I don't understand. You haven't wanted to talk about this before,' she said. 'Whenever I ask you about South Africa, you don't want to discuss it and now you're talking about me going there with you. You can see why I might be confused, can't you?

Tom tramped behind her. 'You should think about taking more risks,' he said at last, not answering her. 'You play it too safe. Don't be so afraid of things – live a little.'

They walked their disagreement away and didn't mention it again when they got back. Instead they luxuriated in the wide space of Jane's double bed, and then lay together on the sitting-room rug, watching a film.

Risks, she thought, as he ran his hand up and down her arm. There were different levels of risk. There was the risk she was taking with Tom: that she'd be hurt or that she'd hurt him. And then there was the kind of risk Bella Balfour was taking, where many more people would be hurt if it all went wrong.

She watched Tom's hand move gently up and down: it fascinated her, with those square-ended fingers, and the strong, wide palm. It made her feel almost unbearably tender towards him. But did she love him? He gave her comfort and pleasure, he made her feel alive again. She could feel old wounds healing every time he made love to her. It was enough. It was all she wanted at the moment. The risk was, that if she let herself love him she would need to be loved back, and she was afraid that if she took that step, it would go wrong, as though he'd suddenly see her through new eyes and say, 'What am I doing with this woman? How can I desire her, let alone love her?' And he'd come to his senses and leave her.

So, she thought, it was better not to allow that to happen. Better to carry on protecting herself in the only way she knew.

'Did Alec tell you our genius plan?' asked Maggie when she called.

'He did. And you're both geniuses.'

'Yes. I was rather pleased with it. He's got big ideas, you know. He thinks he can make a go of the old farm that's falling to pieces down the lane.'

'That's my only worry – I'm not sure exactly what we'll be allowed to do. All I know about the land is that I can't sell it separately from the house. It's all bound up in trusts and protection orders and goodness knows what else.'

'Let's worry about that when it happens. I can't see that anyone is going to stop us renovating buildings that are already there, and bringing jobs and production to the area. But whatever happens, Alec's got a vocation, that much is clear. He just needed a prod to see it.'

'Thank you. I mean it.' Jane smiled into the phone as though Maggie could see her. 'And how are you?'

'I'm fine. I'm glad to be home, back with Gregor, but it's odd – I've come back with quite a new outlook. I'm thinking about making some changes.'

'Really?' Jane felt a quiver of anxiety, then relaxed. She was learning to accept change without the fearfulness she'd had in the past.

'Haven't decided what yet. We'll see. But I wanted to ask if Gregor and I could come down for Christmas with you and the kids.'

'Of course you can!' Jane was delighted. It had always been so hard to persuade Maggie to Rawlston, and now she was volunteering to come. There certainly were some changes going on. 'We'd love to have you.'

It was Tom who put the dent in her happiness. She'd hoped she was imagining the slight chill between them when they next met. They went to a concert in the Sheldonian theatre and came out into the cool night air, wondering where they should go for a drink and settling on the Lamb and Flag pub. She expected him to take her hand as they left the concert and strolled out among the crowd, but he didn't; and when they got to the pub, she found him distant and the aura around him uncomfortable.

They talked for a while about the music but Jane could tell that his heart wasn't in it. She searched his face for what was wrong but could read nothing in it. Finally she said, 'Tom – is something bothering you?'

He looked shifty, took off his glasses and rubbed at the lenses with his shirt sleeve. 'No. Not at all. Why?'

'You don't seem yourself.'

'I'm fine. It's just . . . well, you know, term is starting again soon. Ollie's getting back and he'll be expecting things to be the same as last year. We spend a lot of time together you know, going to parties, dinner, debates at the union. And the lectures will be starting again – I'll need to get on with my D. Phil. The rugby season is beginning too, and I'm pretty sure of getting on to the college team, perhaps I'll even try for the Varsity side . . .'

'Goodness,' Jane said lightly. 'I'll never see you.'

'I know. I suppose that's what I'm trying to say.'

Her happiness sank away from her. 'What do you mean?' She tried to keep her tone as unconcerned as it had been before, but she could hear the flatness creeping into it. 'Are you saying we can't go on?'

'No . . .' He looked at her unhappily. 'Just that we won't be able to see each other so often. We'll have to plan ahead more. You can't just turn up and rely on finding me in. I'm going to be less available. Now, I can see on your face what you're thinking. That this was what you were expecting all along, that I'd turn around and say, Thanks, old woman, I'm back off to my exciting young life now! It's not like that, trust me. But you don't seem as though you want to give up anything for me – so you can't ask me to sacrifice my time here for you.'

'I would never do that. Of course you must enjoy Oxford, I would hate it if you didn't. I'm sure . . . I'm sure we can work it out. Perhaps a regular time every week . . .' Her voice faded away. It sounded terrible, so cold and impersonal, like a gym class or a therapy appointment. The magic was being sucked away, just as she feared. Perhaps it was better to end it altogether – but that idea filled her with bleak misery. She didn't want to go back to the way things were, and a superstitious part of her feared that everything would regress: that Alec would go back to being morose and unfocused, and Maggie distant and hateful. The thought made her panic.

'I thought we should talk about it,' Tom said.

Last week he'd been asking her to South Africa. Now he was telling her he might be able to fit her in occasionally between rugby training and drunken dinners.

'You were right to,' she said. 'It's unavoidable.'

In Cheltenham, Sam had told Becky everything: all her worries and fears and suspicions. At first Becky had tried to laugh it away, and coax her out of it. 'Not Ben,' she'd said. 'He adores you, sweetheart! That much is plain.' But in the face of Sam's vehemence, she'd started to be persuaded. Her eyes anxious, she'd said, 'Don't do anything hasty, love. Remember that thing about revenge being best cold. If he is cheating on you, and you want out, keep an eye to the main chance. You'll be able to take him for everything he's got.'

She added, 'You be careful, darling. You're not yourself, I can tell that just by looking at you. This is really getting to you, isn't it?'

'I'm fine,' Sam had said. 'I'll get through it. It's not the end, I'm sure of that.'

But coming back to Rawlston filled her with black dread. Every mile away from Cheltenham and all it represented – the early days of her and Ben, their wedding – dragged her down into a dark pit. As the car bumped past the lodge, she kept her eyes averted, unable even to look at it in case she caught a glimpse of Bella. The sight of Rawlston House as she turned off the lane into the driveway made her feel nauseous. Ben must still be at work – his little car wasn't there – but Emma's Mini was parked with almost offensive jauntiness by the rhododendrons.

'Great,' Sam muttered. 'That's all I need.' She heaved her bag out of the car and let herself into the house. It was quiet and looked as immaculate as usual, serene in its palette of pastels and caramels. Emma, she supposed, was upstairs, probably salivating over her university prospectus. When was she going, for God's sake? It had to be soon, surely. She threw her bag on to the floor, wandered through to the kitchen and started making a cup of herbal tea. She might have left five minutes ago, everything looked exactly as it had earlier: neat, organized, clean. Here she was, back in the bubble. Why did she ever agree to come to Rawlston? Ben's plans had never come to anything and it was obvious that the woman next door would never sell up. It had been one huge, hellish waste of time.

She ambled into the sitting room and thought about flicking on the television, but she knew what she was going to do. It was as though a little voice was calling her from inside Ben's study, tempting her in. She wasn't going to waste time resisting it, so she took her tea into his office and sat down at the desk to boot up the computer.

As usual, there was nothing incriminating in Ben's inbox but quite a few new messages had come in since she'd last checked. She was scrolling through them when a cold voice from the door-way said, 'What the hell do you think you're doing?'

Emma stood there, arms folded, leaning against the jamb. Her face was even more thin and pointed than usual and her eyes were burning indignantly as she stared at Sam. 'That's my dad's computer.'

'I'm just surfing the Net,' Sam said. 'Not that it's any of your business.'

'You're not. You're reading his email.'

Sam was startled but kept her expression cool and impassive. How did Emma know? She could only see the back of the computer screen.

'Look.' Emma nodded at the window behind her. Sam turned and saw that, quite clearly against the darkness outside, the screen was reflected on the window, showing Ben's inbox. 'You want to draw the curtains next time,' the girl said smugly.

Sam turned back, anger rising. 'I don't know why you're being so superior. What makes you think your dad minds if I look in his email? Actually, we don't have any secrets from each other, if you want to know.'

Emma smirked. 'Oh, really? That's not what I heard.'

'What are you talking about?' Sam demanded sharply.

Emma just shrugged and turned on her heel, throwing back over her shoulder as she went, 'If that's the case, you won't mind if I tell him, will you?'

Sam leapt up from her chair and rushed out of the study after her. 'What do you mean?' she cried. 'What have you heard, then?'

Emma was half-way out of the sitting room, heading towards the hall. She stopped and turned back. Her expression was unreadable but she said calmly, 'Why should I tell you anything? What do I owe you? You've made my life hell for years with your jealousy and your spite and your immaturity. What do you think it was like for me? I was thirteen when you stole my father from us and did you give a shit? No, you didn't. You only ever cared about yourself, what you could get, about having Dad all to yourself. Do you think that was kind? Or fair? Because I don't. You never once showed me any sympathy. All you could do was bitch about my mother in front of me. You never made an effort to find out how I felt, how I might feel better about things. Instead of telling me that my parents loved me, you more or less told me that no mother who loved her daughter would go to America without her. I think it was shitty, actually, to treat a child like that.'

Sam felt herself flaring with rage but didn't know what to say. She didn't want to be sidetracked by some pointless discussion of what was already in the past. She wanted to know what Emma had meant when she hinted that Ben and Sam did not trust each other.

'But,' Emma continued, 'I think things are going to change. In fact, I can feel it in the air, can't you? Ever heard of karma, Sam?' She laughed. 'I'm sure you have, with your yoga class and your eastern garden, I bet you know all about it. So you already know that what goes around, comes around, don't you?'

'What are you talking about?' Sam heard her voice tremble.

'I'm talking about sowing what you reap. Getting your just deserts. Living by the sword, dying by the sword. Get it?'

'Stop talking in fucking riddles!' she shouted. 'What are you on about? What are you trying to tell me?' She wanted to stamp her foot, to shake Emma and wipe that grin off her face.

'It seems you've set a precedent. You taught Dad how to be unfaithful, and he seems to have learnt the lesson very well indeed.' Emma wasn't grinning now. Her face was stony and she jerked out the words as though she took no pleasure in saying them.

Sam's skin turned to ice. This was it, then. She was about to get the proof she'd been after and now it was happening she'd do almost anything not to hear it. She wanted to throw her hands over her ears and block out all of it, sing and shout to stop Emma's cold voice penetrating her brain. But she couldn't, she knew that. She had to listen.

'I don't know if you've noticed anything, Sam. I've always had you down as shrewd but stupid. Cunning but ultimately too dim-witted to see the bigger picture. But I was walking back from the village the day before yesterday and I saw the proof of something I've suspected for a while.'

Sam screwed up her face, her stomach curling in agony. She grasped for words but nothing came.

'I saw Dad coming out of the barn down at the farm, with Bella. It didn't take a genius to work out what they'd been doing – their faces were flushed and they kissed right there on the lane – and I thought, Well, well, what do you know? Time to move on, is it? Time to send old Sam back to where she came from? Shall we take poor Sammy's toys away from her now? All Dad's money and Dad's house and all her pretty bits and bobs?' Emma's voice drip-ped with spite. 'Time to get rid of Sam.'

Sam was convulsed by rage. A scream ripped out of her throat and she felt all control leave her as she rushed forward and snatched at Emma's hair. All the hatred and despair rolled itself up and aimed itself at the girl, to shut her up and inflict back some of the pain she was handing out. Emma shrieked and tried to push her off but Sam had got hold of a hank of her hair, and she pulled it sharply, jerking Emma's head back. She raised the other arm and brought her open palm slamming down over Emma's face. It hurt her to deliver the blow and her hand stung with heat, so she knew Emma must have felt it – from that and from the yelp she gave. It felt good to get some of that aggression back and she raised her hand for another blow, but Emma, strengthened by her fear of being struck again, screamed, 'No!' and grabbed Sam's arm. They wrestled together, Sam struggling to free her arm so that she could gain control again; then she thought of another way and kicked out viciously, hitting Emma square in the shin with her shoe. The girl buckled and fell to the floor, crying out with the pain. Sam aimed another kick, this time on the thigh, and then again, while Emma screamed at her to stop it. She was about to land one more when Ben burst through the doorway and grabbed her by both arms, pushing her roughly away from Emma and on to the sofa.

'Sam, stop it!' he bellowed, at the top of his voice. 'What the fuck is going on here?'

Emma was crying hard from her prone position on the floor. 'She hit me, Dad,' she whimpered. She raised her head and showed the red mark across her face.

Ben spun round to Sam, his eyes as fierce as she'd ever seen them. 'Did you?' he hissed. 'Did you hit her?'

'She asked for it!' Sam shrieked, panicked.

'Emma, go upstairs. Now,' Ben ordered. Emma dragged herself to her feet and, sobbing quietly, went away.

Sam was fearful. What was he going to do to her now? Beat her up? Her rage was beginning to dissipate or, at least, that burning red violent anger was transforming itself into something else. Ben came towards her and she flinched but he just sat down beside her and stared at the rug for a while without speaking. Then he sighed deeply and said, 'I never thought that would happen.' He shook his head. 'I can't believe what I saw – that you're capable of that.'

'You don't know what she said to me.'

'Nothing should make you do that – nothing.'

'She told me . . . about *you*.' Sam's voice cracked on the last word.

'What about me?'

'Oh, come on. Please.' She laughed bitterly. 'We don't have to pretend any more. She told me about you and Bella.'

'I see,' Ben said evenly. 'We'll come to what Emma's based her conclusions on later—'

'Oh, for fuck's sake, she *saw* you! It doesn't get much plainer than that.'

'—but right now I need to say something.' His blue eyes were grave. 'It's over, Sam. I think we both know that.'

Her ears rang and a dizzy faintness rushed through her. It was what she was most afraid of. 'Why?' she whispered, her rage vanished, replaced by fear and desperation.

'I've thought it for a long while and now I'm sure. We don't love each other. I'm not sure you can love anyone, and me . . . well, I loved someone who didn't really exist. I loved an idea of you. But I could never give you enough to fill up the hole inside you, I can see that now, and if I tried to we'd both destroy ourselves in the process. And to see you like that, attacking Emma like some kind of animal. We can never get back from that.' He took her hand. 'I'm sorry. I am. I wish we could have worked it out so it was different.'

Her mouth was dry and her hand, where he was holding it, felt numb, as though it were someone else's. She licked her lips and said croakily, 'Are you going to *her*? To Bella?'

'This is nothing to do with Bella. She's a symptom, not a cause. I think it's obvious that our marriage is over, whether there's a Bella or not.'

'What are we going to do now?'

Ben shrugged. 'There's no point in wasting our time. I can move out, or you can. We'll work everything out as smoothly as possible. There're no kids, so that's a major problem we don't have.'

'Is that it, then? No talking, no trying to work it out?' Sam asked, wretched.

'What is there to talk about?'

'It's our marriage, Ben. Can't you give it one more day? We're both in a state. Let's calm down and think about it.'

'I've made up my mind, Sam. But if you want us to mull it over for one more day . . . well . . . I suppose that's the least I can do. All right, one more day. But I'll sleep in the spare room tonight.'

Sam sat upright suddenly. 'Bella . . . you won't tell her, will you?'

He said softly, 'It won't make any difference if I tell her or not.'

'Please, Ben, promise me you won't tell her till tomorrow night. You owe me that much, at least. Keep it between us for that long. I can't bear it if she knows.'

He stroked her hand again, in a gentle way that made her heart twist. 'All right, Sammy. It's between us.'

Later that night, she lay in bed alone, her heart thumping with fear and fury. Rain pounded against the windows. *He wants me out. He wants her here, in our bed. The bastard. That scheming witch. She was planning this all the time. She and Emma probably cooked it up together in France – the holiday* I *gave her.*

She realized she was grinding her teeth tightly together. Calm down, she told herself. You've got to think clearly. You've got to stop it. You've got to show her she can't get away with it.

There was, after all, one person who clearly didn't know anything about it.

'Hiya, Iain. It's Sam Clarke here.'

Iain sounded surprised to hear from her. 'Well, hello, Sam. How's things?'

'Fine. Fine. Actually they could be better.' She walked to the window and looked out over the misty grey morning. Ben had left early for work without saying goodbye and Emma's car had vanished, so she guessed she'd gone off somewhere too, to avoid her. She'd looked up Iain's company on the Internet and phoned him – a pretty straightforward piece of detective work. 'Listen, you're going to think I'm nuts but I need you to do something.'

'What's that?' He was smooth and jolly, as though he was only half listening to her.

'I want you to go to your boss and tell him there's an emergency at home. Then I want you to get on the twelve o'clock train back here and meet me in the station car park. Will you do that for me, Iain?'

There was a pause. She had his attention now. 'Is something wrong at home?' he said.

'Everything's fine. The kids are fine. Your wife is fine. But I'm serious, Iain. You have to do this.'

'Look, Sam, I don't know what you're getting at but I can't just leave the office for some reason I know nothing about. Now, if you're planning a surprise, I have to tell you it's not my birthday.'

Sam's voice became louder. 'Listen to me, Iain. Go to your boss, leave the office now and come back here. I've got something to tell you, and it concerns your wife and my husband. All right?'

There was another pause and then, 'What are you saying?'

'Just do it.' She put down the phone with a flourish and puffed at her cigarette. She went straight to the office and opened Ben's email. She clicked on the new message tab and in a fresh box, wrote:

Darling
Excuse the message from my normal email – the other one is broken at the moment. Will you meet me today   same time same place? Looking forward to it.
Ben x

Then she typed in *BellaB* and the address book supplied the rest. She pushed send and sat back, satisfied. All she had to hope was that Ben kept his word and didn't tell.

Chapter Twenty-One

It was a dull day. The rain had poured all night and now the
world felt water-logged and mushy. It was a quarter past three
when Sam pulled up in the Mercedes, parking right on the keep-
clear lines in front of the school. A few mothers, early for collecting their children, shot her bloody looks, but she ignored
them. The blue minibus that took the children back to the out-
lying villages and farmhouses waited a few yards on. She needed
to keep her eye on that and she could see clearly from here. Let
them stare at her with disapproval. Who cared about that?

At three-thirty a shrill bell sounded across the empty play-
ground and suddenly it was full of tiny people scampering across
it clutching schoolbags and paintings, hurrying to their mothers
or heading off towards the post office and the village shop. Sam
scanned the crowd carefully, worried she'd miss them. But she
saw them easily enough. Katie came out first, in her red mac,
her schoolbag dangling from one shoulder. She walked towards
the minibus. Sam got quickly out of the car, and called, 'Oy,
Katie.'

Katie looked over and saw her. She smiled and waved. 'Hi,
Sam!'

Sam beckoned to her. 'Come here.'

Katie wandered over, looking towards the school bus. 'What
are you doing here?' she asked.

'I've come to collect you. Your mum sent me. She's busy.'

'We usually go on the bus,' Katie pointed out. 'She doesn't
collect us.'

'I know, but today she said she wanted me to.' A flash of yellow went by and Sam saw Christopher scrambling up into the bus. 'Hey, Chris! Chrissie, over here!'

Christopher turned round and saw Katie standing next to Sam. He got slowly down and walked over. Katie turned to him and said, 'Sam says Mummy said to go with her.'

They looked at each other earnestly. Then Katie said to Sam with a frown, 'Our bikes are in the barn. We have to ride them home.'

'You can get them tomorrow, can't you?'

'Ye-es,' said Katie. She scuffed a shoe along the kerb.

'Don't you want a ride in our car? You can sit in the front if you like.'

'Can I? Can I sit in the front?' begged Christopher.

'We can't both sit in the front, stupid. I'm the eldest, I sit in the front.'

Sam said, 'You can both sit in the front if you want.'

Katie looked at her warily. Two children in the front wasn't allowed. Adults didn't usually suggest such recklessness. She looked as though she ought to take advantage of it. 'All right,' she said. 'Come on, Chrissie.'

The children were quiet as Sam drove them home. She didn't like that. She remembered them as they had been in France: boisterous, dancing little things, always chirruping away. They stared out of the window, pushed close together on the leather seat, the belt making one long black line across the two of them.

As they passed the lodge, the children stared at it, Katie following it with her eyes as it vanished down the lane behind them. 'Aren't we going home?' she asked.

'You're just coming up to ours for a bit. Not long. Mummy will come and collect you from our house.'

They pulled into the driveway, scraping past the dark green rhododendrons as they went. Sam clicked the belt free of them, and opened the door. They got out and stood looking up at the big house. They'd never been inside.

'Come on,' she said. 'Who wants hot chocolate?'

They'd watched television for an hour or so, with hot chocolate and biscuits. The children had relaxed and were absorbed in the afternoon cartoons. Sam sat behind them on the sofa, watching them. They were gorgeous little things. They looked more like Iain, with those blue-grey eyes and fair hair. Not a bit like Bella with her brown hair. They were cute. The kind of children she would have had, if she'd ever wanted them. Precious little things.

'It's funny in here,' said Christopher, suddenly. He looked about him. 'It's messy.'

'It is a bit messy today,' Sam said carelessly. 'My cleaning lady hasn't been.' She regarded them for a moment. 'Come on,' she said suddenly, getting up. 'We're going out.'

'Where're we going? Won't Mummy be coming for us?' Katie asked, guarded and wary again.

'Not for an hour or so. We should go for a walk. I know – you like that stream. You like playing down there, don't you? There's where we'll go.' She went to the chair and picked up their coats.

'We're not allowed at the stream,' said Christopher. 'Mummy said it's dangerous.'

'I'll be with you. She won't mind. Come on.'

The children stared up at her, clutching their mugs.

She felt cross. Why wouldn't they do what she said? Were all children the same? 'Come on,' she snapped. 'Get a bloody move on. We're going to have fun by the stream, all right? Put your coats on.'

They got up obediently and put on their plastic macs.

'You wait here,' she told them at the front door. There was one more thing she had to do. She went down to the cellar and found the paint that the builders had left behind after they'd finished their work. She selected a full tin of pale green gloss that had graced the woodwork in the dining room, and took it upstairs to the kitchen. She pulled Ben's favourite carving knife from the rack, a heavy thing made of a single piece of steel, and used it to force off the lid. The blade juddered and squeaked as she prised the tin open and she half hoped it would snap but it stayed in one piece. The tin was three-quarters full. She lifted it up and approached the vast stainless-steel cooker, Ben's pride and joy. Slowly, she raised the can above the gleaming hob and spotless burners and, with the measured movement of a ritual, poured the gloop all over it. It was surprising how much paint there was in a tin, she thought, as the fountain of gloss continued to come, filling up the wells around the gas jets, slipping over the side on to the units and down behind the wall. The pleasing shade of pale green looked rather pretty against the polished steel, she thought. More and more, until the cooker was coated and dripping, paint finding its way into every crevice.

She stepped back and looked at her handiwork with satisfaction. Then she turned and put the tin carefully on the marble surface.

'Come on, then, kids,' she called, striding back to the hall. 'Stream time!'

Bella hadn't expected to hear from Ben that day. He'd told her he would be in a long meeting off-site, out of contact, so she was surprised to get a message from him suggesting their usual rendezvous at the hotel. Surprised but pleased. His meeting must have been cancelled, she thought. He must have some time he can snatch.

She hurried about the house, tidying up, pushing the children's toys into their box and washing up the breakfast things. If Ben had no work today, perhaps they could spend some of the afternoon together. If she got the housework out of the way, she could relax with him and get back just before the children came home from school.

The drive towards Oxford was the same as usual, although perhaps the sky was a little more lowering and grim than it had been so far this autumn. But when she got to the hotel, parked and went to the bar, there was no sign of Ben. She waited for three-quarters of an hour, in case his schedule was different from normal – if he could arrive later he might be able to stay later – sitting in the bar with an orange juice, ignoring the stares of the barman. She tried Ben's mobile from the lobby phone but it was switched off and carried her straight to his answer-machine where she didn't dare leave a message.

It was past the time they'd usually be saying goodbye when she gave up, and drove home, puzzled. Something must have happened – something he wouldn't be able to tell her until later.

She arrived home, parked the car beside the lodge and let herself into the silent house. She put down her coat and bag, made her way to the kitchen, switched on the light and screamed, jumping violently.

'Oh, God,' she said, with a laugh, clutching her chest. 'You gave me a fright! What are you doing here on your own in the dark?'

Iain had his back to the door, sitting in a kitchen chair and looking out of the window. He turned slowly and stared at her and, from the expression on his face and in his reddened eyes, she knew at once.

She took a step forward. 'Iain,' she said gently. 'Iain . . .'

'Shut up!' he shouted. He slammed a hand on the kitchen table and she saw it was shaking. 'Don't say a bloody word to me. I don't want to hear your filthy, filthy lies. How can you live with yourself? When did you get so . . . *low*? Christ—' His voice broke on the word and he bit his lip, covering his eyes with a hand.

Bella's thoughts were whirling about her head. How did he know? When did he find out? What should she say? How much could she conceal? She advanced slowly and sat on the chair opposite him.

He brought his hand down, looking calmer, taking control of himself with an effort. A deep breath came from his lungs, with a slight shudder in it. 'Okay. I've had some time to think about it. Not long, but enough time to come to some conclusions. I don't know how long you've been sleeping with that man – perhaps you were even sneaking off in France with your own children in the house – but that makes no difference, really. Once is bad enough. The fact is, you've ruined everything . . .' His voice ebbed away as he seemed to understand the significance of what he was saying. 'Everything's utterly spoiled. Us. All of it.' He looked up at her, agonized. 'Why? Why, Bella?'

'I don't know,' she said, feeling the limpness of what she was saying. 'I felt as though I needed it.'

'What didn't I give you?'

Now that he was sitting there, asking to be told all the things she'd been thinking about why their marriage no longer made her happy, she couldn't bring herself to say any of it. What good would it do to kick him when he was down? She had to concentrate her energies on calming him, mollifying him while she worked out what was best.

'I'm sorry,' she said instead. 'I don't know why it happened.'

His face turned cold. 'You could at least accord me the respect of having a reason for cheating on me. You could at least have a reason for fucking over our marriage. Was there nothing in your head when you went to bed with him? Didn't you think of me at all?'

No, she thought. *You are the last thing I think about in bed with Ben.* 'Of course I did. I know it was wrong. I just . . . Perhaps there is something wrong with us, something we need to talk about.'

'You're damn right there's something wrong,' he said roughly. 'I would have thought that was obvious. You've made your choice and now you have to live with it. That's what being an adult is all about it.'

'Isn't being an adult about understanding and talking and forgiveness?'

His voice dropped, trembling with rage. 'Don't you dare lecture me about morals and understanding. What understanding have you shown *me*? You're a cold bitch. Don't you realize what you've done?'

Bella was at a loss. She still didn't understand how the rug had been pulled out from under her in this way. All her power was gone. She'd been in charge of everything all this time and now it had been taken away from her. She was confused and baffled, unsure of what to do. She hadn't decided what she wanted and, she saw now, had assumed that life would continue in the same way until she chose to change it.

Iain pulled his chair closer to hers. 'All right, let me explain something. Marriage is not a three-strikes-you're-out game. You do not have a series of lives to use up. You have one chance to get it right, and if you destroy it you don't get it back. You make a promise when you get married, or have you forgotten it? You promise to be faithful to the marriage. It is a contract between us, and it is legally binding. Do you understand? Do you understand me?'

'Yes, but—'

'No buts,' he said fiercely. 'Don't you understand me? No ifs and buts and I-only-meants. Here's the thing. You've committed the ultimate betrayal, Bella. You've broken our contract. You promised me *life* and you've broken your word. So, all right – the contract is shattered. I shall seek what I'm owed when a legal contract is reneged on.'

'What do you mean?'

'I mean,' he said, slow and measured, 'divorce. I will go to the courts and request that they dissolve all the remnants of our partnership, and I will insist that your adultery entitles you to nothing and I will request custody of our children on the grounds of your moral character. If I had my way, you would never see them again and I would tell them –' his voice faltered again '– I would tell them that you're dead, because it would be easier for all of us that way. I wish you were dead. I wish you could have been killed in an accident rather than that it would end this way. My God! I loved you, Bella, I devoted myself to you and our children. I . . . don't understand this.' Tears rushed to his eyes and he covered them again with his hand.

She was frightened but the tears reassured her that he was in the grip of emotion, saying things he didn't mean, letting his rage get the better of him. She mustn't take anything he said seriously or let him scare her too badly. 'Iain,' she said, 'I'm sorry – let's not rush into anything. We don't have to talk about divorce now, do we? I mean,' she almost laughed. 'divorce! We were perfectly happy this morning.'

'You lying hypocrite,' he hissed, dropping his hand. His eyes were burning with anger. 'Happy this morning? You because you could see your lover whenever you wanted and me because I didn't know any fucking better! Poor bloody fool. No.' He calmed down again. 'I've thought it through and there's no other way. I want you out of here now, tonight. I want you gone before the children get back.'

'Where am I going to go?' she asked, bewildered.

'That's not my problem. Come on,' he said, standing up. 'I've packed a bag for you. You may as well go now, and my solicitor will be available to talk to you. You know his address. I'll drive you to the station.'

'What? Wait!' she protested. 'This is all too fast.'

'You should have thought about it before you did what you did.'

'But . . .' Her mind was racing. She simply couldn't believe that this was happening. She looked at her watch. The children should be home by now. 'Where are the children?' she said, and was struck by a horrible fear. 'Where are they? What have you done with them?' She jumped to her feet and ran out of the kitchen, along the hall and into the sitting room, calling, 'Katie! Christopher!' but the sitting room was empty. She passed Iain in the hall as she pounded up the stairs to their bedrooms, hoping that they'd come back somehow without her hearing them. 'Katie! Are you there? Chrissie!' They were not. She came back to the top of the stairs. 'Where are they?' she shouted, her fearfulness coming out as anger.

'They're fine,' Iain said, looking up at her. 'You might as well realize you're not going to see them until some damn court forces me to let you.'

'Iain! Where are my children?' she yelled.

He gazed at her. 'They're fine, I told you. Sam offered to look after them. They're with her.'

She gasped. 'Sam? She told you, didn't she? She told you about Ben. Oh, my God, and you've given her our children. What have you done? Oh, my God, oh, my God.' She raced down the stairs and opened the front door. The lane was silent and empty. 'We've got to find them!' she said frantically, and ran out.

Bella tore up the lane, her heart pounding, ignoring the mud and the puddles. She rounded the drive to the Clarkes' front door and saw the Mercedes in the driveway. A throb of relief filled her as she thought, *She must be home, they must be here.* But the lights were off inside and there was no answer to her thumping on the door and ringing of the bell.

'Sam! Katie! Christopher!' she shouted, but there was no response. She looked about, as though she would see them rounding the side of the house at any minute, and then she set off again back down the drive. She saw Iain walking up the lane towards her. 'They're not there!' she shouted. 'She's taken them!'

She ran up the driveway to the Fielding side and round to the kitchen door. This time the door opened to her panicked knocking. Jane Fielding stood there, looking bemused to see Bella, damp and wild-eyed, on her doorstep.

'Have you seen my children?' blurted out Bella. 'Sam Clarke has them – have you seen them?'

'No . . . no. Not today. You look awful – come in.'

'I can't – there's no time. I've got to find them!'

'Calm down now – tell me what's wrong.' Jane put out a hand and pulled her gently into the kitchen. 'A few minutes can't hurt. What's this about the children?'

'Oh, something terrible's happened.' Bella's voice cracked for the first time. 'She found out!'

'Oh dear,' Jane said, in a measured voice, trying to keep Bella calm. 'Yes, that is bad.'

'She's found out and she's told my husband and he's going to take the children away,' Bella's voice rose in panic, 'but she took them first and now I can't find them!'

'Is her car there?'

'Yes, it is.'

'Have you called Mr Clarke?'

'His phone's off.' Bella stared up at the other woman with beseeching eyes. 'What am I going to do? Where can they be?'

Jane said, 'If the car's there, they can't be far away. It's a long walk to anywhere in either direction. Let's go and look for them. I'm sure there's a simple explanation. She would never hurt the children. You mustn't worry about that.'

'All right.' Bella took a deep breath and tried to calm herself. 'All right. Let's go and look.'

In the driveway they met Iain, who was walking towards the house.

'We're going to look for them,' said Bella, 'they must be around here somewhere.'

He looked puzzled, the first signs of worry in his eyes. 'I'm sure there's nothing to be concerned about. She said she'd take care of them. She wouldn't hurt them.'

'Your wife is very upset,' Jane said. Her voice was calm but there an anxious edge to it. 'She needs to find the children.'

'She should have thought about her precious children before,' Iain replied, with a cold spite in his voice.

'I think we ought to look for them.' Behind her, Bella was crying tearless, panicked sobs.

Iain frowned. Jane's quiet insistence seemed to be convincing him that he should be anxious. 'I'm sure it's fine,' he persisted, though he sounded a little less certain.

'You stupid man!' screamed Bella, furious. 'You're so blind! Can't you see anything at all?' She ran out on to the lane and looked up and down, trying to guess where Sam might have taken them.

Jane came up beside her, tying a scarf round her neck. 'Your husband has agreed to search the woods,' she said. 'He's going off now.'

'You try down at the farm,' Bella said. 'They could be there. I'll go to the stream.'

Jane nodded and headed off down the lane towards the old farm buildings. 'Call if you need me,' she said.

Bella climbed the fence into the meadow at the side of the lane and ran across it towards the woods. It was sopping wet and the long grass soaked her trousers while her shoes were soon heavy with mud. The surface of the ground was uneven, with hillocks and pits concealed under tufts of grass. Her breath burned in her chest as she tried to keep her footing. On the other side of the meadow, she climbed the fence and found the muddy track that led down to the stream. Everything was slippery and unsettled. How far was it to the stream? She'd only been there once or twice when the children wanted to show her something. She went down the track as quickly as she dared. The light was failing and it was gloomy once she was under the tree canopy. The twilight felt menacing. There was no sound, apart from the panting of her own breath and the tapping of raindrops falling from leaf to leaf.

As she approached the gully that the stream ran through, she called, 'Katie, Christopher!' There was no reply. It was dark and cold here. Why would Sam bring them to the stream? Iain was right. This was ridiculous. There was no one here. It was deserted. She walked more slowly towards the bank, then noticed that the stream seemed to be blocked by something. She approached, straining to see what it was in the darkness. It looked like some old tyres or a mound of plastic . . . then she caught sight of the colour: a flash of canary yellow and the darker smear of red. She knew at once what it was, and unable to do anything else, began to scream.

This is very bad, Jane thought, going into the broken-down barn. She was much more frightened than she'd dared let on to the Balfours. The husband had no grasp on the situation at all, though she'd tried to convey to him how important it was that they find the children. But Bella knew. Her terror was obvious, and Jane couldn't help fearing that she was right to be so scared. She only had to think about Sam in her kitchen that day, twitchy and peculiar, harping on about Bella's faults. Perhaps she'd known about the affair even then. It was clear that she knew now. They all knew.

Jane shook her shoulders in a cold shiver. It was awful, dreadful. What would happen now? But first things first – those poor little children. The idea of something happening to them, of Sam hurting them, was too dreadful to consider. They had to around here somewhere.

She went into the barn. It was dry inside at least, but there was no one there. She hadn't expected that there would be, it was far too quiet. Coming out, she wondered where she should look next. The place was deserted, that was clear. Then she heard a shrill, high sound and realized a woman was screaming.

'Oh God,' she said aloud, and began to run towards the sound. She knew where the stream was – her own children had played there when they were young – and she hurried towards it as fast as she could, chilled by the cries echoing from the wood.

When she got under the trees, she could hear that the shrieks had diminished to sobbing. Running as fast as she dared along the muddy track, she came up to the stream and saw Bella's head above the linc of the bank. She had something with her in the water.

What is it? wondered Jane, then thought, with despair, *No, no, not the children, don't let her have the children, please.* The horrible idea came upon her: the Balfour children had been drowned in the stream. She went to the edge of the bank and looked down.

Bella was sobbing uncontrollably. She looked up and saw Jane. 'Look!' she wailed. 'Look what she's done!' She held up the small yellow mackintosh. 'Look . . .'

The other mac lay plump and round in the water while the one in Bella's hands hung limply, and scattered round it dark rags and clothes that had been stuffed into it. It was empty now. 'Look what she did,' Bella said brokenly, between sobs. 'Oh, my God. I thought they were dead.'

'Come on, get out of there,' Jane said, horrified by the sight of the children's clothes deliberately left like that. 'We'll look for them somewhere else. Come on now, come out of the water.'

'But Katie's coat, she loves her coat . . .' said Bella.

'Come on, come with me. We can get them later.'

Bella insisted on leaving the macs carefully at the side of the stream. She was shaking all over with fright and cold. Jane led her out of the woods, an arm round her shoulders, trying to comfort her. 'Is there anywhere we haven't looked?' she asked.

'Only the cottages,' Bella said.

'Trudy does Mrs Clarke's cleaning, doesn't she?'

Bella looked at her, eyes suddenly hopeful. 'Yes, yes, she does. She knows Trudy. Of course she does. Come on.'

They hurried to the cottages. The short-cut from the stream to the lodge led directly past them. They looked solid and homely in the gloom, their yellow windows bright in the darkness. Bella ran to the cottage where Trudy and her family lived and pounded on the door.

It opened at once. Trudy's mother stood there, frowning, holding a yapping dog back by its collar. 'I should think so too,' she said. 'What time do you call this?'

Jane came up behind Bella. 'Hello, Mrs O'Reilly.'

The old woman's face cleared. 'Oh, hello, missus. I didn't see it was you. I was just surprised that the lady here hadn't been to collect her children before now. It's over two hours we've had them and I need to get the tea on.'

'Are they here?' panted Bella, hardly daring to hope. 'Are they?'

Mrs O'Reilly stood back and opened the door wider to reveal Katie and Christopher sitting at her kitchen table, muted and frightened. 'Mummy,' said Katie, with relief, when she saw Bella, and Christopher got down to run towards her. Bella put her arms out to them and felt tears running freely down her face as they pressed close to her.

Chapter Twenty-two

'Aren't we going home, Mummy?' Katie asked, as they passed the lodge.

'No, darling, not now. Not yet. Mrs Fielding has kindly said we can go to her house.' Jane was walking beside them. She'd murmured to Bella that it might be best if they came back with her until things had calmed down. Bella held the children tightly by a hand each. 'We're going to have tea there. Won't that be fun?'

'I want to go home,' moaned Christopher. He looked exhausted.

'Why did Sam collect us today?' said Katie.

'It's all very complicated, darling. I'll tell you later.' She was watching out for Iain. But she had the children, was physically holding them. He couldn't take them away now.

He was coming round the side of the house into the driveway as they walked up. 'I see I was right,' he called, as they neared him. 'They look fine to me.'

'Go away,' Bella shouted warningly, clutching the children's hands more tightly. 'Go home!' she called, as though talking to a bad dog. 'You're not having them.'

Katie looked up at her, frightened.

'Come on, kids. Don't you want to come home?' Iain said. 'We can have my special supper and watch TV. Don't you want to?'

They looked from mother to father, eyes wide and scared.

'Come on,' Iain coaxed again. He beckoned to them, holding out his hands.

'They're not coming,' Bella yelled. 'You're not getting your hands on them!'

Christopher stuttered, 'Da-daddy' and started to cry. Iain

305

rushed forward and grabbed him, yanking him suddenly upwards and out of Bella's grasp before she realized what was happening. With the boy tucked under his arm, he reached out, took hold of Katie's arm and pulled her away as well.

'No, no!' Bella shouted. 'Give him back! Let go of her!'

Katie began to cry with terror and pain as they pulled back and forth between them, Iain wrenching at one arm and Bella tugging at the other. Tears streamed down Bella's face as she sobbed, 'Stop it! Give them back! Give them back!'

Jane tried to intervene, flitting helplessly round them, begging either of them to let go, but neither was listening. Christopher howled at the top of his voice and, with one strong tug, Iain forced Bella to let go of Katie or have the child's arm torn out of its socket. He scooped her under his other arm and strode off down the driveway, leaving Bella shaking and desperate, only able to watch him go, the two children crying hysterically for her as he went.

She couldn't stop trembling, even wrapped in a blanket in front of the fire in the sitting room, with a glass of brandy in her hand, put there by Jane. She was in a kind of shock, she knew that, for all it helped. The events of the day replayed themselves over and over again in her mind, the horror unfolding afresh each time.

'How could she do that?' she whispered. 'How could she? Even if she hated me . . .'

Jane sat with her, offering her what comfort she could, but Bella could see in her eyes that she considered the situation serious.

'Will he give me back the children?' she asked, through chattering teeth.

'We'll see,' answered Jane, clasping her hands round her knees. 'He can't stop you seeing them, at any rate. You'll have to find a lawyer. Get some advice. I'm afraid I don't know much about custody law.'

'How did this happen?' Bella murmured in disbelief. 'This morning everything was fine, everything was normal, and now . . .' She sighed a long, juddering sigh, the result of exhaustion and hours of crying.

'You're very tired. I think you should go to bed. I've made up the spare room for you.'

'Ben.' A light of energy came into Bella's eyes. 'I must see Ben, talk to him.' She struggled to her feet, casting off her blanket.

Jane caught at her arm. 'No,' she said. 'You're too done in. Leave it for now. Look at everything fresh in the morning.' Her tone was firm.

Bella's energy leaked away under her command; in a way, she was grateful to let go of responsibility for herself. 'All right,' she said, in a small voice. 'I'll go over there tomorrow.'

She woke in the morning and enjoyed a moment of happy ignorance, wondering where she was and why, before everything came rushing back to her. She sat bolt upright with a gasp, staring round at the small white-painted room. It was early, but she got out of bed at once. She had to see Ben as soon as possible.

It was still almost dark as she set off to the house next door, and a rough, cold wind cut through the trees. She walked quickly, ignoring the chill. In the driveway, the dark Mercedes was gone but Ben's car was there instead. She felt a rush of relief and knocked on the door, pounded on it, and called his name. When it opened and he was standing there, she fell on to him, engulfed with relief. Ben would make it all right – he was so tall and strong and capable. She didn't have to worry any more.

'Ben . . . I'm so glad to see you.' She hugged him.

He didn't seem surprised to see her, but hugged her back quickly, then stepped away to let her into the house. 'Emma and I are cleaning.'

'Cleaning?'

'Yes. Look at this.' He gestured for her to come in. 'Sam's gone.'

Bella stepped inside. The hall was a mess. The immaculate pale emptiness of the house was ruined. Every object that could be knocked over had been; the vase lay shattered on the table, flowers and water all over it. The mirror was hanging askew and the floor was covered with rubbish.

'I got home last night to find the place looking like this, and no Sam. It looks like a typhoon's been through it.' They walked into the sitting room, where the destruction was even greater. The leather sofa was ripped, the photo frames smashed, the glass shelves smeared with dirt and what looked like honey. Emma was there, scrubbing at a dark stain on the floor. She looked up and nodded at Bella in acknowledgement, then went back to her work.

'My God,' Bella said, stunned. 'She's gone mad.'

'You haven't seen her *pièce de résistance*.' He led her to the kitchen and they looked in silence at the vast, ruined stove, the paint now dry in places, or lying in wet puddles with a saucer of skin on top.

'Bloody hell.'

'I don't know if the insurance covers wilful paint attack, but I have a feeling it doesn't.' He sighed, looking sadly at his expensive cooker. 'I should have foreseen this, that she'd take some revenge. She found out about you and me, and attacked Emma for telling her. I told her plainly that I felt this was the end of the road for us but she begged me for twenty-four hours, so I gave in. I thought it was the least I could do. Stupid. I didn't bank on this.'

Bella said bluntly, 'That's not all. She told Iain. He's thrown me out.'

'What?' Ben looked serious. 'Come with me.'

They went into his study, sat down and Bella told him everything that had happened the day before. 'When I got your message, I did think it was odd – coming from your official email and not sounding exactly like you, but I just believed it. She must have been planning to get me out of the house so that she could get Iain back here and tell him everything.'

Ben was white-faced and horrified. 'But the kids,' he said. 'I can't believe she'd be capable of that. God, Bella, I'm sorry. I really am. If I'd had even the faintest inkling that she'd be capable of turning against them, I'd never, never . . .' He paused, lost for words. 'I'd never have let that happen. I told her plainly that it wasn't because of you that we were splitting up. I thought she understood that.'

'I don't think that displays much knowledge of the female mind,' she said drily. A tiny, selfish voice at the back of her mind asked why it wasn't for her he'd decided to leave Sam. She suppressed it.

'This is terrible. I don't even know where she is.'

'Do you really care?'

His eyes were hooded. 'Of course I care. You must hate her guts but she's still my wife.'

They sat in silence for a while. Then he looked up at her and said, 'What are you going to do?'

Grateful that he was thinking of her at least a little, she shrugged helplessly. 'I've no idea. I've got nowhere to go, no money and Iain has my children. It's not a great situation.'

Ben stared at the carpet. 'I'll do what I can to help,' he said finally. 'I can give you some money, and put you in touch with my lawyer if you need legal advice. But you can't stay here. You understand that, don't you?'

Was it just the other day that they'd been locked into each other in that barn, panting in time, passionate? She remembered it so clearly. Now, here they were, and the last thing she could expect from him was somewhere to stay. Everything was transformed but how, and why, she didn't understand.

When she didn't reply, he said, 'I've got to think of Emma. I can't move Sam out and you in, just like that, even if it would be to do you a favour. She's been through too much. It wouldn't be right. I've got to think of her.'

'What about *my* children?' Bella asked, her voice shaky. 'What will they think if I just disappear?'

He put his hand over hers and squeezed. 'He can't stop you seeing them – no court in the land would allow it. I'll get you some top-notch advice. It'll be fine, you'll see.'

She gazed up into his handsome face. It had been everything she desired for so long and suddenly, and with complete clarity, she understood that their affair was over.

She went back to the Fielding house, pale and muted. Jane was in the kitchen in her dressing-gown, making fresh coffee. She seemed to know at once that there was nothing more to be said about Ben. She gave Bella a mug and hugged her lightly. 'You know you're welcome to stay here as long as you like. I've got more room than I can possibly need.'

'Thank you,' Bella said, with a small smile. 'I don't know what to do. I simply have no idea.'

'I could go down and get some things for you later,' suggested Jane. 'And you ought to think about talking to a solicitor about access to the children.'

'Do you think I should stay away? They're so close – they'll be going to school in a little while, I could see them then . . .'

'I should think Iain's thought of that. Look, it's in the children's interests that they're spared the kind of scene we had yesterday.'

Tears rushed to Bella's eyes at the memory of it. She covered her face with her hands and began to cry. 'What have I done?' she said. 'I had no idea . . . Oh God, if I lose the children . . .' Seeing Ben had made her feel so desperately empty. It had been such a wonderful fantasy, the day that she and Ben were together without their partners. How had it turned out to be that limp, half-hearted affair? It was as though she'd been promised the most wonderful Christmas present in the world, and had opened it to find it was just an empty box. What on earth had it all been for?

She felt Jane's arms around her, buried her face in the soft flannel of her dressing-gown and wept.

Later that day, she was more in control of herself, quivering with nervous energy as she considered her options. She called Nicky to explain the situation. To her credit, Nicky never so much as hinted at an 'I told you so'.

'Oh, love,' she said, sympathetically. 'What a terrible thing to happen. You can come to me if you need to, you know that, don't you? And don't worry about Iain, he hasn't got a chance if he really intends to fight you for the kids.'

'I might have to throw myself on your mercy, at least for a little while,' Bella said. 'I can't stay here in Rawlston.'

'What about your . . . that man – Ben? What's happening with him?'

The pause before Bella answered was enough to tell Nicky what

310

she wanted to know. 'Right. I see. Great. What a shit! Can't he see you've ruined your marriage for him?'

'It's not that simple. He's not a shit, really. Things are pretty rough for him as well.' Bella wondered why she was rushing to Ben's defence. Nicky was right in a way – Ben owed her something and, apart from recommending his lawyer, he'd made it clear that she was on her own. The fall-out from their affair was her concern alone. Yet she couldn't be angry with him, even if it appeared that he would escape from the whole mess much more lightly than she would. She had nothing to rebuke him with: no promises were made, no vows were exchanged. They were always at liberty to walk away at any point. She understood that the rules hadn't changed because the situation had imploded so spectacularly.

'What's he got to lose, apart from his barmy wife?' demanded Nicky, indignant on Bella's behalf. 'A bit of alimony? Poor lamb! Whereas you've lost your home, your kids, your husband . . .'

'But,' said Bella miserably, 'I knew that was the risk from the start. I can't pass the buck now.'

'You come to me. We'll make plans. We'll sort this out.' Nicky was firm and decisive. Bella followed her lead obediently, grateful for her strength.

Jane couldn't shake the image of Iain carrying away his screaming children. It haunted her, making her skin crawl with a cold chill. She tried to banish it by recalling Katie and Christopher coming into the kitchen looking for biscuits, boisterous and high-spirited, but instead she saw them white-faced and crying, looking with confusion at their parents.

When Alec came into the kitchen, she grabbed him and hugged him tightly until he pushed her off, saying, 'Oy, Mum. That hurts.'

Later, while she was making lunch, she heard the telephone extension bing, telling her that the phone had been put down in another room and a few moments later Bella came in.

'How is everything?' Jane asked. They sat down at the table together.

'I've made some decisions,' Bella said, running a hand through her dark hair. 'I'm going to stay in London with my friend Nicky for a while. I've got to get things sorted out.'

'Are you sure?'

'Yes. It's very kind of you to invite me to stay here but . . .' Bella looked strained. 'Ben next door, Iain down the road. It's too much. I think I need to get away for a bit, clear my head. But I'm going to see the children first, explain to them what's happening, and I will need your help for that.'

'What can I do?' Jane asked, apprehensive.

'Iain will have to behave like a human being if you're there. Would you mind? Would you be able to do that? I know it's a lot to ask.'

'No, no. Of course I'll come. We'll go down after lunch. Do you think he'll be there?'

'I shouldn't think he's gone to work today. Thank you, Jane. It means a lot, particularly as there's no earthly reason why you should get involved in this mess.'

Jane thought of the children's faces again. 'I'm happy to help, if I can,' she said.

They went down the lane together that afternoon, Bella wide-eyed and silent, absorbed in her thoughts, while Jane walked beside her, apprehensive. When they got to the red-brick house, they stood for a moment in front of it.

'Perhaps you should knock,' said Bella. 'I don't want to start a furious row on the doorstep – you might be able to prepare him a bit.'

'All right.' Jane went to the door and banged the knocker. She waited a minute or so, then it opened slowly and she saw Iain's white face in the gap between the door and the jamb. He immediately looked beyond her to where Bella stood in the lane.

'What do you want?' he said in a high, trembling voice. 'Why is she here? I've already made it perfectly clear that we don't want her.'

'Hello, Iain.' She dropped her voice to a low, comforting tone, the kind she used to a frightened animal. 'We've come down

312

because Bella needs to pick up a few things, and she wants to see the children.'

Iain's eyes hardened. 'No,' he spat.

'Now, come on, I think we all need to be reasonable,' she said calmly. 'It's not right to deprive the children of the chance to see their mother, no matter how you feel about your wife right now. I have every sympathy with what you must be going through, I really do. But it's not going to improve your cause if you prevent Bella seeing the children. It won't take long. Will you let us in? Are the children here or are they at school?'

He stared straight at her. Jane was disconcerted by his suspicious gaze and hard-set mouth. He probably thinks I was in on it, she thought. He thinks I'm her cohort. Then his eyes slipped away back to Bella and his air became distracted and sunken.

'They're here. But I don't want her inside,' he said. There was a tone of wretchedness under the steel.

'I know, I know.' Jane put her hand on the door as though she was reaching out to comfort Iain himself. 'I know it must be painful, difficult . . . but I promise, if you let Bella see the children, you'll be doing the right thing.' His reluctance was almost tangible. I must push him gently, she thought, or he'll suddenly turn to stone and then there will be no shifting him. She hoped Bella would keep quiet and not take it into her head to say anything to disrupt the delicate balance of the situation. 'Think of Katie and Christopher. It would be very wrong not to let them say goodbye to their mother.'

Iain said quickly, 'She's leaving?'

'She's going to stay with a friend in London.'

'She's not going to stay with . . . *him*?' Iain's voice strained over the last word.

Jane shook her head. 'I think that's all over.'

They stood looking at each other for a long moment, then Iain slowly pulled the door open. 'She can come in for ten minutes,' he said. 'But I don't want to talk to her. I'll be in the back.'

He turned and strode off down the corridor as Bella darted forward, encouraged by the sight of the door opening.

'Thank you, thank you,' she said to Jane, as she brushed past, eager to get upstairs. 'He'd never have let me in if you hadn't been here.'

Jane waited in the sitting room while Bella went upstairs to pack her bag and talk to Katie and Christopher. She came down twenty minutes later, a heavy bag over one shoulder, weeping.

They walked back up to the house together, Bella unable to speak through her sobs.

Here I am, back in London, Bella thought, as the taxi took her from Paddington to Nicky's flat.

Odd, how the situation was reversed. Now leaving Rawlston felt like leaving her life behind and the city had an atmosphere of unreality and foreignness about it. Nicky had left the key to her apartment with the doorman, along a with note telling her to make herself at home. Bella wandered about the tiny, silent little flat, wondering what to do. Had she done the right thing, coming away like this? But what choice did she have? Staying with Jane Fielding hadn't felt right, and she didn't know how she'd be able to stand being so near the children without seeing them. Saying goodbye to them had been heartbreaking enough. Their confusion had cut through her heart like a knife. It was so evident that they had no idea how their world had come to be slung upside down like this.

'When are you coming home, Mummy?' they'd begged.

She hadn't known what to say. 'Soon,' she'd replied. 'As soon as I can. And Daddy will look after you until then.'

Getting up and walking away was one of the hardest things she'd ever done. She was determined to establish her access quickly and speedily but she could see that, as things stood, she was in a difficult position. Iain was in the family home, near the children's school, offering them familiarity and continuity. She had nowhere to live and no job: she could hardly demand that Iain hand them over when she didn't have a roof over her own head.

Not knowing what else to do, she went to the spare room, lay down on the bed, curled herself into a ball and slept.

Ben was as good as his word. Two days later, Bella had a phone call from his lawyer, and then an email from Ben delicately offering to pay all her legal fees. She wished she were in a position to refuse, but she wasn't.

I'm going to be in town later in the week. Do you want to meet for a drink? he wrote.

Bella almost laughed when she read it. It was only a short time since they'd been grasping every opportunity to meet, sending each other messages loaded with desire and heavy with sex. They were like strangers again, she thought. She wondered why she wasn't furious with him; after all, they were both free now – able to do anything they wanted, wherever and whenever they liked. Ben took it for granted now that she understood nothing like that would happen.

They arranged to meet in a wine bar beneath Leicester Square. He was waiting for her when she arrived nervous and in need of a glass of wine. He kissed her cheek, smiled and said, 'It's good to see you.'

'Good to see you too.' She took the glass of wine he offered and they found a table. They both looked different, she thought. Ben was washed-out, somehow, and grey-faced. His eyes had lost some of their intensity.

'How are you?' he asked, when they were settled at a small table, crammed hard against the wall.

'All right. Nicky's being lovely – it can't be much fun coming home to me moping about every evening. I'm trying to find some temping work but it doesn't seem as easy as it did when I was younger. Otherwise, I'm learning a lot about daytime television.' She felt awkward. A few feet away, a couple were bent close across their table, murmuring to each other over their clasped hands, oblivious of everyone else.

'It's a shame about your business,' he said. 'I suppose that's no good now. I thought that was a goer.'

'I know.' She shrugged. 'But I can't run a business without a permanent address. It's just not possible. I'm doing all right, really. I'm sure I'll be able to see the children soon, your lawyer's rushing it all through for me. We should have something sorted out by Christmas anyway.'

'That's great. I'm pleased for you.'

'And you? What's happened with Sam?'

He sighed. 'I've spoken to her, I haven't seen her. She sounds in a very bad way – she's staying with her parents, which amazed me as she can't stand them, and when I called she was doped up to the eyeballs.'

'Coke?'

He shook his head. 'Some kind of tranquillizer, I should think, or anti-depressant. I imagine Sam's mother is feeding them to her like sweeties, just to keep her under control. Still, she was composed enough to tell me she'd be after everything I've got in the divorce.'

'Oh, Ben . . .'

'Don't worry. There are more important things than money, you know. I've tried to look at all this as an opportunity to make some changes. I've been thinking hard, talking to Emma, working out what we're going to do.'

'Yes?' She felt a flicker of interest, as though these changes might involve her, and then rebuked herself quickly. She wasn't going to be a part of Ben's life, that much was obvious, and even if he asked her to, she didn't think it was what she really wanted. She'd know for certain if she did.

'I've decided I'm going to sell the house at Rawlston and buy Sam off with as much of the money as it takes to satisfy her. All of it, if I have to. Then I plan to move up to Edinburgh, buy a small flat, do something new. I can let the business run itself – I pay some good people very good money to do just that. I took Emma up to university the other day. It's absolutely beautiful, and she loves it there. Just breathing in that air . . . it felt like a new place, a place to get clean in. Fresh beginning and all that.'

Bella felt a stab of envy. Ben was so free, while she felt like a prisoner. She laughed lightly and said, 'Most students wouldn't appreciate their fathers moving to the same city as their university.'

'Perhaps. But most students aren't Emma. We've lost years along the way and I want to make it up to her, if I possibly can. I won't crowd her, I'm not that stupid. But I want her to know I'm

316

there for her any time. In fact—' he smiled almost to himself – 'I think she quite likes the idea.'

'Perhaps all this was a blessing in disguise, then.'

He put a hand on hers, his gaze apologetic. 'Better for me than for you, eh? I know how it must seem. You've every right to be bitter about it. I really didn't want you to suffer because of me, that's why I want you to accept whatever you need to pay for the lawyer.'

'Do you think that's all it takes?' she said abruptly. 'It seems like you're buying me off the same way you're doing with Sam.'

'Does it? I'm sorry if that's the way it looks. I think of you very differently. If I could make it all better for you, I'd do it in an instant. But I can't, you know that. We both know that. We could pretend we were in love and that being together would work out for us, but it's obvious that we're not and that it would be a disaster if we tried to force it. I don't know about you, but I need some time on my own, to get my head together.'

'Of course,' she replied, embarrassed that it might seem she was begging him to be with her. 'So do I. And I'll be fine, don't worry about me. I'd like us to be friends, if we can.'

'We are friends, no matter what. And I know you'll be all right. You're strong, no matter how bad and low you're feeling right now. You'll make things work out.'

She smiled. 'I'll try. I suppose it's a question of flexibility – and I've always been ready to change my future. It's been the story of my life. And you're going to have to let go of all the dreams you had for Rawlston.'

'Well, it's not so bad. I'm the same as you, in a way. Gotta keep moving on,' he said, and took a sip from his glass. 'You stand still, you die.'

They said goodbye in the throng outside the tube station. They said they'd meet up again some time but Bella knew this was the last time she would see him. Once, she thought, we would have been haring off to a hotel, unable to keep our hands off each other.

Now they kissed on the cheek sedately, almost sadly.

317

'You take care,' Ben said. 'I know it will work out for you.'

'You too,' she said. 'Good luck. I hope you enjoy Edinburgh.'

'Keep in touch. Let me know if I can be of any help. Okay? 'Bye, Annabella.'

''Bye.'

Chapter Twenty-three

Whenever she drove past Holly Lodge, Jane was struck by the mournful air that seemed to surround it. It had to be her imagination, as there was no real change. It looked the same as it ever did. The difference was that she never saw the children now. They'd stopped coming to visit and she hadn't seen them on their way to and from school. Iain must have made some kind of childcare arrangements for them while he was at work.

Next door was quiet too. Ben Clarke had come round one evening to tell her that he was intending to sell his half of the house. It had been a quick, courteous visit, where they pretended that Jane didn't know about what had gone on. Bella wasn't mentioned. Nor was Sam.

The things that happen when it turns bad, Jane thought. Two families destroyed. Three motherless children. People floundering about in terrible pain – she thought of Iain Balfour's evident suffering. How on earth could it all have been worth it?

What's happened to Bella is a salutary lesson, she told herself. It's what I've been protecting myself from. But, nevertheless, she couldn't help herself thinking with longing of Tom. Their relationship was different to Bella's with Ben: it was illicit only because they chose to keep it a secret. If it were known, there was no one who could truly be hurt. The children might be surprised, even possessive, but it wasn't going to alter their lives or make them miserable if Jane had a lover.

The problem was, she didn't know if it was already too late. Perhaps she'd loitered, undecided, for so long that her opportunity had passed by.

How stupid I am, she thought. I imagined I was protecting myself from being hurt by keeping him at a distance. It just isn't possible. If it's going to get you, it's going to get you, whether you like it or not. And now I'll end up with nothing at all, back where I started, if I'm careful.

To think about turning her back on the sweetness of life she'd tasted lately was terrible. She knew that she couldn't give it up now.

When Maggie called, Jane surprised herself by telling her everything. Once she began talking about it, the whole story of Tom and what had happened between them up until their last meeting came flooding out.

'Jane,' she cried, 'I'm so glad! Why didn't you tell me before? I think it's wonderful!'

'Do you?'

'Of course I do! It's against nature to have you withering away in that great place all alone, I've always thought so. I wanted you to find someone years ago but how could you when you never left the house? And a student! I can tell you, there are some pretty tasty specimens walking round here that I'd love to get my hands on – if it weren't for Gregor and professional ethics, of course. Oh, lucky you! I bet he's got bags of energy as well.'

Jane laughed. 'Is that what matters?'

'Oh – don't try to over-analyse what matters and what doesn't. Jump in! Seize it! Why not? We don't have too long in our lives for rolling in the hay, you know. Your first instinct is always to say no to things, isn't it? God knows why. Come on, Jane – live a little. What have you got to lose?'

Live a little. It was what Tom had said. 'You're right,' she said to Maggie.

'Of course I am. Now go and find that boy before some little undergraduette snaffles him from under your nose.'

'Do you think I can?'

'You don't need my permission! I can tell it's what you want. Just do it.'

*

Gathering her courage, she called Tom and arranged to meet him outside the Botanic Gardens. He was waiting for her when she arrived, perfectly and – she thought – rather adorably turned out in a tweed jacket and cord trousers worn to a velvety softness. With his little gold-framed glasses and his curly hair, he could have stepped out of almost any decade in the last century. He greeted her with a kiss and, a little awkwardly, they walked through to the walled garden and a bench in a little clearing dominated by a fountain. It was a chilly day and not many other people were about as they sat down.

'I wasn't sure I'd see you again,' Tom said, not looking at her. Instead he examined the arm of the bench they were sitting on. 'You didn't seem to mind too much last time when I said that we wouldn't be able to see as much of each other as before.'

'Didn't I?'

He shook his head. 'Nope.'

'Well – I did mind. I suppose I've just become very good at protecting myself and hiding what I really feel. I've been working at it for fifteen years, after all.' She wrapped her scarf tightly about her, as if trying to hold in her courage. 'Now, listen. I want to tell you something. It might be too late, and I'm prepared for that.'

'What?' He looked nervous.

She resisted the urge to reach out and stroke his cheek. 'I'll try to explain. I've held back with you for lots of reasons, many of them sensible. But the main one has been because I've been afraid that if I let myself go, I'll get horribly hurt. I suppose it must be like falling off a horse and being too scared to get back on again. You either face your fear or become morbid about it, and I went the way of the coward and decided to wrap myself in cotton wool to prevent anything like the pain I had when Theo died happening again. It's worked quite well so far but I had the children and the house to think about, to focus all my energy on. And, of course, I never met anyone who might seriously challenge my way of behaving.' She looked out over the muted, wintery greens of the garden. 'And when you came along, there was the perfect excuse not to take it seriously.'

'You mean – the difference in our ages?'

'Of course. It was a bit of a get-out clause for me. It meant that there was definitely no future for us, so it was easier to let it happen. And you appeared to want to keep parts of your life private from me which made me think that we shared the same attitude. Then, before we knew it, we were getting in much deeper than I'd expected. We reached a crossroads where we had to decide what to do.'

'That was me.' Tom reached for her hand and held it tightly, running a finger over her palm. 'I wanted us to decide.'

'Because you can see endings coming.'

'Of course – the end of my time in Oxford. A time when I'll have to leave. Perhaps the end of my time with you. Even though you probably think I'm full of youthful carelessness and won't give a damn about going on my way, that's not the case.'

'I think I can see that now, but it was hard for me to understand that you took this seriously. You must see why.'

'Why?'

'Because I'm so much older than you. Isn't it obvious?'

He looked anguished. Then he burst out, 'I feel I've failed if that's what you think. Can't you see what you've done for me? First, I've been lonelier than I can say here. I know it's fun living it up with Ollie and the crowd, wearing silly clothes and going to parties, but it doesn't mean anything. It doesn't touch the real me, like you do. You brought some real warmth and humanity into this place.'

She went to speak but he rushed on without letting her. 'And you're everything I admire. A beautiful woman – no, you are beautiful, I can't get over it –' as Jane made a face '– and you're kind and good and real. It always seems to me that you have some kind of secret about how to live . . .'

Jane burst out laughing. 'But that's ridiculous! That's how *I* feel about *you*!'

'Well, isn't that the best kind of relationship? You make me feel like a better person when I'm with you, like I'm learning how to . . . how to *be*.'

She put her hand to his cheek and he leant into it, rubbing his

322

face against her. She savoured its soft, rough warmth. 'What are we saying?' she said. 'Are we saying that this really is something?'

'I don't see why it should end, when neither of us want it to.'

'Except that—'

'Don't you dare say it!'

'Say what?'

'The O word. You know. Old. I never want to hear it again.'

'I can't promise that. We can't make it go away, you know.' She took her fingers up through his curly hair. 'But I won't go on about it. You've told me you don't mind and I have to trust you – I must trust you.'

'I'm glad. Very glad.' He kissed the tip of her nose lightly. 'That's a bit cold. Let's go and get a hot drink. Now, I meant to ask you . . . We've got a black-tie dinner next week at the Union – some ridiculous society or other – and we have to take a guest each. I wondered if you'd like to be my date, if you can bear the company of lot of loud, opinionated and rather drunken under-graduates . . .'

They got up and wandered back slowly towards the entrance, holding hands.

This feels too easy, she thought with a stab of trepidation. Then she caught herself up. *Enjoy it! If it feels easy, perhaps that's because it is.* 'Black tie? Goodness . . .'

'I wouldn't get too excited. Most of the people I know would gladly wear black tie to lectures if they could. Any excuse. But it might be fun.'

'Perhaps I will. Will there be dancing?'

'Very likely on the tables from about one in the morning.'

'Then I'll definitely be there. Will we stay up all night?'

'We'll kiss on the bridge at dawn.'

She smiled at him. 'It sounds like heaven.'

Nicky was out at a work do, as she seemed to be almost every night, and Bella was in the tiny Mayfair flat on her own. It felt as though she'd been living out of a suitcase and sleeping in a cramped single bed for years. Holly Lodge, the spacious sitting room, the sofa, the children round her seemed like a distant dream now. London was impossibly crowded and despicably dirty in a low, unhealthy way. Perhaps once you were set free of London, there was no going back happily into its sweaty embrace. The whole place was dedicated to money and a kind of false enjoyment based on spending it: eating it, drinking it, wearing it, preening with it, insulating oneself with it.

That wasn't much fun when you had very little of it.

She sat in the sitting room watching cable television in the dark, listening to the raucous customers leaving the pub opposite. When the phone rang she left it for the answer-machine to pick up. She stiffened when she heard Iain's voice.

'Er . . . yes, this is a message for Bella. Um. It's Iain. I wondered if you were there, I felt like having a word with you . . .'

She shook herself into action and plucked up the receiver. 'Hello? Hello, Iain? It's me.'

There was a pause. 'I thought you weren't there.'

'I assumed the call would be for Nicky.' She waited for him to speak, but there was a long silence on the other end. 'Are you still there?'

'Yes, yes, I'm still here. Don't hang up. Listen . . . Bella . . . I wondered if you wanted to meet to – talk about this. About everything that's happened.'

'Well. I don't know. Is there any point? I thought you said there were no second chances. No three-strikes-and-you're-out.'

'I know. But I need to see you about this, about all this . . .' His voice wavered. 'I'm finding it very hard. Harder than I thought I would. I thought it would be possible to shut you out, but everything here reminds me of you. And the children . . . the children miss you. I wish they didn't but they do, and I can't do anything to make it better for them.'

'Where shall we meet?' Bella asked quickly, sensing how much effort it was for him to say these things. A tiny window of possibility had opened and she needed to wedge it in place. 'Shall I come to you?' The idea of seeing Katie and Christopher, of smelling their hair and skin, filled her with yearning for them.

'No.'

'Do you want to come to London?'

'No. Not London.'

'Then let's meet in a half-way house. Let's meet in Oxford.'

'Yes. All right. We'll meet in Oxford.'

She was absurdly nervous on the train, a slow, chuntering thing that stopped at every tiny station along the Thames before it reached Oxford. Staring out of the window, she saw her own white face, distorted in the glass, looking back at her through over-large eyes. She was too apprehensive to imagine scenarios for the evening. When she'd seen Ben, she'd wondered if they might end up in bed together: the physical pull between them was still new and strong. She couldn't imagine that for a moment with Iain.

He was waiting at the station. She saw him before he saw her, and when she did, her heart clenched with pity and tears started in her eyes. He looked so alone, in the small station concourse, standing near the doorway in his work suit, clutching a newspaper in one fist. His eyes were flicking nervously up and down, scanning the other people walking past; by the time he saw her she'd got control of herself and was walking towards him with a smile.

'Hello.'

He cleared his throat. 'Hello, hello.' He leaned forward awkwardly and kissed her quickly on the cheek. 'Where do you want to go?'

'I don't mind. Where do you recommend?'

'There's nothing much round the station. But there's a Chinese place up the road, if you fancy that.'

'All right. Let's go there.'

Small talk was difficult while they walked to the restaurant and then were seated. Bella tried but Iain couldn't respond, so they fell into silence until after they'd ordered.

'How are the children?' Bella asked, when the waiter had left them.

'Fine. Well . . . Chrissie's been wetting the bed. Katie's very good – she acts quite like the little mother, taking off his sheets in the morning. She knows how to work the washing machine. I don't know what I'd do without her.' Iain fiddled with the small revolving dish of soy sauce, salt and pepper. 'It's really because of them that I'm here.' He stared at the white table linen and then said suddenly, looking at her carefully, 'Clarke's gone, you know.'

'Has he?' she said calmly. She wasn't going to react or even hint that she had a breath of Ben's plans.

Iain chewed his lip, then said, 'I take it that it's over.'

'Yes.' Bella looked him straight in the eye and spoke as firmly as she could. 'It's over.'

His face lightened for the first time in the evening. 'Good.'

Is this about me coming back? she wondered. She wanted to ask him straight out but her years with Iain had taught her that it was best to wait. She bit her tongue and made a conscious effort not to speak.

'I wanted to talk to you about the children,' he said, at last. 'If you were still seeing Clarke, there wouldn't be any question of what I'm about to suggest. I want to make that perfectly clear.' He waited, then, when she didn't speak, continued. 'I'm not a monster, no matter what you think. I don't want to punish the children for what you've done. But it's very hard for me. I find it difficult to . . . not to lash out, especially when I've been attacked and damaged the way you've attacked me. I've been trying to overcome it and I've come to a decision. I think you should come back to the lodge.'

'You want me back?'

'The children want you back. I . . .' He took a deep breath. It emerged shakily. 'I'm prepared to leave the lodge and stay in London for a while, until we've come to some decision about our future. I work in town, you don't. It seems crazy for you to be there, when they need you. Obviously we can't live together, so this way makes sense.'

Bella felt unbearably small in the face of his generosity. He hated London. He loathed being away from the children for any length of time. And here he was, offering her the lodge, a place with Katie and Christopher, when all his instinct must be telling him to take away everything she held dear. It was, she knew, an act of supreme sacrifice for him.

'Thank you,' she whispered.

He looked away, blinking hard. 'I'm not thinking of you. I'm thinking of the children.'

'I know. But thank you.'

They sat in silence, waiting for their food.

'I think it's pretty awful that you didn't tell me earlier,' Jerry said, his voice unmistakably sulky down the telephone line. 'I was planning to find you lots of lovely sex, and there you were, having it without telling me.'

'I couldn't have had it without you, could I? You were the one who brought Tom here,' Jane said soothingly.

'I suppose that's true. Well, if I can take a little credit for it, then I feel much better. Oh dear, you are lucky.' Jerry sighed. 'Think of poor me and the divine Ollie. A fortress yet to be breached. But I haven't given up yet.'

Jane laughed. 'Darling, you keep trying. You know that's at least half the fun.'

When she'd put the phone down at last, Tom came in with some sloe gin. He handed her the glass of rich, plum-coloured liquid. 'How did he take it?' he asked, sitting down beside her on the sofa.

'Very well, considering how much he hates being the last to know anything.'

Tom grinned. 'He'll get over it.'

Alec put his head round the sitting room door. 'Mum, you've got a visitor.'

'Have I?' Jane was surprised. It was cold and miserable outside. She wasn't expecting anyone at this time of night.

'The lady from the lodge,' explained Alec.

Jane exchanged a look with Tom and then went to meet Bella in the kitchen where she was nestling gratefully against the Aga.

'This is lovely and warm,' Bella announced as Jane came in.

'Hello.' Jane went forward to greet her with a kiss. 'What a surprise! What are you doing here?'

'I've moved back.' Bella smiled at her. She looked a different woman to the broken, dazed one who'd last been here. They sat down at the table together. 'Iain's offered to let me stay with the children while we resolve everything. Oh, thanks –' she took the wine Jane offered her – 'so I got back yesterday.'

'I'm very pleased to hear it. It's felt quite miserable round the lodge while you've been gone.'

'Yes. I can't say it's been magically restored. The children had one glorious moment when they thought everything was back to normal and then, when they realized that Iain was leaving, they were in despair again.' Bella's expression darkened. 'There's been nothing good for them from all this. But I wanted to say thank you for your help and support while it's been going on. It meant such a lot. I don't know what I would have done without it.'

'You're welcome.' Jane swirled the ruby liquid around her glass. 'I know we don't know each other very well but do you mind if I ask you something?'

'Not at all.'

'Do you think you and your husband will get back together?'

Bella considered. She sighed deeply. 'I don't know. I can't see how it would happen at the moment. Iain is so very proud and I know I've hurt him at the most profound level possible. I don't know if he'll ever recover enough to be able to bear being around me. I don't know if I'll be able to go back myself. I was so unhappy towards the end – that's why I became infatuated with Ben, because of the miserable, lonely irritation I'd been feeling for so long. When Ben came along, it was impossible to resist him. Despite all the awful things that have happened, I know I wouldn't – couldn't – do it any differently because I just didn't have a choice.'

'I see.'

'Do you know what that's like?' Bella looked at her beseechingly.

'I know a little of what it's like.' She thought of Tom, sitting in the other room, waiting for her. It was like a pulse of happiness beating away nearby. 'There's something else I wanted to say. I've been thinking about you lately, and what happened. As you say, it's too late to change it all now. But if, despite all the hurt and pain and suffering, it's opened a door to a new life, a life that you really believe will be better, then don't turn your back on it.'

Bella looked surprised.

'I know – you were expecting me to say, go back to your husband, put your children first, atone for your sin.'

Bella stared down at the table. 'That's how I feel, though. As if I've been terribly wicked, taking another woman's husband, breaking up her marriage, betraying my own. I feel as though everyone expects me to put on a hair shirt and be punished for the rest of my life.'

'Perhaps I would have thought that once. But, obvious as it may sound, life is short and unpredictable, and nothing is as simple as it looks. I can't begin to judge you. I wouldn't dream of it.'

'Really?'

'Absolutely. It would be wonderful if we all had happy endings all the time but we don't – so seize anything you need to seize while you can. The main thing is, you mustn't waste your life. I've wasted years, and I was on the point of wasting even more before I realized that you can't let these chances go by. If going back to your husband and trying again is the best way, then do that. But whatever you do, it must be what you really want, or it will be doomed, and so will you.'

Bella absorbed this for a moment. She said, 'In some ways, I can see Iain's changed. Perhaps we have a chance. I honestly don't know.'

'Then take your time. Don't rush into anything. And come here any time you want to.'

'You said that before, when I first came to Rawlston.' Bella smiled at her. 'It's nice to know you're always here.'

Jane shrugged. 'I may not be. I'm thinking of travelling, actually. My daughter went Interrailing in September and loved it so much, I wondered if perhaps I should give it a go myself.'

'Sounds wonderful. Anywhere in particular?'

'Not sure. I haven't decided. Perhaps . . .' She paused and said casually, 'Perhaps South Africa.'

'How exotic! Well, good on you. But it won't be the same here without you. I've got used to knowing you're here, like a guardian angel.'

'If I'm not here, someone will be. My sister and her partner may come and live at Rawlston for a while. They're talking about leaving London, making some life changes. Perhaps even buying the other side of the house.'

Bella smiled. 'That would be lovely for you, wouldn't it?'

Jane nodded slowly. 'It would be. Things are going well at the moment. Having Maggie here would be very good indeed.'

'I'm glad for you.'

Jane reached out and put her hand over the other woman's. 'Things will get better for you, too. I know it. It's hardly ever the end of the story, you know, even when you want it to be. Life just keeps on happening, no matter what.'

'You know what? I'm very glad to hear it.'

The kitchen door opened and Tom put his head round. 'Jane, where do you keep the coal? The bucket's nearly empty.'

'There's a bag inside the cellar door.'

Bella turned to Jane as Tom disappeared, raising her eyebrows. 'Who is that?' she asked, with a grin.

'Ah, well . . . that's a whole new chapter.'

THE END